The Magic Mooncat

To Ann,
Best wishes
Lois Jenn
Sept 2003.

face her companion. 'Another one!' she exclaimed. 'That's not fair. There are three of you already.'

Sally grinned, jubilant in her news. She rarely had grounds to boast. 'Now you've made me tread on a crack,' she giggled. 'The big bear'll get me.' She ran the short distance to the corner of the next street and screamed in mock terror as she disappeared out of sight.

'Don't be so stupid,' Hannah shouted. 'Anyway, how do you know?'

'I heard my mam telling my dad. She said, "That's the third time I've been sick and you know what that means." '

Hannah carefully stepped over the cracks, not believing in the bear story any more but unable to disobey the rules dictated by this stretch of the route from school. 'What's that got to do with babies?' she protested. 'My mam gets sick sometimes. You're just making it up. You do tell big fibs, Sally Blenkin.' She glared and ran ahead. Sometimes, she didn't know whether she liked Sally. Her mother described her as being a stranger to the truth, and they did live in Liddon Street before they were bombed out and moved in next door. According to her dad, Liddon Street was one of the slummiest streets around.

'Just listen, will you,' Sally yelled, her face flushed with the exertion of the mock terror, and her blue eyes wide with indignation. 'It wasn't just being sick. She said, "Another mouth to feed and with a bloody war on as well." And then she said that it had better be a girl this time and if it was another boy she would go mad.'

They crossed Sedgemore Street and continued along the concrete path that cut through to Tennyson Street.

'Did she really say that word?' Hannah asked.

'What word?' Sally's voice was full of contrived innocence.

'You know. That bad one about the war.'

'Oh that one. She didn't mean that word. She meant the other one when you're bleeding. She meant about people getting killed and bleeding and things.'

Hannah gave her the benefit of the doubt. Sally was the best friend she had ever had, and the fact that they were born on the same

1

Tennyson Street

It could have been any weekday in any September. The trees and shrubs in the town gardens were displaying their autumn colours, and dead leaves caught up in sudden small winds rustled across the paths and pressed against the walls. Women were doing last-minute errands, and children were behaving as children do at the end of the school day. Yet, in other Septembers, dust did not hang in the air, nor did Bonfire Night appear to have come early with its pungent smells of burning timber. The words 'blackout' and 'shelters' would not be present in everyday vocabulary, nor would gas-mask drill be part of the school timetable. But then nothing would ever be quite the same again, for this was September 1941 and Hull was on fire.

The two friends laughed and skipped along as though it was any day in any September. They still had a blissful ignorance; an ability to cast aside memories of the previous night when they had shivered in the air raid shelter. Life was lived in moments, and each day was so crowded with moments that there was no time for looking back.

'We're getting another baby,' Sally Blenkin suddenly announced, her thick blond pigtails bouncing in rhythm with her legs as she shared in the daily ritual of dodging the cracks in the pavement.

Hannah Flynn stopped dead in her tracks and spun around to

*Dedicated to my husband Ralph with love and
in memory of my dear mother Lilian Lois.*

*Thanks to our children, Lisa, Andrew, Ian, and Karen,
and to my friends Norma Sedler and Marion Ware
for their love and support.*

Copyright © Lois Fenn 2003
First published in 2003 by Crow's Nest Books
33 Townend
Wilsford, Nr Grantham
Lincolnshire NG32 3NX

Distributed by Gazelle Book Services Limited
Falcon House, Queen Square
Lancaster, England LA1 1RN

British Library Cataloguing in Publication Data
A catalogue record for this book is available from the British
Library

ISBN 0-9542884-0-8

Typeset by Amolibros, Milverton, Somerset
This book production has been managed by Amolibros
Printed and bound by T J International Ltd, Padstow, Cornwall, UK

The Magic Mooncat

a novel by

Lois Fenn

Crow's Nest Books

day, the ninth of September and had recently shared their ninth birthday, seemed to have some significance.

They had reached the beginning of the track known as the ten-foot, which ran along the back of the terraced houses. It was easy to pick out their garden gates about a third of the way along the ten-foot. An ash tree grew near to the boundary fence, spreading its branches into both the Flynns' and the Blenkins' gardens. 'It's shedding its leaves in a great hurry,' Martin Flynn had commented that morning with a British pre-occupation with the weather. 'We're in for an early autumn.'

'That's the least of our problems,' Sylvia Flynn had replied, dragging the brush through her daughter's hair with no regard for the yells of 'Mam, you're hurting me.' She was never in a good mood in the morning and now, with every night spent in the shelter, tempers were becoming more and more frayed.

'Get down,' Sally hissed. 'My mam's in the garden talking to your mam. She'll find a job for me.'

'She doesn't look any different,' Hannah whispered. 'She doesn't look sick. I'm going to have four children when I get married. Two of each. What are you going to have?'

'I don't want any. I'm going to marry a rich man and have a fur coat and servants. If I did have any, they could go to boarding school like in *School Girl Annual*. I don't want to spend ages washing up. It's always me. Michael and Gavin never have to do it. They drop things and leave bits on. Crafty little devils.'

'My mam says it was a miracle when I arrived. It was in a thunderstorm and the waters broke,' Hannah said in dramatic breathlessness, her knees pressing into her stomach. 'She said I'm so special that she didn't want any more.'

'It couldn't have been a miracle. They only happened in the Bible and that was millions of years ago.'

Hannah grunted, not being too sure of her facts, although she wanted to elaborate on her belief that somehow it had been like God holding back the water for the Children of Israel and then letting it go again. But then Sally would laugh, and, in spite of their friendship, Hannah liked to keep her innermost thoughts away from criticism and possible ridicule. She wished she hadn't mentioned the miracle now.

The two women were deep in conversation, and Hannah noticed how her mother pushed at her hair, a habit of hers when she was upset. She wished she had hair like her mother's, black and curly. Her hair was blond and apparently as straight as a poker. Sometimes she had it in rags; strips of old sheet wound around and around strands of hair, twisting them into corkscrews; not conducive to a good night's sleep.

'I bet they're talking about Sunday,' Sally whispered. She altered her position, straining to hear the adult conversation and losing her balance.

'There you are, Sally,' came Millie Blenkin's harsh voice. 'That's a clean frock. Come on in and put your old one on. And I want some errands. Where's the lads? Little flamers! If they're on that railway line again I'll skin their backsides!'

Sally stood up and smoothed the dust and creases from her dress. 'I'd better go in,' she sighed. 'Roll on Sunday.'

Hannah wandered a little way up the path and thought of Sunday. She picked up a ball and began to throw it against the brick wall of the air raid shelter. A raucous voice broke her concentration, and the ball escaped her hands and rolled along the path.

'Rag Bone. Rag Bone.' The words gave the voice identity. Hannah was about to alert her mother but remembered how last time she declared that they needed all their clothes, raggedy or not. 'Make do and mend,' she'd said, quoting a recent government directive.

Martin Flynn likened old Sam to a modern-day Pied Piper. He told his daughter how first the rats and then the children were enticed away by his music. Hannah shared her father's love of poetry and didn't follow old Sam too closely after that.

A scream of anguish competed with the hoarse cry. It was followed by the sound of a resounding slap on bare flesh. Janet Pearson was dragging her little brother Kenny along by his only garment, a heavily soiled vest.

'Who's got a bare bum then?' Hannah heard the big girl shout.

'Stop struggling, ya little bugger. Me mam'll kill you! That's her best jumper.'

Hannah took a few steps towards the back gate and giggled, remembering how last time little Kenny had made off with his grandfather's trousers to exchange them for a balloon.

'Seen enough, gal?' Janet Pearson pulled a hideous face and stuck out her tongue. 'Made you look. Made you stare. Made you cut the barber's hair,' she jibed.

Hannah turned and ran back into the shade of the shelter. She knew the rest of the rhyme about crawlies in the hair and put her hands over her ears. That was Sally's voice now.

'Who wants to stare at you face aches,' she heard her shout at the retreating Pearsons. 'You're the ones with fleas.' She gave a jeering laugh before joining Hannah behind the shelter. 'They've gone in now,' she said. 'You can sound the all-clear. Just give 'em as good back again. Shout "sticks and stones" next time.'

Hannah didn't speak. Words did hurt even more than sticks and stones. Words stayed locked up inside, escaping into her thoughts when she couldn't sleep, and refusing to be banished from her mind. She still didn't believe Sally about that bad word. 'Bloody war' her brain reminded her. She found it hard to concentrate on the game that followed, dropping the ball so many times that they both became bored.

Sylvia Flynn watched them playing and thought of her conversation with her neighbour. She'd taken pity on her and asked her in for a cup of tea. Pregnancy was bad enough in peacetime, she thought. Hannah didn't look well. The child worried her. Mrs Blenkin had commented on her delicate build and it seemed to Sylvia like a direct criticism of her ability as a mother. Why wouldn't she eat more? Where would she end up on Sunday? What if they didn't care whether she ate or not? And then there was the problem at night. She'd thought it was a thing of the past, but disturbed sleep sometimes twice in a night and taking refuge in that cold shelter seemed to have triggered it all off again. 'Does the child wet the bed?' it had asked on the evacuation papers. She'd ticked 'No'. She'd heard that bedwetters were put in communal hostels and she couldn't bear the idea.

'Why don't you go with Hannah?' Mrs Blenkin had asked. Sylvia sighed. If only it was that simple. She would love to escape from the monotonous rows of houses and the vulgar way of life which pressed in on her from all sides. 'Roses round the door. Babies on the floor.' The words of a popular song of her childhood drifted across her thoughts. No, she didn't want the babies, but the roses would be wonderful. The bitterness was back with a vengeance, creating ugly thoughts of her sister Vera in her big house on the city boundary. She'd never offered to accommodate their parents and all their possessions after they were forced to abandon their home.

She wandered into the front room brandishing the remains of a cotton vest which now served as a duster. Martin frequently commented that she must have been born with a duster somehow welded to her wrist and had asked her on the previous day if she had dusted the shelter. Oh well. Let him have his silly jokes. She looked around her best room with little pleasure. The piano was trapped behind her mother's settee, and the chairs were crammed in a continuous row giving the area the appearance of a doctor's waiting room. Her small china cabinet, which housed a few precious items from their wedding day eleven years ago including two fluted cups and saucers and four plates, now thickly wrapped in newspaper, was totally obscured by one of the chairs. Pictures and mirrors were propped against the walls, casting strange reflections of the worn carpet square and chair legs.

She reached over to dust the piano, flicking the duster as far down the back of the settee as she could reach. A shaft of late afternoon sunlight suddenly entered the net curtain, and illuminated the room with transfused light. Particles of dust hung in the air, and sprang from her cloth.

'Oh tittle!' she exclaimed, and decided that it was a job for Monday after Hannah had gone. The thought of having a spare bedroom to house some of the excess furniture and a chance to restore her front room to its former glory cheered her for a moment, but then the guilt of having such feelings and a sense of a kind of future bereavement, dulled her mind back into depression.

She returned to the kitchen and tipped some potatoes into the washing-up bowl. Two ounces of stewing beef simmered in the pan on the stove together with a marrow bone. She tutted impatiently as she cut the black areas from a large potato. 'Only fit for pigs,' she muttered. The second one also revealed blighted areas under the peel. She threw down the knife in exasperation and sighed, her shoulders drooping with weariness.

The two girls were squealing with the joy of kicking their legs up against the shelter wall. Their skirts were tucked into their knickers with a total disregard for modesty and the world outside of their youthful exuberance. Sylvia envied them their forgetfulness of the previous night's terror, yet at the same time pitied them for their insecure future. She wanted so much happiness for Hannah. If it wasn't for the war, she mused, she would not encourage this friendship. The likes of Sally Blenkin were not part of her plans, although to hear Millie Blenkin speak, her daughter was a genius. Sylvia snorted in humourless mirth. No doubt Sally would end up in a factory she decided, whereas her Hannah was destined for greater things. She'd told her neighbour as they shared a pot of tea, that her daughter always had her head in a book, and what she didn't know about the Romans was nobody's business.

Her attention returned to the potatoes. War or no war, it shouldn't be allowed. She rapped on the window, bringing down two pairs of legs from the shelter wall.

Hannah pushed her hair out of her eyes. 'Oh Mam,' she wailed, 'can't we have another five minutes?'

Sally cast a nervous glance towards her own back door. 'I'd better go in and find our lads. They'll be belted if they're out after blackout,' she said.

Moments later, Hannah set off clutching the condemned potatoes, with strict instructions not to return without a fresh quarter of a stone. She ran her fingers along the brickwork of the passage, enjoying the musty smell and reminded as always of imagined secret tunnels. As far as adults were concerned, a passageway was an added bonus, providing an extra foot or two to the bedroom space above and a drying area on wet wash days. Sheets and towels were draped over a clothes line suspended between two rusting hooks and left to drip the worst of their wetness, creating soap-scented puddles. Hannah and Sally were proud of owning a passage. There were only a small number evenly spaced along the terraced row. House-proud mothers, intent on keeping the front step clean and the front room free from dusty feet, locked the door, enforcing entrance from the back only. This could mean a lengthy trek to the end of the street and back along the ten-foot.

Hannah responded to the change in the atmosphere as she left the dank gloom of the passageway. Life was noisy at the back. Doors were left unlocked; children played; dogs barked; women gossiped over the fences; cats scavenged amongst rubbish and sparrows and starlings joined by seagulls in hard winters, flew down to gather up food from scraped pans and plates. In contrast, the front way had an air of hostility; an expectant silence as the closely netted windows seemed to spell out 'Private. Keep away'. Repeated rappings on a door sometimes echoed along the row and curtains twitched. The paperboy, the milkman and the postman were welcome, but the rent man, the club-man and debt collectors were often ignored. The rat man, as the truant inspector was known because of his long thin nose and meanness of disposition, fooled the system by sneaking around the back and pouncing on freedom-seeking kids along the sides of the railway track.

Hannah giggled as she passed the Higsons' house. Paul Higson was clutching his trousers with one hand and hammering on the door with the other. 'Go round the back,' came Mrs Higson's voice. 'But Mam,' Paul wailed, 'I want the lavvy.' His cry went unheeded. Hannah dawdled, watching at the gate and then looked quickly ahead and broke into a run as young Paul relieved himself in the privet. 'Ugh, boys!' she exclaimed under her breath.

It was a relief not to have a scene over the potatoes. The greengrocer lady made no objections. 'Tell your ma I'm sorry,' she said. 'We get all sorts these days.' She shivered and clutched her woollen cardigan across her chest.

'Someone just walked over your grave,' Hannah said.

'Cheeky monkey! More like you've left the door open. Make sure you shut it on the way out.'

It was a funny expression, Hannah thought as she dawdled back along the street. Her mother had said it that morning and she didn't understand it at all. You'd have to be dead first, she mused. A huge shiver ran up her spine. The sun was out of sight now behind the houses and a grey mist dulled the sky into early twilight. Now, as coal fires were stoked up, rows of chimneys belched out black smoke adding to the gloom.

'Want a ride?'

Hannah spun around at the sound of a familiar voice. 'You're early, Dad,' she yelled, her face flushing with pleasure at the sight of her father on his ancient 'sit up and beg' bike.

Martin Flynn stopped and steadied himself against the kerb. 'Now then, Poddletoes. Had a good day?'

'Don't call me that!' Hannah chided, although she didn't really mind. She perched on the crossbar of his bicycle and held on to the middle of the handlebars. 'I had to go for some more spuds. Me mam's in a bit of a mood.'

The smile left Martin's face. Sylvia was not going to like his news. He concentrated on steering the bike, vaguely aware of his daughter's chatter. They wobbled to a halt, level with the small front garden.

'What's the book?' Hannah reached into the front basket.

'It's poetry. I thought you would like it.'

His daughter gave a squeal of delight and had scarcely put her feet on to the pavement before she opened it, scanning the first page. Martin pushed the bike into the passageway, scraping the handlebars against the flaking brickwork.

'Me dad's here,' Hannah announced as she burst in through the back door.

'Been entertaining?' Martin enquired with a forced brightness.

'I expect it was Mrs Blenkin,' Hannah said, innocent of the repercussions.

Sylvia jumped up, grabbing the cups and saucers and made for the kitchen sink.

'What's she doing round here? On the scrounge?' Martin snapped. 'Jerry's done her a good turn. It's a pity all of Liddon Street didn't get it.'

'Don't be awful, Martin. How can you say that? I thought it would do her good to get out of the house for half an hour. Those kids of hers are a right handful.'

'Give 'em an inch and they'll take a mile. I know their sort. I bet they're paying less rent than us. Perhaps not paying any.'

'Poor soul,' Sylvia said defiantly.

'Poor soul! What do you mean poor soul?'

'She's pregnant.'

'Good God! Still, you know what they say: new house, new baby. Didn't work for us, did it?'

The sudden scraping of the chair as her mother got to her feet alerted Hannah to caution. She kept her head bent over her book and wondered about the word 'pregnant'.

Sylvia's eyes, dark with anger, focused on the small shabby book. 'Get that put away and set the table,' she yelled. 'Anyway. Where did that come from?'

'Me dad gave me it.'

'Honestly, Martin. Fancy giving the kid that. It looks filthy. You've no sense. Put it in the ashcan, you Hannah. I'll use it to light the fire. It looks as though it's been in someone's outside privy for donkeys' years!'

Martin thought of the first entry 'Ode to Autumn', and wondered what Keats would make of this autumn. 'Season of mists and mellow fruitfulness'! More like season of bombs and bloodymindedness! The picture of the pile of rubble, the remains of the back street antique and bric-a-brac shop which had given him a living for the last seven years, was clear in his mind. He had picked up the small first edition anthology from amongst the bricks and broken tiles. It was an old friend, which he had kept away from public scrutiny. How could she be so obsessed with cleanliness when generations of dust and decay hung in the air over the city? He saw the pain on his daughter's face and wanted to defend her right to keep the book but he knew that his wife's anger was aimed at him. Oh well, he thought, she'll be rid of me soon. His call-up papers should be arriving any day now.

He ran his fingers through his wiry, sandy coloured hair, and, turning away from her anger and Hannah's misery, reached in his pocket for his cigarettes. He would tell her when she had calmed down. Poor old Charlie. He'd refused to go in the shelter in case of looters. He'd always said he would die with his boots on. Martin imagined him reaching for his cash box as the bomb blew him to kingdom come. All those years of scrimping and saving for his old age. All those coins counted and hoarded. 'Bloody Germans,' he muttered.

'What did you say?' Sylvia asked, half turning from the potatoes which were adding to her feelings of frustration, being little better than the rejected batch.

'Nothing.' Martin drew the cigarette smoke sharply down his throat and blew it back out in the direction of the ceiling.

'Have you got the sack? Is that why you're home early? Can't afford to keep you, I suppose. He could have waited until your call-up. Still, who wants useless ornaments these days? You should have taken that job on the railway. Look at my father. A good job and maybe you wouldn't have to go. But no! You have to work in a junk shop!'

Martin sighed. On good days he was an antique dealer.

'Get away from the fire, Hannah.' Sylvia hung on to her aggression. 'I've told you before about sitting with your back to the fire. You'll melt your spine, and go out to play. You're getting on my nerves. These potatoes are no better. Couldn't you see?'

'Just made it before the blackout!' The entrance of Hannah's grandparents through the back door was greeted with strained glances. Hannah scanned the pages of the little book and listened to her grandmother's description of Auntie Vera's new carpet. She knew from her mother's tone of voice as she replied, 'Oh well, I don't suppose they're worried about bombs where they are,' that she didn't approve of her sister's ways.

Her grandfather gave her a quick look. 'The place is too big for me,' he said. 'There's nowt like a good fire and a cosy room.' He coughed over his pipe and grinned.

11

Hannah ate her bread and jam slowly, squeezing the jam through the sides and licking it. Her mother returned to the potato problem glaring accusingly at Hannah and suddenly became aware of her bad table manners. 'For goodness sake, Hannah! If you can't eat properly you can do without. And you can have an early night. Catch up on your sleep. We've got a lot of sorting out to do tomorrow and shut the door after you.'

Her mother said that every night, but tonight Hannah sensed an urgency in the words and stayed close to the other side of the stairs door listening. It was a habit of hers when she couldn't sleep. Her favourite place was on the third step up where there was room to stretch her legs yet be within listening distance. At bedtime, the stairs door was a solid reminder of the division between childhood and the world of the grown-ups. She pressed her ear against the door and listened.

'It was a direct hit,' she heard him say. 'A landmine no doubt by the size of the hole. Poor old Charlie. We dug down but it was hopeless. No trace of him. Blown to kingdom come. Everything smashed to bits. Just that little book. But you were right, Sylvia. It's in a bit of a state now. I'll get her another poetry book sometime.'

The sounds of dishes clattering and water running competed with the voices and Hannah, afraid of exposure, trod carefully up the stairs, taking a big stride halfway up to avoid the creaking step. She huddled under the blankets and thought of old Charlie. He'd given her a tiny wooden doll, apparently the smallest in the family of painted Russian dolls who lived together one inside the other. 'She's lost all her folks,' he explained. 'She's an orphan. You must take care of her.' Now he was gone, to kingdom come, her father said. She gave a little moan. Death had come into her life for the first time.

2

Dreams and Daydreams

Hannah pulled the blanket over her ears trying to blot out the sounds of bombs exploding and the moaning of her grandmother, who was sitting in an old fireside chair. Her mother had lit a candle, which had been rammed into the neck of an empty beer bottle. This was the second raid of the night, the last fling of the German pilots before they high-tailed it back across the North Sea.

'Bastards!' exclaimed Mrs Randall.

Sylvia Flynn put her fingers to her lips and nodded in the direction of the child lying on the bunk bed.

'That's not very ladylike, you Mother.'

'Well, I don't feel very ladylike. More like a rabbit down a hole. Are you awake, Hannah?'

Hannah didn't answer, although she had been listening to the adult conversation for the last few minutes. Another 'B' she thought. Nearly all the bad words she knew began with 'B'. She stretched her arms and yawned.

'It's all right, pet,' her mother continued. 'I think they have gone over now. We'll wait for the all-clear and then we can go and put the kettle on.'

Her attempt to sound cheerful and reassuring gave her voice a shrill tone and her words echoed around the bare walls of the shelter.

The flickering light from the candle cast strange shadows, and Hannah watched as the contours of her grandmother's profile enlarged and shrank on the back wall. She gave a sudden shiver, recalling 'the dream'. The doll's-house dream she called it. She'd experienced this dream before when a house was opened up as though it had a hinged section like her doll's house and she could see all the rooms at a glance. But this dream had differed in that she recognised the rooms. It was the back of their house. She could see inside her bedroom and inside the room which her grandparents occupied now that they were homeless, but the kitchen had gone. She shivered again and sat up, rubbing at the stickiness of her eyes. 'Do your eyes stick together, Grandma?'

'You've had a blast in them and no wonder sleeping in this draughty place. It's killing me, Sylvia! It's no good. I can't stand much more of this.' Enid Randall suddenly found some energy, abandoning her resigned posture and stamping her feet aggressively on the bare concrete floor.

'I know, Ma,' her daughter responded wearily. The sound of the 'all clear', that long uninterrupted wailing, so good to hear after a night of terror, was like a shot of adrenaline. 'Come on! Cheer up. Let's see if we still have a kettle to put on.' Sylvia struggled to her feet and held out her arms to her mother.

Hannah groped around for her shoes, carefully avoiding the large chamber pot under her grandmother's chair. 'I dreamt our house had changed into a doll's house,' she said in a chatty kind of a way. 'Can you see? Has our house still got a back on?'

'I hope so.' Sylvia gave a hoarse laugh. 'Anyway, it's pitch black, you know. I'm not a cat. You and your dreams.' Although she made light of it, an uneasy feeling moved down from her head, prickling her spine and causing flutters of anxiety in her stomach. Just lately, Hannah had been having the strangest dreams. It was to be expected she supposed, with all the comings and goings into the shelter and constant disturbed nights, but on at least two occasions during the past few weeks her dreams had seemed to precede happenings with an uncanny accuracy. What did Martin call it? 'Prem' something or other. Sylvia wasn't good with long words. Anyway, whatever

14

the word, apparently his mother used to do the same thing. 'A bit of a witch,' Martin laughed as he recounted tales of his childhood back in Ireland.

All three of them were relieved as they stumbled in over the backdoor step. After Sylvia had closed the door behind them, her mother turned on the light and they blinked in the brightness of the overhead bulb. Everything was as they had left it, the normality making a strange contrast with the bizarre night-time ordeal, and the fact that this was commonplace now did not diminish the stress of it all.

Sylvia methodically filled up the kettle and struck a match for the gas ring. Her hand shook as she waited for the familiar plop and rush of flames. God, I'm falling apart, she thought. Still, was there any wonder? It was such a relief to see another day, but it was not one she had anticipated with any pleasure. She knew it had to be faced. She'd resisted it for a long time, hoping that it would all go away. They'd survived the worst of it in May and things had calmed down a bit but now the hell was back and she couldn't pretend any more. Hannah had to go. They'd not had a good night's sleep for weeks. She shivered as she recalled the scene that had met her eyes after the raid two nights ago. The back bedroom window took the blast of the Storton Street bomb, and fragments of glass littered Hannah's bed. Shock waves of horror zigzagged through her at the thought of what might have happened. She could hardly bare to go in that bedroom now with its boarded up windows, and her child gladly snuggled down in her parents' double bed before the nightly shelter routine.

Hannah, unaware of her mother's tormented thoughts, was checking the well-being of the two goldfish. 'Mam,' she called out for the second time, 'I'm just wondering if me dad'll be back in time. I don't want to miss the train.'

'You're in a great hurry to leave me. Don't worry. It's only just gone half past six.' Sylvia sat down and picked up her cup of tea, pressing it against the side of her face. Don't worry! She repeated her words silently. That was all everyone kept saying these days. It was impossible not to worry. Each night, when it was Martin's turn to go on fire watch, she worried. How on earth was she going to cope? She felt a surge of affection for him which was quickly replaced with a sense of frustration. She hoped that he would have a home posting and leave the fighting to the youngsters but apparently such an arrangement was farthest from his mind. He couldn't wait to get into the thick of it and avenge his dead boss and the loss of his livelihood. Selfish, that's what he is, she thought accusingly.

Hannah dipped her finger in the goldfish bowl and stirred the water. 'Will there be snakes and wild animals where I'm going?'

'For goodness sake, you're only going to Lincolnshire! It's not a foreign country, you know. Anyway, stop chattering and get on with your breakfast. Never mind pulling a face, young lady. It could be hours before you get a decent meal, and then get a good wash and put your clean clothes on.'

'It must be a long way then, if it's going to take hours. There might be different animals, you know. Do you think there could be wolves?'

'Oh I don't know. I've never been. Here, get this down you. Every time you open your mouth put something in it, otherwise you won't be ready.' Sylvia pushed the bowl of cereals in front of the child and sighed, turning her head away quickly as her eyes filled with tears. This was not as she had planned. She had been determined to make these last hours a time of loving and yet here she was again, tense and irritable. 'Come on, Martin,' she breathed, longing to escape to her bedroom and to a release of all this bottled-up emotion.

Hannah toyed with her cereal, suddenly in tune with her mother's anxiety. During the last few days, she had pretended that she was going to boarding school like the girls in the stories that she read so avidly. Their mothers packed them up with all kinds of goodies and waved goodbye without shedding a tear. And then she started to think of herself as 'she' as though she were writing a story and she rehearsed various possible outcomes of her evacuation; the lady who looked like the Queen, and welcomed Hannah into her grand house with its wide staircase and spacious rooms; the tall gentleman with a moustache and a large dog, showing her the rolling lawns and flowerbeds; the kindly lady with identical twin daughters who offered to share all their books and toys with her; the haunted house with crooked rooms and secret passages. Now, all her thoughts were becoming confused into a mix-and-match kind of game and she was beginning to dread the consequences.

'Mam,' she said, resting her spoon in the dish, 'I wish you were coming with me. Why can't you? Mrs Green's going with her kids.'

Sylvia's expression softened. 'I wish I could, sweetheart, but who would look after your grandma and granddad? Anyway, it won't be long, you'll see. It'll be like a holiday with all those cows and things.' She clapped her hands in an attempt to appear jocular. 'Come on, now. Anybody would think I'd poisoned your breakfast. You won't grow, you know.'

Hannah giggled at the idea, relieved at the relaxation in her mother's attitude. 'I would be able to live in a tiny house, wouldn't I?' She stopped laughing as memories of the doll's house dream came flooding back. She bolted the last of her breakfast and jumped up, pushing the chair back away from the table, dragging and scraping the legs across the linoleum.

'Don't do that! Lift it! If I've told you once, I've told you a thousand times!'

They both sighed.

3

Cragthorpe

Jane Spencer hurried down the hill towards the village hall. She was 'wearing the hat' of the area billeting officer today, instead of that of the village school headmistress. She had instructed the small number of selected foster mothers to be there for midday. Six children were allocated to the parish. It would seem to be an acceptable figure for a community of this size, but previous experience of evacuees at the onset of the war had now tarnished initial patriotic fervour. The first batch had consisted of orphans or rejected children from a city orphanage and the stories of their bad habits and unsociable behaviour were still repeated. After the first few months, when life seemed to be going on as normal in spite of the war, most of these children returned to their familiar surroundings much to everyone's relief, but with the onset of heavy bombing raids, the policy of evacuation was resumed. Now, it was the turn of Cragthorpe. Some of the local people, alarmed by stories of rough little city kids as they were called, were loath to open their hearts but were obliged to offer accommodation if they had room. The allowance of ten shillings and sixpence a week and the extra rations were a sweetener in some cases, but even so it was no simple task. Jane had eased her conscience by accepting the role of billeting officer. She had no wish to share her home. Children belonged in the nine until four part of her day.

As she rounded the corner at the foot of the hill, she could make out a group of women waiting by the door. The hall, or village hut as it was generally called, was a single storey, wooden, creosoted structure. The window frames and the door were desperately in need of paint. The original green coat showed under a peeling brown layer in irregular patches giving it an unintentional camouflaged look. The weeds and grasses were left uncut, and the responsibility of maintenance was an unresolved issue on the last three agendas of the monthly parish committee meeting. Energy was channelled into self-sufficiency and the war effort.

The large shape of Mrs Callum, a farmer's wife, was easily recognised. She generously offered accommodation for two children, preferably strong boys. No doubt land work was on her mind. Mrs Hind was talking to her: she's a pleasant little body, Jane thought, remembering her hospitality and the neatness of her small house down Drovers Lane. As she drew nearer, she recognised Mrs Turner standing apart from the rest. She was the village shopkeeper's wife and a bit of a tartar by all accounts.

'Hello, Miss Spencer,' called Mrs Callum as Jane approached the group. 'I'm taking three today. Lily's kids have got the measles so she thought it best not to pass it on.' She laughed at the idea, as though it was a huge joke.

Jane didn't share her sense of humour. She had a mental picture of sickly children in the classroom. It was scarcely two weeks since the diarrhoea and sickness bug invaded all and sundry, and the bucket of sawdust had only just been returned to the cupboard.

She made no comment as she groped in her handbag for the key and proceeded to turn the rusting, reluctant lock. She stood to one side as the others filed past her and glanced at the list in her hand, mentally ticking off the names. There was no great arithmetical necessity to make such a labour of her task, but lists were there to be ticked. As if justifying her zeal she asked, 'Has anyone seen Mrs Porter?'

'I saw him on his way to the pub,' Mrs Turner said. 'She's probably forgotten. You know what she's like.'

Miss Spencer didn't know what Elsie Porter was like. She made no contact with her through school as Elsie was childless, but stories abounded of her husband's drinking sessions at The Three Bells. Perhaps the responsibility of a child would do them good, she thought, but with little conviction. She gave Mrs Turner no satisfaction however, and merely commented that no doubt Mrs Porter would soon arrive as it was only just striking the hour.

'We might as well make ourselves comfortable,' she said, pulling a chair away from a pile stacked against the wall. The others followed suit, grouping their chairs a short distance away from the teacher, establishing the feeling of separation between them and her.

The atmosphere was strained. Jane Spencer enquired about their families with scant enthusiasm. Her stomach, as if sensing neglect, began to complain loudly, and to cover her embarrassment she got up and went outside. 'Just for a quick look,' she explained. She listened for the sound of the bus. There was little traffic on the roads these days, particularly on a Sunday. The train was due in Grantham at eleven o'clock. 'Any minute now,' she muttered, looking at her watch. There was still no sign of Elsie Porter. She turned and walked back into the hall as a cold gust of wind whipped against her face, and a sudden feeling of loneliness lurched in her stomach, joining the hunger pains.

The following half an hour seemed to pass at a snail's pace, but at last the sound of a noisy motor engine signalled a possible end to their waiting.

'Wait here, everyone,' the teacher ordered. 'I'll go and check them off. It shouldn't take long.' She breathed in deeply as she strode to the door, the shabby floorboards creaking under her determined tread.

The single-decker green bus was pulling to a halt on the gravelled patch at the roadside opposite to the village hall. She could see children standing up and walking along the gangway. They were an unknown quantity. Miss Spencer, with school in mind, prayed for some decent brains, whereas the waiting women inside were no doubt considering the disruption these arrivals could bring to their lives.

Hannah stood up when her name was called. The boy and girl, whom Sally had recognised, were getting to their feet. Sally had whispered that they came from a rough family down Liddon Street. It was exciting on the train: a glorious adventure that needed no ending. But the next part of the journey along twisting badly surfaced country roads, as the bus travelled through a succession of villages, had made her feel quite sick. Added to this was a great feeling of loneliness. She tried to keep a picture in her mind of her last sight of Sally as she got off the bus, but all she could recall were trees. She reached out to steady herself and looked across at the small groups of houses that clustered around a wooden building. 'I can't see any cows and things, can you?' she whispered to the quiet girl with pigtails.

The Liddon Street boy answered, giving a hoarse laugh, 'Here's one coming now. She looks a right cow.' Jack Clayton was feeling as tired and disenchanted as Hannah, but he wouldn't admit it. 'Is that a cowshed, missus?' he called in a jaunty voice.

The two other boys, David and Peter Brown, giggled, but the smiles left their faces when the tall, thin lady glared in their direction.

'Indeed it is not,' she replied sharply. 'Speak when you are spoken to, boy. I can see you need your knife box squaring up.'

Jack mouthed, 'What knife box?'

Her dark eyes continued to focus on him, and he shuffled uneasily, turning his attention to the gravelled surface and stirring up the stones with the toe of his boot.

The WVS lady made a final check and handed over the appropriate ration sheets and identity cards, before shaking her colleague's hand and waving goodbye to the six children. 'Just behave yourselves,' she felt obliged to say, although she had passed the point of caring some time ago. All she wanted to do was to get the next train home before the raids started. The German pilots were in the habit of following the railway tracks into the industrial sites.

'Right! Follow me,' their new guardian commanded. The children responded without thinking, programmed to the words and to the tone of voice. The teacher's stomach churned and gurgled, and she struggled to compose herself, glancing at the list of names and matching them to the labels pinned on the coats. For a brief moment, she likened them to so much lost luggage, but that little surge of compassion vanished as Jack Clayton kicked out at the small girl in front of him. I know who's getting him, she thought with a tight-lipped smile.

She scanned the list again, as she herded the children towards the seated adults. Apparently, the older girl was that little renegade's sister, Gloria. What did she glory in? Perhaps separation from her brother would brighten her life and ease the workload for Lily Winter with her toddlers. The two Brown brothers would fit in splendidly with life on the farm. Mrs Callum, she hoped, would be pleased with that arrangement. Mrs Turner, the local shopkeeper, wanted help in the business, particularly in running errands now that her two grown-up sons were conscripted. Jack Clayton was the only available choice. Well, if anyone could square him up, she could. The neat little girl with pigtails, Rosie Dent, seemed the ideal choice for quiet Mrs Hind, and that left one name. Ah yes. The small fair-haired girl, Hannah Flynn. She ticked down the list, as though she was marking a column of sums, linking each child with an adult. That's the best I can do, she reasoned, drawing in the last line joining Hannah Flynn with Elsie Porter. There was still no sign of the wretched woman.

'No Mrs Porter yet.' The tone implied a matter of fact, rather than a question and no one spoke. The atmosphere was tense. The women regarded the children, and they in turn studied their future 'mothers'. Hannah liked the look of the fat lady who exclaimed, 'Oh! Bless their little hearts!' as they walked into the hall. She reminded Hannah of a jolly version of Mrs Blenkin, and such an association with home comforted her.

'Now children. These ladies have kindly offered to look after you for a while.' Miss Spencer cleared her throat. 'Mrs Callum, you wanted two boys, which is splendid as David and Peter are brothers, so I'm sure you will all be happy with that arrangement. Mrs Hind, Rosie Dent has been allocated to you. Gloria Clayton, you will eventually be with Mrs Winter. We don't want you catching the measles, do we?' She ignored Gloria's puzzled look and hurried on, not allowing any space for differences of opinion. 'Jack Clayton, you're to go with Mrs Turner.' She indicated each lady in turn.

Hannah gave a small sigh of relief. She had taken an instant dislike to the formidable looking Mrs Turner. She didn't like people who wore spectacles. 'Four eyes' they called them at school. This woman seemed to have a permanent glare on her face like the teacher in class three. However, the feeling of relief was quickly replaced with that of concern as she realised that she appeared to have been left out. This was always happening to her. When they picked teams for races, she was left until last with the fat boy, Piggy Steele. A voice inside her head began to wail. Her cheeks flushed and a sudden sob choked in the back of her throat. Before she could squeeze her eyes together, tears began to run down her face. She stared down at her feet in an attempt to hide the evidence and tried to sniff quietly.

No one seemed to notice. The adults struggled to their feet, their limbs stiffened by the long wait.

'Every picture tells a story,' laughed Mrs Callum, 'I feel as though I've been sitting here for hours. It'll be milking time before we know it.'

Hannah looked up as far as she could, without raising her head. She watched an assortment of legs and lower bodies pass by on their way to the outside door.

'I will see you all in school tomorrow. Don't be late.'

Hannah gasped. The woman in charge must be a teacher. She could think of nothing worse in life than living with a teacher.

Miss Spencer was making a valiant attempt to sound interested in the children's welfare. 'I expect they will need an early night tonight,' she called as the door creaked open. She turned away, war effort completed for another day apart from solving the problem of the missing Elsie Porter. 'Now. What are we going to do with you? Come on. Turn off the waterworks. We can do without that, thank you. You haven't been missed out. Mrs Porter hasn't arrived yet.'

'I thought I was coming to live with you,' Hannah croaked, the tension still affecting her throat.

'Goodness me, no! I'm the head teacher at the school. I'm far too busy to look after an evacuee. Oh no, indeed not. You are to be with Mr and Mrs Porter up Eastfield Lane. I can't think what's happened to her. She knew you would be here by twelve. We'd better go and find out. Perhaps we'll meet her on the way.'

The cold wind buffeted against their legs. Hannah stumbled, the brown cardboard box housing her gas-mask bouncing on her hip, as she caught her foot on the uneven pavement.

'Come on, child,' the teacher said impatiently. 'Don't dawdle and pick your feet up! Time is pressing.'

Hannah wanted to ask about her billeting. Was it a farm or perhaps a big house with an attic? She had given up hopes of castles and secret passages, but the tone of the teacher's voice was rather daunting, and she walked behind in silence, her short legs outpaced by her companion's manly stride. She broke into a run every now and again, and there was no time to study the stone houses on either side of the village street. She focused her eyes on the pavement instead, dodging the pot-holes flooded with water from the earlier showers. Her imagination was locked in the back of her mind. This was grim reality with nothing to lend itself to fantasy. There was no escaping it.

They seemed to be leaving the village behind now. For a moment the fantasising returned, ugly and threatening. What if this Mrs Porter was old like a witch? Pictures of Hansel and Gretl and the gingerbread house came into her mind. Why hadn't she come to meet the children? She glanced fearfully into a large spinney on their left. The branches creaked in a sudden gust of wind. She tried hard to think of home. What would her mother be doing now? Making a cup of tea for Grandma perhaps. What time was it? She had no idea. It didn't seem like the kind of day that had time. There was a nothingness kind of feeling about it and she couldn't believe that it was only this morning when she woke up in the shelter and got ready to go on the train. It was difficult to visualise things. She tried to conjure up a picture of her mother. It came through in separate parts like pieces of a puzzle and reminded her of the Cheshire cat. She liked Alice books. Sometimes she would stare into her dressing-table mirror and wish that she could go through it into a magic land, or she would press her eye against the torch during illicit bedtime reading under the covers, imagining strange fairy-tale realms beyond the twinkling bulb.

'Nearly there now, dear,' said Miss Spencer, breaking into Hannah's contemplations. The teacher had a sudden desire to console. There was something about this child which stirred feelings very foreign in her austere disciplined life.

Hannah, receptive as ever, latched on to the sympathetic tone.

'That's okay,' she said. 'I'm not tired. Well perhaps just a little bit. I expect you are. My grandma gets tired but she has bad knees. Do you know, they swell up like footballs.'

She emphasised the last word and the teacher half smiled and half winced at the idea, although the association with an elderly lady was not exactly flattering. They continued in silence once more. Hannah regretted her impulsive chatter. Fancy talking like that to a teacher, she thought. But then she had never been in such intimate company with a teacher before.

Their steps now led down a narrow lane that was little more than a cart track.

Goodness me! thought Hannah. How much further?

Come on, Mrs Porter, thought Jane Spencer, her stomach gurgling loudly.

4

Elsie Porter

Elsie Porter dabbed at her eye with a piece of wet rag. She was still feeling dizzy after the blow to her head, but her chief concern was with the outward signs of violence. She rummaged through the deep drawer at the bottom of the kitchen chest of drawers which was filled with a tangle of clothes pegs, lengths of string, cotton reels with needles pushed under the cotton, candles, pencils—in fact one could say everything under the sun, without feeling that it was a gross exaggeration. After stabbing her fingers twice, first on a darning needle and then on a stray drawing pin, she gave an 'ah' of triumph. She had hunted for this little round box for a long time. 'I knew it was in this drawer,' she said to the cat. 'I don't know how I missed it.'

She scrutinised her reflection in the small mirror that hung over a shelf near to the kitchen window. It wasn't easy to get the whole picture as the damp steamy atmosphere on wash days had caused patches of the silvery backing to peel off. She twisted her head from one side to the other, trying to detect any sign of swelling, and patted the pink face powder over the inflamed area around her right eye.

Elsie was the victim of a bad marriage, wretchedly unhappy, but with nowhere else to go and in any case, no spare money. She looked considerably older than her thirty-five years. She was always small and slim, but after eighteen years of marriage to Tom Porter, the words downtrodden and skinny came more readily to mind. Her light brown hair leapt wildly from her scalp after being released from the nightly grip of steel rollers. She had been dragging the hairbrush through it when the quarrel started.

Tom looked forward to his Sunday breakfast and particularly this Sunday's when he expected a sausage to accompany the fried egg and fat bacon on his plate. During the week, there was little time to indulge in a good breakfast and he had drooled over the sight of the sausage in the meat safe for two days.

Usually, Elsie cooked extra potatoes on a Saturday and used the left-over for frying up on a Sunday to keep Tom going until he had slept off his usual Sunday drinks at The Three Bells. All of her efforts during the last few days to tidy up had completely confused her thinking processes. Tom wouldn't need another hot meal until later on, but the child would be hungry after the long journey. Elsie desperately wanted to make a good impression. Bangers and mash! That's what kids like. She rejoiced in her brain wave and hid the spare mashed potato under an upturned dish in the pantry. Tom could have fried bread for a change and he would be too sleepy to notice the absence of the sausage.

However, she was wrong. After demolishing half of the egg and most of the bacon and fried bread in three greedy gulps, he shouted, 'You've not put the potato out and where's that sausage? Come on! Never mind titivating yourself, woman.'

Elsie didn't move for a few seconds. Her brain was working overtime in the deceits department, a highly developed area of grey matter. Then she turned, story ready. 'That mouse ate it. You know. The one that's too bloody clever to be trapped. It's such a pest, Tom. We'll 'ave to catch it.' She gabbled on about chewed sugar bags and mouse droppings, not wanting to give him space in the conversation. 'I'll do you a real big dinner tonight. Lamb stew. I haven't got time now. I have to be at the village hall by twelve.'

'What have you got to be there for?' Tom's mind was still blanketed by sleep.

'You know. The evacuee. They are getting here at about twelve. The school teacher told us not to be late.'

'Bossy cow! Who the hell does she think she is? Well she'll just have to wait, won't she?'

'Don't talk so stupid!'

Elsie turned back to the task of taming her wayward hair, too late to avoid the plate dripping with grease and the remains of the fried egg. It struck her at the side of her face and she fell to the floor, knocked off balance. She wanted to remain there, safe behind her closed eyes, but felt obliged to squint through her lashes.

For a moment, Tom regretted his action. He hadn't intended to hit her with the plate. He just wanted her to know who was boss. He stared down at her. She had applied a thick layer of lipstick, knowing that she would lick most of it off on the way to the village, and the red gash in the white face, surrounded by corkscrews of hair, gave her a clown-like look. However, he felt no inclination to laugh, and it was a great relief for him when Elsie squinted through her lashes. Now, with the danger apparently over, he continued where he had left off. 'You've eaten that bloody sausage, haven't you?'

Elsie struggled to her feet, wiping a piece of fried egg from her face, and kicked the broken pieces of plate to one side. She had seen the fear on his face and felt secure in the safety of his cowardice. 'I'm going to the lav.'

Tom could only stare at his bizarre-looking wife. This was an Elsie he didn't know and he made no attempt to stop her. Elsie quickened her pace as she reached the kitchen door and headed towards the safety of the outside lavatory. She was shaking with nervous tension and physical shock. She perched on the wooden seat of the earth closet, merely using it as a resting place, and listened for any sounds of her husband in pursuit. There were no footsteps, but the sounds that did reach her ears made her gasp hysterically.

'Oh my God! Oh my God! What the hell's he doing? He's breaking the place up. Oh my God! Whatever am I going to do? I'll kill him! I will. I'll kill him!'

The noises stopped, and she listened, hardly daring to breathe in case she missed hearing him creeping up the path. The wooden earth closet must have been designed with larger bodies in mind for her legs dangled and her feet were beginning to throb. A hen clucked outside, its beak and little head appearing briefly in the gap under the door as it pecked at some groundsel growing near to the doorframe. Elsie had no idea by now what the time was. It seemed that she had been huddled in this spot for ages. At last, after hearing no further sounds, she plucked up the courage to open the door wide enough for a view up the path. She sensed that he had gone. There was an atmosphere of desertion and solitude. No doubt he was well on his way to The Three Bells.

The sight that met her eyes as she went into the house was chaotic. Her mother's vase was smashed to pieces, the jagged evidence scattered in the hearth. He'd thrown the kitchen chairs across the floor and scattered her piano music in all directions. The piano itself looked unscathed.

'Just let him damage my piano and I will kill him,' she fumed as she set the chairs back and gathered up the pieces of the broken pottery. She paused at the foot of the stairs, still not able to trust her instincts fully, and sniffed the air like a wild animal, her nostrils straining to filter out his scent. His jacket was gone from the hook on the kitchen door, and she relaxed her shoulders and took a deep breath.

Now, as she dabbed at her eye with the face powder, she began to doubt her good resolutions. The clock hands pointed to a quarter to one. Perhaps the teacher had made other arrangements. Perhaps they didn't need her any more. She relaxed with that idea but felt saddened as well. She'd always wanted a family. The swelling was going down now and if she ran all the way she might be in time. She combed her hair down the sides of her face, ignoring the frizzy mass at the back. She'd planned to look so glamorous to spite the village women who could be very uncharitable at times.

'I'll show them,' she declared to the mirror. She put on her headscarf, pushed her thin arms into her tweed coat and shuffled off her grease-stained slippers. The lane was very muddy after the heavy rainfall. It would have to be wellingtons.

5

Eastfield Cottage

Such was the figure who rounded the bend in the lane, as Miss Spencer and her small charge approached it from the opposite direction. Elsie began to raise a hand in a wave of acknowledgement, but on second thoughts dropped it again. Such familiarity seemed out of place between the likes of her and the village head teacher. She quickened her step, weaving around the potholes, and Miss Spencer stopped in her tracks.

'Wait,' she ordered. 'There's no point in me going any further than I have to.'

Hannah stood next to her latest acquaintance at the side of the lane, with a feeling of safeness and reassurance in her company. The figure new on the horizon represented the next hurdle of the day.

As she drew closer, Elsie began to call out in nervous incoherent bursts of sound, her stammering speech regressing to that typical in a pupil/teacher relationship. 'Sorry I'm late, miss. One of those days, you know. I expect you get them although I don't suppose you do. You not being married. You know how it is. Still better late than never as they say.'

Miss Spencer gave a loud sniff, a habit which manifested itself in times of stress. Her long thin nose, now reddened with the cold east wind, was a yardstick to her moods. The children knew to watch out when Miss was sniffing.

'Well, you're here now so I can go home and get my dinner. At this rate it will soon be teatime.'

Elsie gave a crooked grin, exposing a row of yellow teeth. Like the teacher's sniff, it was a nervous habit. People found it most irritating and Miss Spencer was no exception. She nearly said that it was no laughing matter, but replaced that comment with a loud sniff as she handed over the last envelope from her bag.

'You'll find her name and address and medical details in there and an emergency ration sheet. Write to your parents, dear and let them know you are all right.' Her voice took on a kinder tone but her chief concern was for her own well-being. She turned and strode off into the wind, which blew her long coat against her legs and billowed it out behind her. Hannah felt a sense of loss as she watched her go, the distance between them widening rapidly.

'My, she's a tartar. I can remember one we had just like her. Anyway, come on, duck. Let's get home. You look frozen to death.' Elsie tugged at Hannah's arm. She was pleased with her new possession. She's like I was, thin and quiet, she thought. She looked behind her. The teacher was out of sight and she felt a surge of joy pressing against her fears of failure and rejection.

Hannah didn't respond. The name 'duck' puzzled her. Still, she didn't argue with the idea of reaching a warm resting place. There seemed to be no shelter from the biting gusts of wind, no buildings to dull the edges. She had given up trying to come to terms with the day. Misery now solidified in a hard lump in her chest. She cast sideways glances at her new companion as they trudged along, the silence broken only by the squelching of the woman's wellingtons. They were streaked in yellow slime, a layer of mud becoming softened by the splashes of water from the puddles. Hannah would learn later that this end of the village was called 'The Clays' and that the fields were either water-logged or baked solid in the high summer.

She sighed and gave a shudder. The awareness of the rough bony fingers, which held her hand in a tight grip, seemed to be the only physical reality, and, fearing the loss of it, she allowed herself to be tugged along.

'What's your name, duckie? The teacher didn't say. Well I didn't hear her if she did. This wind blows everything away.' Elsie broke the silence, dragging her thoughts away from her own childhood. She was feeling at a loss for words, suddenly uneasy in the company of her dream child.

Hannah smiled at the idea of her name blown away by the wind and travelling to strange places. Elsie's fingers tightened on hers to remind her of the question.

'Hannah, Hannah Mary actually but Hannah will do.'

'Hannah. That's a nice name. You can call me Auntie if you like— Auntie Elsie. That sounds good, doesn't it?'

Hannah didn't answer. A small wood at the side of the road caught her attention. Night-time seemed to be there already in its dark shade. She could feel the prickling of goose-pimples under the sleeves of her jumper and her leg muscles strained against the steady walking pace of her foster mother. A building came into view behind the last of the tall elm trees and she tightened her grip on the captive hand.

Elsie laughed. 'Not there yet, duck. You wouldn't want to live in that place, I can tell you.' She laughed again in a hoarse kind of cackle and Hannah's heart leapt in fear as they drew near to the house. She could see now that it was a ruin. It stood sideways on to the lane, its windows gaping holes and its door ever open. The two bedroom windows seemed like sightless eyes, blind from lack of tenants.

'That's not going to see many more winters now the roof's going. A crying shame I call it. It was a good warm house, but folks don't seem to care any more.'

Hannah twisted around to see the back of it. A drystone wall formed the boundary of a garden now overgrown in a tangle of years of neglect.

'Poor old Mrs Knight,' her companion continued. 'The place went to rack and ruin after her husband died, and she never got no help. I used to go and give her an 'and but I had all my jobs to do and she was a funny old stick at times. Only fit for rats and mice now.'

'Can't somebody mend it?' Hannah asked, trying to sound matter of fact.

'I suppose they could, but then no one would want to live there. They're frit to death of the place. Reckon as how it's haunted. I've never seen any ghosts but then I don't come down here after dark. Not if I can help it.'

'Do they think it's the old lady?'

'What, haunting it you mean? Oh no. She lives in the village now. I haven't seen much of her lately, but she's still on the go. People think she's mad because she talks to herself and keeps cats. They reckon as how she has twenty of them all living inside, but I don't know. The elderberry has grown like a thicket around the place. You nearly have to fight your way in.' Elsie gave another of her coarse cackles sounding like an old crone herself.

Hannah, curiosity whetted in spite of her misery, turned to have a last look at the old house, part of it now silhouetted against the dull sky.

'Nearly there, duck. That's our house. Look, the one with the hawthorn hedge and the sycamore tree.'

Such observations were wasted on Hannah. She had no idea what hawthorn or sycamore trees looked like, and in any case the details were unnecessary, there being only one house in sight.

A large black cat appeared from under the hedge and ran towards them.

'It's all right, duckie. She won't hurt you,' Elsie reassured. 'She always thinks it's time for her milk when she sees me. Don't you, greedy guts?'

The cat rubbed herself against Elsie's wellingtons ignoring the wet mud in her purring exuberance.

'She's very fat. Do you think she has too much milk?'

'Oh no. That's not milk. She's pregnant. You know. Having kittens. It'll be a job for Tom soon.'

Hannah repeated the word pregnant to herself and wondered about Mr Porter's part in it. The cat ran ahead in the direction of her empty saucer and disappeared under a wicket gate about halfway along the hedge.

Elsie laughed. 'She'll have to wait. I bet you're starving, aren't you?'

Hannah didn't answer, leaving any commitment until some food was produced, although she had to admit that she was ready for something.

Elsie pushed open the gate with some difficulty. Like everything else around here, it had seen better days. The horizontal bar at the bottom which secured the upright palings had come adrift at one end, and in consequence the whole gate was suffering. As if to emphasise its dilemma it creaked loudly. A gravelled pathway led from the gate up to the back door.

'Here you are, duck. Your new home. You go upstairs and put your things in the back room while I put the kettle on. I've got sausage and tates for your dinner. I bet you like that, don't you? I know I always did.'

Hannah tried to disguise the shudder and gave a forced smile. She hated sausage. At the same time she wrinkled her nose at the dank smell. It reminded her somewhat of the outside passage at home with an added indefinable addition.

'Go on. Take your case upstairs. Through there at the end of the passage.'

Hannah looked up at the dark uncarpeted staircase. A small window high in the landing wall appeared to have never experienced the cleansing touch of a wash leather. The light struggling through the layer of grime had a greenish cast, and she groped for the handrail, bumping the case on each tread. She was breathless when she reached the landing and rested her case on the bare boards while she decided which door would open into the back room. Her brain had an illogical twist when it came to directions and as usual she made the wrong choice. This obviously was the grown ups' room she reasoned, for a high double bed dominated the room. She noticed nothing else, intent on closing the door as quickly as possible to trap in the awful smell. It was the same as downstairs. She ran her tongue over her lips. She could taste it whatever it was. The other

34

door was directly opposite, a few steps across the landing. 'Please don't let it be smelly,' she prayed, slowly turning the knob.

There was little space on the other side of the door but the air was fresh. A narrow single bed fitted into the gap between the door and the wall, and a chest of drawers stood in the opposite corner next to the window. There was no mirror to reflect any images, but this room even viewed through the looking-glass would have been just as austere and dull. The walls were distempered in a drab cream and, as with the rest of the house, the paintwork was dark brown.

She went to the window, lifting the bottom of the frayed net curtain to get a clearer view of the back garden. It was as uninspiring as the house. A concrete path led down to a small pantiled shed and a few rows of Brussels sprouts stood stark and ugly against the brown compacted soil. A number of hens scratched amongst some kitchen refuse, their little heads bobbing and turning in their constant pursuit of nourishment.

She watched them for a while with fascination and then turned to study the small room, thankful to be alone with her thoughts. However, her reverie was short lived.

'There's a cup of tea here for you, 'annah,' Elsie's voice echoed up the stairs. 'And I've got your sausage and mash frying.'

Hannah was frowning as she went down into the kitchen. She hated it when people missed the 'H' off her name. Still, it was better than being called 'duck'. Fumes from the hot lard in the frying pan competed with the stale smell of dirt and body odour. Elsie didn't notice the bad smells. She was part of them, her major contribution coming from her abandoned wellingtons and her slippers, which were now back on her feet.

'Nearly ready. Here. Get this hot tea down you and go and sit in the other room by the fire. It's got a bit low what with one thing and another, but I'll put another log on in a minute.'

Hannah gratefully accepted the tea, although it looked, as her mother would say, stewed to jiggery. Elsie liked strong tea, and for quickness sake and economy had made do with the left over from breakfast by standing the teapot on the top of the oven at the side of the kitchen range. She scraped the sausage and potato onto a plate and placed it carefully on the so-called scrubbed top table. It rarely, if ever, saw a scrubbing brush, and was used as a resting place for anything which came to hand, albeit a hen for plucking and drawing or a pile of dirty washing ready for the dolly tub, as well as for the general preparation and eating of food.

Hannah looked around the small living room, sipping her tea and trying to avoid the numerous chips on the edge of the cup. The piano caught her eye, its highly polished walnut veneer reflecting the light coming in through the casement window. It didn't seem to belong amongst the shabby furniture, and the sight of it raised her spirits. She longed to have piano lessons. Her father couldn't read music but that didn't stop him from rattling through all the latest popular songs as well as the music hall favourites of the 'twenties and 'thirties. She was promised lessons, but they never materialised. The outbreak of war put a stop to that and, since her grandparents had moved in with their possessions, it was impossible to get near to the piano.

She took her tea into the kitchen when Elsie called and valiantly struggled to eat the crispy potatoes and the charred sausage with its pink undercooked interior. Her mouth was so dry with tiredness and anxiety that each mouthful was taking a lot of chewing. The heavy grease which clung to every morsel was cloying on her tongue. She put down her knife and fork and sipped the strong, now tepid, tea.

Elsie was watching her eat as though the child was a new pet at feeding time. 'Don't you like it, duckie?' she asked anxiously.

'Oh yes, it's lovely,' lied Hannah. 'I can't eat quickly. I'm a right slow coach. I have to have drinks in between.' She took the opportunity to converse instead. 'Can you play the piano, Mrs Porter, or is it Mr Porter? I was going to have lessons but our piano is behind my grandma's settee.'

'That's a funny place to keep it. Yes, it's me what plays. Tom...er Mr Porter doesn't know one note from another. Hurry up and finish your dinner. I'll play you a tune and I can give you lessons if you like.' Elsie seemed to grow with importance. Fancy, she thought. Me a piano teacher. She got up and went into the living room, returning with a photograph. 'This is me, look, when I got my last certificate.'

Hannah studied the image of a young woman in a long dress, her hair curling down over her shoulders. 'Was this in the olden days?' she asked, staring in disbelief at the shabby little woman beside her.

'I was fifteen. Like a film star, wasn't I?'

Elsie's pride was short lived as the back door burst open and Tom fell over the cat.

'What the bloody 'ell,' he shouted, kicking out at the terrified creature who shot past him, ears flattened and body low to the ground. Elsie's face registered the same feelings of panic. Her cheek bone throbbed from the earlier encounter with her husband's ill temper, which now had become even worse with the effects of alcohol. She gestured to Hannah across the table.

'Go upstairs and put your clothes away, duckie.' Her voice was little more than a whisper.

Hannah needed no second telling, pushing her unfinished meal to one side and struggling to her feet. She recognised the smell of liquor. Her father came home sometimes like that, although usually he was in a joking kind of mood. Nevertheless, he soon felt the sharp edge of her mother's tongue. Her heart was beating as fast as her legs were mounting the stairs.

'So that's what happened to it then,' she heard him shout. 'Bloody mice indeed. What's the matter with bread and dripping for the kid? It never did me no harm.'

There was a loud crash followed by a scream. Then Elsie's voice yelling, 'Don't, Tom! You're hurting me!'

Hannah reached the bedroom and slammed the door behind her. She ran to the window not knowing what to do. Her teeth began to chatter and she couldn't take in a full breath. 'Mammy,' she cried, reverting to her infant speech, 'please come and take me home.'

Then she froze, hearing a heavy tread on the stairs. The only place to hide was under the bed. She crawled under the over-hanging blanket and pressed herself against the wall, holding her breath, the whole of her being focused on listening. A door slammed and then there was silence, a blankness which stretched her awareness into even greater tension. She had the sensation of being in a nightmare, and her chest began to ache with the unevenness of her breathing.

What if he had murdered Mrs Porter? What if her body was lying on the kitchen floor covered in blood? Hannah had read of such things in books smuggled upstairs at bedtime, which created such lurid images in her mind that she stayed awake for hours. She pressed her ear to the floorboards, straining to hear any sounds of movement, and jumping violently when the bedroom door creaked open.

"Annah. It's only me, duckie. Wherever are you? Oh! You're under there. Silly billy! He wouldn't hurt a fly. You can come down now. There he goes, snoring his head off.'

The sound of Elsie's reassuring tones, although not her words, released the tension. Hannah struggled out from under the bed and looked up to see her foster mother apparently none the worse for wear and not a drop of blood to be seen.

'He always goes to bed for a bit and wakes up in a good mood. You'll see,' Elsie continued. 'I think we ought to have a walk while it's dry. I'll show you the way to school for the morning.'

'Can't you show me tomorrow?' Hannah didn't particularly want to face that windswept lane again, but the sudden sound of very loud snoring from behind the bedroom door made her clutch at Elsie's skirt. 'All right then,' she agreed. 'I'll get my coat.' Her voice seemed small; lost somewhere in the back of her head.

Elsie appeared not to notice.

'Yes. You do that and you'd better go to the lav or you'll want to go on the way and then you'll prick your bum on some thistles or something.' Elsie giggled hysterically at the idea.

Hannah didn't find it amusing. She hated that word. Her mother said that only common people talked like that.

'Go on, duckie. I'll just get this in the oven with some onions.' Elsie scooped some pieces of scrag end of mutton into a stoneware dish and then began to peel a large onion.

'Where is it?' Hannah asked, looking for another door. At home, the bathroom and lavatory were next to the back kitchen. 'It's not upstairs, is it?'

'Oh bless you, no. We ain't got a bathroom. Nothing as posh as that. No, the lav's down the garden. The door's a bit stiff. Give it a good pull and I wouldn't try and close it if I were you. You might not be able to get out and it's a bit dark in there.'

Hannah walked slowly along the path, glancing back once or twice at the house. She imagined herself behind the bedroom curtain looking out, as though part of her was like a ghost reliving those recent fearful moments. The small tiled shed, which she had seen on her first appraisal of the back way, apparently was the outside convenience. She reached up to the rusty sneck[1], pressing her thumb down as hard as she could. The latch suddenly yielded in a noisy click and she put her hands around the edge of the wooden door, pulling against its weight with some difficulty. The sight that met her eyes, as she peered into the gloomy interior, filled her with astonishment. Where was the lavatory? All she could see was a high wooden box with some newspapers piled up in one corner. A round lid with a knob in the middle invited inspection. She lifted it up and her face twisted in distaste. Why hadn't it been flushed away? Where was the chain? She balanced on the edge, legs dangling, terrified in case she fell down this dark, evil-smelling hole, and decided that she would rather have taken her chances with the thistles.

Elsie was pegging some towels on the line, anxiously keeping a check on her small charge. 'All right, my duck? Did you manage? It's a bit dark in there. You'll need a torch later on. This is our bath, look.' She pointed to a zinc bath hanging on a nail against the house wall. 'I have to boil some water up when we use it, which isn't very often, I can tell you. It takes a bit of filling especially if the tubs are low. I get worn out trekking up and down to the farm pump. That can be your job sometimes. Still, we usually manage with a bowl and a flannel. Won't be a minute, duck.'

Hannah turned and looked back along the garden. Just beyond the earth closet, the path disappeared through a gap in the hedge.

_____

1 Part of a latch

'Is the farm down there?' she asked, as Elsie reappeared resplendent once more in her tweed coat, headscarf and wellingtons.

'No. There's only our barn, such as it is. We just use it for straw and feed. It lets in the rain. One of these days the farmer might mend the roof before it falls down. No, it wouldn't be so bad if the pump was there. It's about half a mile up the lane. I'll show you that another day.'

Hannah couldn't think of another day. All she could think about was going home. 'Where does the teacher live? 'she asked. 'You know. The one who came with me.'

'Oh that Miss Spencer. In the school house, of course; I don't know whether we'll get that far. The hill's a killer in rough weather. Still, we'll see.' Elsie had Tom on her mind. 'Do you like bread and jam? I've got some of this year's plum.'

Hannah plodded along, a little cheered by the promise of more palatable food, while Elsie's thoughts turned to the end of her responsibilities for the day and the chance to put her feet up. They walked in silence now, both quickening their pace as they reached the wood. Then Elsie began to explain who lived where, pointing out the cobbler's workshop and the blacksmith's forge. They stood on the bridge watching the flow of the beck and catching their breath before following the road past the church and continuing up the steep hill towards the school.

Miss Spencer, in the act of drawing the curtains against the fading light, peered out at the two hunched little figures standing at the school gate. For a moment she experienced a pang of anxiety. Surely Mrs Porter hadn't changed her mind. The child took a step forward when she caught sight of the teacher's face at the window, and Miss Spencer ducked behind the curtain and then peeped through a narrow gap. She breathed more easily as they turned around and headed back down the hill.

'It will be pitch dark soon,' Elsie said, pushing open the rickety gate. 'Stay out in the garden for a bit longer and get the last of the daylight. I'll see to Mr Porter's dinner. Hang on. Perhaps you could do with the torch. Don't flash it around. Still, you know that, don't you?' She looked towards the front door, a frown creasing between her eyes. The walk had taken longer than she had anticipated, not being used to the slower gait of a child, and she had made little conversation on the way home, her mind preoccupied with thoughts of the Irish stew drying up in the oven. A burnt offering would be like a red rag to a bull.

Hannah welcomed the gaps in the conversation. As usual, fantasy had the upper hand, and she imagined herself journeying through dark landscapes encountering many perils, until she reached that familiar row of terraced houses. It was so easy to be resolute inside her head but now the real world, cold and strange, brought shivers of apprehension. In truth, she didn't know how to make her escape. She was in the proverbial cleft stick, afraid to be outside in the dark, yet equally fearful of the interior of the cottage and its tenants.

She wandered down the garden path past the earth closet and through the gap in the hedge. The barn was situated at the end of the next stretch of garden. The hawthorn hedge that bounded the property looked black and solid in the half-light. In the corner opposite to the barn was a collection of sheds made from an assortment of rusting sheets of corrugated iron, some lengths of rotting timber and several old doors. The whole area had a look of desolation and neglect.

The wide wooden doors under the front gable of the barn were hanging out of line, the hinges pulling away from the rotting frame. One was pulled open sufficiently to allow entrance, and Hannah squeezed into the gap, standing half in and half out, now feeling at liberty to direct the torch light up and around. There was a dank smell of rotting timber, and here and there puddles of water gave credence to Elsie's complaints about the leaking roof. Curiosity overcoming fear, she took a few steps over the cobbled floor, layers of straw and dead leaves crunching under foot. There was a trough fastened to the back wall and Hannah's thoughts turned briefly to the Christmas story, but no angels proclaimed glad tidings from the loft piled high with straw. Only a number of spiders, whose black cobwebs hung from the beams above her head, gathering in great clumps down the corners and across the stonework, were aware of her presence. Two small glazed windows, one on each side, were coated with a thick layer of grime denying their purpose of illumination and merely providing deeper ledges for the accumulation of dust.

A zigzag of shivers travelled down Hannah's back. The dereliction was no threat. She had been experiencing a certain sense of comfort in the privacy of this place, but suddenly a fear of something she could not name sent a lurch of adrenaline across under her ribs. She turned in a panic, pushing her body through the gap between the doors, forgetful of the wildly waving flashlight, her mouth dry and her heart beating fast.

She stood outside for a moment or two trying to quieten her fears, but an unfamiliar noise to her right set her heart bouncing again. She ran back along the path almost colliding with Elsie, who appeared in the gap carrying a large zinc bucket and an enamel bowl.

'The hens have put themselves to bed by the look of it. I bet they think I've forgotten their tea. It's a wonder Molly isn't complaining. Ah! There she goes.'

The same noise that had put Hannah to flight was coming from one of the ramshackle sheds.

'Who's Molly?' Hannah asked, shadowing her welcome companion as she stumbled along the muddy path.

'The pig, of course. Can't you hear her grunting?' Elsie swung the bucket backwards and forwards in an effort to keep her balance. 'This'll fatten her up,' she continued with some feeling. 'Do you like pig? I reckon there's nothing to beat a bit of fresh pig.'

Hannah didn't associate the word pig with meat. If Elsie had said pork it would have been different, but even so she was very ignorant about the source of meat, chose to be in fact, and until recently she linked pork with porcupines. Elsie grabbed the torch and directed the beam inside the chicken house lighting up a collection of Rhode Island Reds clucking in nervous anticipation of their food.

The child's excitement grew as they left the hens pecking at the grain and approached the second shack with its corrugated roof and small brick built enclosure along the side. A large snout snuffled over the top of the wall and Hannah clapped her hands in a brief moment of happiness.

'Have you had her for some time?' she asked.

'Hold your horses, damn you!' Elsie yelled as the pig pushed its head into the bucket. 'Quite a while,' she said, turning to answer Hannah's question. 'Since the garden fete. Tom won her at the bowls.' She hit Molly on the end of the nose with the bucket. 'Your greedy ways will come to an end soon, madam. She'll soon be fat enough to slaughter. It'll be good to have a side of bacon to cut at and plenty of lard. If you ask Tom nicely he'll blow up the bladder and you can play football with it. Then there's the fries. You can collect up some pennies taking plates of fry round. It don't keep long and folks are glad of extra rations. They do the same back to us. That's country ways for you.'

Hannah was staring wide-eyed. 'You're not going to eat her, are you?'

The pig looked up, disturbed by the high-pitched tone of an unfamiliar voice, suddenly aware of a stranger in their midst. Hunger had reduced her vigilance. Now she fixed a pale eye on the child and grunted nervously.

'It's all right, Molly. She won't hurt you, even though she is a townie. Of course we are going to eat her, silly! Why do you think we've got her in the first place? If it wasn't for the hens and a pig each year and the rabbits Tom gets in his snares, mind you, that's between me and you, well we'd be in a sorry state I can tell you. What with the rationing and the money Tom earns.'

Hannah turned away. All that people seemed to think about was eating. She was curious about bladders and fries but was determined not to appear to share in Elsie's enthusiasm.

The dark shape of the cottage came back into view. Its squatness looked brooding and sinister, reminding Hannah once more of the witch's house, and she cast a nervous look in her foster mother's direction. A band of light showed under the kitchen blind. Back in their street the air raid warden would have been knocking on the door and shouting, 'You're showing a light,' but this place seemed remote from everywhere and everything.

Elsie turned around, shining the torch at the door of the lavatory. 'You'd better go again before you get ready for bed. I'll wait for you. Be quick. I'm getting perished. Then you can have some bread and jam and a cup of cocoa.'

Hannah didn't want to go and protested but Elsie was adamant and clicked her tongue impatiently at the child. The woman's legs ached with the unaccustomed walk and her stomach was crying out for food. She pulled at the door, cursing under her breath at its stiffness, and gave Hannah a less than gentle push inside.

Hannah held her breath and felt for the knob on the lid, encountering instead the rim of the hole. She drew back her hands shuddering in disgust and rubbed them down the side of her coat.

'Be quick!' came the impatient voice.

The child kicked at the wooden front and waited for a few seconds before turning her back on the black hole.

Elsie removed the thick mud from her wellingtons on the scraper by the door and told Hannah to do likewise.

'We don't want muck all over the floor, do we? Come on, duckie, hurry up. Let's get the door shut else there'll be rats in. Mice is bad enough.' She raised her voice as though anything lurking in the undergrowth would be deterred by aggression and without realising that she was adding yet one more fear to those already established in Hannah's mind.

'Have you got Black Clocks in your house, Mrs Porter?' she asked, peering into the shadows.

'Black Clocks? Whatever are those?'

Hannah hesitated, remembering her mother's anger if she ever spoke of them.

'They're a kind of beetle,' she said. 'Some people have them under the floorboards.'

'Dirty people, I expect. We've not got any.'

Hannah winced at the word dirty. Her mother would go mad if she heard about it. Her Dad had creosoted under the floor, but said it was a waste of time as they were all up and down the street.

She thought of Sally laughingly telling her how she and her brothers screwed up fish and chip paper and put it under the bath to lure the beetles, and then listened to them popping as the paper burnt at the back of the range. She shuddered at the thought of them, but would have swapped her new fears for those of her recent past.

She looked around the kitchen again, realising, now that her eyes were accustomed to the light, that the corners of the room were still in shadow. An oil lamp hissed away on the chest of drawers. She stared at it and then looked up at the ceiling, noticing the absence of a light bulb.

'Why haven't you got a bulb, Mrs Porter? Is it broken or something?'

'A bulb? Oh you mean electric. We ain't got none of that. We were supposed to get it, and then the war broke out so that was that. They've got it down in the village but we get nothing up here.'

Hannah couldn't imagine life without electricity. 'We've got it,' she said smugly, 'and a sink and a bath with taps and a chain to pull.'

'Well you're lucky aren't you, miss!' Elsie snapped. Her varicose vein throbbed in the back of her leg. 'We have to work hard here, you know.'

Hannah couldn't see what that had to do with it, but Elsie's expression reminded her of her mother on a bad day. She sat down and ate the bread and jam which Elsie thrust in front of her, washing the last of it down with the cocoa. Elsie scooped the remains of the stew on to her plate, weariness fighting her appetite.

Meanwhile Tom sat in the small living room at the fireside, one ear concentrating on the radio programme and the other catching an occasional word or two of the conversation between his wife and the evacuee. The fleeting glimpse he'd had of the fair-haired child was a vague memory, almost lost in the drunken haze of earlier hours, but it had whetted his appetite for better acquaintanceship. In that way in which country folk regard young creatures, he was capable of great tenderness—a gentleness which showed itself when he helped to deliver a lamb, or watched the yellow chicks emerging from a clutch of eggs. In the next instant, he could begin to drive a herd of beast ready for slaughter or quite happily pull the neck of a rabbit caught in one of his snares. It was all about survival, each mood playing its part. He would have been as surprised as his wife when Hannah expressed horror at the fate of the pig.

He longed for children of his own. A boy to rear to manhood and a girl to love him and fuss over him. He couldn't express his feelings, appearing hard and uncaring, yet he needed to be cared about. Elsie did her best but her humility irritated him. He was surprised by her behaviour earlier on, and, although he reacted violently, he felt a spark of affection. Of course, he couldn't let her get away with it. Now, as his stomach gurgled and erupted, producing loud belches, he was feeling left out.

'Let's have a look at this evacuee then,' he shouted above the noise of the radio. 'Never mind telling secrets behind my back.'

Elsie did not recognise his attempt to sound jovial and jumped up, abandoning the last pieces of meat and potato. 'Just making your tea. I won't be a minute. Leave your cocoa, duckie. Come and say hello to Mr Porter and then you'd best go to bed.'

Hannah scraped her chair across the floor and looked apologetically across at Elsie, waiting for a rebuke. None came. She was propelled towards the living room, the force of Elsie's hand in her back increasing as her legs began to falter. She took one step beyond the open door and then came to a halt. Elsie pushed past her, and stood part way between her and the waiting Tom as though settling a dispute between two boxers in a ring.

'This is Hannah Flynn,' she said, being at a loss for words, and getting the name right in her nervousness.

'That's a posh name,' Tom remarked, grinning broadly in an attempt to look genial. 'Is it a family name or something, or did your mam read it in a book?'

'No.' Hannah smiled, seduced by his flattery. 'It wasn't in a book, I mean. I'm called after my grandma in Ireland, but she's dead now, so I'm the only Hannah Flynn. Me mam wanted to call me Janet.' She gave a little shudder in remembrance of the Pearsons. Their absence here was one blessing.

She waited for him to speak, and in her way, which often drew sharp comments from her mother about it being rude to stare, she studied his features. The earlier impression had been of a dark-haired, morose, scowling man, but on second acquaintance she could see that he had grey eyes wrinkled at the corners, a long straight nose and a wide mouth which looked ready to laugh. His skin, brown from constant exposure to the elements, had an attractive healthy look. She was pleasantly surprised. Perhaps, as Elsie said, he was all right really. Just been in a bad mood after all.

'You've helped with the feeding, haven't you, duckie?' Elsie said, also reassured by the tone of his voice. He could be nice if he tried, but she seldom saw that side of his nature. It belonged to the Tom she had fallen for eighteen years earlier. Why couldn't he speak kindly to her? Her mother didn't like him. A proper Jekyll and Hyde she'd called him. Ah well, give him a day or two.

Tom was asking Hannah whether she had any brothers and sisters. 'That's a shame,' he said, when she told him that she was an only child. She wanted to explain abut the miracle, but decided to save that for another time.

Elsie was getting impatient. She'd had enough for one day. 'I think it's past your bed time,' she said reaching forward and possessively grasping the small hand.

'Stop wittering, woman,' Tom snarled. 'She's like a clucking hen isn't she?'

Hannah shuffled her feet uneasily.

'She's not a baby. Not that you'd know anything about that. Go and make the tea and do the washing-up or whatever else you haven't bothered with.'

Elsie, desperate to avoid another scene, did not rise to the bait. She pushed past Hannah and went into the kitchen, her slippers dragging on the linoleum.

'Come and sit on my knee and tell me about your folks. You're a Yorkshire lass, aren't you? So that makes us kind of related. I'm Yorkshire as well.' Tom's voice, well oiled at The Three Bells, was oozing with good will.

Elsie snorted, viciously stacking up the plates and dishes.

'Yorkshire, my eye,' she muttered. He was as Lincolnshire as she was. Admittedly a babe in arms when he came here, according to his cousin Freda. Born in Leeds he was, but most definitely conceived and carried most of the way in this county. Apparently it was common knowledge that his mother was sent to an aunt in Leeds for the confinement. A bastard, that's what he was.

Tom patted his knee and the dust from animal feed rose up like smoke. 'Come on, duckie I won't eat you.'

Hannah regarded his trouser leg dubiously. It was all right sitting on her grandfather's knee but she didn't think she liked this man after all. She could hear Elsie clattering the dishes in the bowl and shared her resentment.

'Well actually,' she said, 'I want to write to my mam. She said as soon as I got here. I want to draw her a picture as well which will take me ages.'

'We ain't got no paper and envelopes,' Elsie called from the kitchen. 'I'll get some tomorrow. Your mam will know you're all right. That Miss Spencer will tell her.'

'I've got some in my case and an envelope with a stamp on. I want her to get it tomorrow. I could do it in bed if you like.'

'She won't get it tomorrow, my duck. Best do it on the kitchen table. You won't see upstairs. I can help you with the words.' Tom raised his voice and Elsie snorted again over the greasy water.

'I'll just get it then. I can manage, thanks. I'm good at spelling.'

Tom waved Hannah away, tiring of his new 'father' act, and returning his concentration to the radio.

'I'll get it for you. In your case, did you say?' Elsie's voice had a harsh ring to it. 'I'll bring your night things down. Go and get a quick wash. There's clean water in the jug. That'll do until the morning.' She indicated the bowl, now emptied of plates and pans but with the greasy evidence still ringing the enamelled surface and reached out along the chest of drawers for the soap dish and flannel. 'The towel's on the door, look. Pull it round and find a clean bit,' she called on her way up the dark staircase.

Hannah poured some water into the bowl and dipped her fingers in, wincing at the coldness. The flannel smelt of stale soap and felt slimy against her face. She wiped her forehead and cheeks, avoiding any contact with her mouth and nose, and then pulled at the roller towel as instructed but no clean bit came into sight.

Elsie came down with the night-gown and stationary and rummaged in the top drawer for a pencil. She had seen one in her earlier searchings for the face powder, and experienced a few moments of confidence before giving an exasperated moan and extracting a chewed stump from the chaotic contents. 'Can you manage with this one?' she whispered, not wanting to give her husband further room for criticism. She pressed her nail against the point, breaking away some splinters of wood to expose the lead.

In spite of her boasting, Hannah had never written a letter before, except as an exercise once at school. 'The address comes first, doesn't it?' she asked, chewing on the stub.

'Yes. Go on then. Eastfield Cottage. Cragthorpe. That's it. Everyone knows where that is. Now, just a quick note to say you are here, and stop chewing that pencil. Just look at the state of it.'

'Stop breathing down her neck, woman,' Tom Porter grumbled, giving his wife a hard push on his way to the back door.

Elsie reluctantly stepped to one side and Hannah bent low over the paper, screening it with her hand as though in the classroom during a test. She wanted to tell her mother that she was not happy, that she hated this smelly little house, and to come and take her home, but she was afraid, and it wasn't just Mr Porter. There was something about Mrs Porter that was just as frightening in spite of her efforts. As soon as Mr Porter closed the door, that lady was back leaning over Hannah's shoulder.

'Just ask me if you get stuck.'

'It's all right, thank you. I can manage. You can finish tidying up.'

'Yes, why don't you?' said Tom, catching Hannah's last words as he came back into the kitchen. 'Don't ask her for any spellings, duckie. She's hopeless. Can't even spell her own name half the time.'

'Of course I can!' Elsie's face reddened with anger. 'You're a fine one to talk. At least I went to school. Not like you, dodging off and getting into trouble half the time.' She took a step backward as his

49

sneer became a look of pure hatred and quickly picked up Hannah's night-gown, shaking out the creases and holding it in front of the range.

Hannah listened to their voices nervously, and scribbled a message to her mother. She hoped that she would understand how desperate the situation was, and wouldn't think that she was being a baby. She folded the paper and pushed it quickly into the envelope, licking the gummed flap and pressing it hard down.

'Well done,' Elsie said, relieved that her husband was now safely back in his chair. 'Just leave it on the dresser top. Old Mr Bentley will take it tomorrow. He brings the post up here along with the papers and doesn't mind taking some back. It saves us a long trek.'

'Do you think my mam will get it tomorrow night?'

'Good heavens no! A few days I should think. Even longer. Don't forget there's a war on. Nothing's quick these days. It could even get lost but don't worry. I'm sure folks get told where their kids are billeted.'

Hannah's feelings of relief turned to dismay. What if it never got there?

'Right, bed-time now, or you'll never get up in the morning. Just shout goodnight. You needn't go in.'

'But I haven't cleaned my teeth yet,' Hannah protested as the night-gown was pulled roughly over her head.

'Oh it won't hurt for one night. Give 'em a good scrub in the morning.'

These were Hannah's sentiments normally, but the thought of that dark staircase and cold bedroom called for delaying tactics.

'My mam always lets me read until ten o'clock,' she said, stumbling on the stairs in the dim light of the torch.

'I'm sure she doesn't,' Elsie laughed. 'Anyway, I'm not letting you have a candle. You not being used to it. We don't want to burn in our beds.'

'Couldn't I keep the torch then?'

'And what are we supposed to do if we want to go outside or when we come to bed? Anyway the battery's running down and that's more expense. You'll be as snug as a bug in a rug,' Elsie cackled, and jabbed Hannah in the ribs.

The bed was cold and hard and Hannah shivered, pulling the covers up to her neck. She waited until she heard the kitchen door closing and then pushed her feet down on to the bare boards and leant forward, feeling for her case. She was very proficient at 'seeing in the dark'. As well as creeping down to the stairs door when she couldn't sleep, sometimes during daylight hours she pretended that she was blind and, with her eyes tightly closed, she would try to avoid obstacles usually resorting to squinting in the last few seconds.

The case was already open and she panicked at the thought of Mrs Porter poking around amongst her possessions. Then she relaxed as her fingers curled around the shape of a torch. It was part of her emergency plans. Penelope Horton in a *School Girl Annual* story had gathered up numerous items before being packed off to boarding school. Just before she left, Hannah was beginning to panic and smuggled her grandmother's torch into her case, slotting it up the sleeve of her red jumper. She would have to be careful and keep it for special occasions. She pressed the switch forward and shone a beam of light up to the ceiling and around the walls, skipping quickly past the window which was curtainless except for the drab piece of net. Reassured by the apparent normality of the room, she turned off the torch and pushed it under her pillow. She would have to find a permanent hiding place for it but that would have to wait until tomorrow. Tonight she had to admit that all she wanted to do was sleep and she didn't hear the door creak open and Mrs Porter's husky 'Are you asleep, duck?'

Elsie, relieved by the lack of a response, crept back down the stairs and gave a quick look around the living-room door. Tom, lulled by the effects of a full stomach and the droning voice on the radio, was lying back in the chair with his mouth open, his snores competing with the voice of the news reader. Elsie wasn't interested in the news. What could she do about anything? Her immediate intention was to read the child's letter. She put the kettle on the hob and when the water came to the boil she expertly steamed open the envelope flap.

The writing was neat and easy to read.

Dear Mam,

I have arrived safely. I don't like it here. Please come and take me home. Please don't be long. I miss you.

Love Hannah.

Elsie read it twice and tutted. Such ingratitude! After all her efforts and giving her Tom's sausage as well. Well she was here now and she would have to get used to it. Been spoilt, that's what. She put the letter back in the envelope and pushed it down into her apron pocket. She would rewrite it tomorrow when she was on her own. Poor Mrs Flynn had enough to worry about without getting a letter like that.

6

'Them Townies'

Hannah slept fitfully that night. Even during the periods of deeper sleep, she was aware of the unfamiliarity of her surroundings. The sound of Tom Porter staggering down the stairs at half past six, followed by a yawning Elsie, found a place in her last nightmare, and she awoke moments later shaky and disorientated, still too sleepy for rational thought. The bang of a slamming door brought her fully to her senses. She turned over and stretched her legs down the bed.

'Oh no!' she gasped. She hadn't wet the bed for the last two nights. She thought she'd grown out of it. Her mother had said she would. What was Mrs Porter going to say? She lay still, panic flooding through her. The cocoon of stored comfort was being drained from the bed by the cold morning air. The blackness around her suffocated her senses and she began to cry, suppressing the sounds behind closed lips. Her stomach cramped in pain. She felt desperately alone. The familiar things, her home and family, were remote, part of another world which had stopped turning from the moment she'd left it.

Her convulsive shudders eased, leaving behind a universal aching. Her fingers came in contact with the torch, which was now balanced on the edge of the mattress. She pressed against the switch, and a shaft of light illuminated the chips and runs in the roughly painted door.

From beyond it came the sounds of voices and activity in the kitchen. Was it still night or morning? She heard Mr Porter's voice and the click of the garden gate, and the panic returned, demanding action along side the fear.

She pulled back the covers, her teeth chattering. Her night-gown clung to the back of her legs and she peeled it off, dropping it on to the floor. By the light of the torch she took her clean clothes out of the case and got dressed. Then she directed the beam of light on to the bed. The telltale patch was only too evident. She pulled the sheet away and looked despairingly at the mattress. If she turned it over it might dry unnoticed. That was easier said than done. The top sheet was only slightly damp and she turned it around and spread the blankets back in place. Now only the night-gown and sheet were left in sight. She rolled one up in the other and pushed the wet bundle as far under the bed as she could reach.

She stretched herself out on top of the covers, pinning down her dreadful shame. Noises came from the room below; the rattle of dishes, the raking of ashes. The crowing of a cockerel made her jump. It was the first cock-a-doodle-do she had heard outside of nursery rhymes. Time went by slowly, each moment straining against the last. She became transfixed with cold and tension apart from the rise and fall of her chest, which every now and again gave a convulsive jerk, the remnants of her sobbing.

'Hello, duckie. You've done well!' Elsie exclaimed as she peeped around the door. 'Fancy! All dressed and ready. I've made porridge for your breakfast. I bet you like that, don't you? I know I always did.'

Hannah nodded. 'That'll be nice. I woke up early so I've made my bed. Mam told me to do that to help.'

'Bless you. It is a big help and no mistake. It's wash day today and the copper fire doesn't want to light. Damp sticks. Anyway, let's get you sorted out. I hate these dark mornings. Come on, duckie. Not much time.'

Elsie spoke quickly and Hannah had to guess at her words as

she trailed behind her down the dark stairs. The kitchen was warm from the glowing coals in the range. Hannah ate the porridge, letting it slide down her throat and resisting the impulse to shudder. Her shoulders relaxed in the warmth and with the sense of relief that her plan seemed to be working. Perhaps the sheet and night-gown would dry before bedtime.

Elsie glanced at her from time to time as she sorted through the washing. She was proud of her efforts. The best porridge she had ever made and not a lump in sight.

'You've made short work of that,' she said smugly, as Hannah put her spoon down in the dish. 'I've done you some sandwiches. It's too far to come home at dinnertime. That's the last of the boiled bacon and there's a jam tart for afters.'

She chattered on, taking the child's reluctance to respond as a consequence of tiredness. 'Was the bed comfy, duck? Did you have enough covers on? I'm a bit short of blankets you know, there just being the two of us, but there's an old cover I use when I'm ironing or I might have some curtains somewhere you could have on top.'

'No! I mean, thanks, Mrs Porter. I was warm enough I mean. You don't have to bother.'

'Well, that's all right then. Perhaps you're a sleepy head like Mr Porter on a morning. Still, you'll soon wake up when you get outside. It's a cold un out there. The washing'll blow off the line I shouldn't wonder. I hate wash days!'

Hannah sat at the table and ran her finger around and around the rim of her cup. 'Did the man take my letter?' she asked suddenly.

Her question caught Elsie off her guard and she burnt her fingers on the flaming match as she struggled for the umpteenth time to light the copper. Her face flushed both with guilt and pain. 'Of course he has,' she snapped. 'Your mam will get it in a day or two, he thought.' She pressed her hand against the stiffness of her apron pocket.

Hannah continued to trace the rim of the cup. Perhaps the teacher would know how she could get home she thought, but then remembered the impatient sniff and later the swish of the curtains, and felt the flood of depression surging back.

'Are you going to finish that tea? I expect it's cold by now. Come on. I've got the bed to change. Just ours. Yours should last for few weeks. Soap's such a problem. Have you had enough? I don't want you complaining to your mother.'

Hannah nodded, gulping down the last of her tea.

'I'll only come to the end of the lane with you, duck. I must keep this fire in and I haven't fed the livestock yet.'

Her excuses were genuine enough but in truth the most pressing reason for her reluctance to go any further was her unkempt appearance. The night-time curlers were still in her hair, protruding out from her scarf and giving her head a strange lumpy shape.

Hannah nodded. Traces of porridge, which had escaped the gulping, clung to her teeth reminding her that she hadn't cleaned them.

'Oh there's no time for that now. It won't hurt. Give them a good scrub tonight. I always reckon once a week is enough. What did folks do before they invented toothbrushes?'

Hannah put on her coat and pixie hood, leaving her mittens to dangle on the tape which slotted through the sleeves of her coat. She looked around for her gas mask, but Elsie laughed at the idea. 'No one bothers out here,' she said. 'Hitler's not going to mess about gassing the likes of us.'

They walked to the end of the lane and she stood for a few minutes watching the small figure reach the bend in the road and disappear out of sight.

Hannah had no desire to look back. Other houses were coming into sight now and she quickened her pace, relieved to put some distance between herself and Eastfield Cottage, yet feeling vulnerable in her loneliness. She overtook a group of children who were in less of a hurry to reach school. They blocked the path, and as she stepped out into the road they regarded her with curiosity.

'That's one of them townies,' she heard a boy say.

'Don't speak, will you?' came a girl's voice, reminding Hannah of her old enemy from down the ten-foot. She tossed her hair back and walked quickly on.

'Stuck-up little bitch. Wait until playtime,' the girl shouted.

Hannah's legs began to ache. It was a steep climb up to the school, but she didn't lessen her pace and was short of breath by the time she reached the school gate. She stood close to the wall, which separated two playgrounds, and cast quick glances around for her companions of the previous day. A vigorous game of tag was in progress, and screams and shouts of exuberance filled the air, whilst bodies ran past jostling for space. The noise came abruptly to an end at the sound of the school bell. Everyone froze like statues waiting for the command. A tall boy shook the heavy brass bell for a second time and the children marched, arms swinging like soldiers on parade, into four lines. The smaller children did likewise at the other side of the yard. Hannah waited, now aware of the other evacuees who were standing at various points, unsure of where to go. A strident voice startled her.

'Evacuees. Come over to me, please.'

Miss Spencer strode out of the school porch. She had her Monday morning voice, strong and refreshed after the weekend break. All eyes were on the newcomers, a ripple of conversation being quelled by a stern glance.

'Attention, everyone! These children, as I expect you all know by now, are evacuees. You'll remember some came before but went home again. Well perhaps these will be here for a bit longer now that lots of bombs are being dropped on their town, so I want you to welcome them and be as helpful as possible. We have four teams as you can see,' she continued, turning to the evacuees. 'Everyone tries very hard to gain points for their team and we count them up at the end of the week. Now. Is anyone missing today?'

'Michael Brent's got the measles, Miss,' said the blue team leader.

Miss Spencer sighed and counted along the rows.

'I think you have space in your team for two more. David and Peter Brown, blue team. Jack and Gloria Clayton, red team. Rosie Dent, yellow team and Hannah Flynn, green. That has worked out very nicely. Nine in each team.'

'Trust us to get the little kid,' came a voice from the green line.

'Who said that?' the teacher demanded to know, her face grim.

57

'Please, Miss, it was Jimmy Parker, Miss. Should he lose a team point?'

'No, but you can for telling tales. I've told you before, Jimmy Parker. Size has nothing to do with brains, otherwise you would be a genius.'

The lanky Jimmy scowled and the Parker clan, who had jibed at Hannah en route, closed ranks even more tightly against her. The rest of the children, somewhat subdued, marched into the classroom, casting backward glances at the strangers as they hung their outdoor garments on the pegs. After spaces had been found for the extra clothes, not an easy task in such a confined space, the evacuees went into their delegated places in the larger of the two classrooms. Hannah squeezed in beside a small fat girl who grinned at her, showing gaps top and bottom where milk teeth had recently fallen out. Hannah returned this gesture of friendship with a tight-lipped smile. She was still smarting from the comment about her size. She looked around at the cream distempered walls, bare of any information other than a map of the world and a team points chart. There were windows on two sides of the room, church-like and set high allowing only a view of the dull autumn sky. Empty jam jars were stored on the sills waiting for the seasonal sprays of flowers or fruits of the hedgerows. The wall opposite to the rows of desks was partly obscured by two large blackboards balanced on easels, the teacher's high desk and stool and an upright piano. The fourth wall was constructed of wooden hinged sections and from beyond it could be heard the sounds of another class.

'Water monitors, don't dawdle,' the teacher was saying. 'The vicar will be here soon. We don't want a repeat of last week with buckets and wash bowls clanking. Everyone else, get out your reading books. We'll have silent reading and I mean silent, until he gets here. Evacuees. Go and choose a book from the shelf. Monitors. Give out the hymn books.'

Two of the big children left to collect the buckets, which were filled from the pump about two hundred yards from the playground, and the hymn books were distributed. There was some silent protesting and face pulling at being given shabby ones. The register was called. All present except for the measles victim.

Hannah chose a book called *Under the Lilacs*, and within moments she became absorbed in the story. She was a fluent reader and turned the pages over quickly. Miss Spencer, registration figures completed, regarded the latest members of the class. Jack Clayton, as she expected from her earlier encounter with him, was paying little attention to his book.

'There is a certain person who is not concentrating,' she said in that practised way when anyone who fitted the bill was alerted and guilty. Jack made a stab with his finger at some words, his head down so low to avoid eye contact with her that the black letters became even less meaningful.

He relaxed as she called out, 'Hannah. You seem to have found an interesting book. What is it called?'

Hannah didn't answer. Sounds made little or no impact on her when she was reading.

'Hannah Flynn! Can you pay attention, please?'

Her neighbour gave her a nudge. 'Miss is talking to you.'

Hannah looked blankly at the teacher.

'It must be a good book.' Miss Spencer understood that look and rejoiced in it, but the children began to giggle.

'She must be deaf or daft,' sneered Dorothy Parker in a loud whisper.

'Could you read out the title, dear?' the teacher continued. Everyone noticed the 'dear'. Miss Spencer was not given to using words of endearment. She was very fluent in derogatory ones, her favourite being 'nit wit', and the past holders of this title now cast hostile glances in the direction of the newcomer.

'It's *Under the Lil-acs*,' Hannah said, mispronouncing the last word.

'*Under the Lil-acs*?' the teacher repeated, puzzled.

'She means lilacs, Miss,' said the gappy-toothed girl.

The children roared with laughter saying the word over and over like parrots.

Hannah slumped in her seat and looked down at her fingers.

'Be quiet!'

The sound of the teacher's voice had the same effect as a gun shot, stunning the children into silence.

'It's a pity a good many of you don't concentrate on your reading. That must be a new word for you, Hannah. Lilac is a tree with beautiful purple or white flowers. We've got some in the school house garden but they won't flower until the spring. I expect the evacuees can tell us about things in the city that are strange to us. That can be something for them to write about after playtime.'

She stopped talking as the door burst open and the Reverend Cole strode in followed by the water monitors who scurried to their places, their eyes avoiding the accusing stares of the teacher. Hannah looked up as the lofty figure swept past her, blinking at the impact of the sudden rush of air against her eyelids. She studied the back of his head before he turned and focused his small blue eyes on his nervous audience.

'Good morning, children,' he boomed in a voice grown accustomed to the acoustic properties of the parish church.

'Good morning, sir,' the children dutifully replied in practised unison, and in the same sing-song tone which they used for their times tables.

The Reverend Cole had spent a little more time than usual in contemplating on the lesson for the week. This was the only contact which he had with the majority of the children. He didn't believe in Sunday School, having no wish to compete with the chapel preacher and his wife, who, in his opinion, degraded the faith with juvenile song and dance routines and yearly anniversaries and outings. Needless to say, the children, faced with the choice of long and dry sermons in an unheated dark church or stories and action songs, chose the latter. Parents who professed to be 'Church of England' put aside their criticisms of the 'Chapelites' as they called them for the benefits of a peaceful Sunday.

The previous evacuees had caused a good many problems, and the Reverend Cole had decided to put the fear of God into this fresh batch. There were enough sinners in the parish without swelling the numbers. He cleared his throat and looked slowly around, focusing his eyes on each strange face in turn. Those of a very nervous disposition jumped at the sound of his voice. 'We are going to think about two of the commandments today. To whom did God give the commandments? Do you know, boy? The evacuee in the brown jumper. Yes! You boy!'

Jack Clayton was in the act of persuading a money spider to commit suicide in the inkwell. He didn't know the question, never mind the answer.

'What?' he asked.

'What? Don't you "what" me, young man. Give this boy some lines at playtime, Miss Spencer.'

The teacher sighed. 'Suffer little children': the first few words of Christ's directive always seemed so apt when the vicar came.

'Does anyone know the answer? Come on! Are you all asleep?'

No one volunteered to risk the penalty of lines at playtime. Hannah didn't have the courage of her own convictions. Her throat had gone so dry that she was sure the words would stick in her throat. Anyone knew it was Moses.

'Some work is needed on Exodus, Miss Spencer. I would have expected every hand up. There'll be no excuses next week for such appalling ignorance. Honour thy father and mother. Stand up the evacuees. You've all got new fathers and mothers, haven't you?'

The six children nodded, temporarily struck dumb by his aggression and the sudden uprooting of their bodies from the safety of the masses.

'What does honour mean, girl?' He pointed to Gloria Clayton, who was nervously twisting a strand of hair around her finger.

'Is it somebody important like a judge?' she suggested.

Miss Spencer's lips curled at the corners. She was still smouldering from his sly criticism of her teaching ability.

'No!' His face twisted with impatience. 'It means to treat with respect. What does it mean?' The children repeated the words mechanically, their faces matching their brains in vacancy. The voice continued. 'It means to be helpful and thoughtful and not cause any trouble. You are giving your new parents a lot of extra work so you don't cause them any problems. Make no mistake about it, I shall know.'

Hannah shuffled uneasily, thinking of the wet sheet and wondering whether Mrs Porter had looked under the bed. She squinted out of the corner of her eye at Gloria and her brother. Jack caught the look and half shrugged his shoulders. He glanced back towards the stern figure who had paused to pass some comment to the teacher, and quickly put a finger to his head, making a winding action. Hannah smothered a giggle. He was common and incorrigible, an unlikely bosom friend but an ally.

The vicar turned his attention back to the class. 'Thou shalt not steal. Do you steal, girl?' He directed a long thin index finger towards Hannah.

Her face coloured up. Guilty or innocent, it always did when she was frightened. 'N—no, sir,' she stammered.

'I should think not as well,' he continued in a tone which implied guilt, and giving her a long, watery, blue-eyed stare. 'God knows everything we do. He is always watching us. Now, Miss Spencer. The morning hymn, please.'

'Number one hundred and thirty-six. "He who would valiant be, 'gainst all disaster". Stand, children.' The teacher sat down at the piano and played the opening bars. The children breathed in deeply with great relief that no further punishment was likely, and the first line of the hymn was sung gustily with the help of their expanded lungs. Hannah loved this hymn. It was all about giants and battles. 'To be a pilgrim,' she sang triumphantly in her tuneless little voice.

The Reverend Cole went on his way, the path of an academic rather than an evangelist, and with little affection for his neighbour. The children chanted the catechism and the Lord's Prayer, dutifully bowing their heads at each reference to the Deity, enjoying the ritual, even though the significance of it all only brushed vaguely against their awareness. Miss Spencer sighed. Some children were still saying, 'We chart in heaven,' but there were no 'Harold be thy names', which was an improvement on the previous week. She decided to leave the service and Exodus for another day and concentrate on the greater needs of mathematics. Sums test, like wash day, was always on a Monday. Both blackboards were already filled with mechanical arithmetic, testing the four rules in a sequence which became progressively harder. It wasn't easy to teach a class of such varied age and ability, but the teacher had her tried and tested methods, repeating them year in and year out, sunshine or rain, war or no war.

Hannah accomplished the task with ease, and queued at the high desk waiting for the gloriously satisfying ticks with no expectation of crosses. She felt pleased with herself being close to the front of the line with some of the big ones. Jack had filled in the answers at nearly the same speed. Think of a number was his philosophy. His numeracy was little better than his literacy, and he accepted failure as inevitable. He could cope with simple addition and subtraction, particularly when it involved any money which came his way, but when the answer went into double figures with all the complications of carrying or borrowing tens, he began to flounder. Now, he stood behind Hannah and occupied himself with picking at a scab on his knuckle. Then he gave Hannah a conspiratorial nudge and cast a practised eye over her shoulder at the neat page of sums. He rubbed at his answer to number six with a grubby finger, and licking the lead of his pencil to add to its blackness, he altered the answer, before moving his finger along to check the next figures. Hannah, aware of his intentions and eager to please, held her book to one side to allow him a better view.

'Please, Miss, they're cheating,' came a triumphant tell-tale voice from further down the line.

'Who's cheating?' Miss Spencer's nostrils dilated in preparation for a sniff.

'Them evacuees. They're copying, Miss.'

'Are you cheating, Hannah Flynn?'

'No, Miss Spencer!' Hannah's voice registered indignation. Jack had already disappeared out of sight behind her.

'I've told you all before. It's stupid to copy someone else's work. It could be wrong.'

'Well done, dear!'

Miss Spencer recorded twenty out of twenty, first on Hannah's page and then in her neat Monday test column in her large hardback mark book. She'd said it again! The class glared in unison, apart from the other newcomers who were not yet familiar with the teacher's turn of phrases. Dorothy Parker, hovering near to the teacher's desk and with 'stupid girl!' ringing in her ears, trod hard on Hannah's foot as she turned to go back to her place. The following act of retribution was swift. Hannah's squeal of pain activated Jack's boot and her antagonist hobbled across to her desk, her eyes dark with hatred.

The children sensed the unspoken promise of revenge like a pack of wolves scenting the prey, and a wave of excitement travelled around the room. The Parkers were regarded as a kind of village Mafia, a long-held position of countless generations.

Hannah didn't give them the satisfaction of seeing her cry, although her foot was throbbing from the weight of the size seven shoe. She sat down and pushed the exercise book under the desk lid on to the ledge. She looked at Jack who had returned to picking at the scab as he waited for the teacher's response to his contribution. Dorothy also watched, abandoning her dozen corrections. He was in the firing line and all she needed was the ammunition.

'Not bad, Jack. Do try to be a little neater and use a rubber, not your fingers.' The teacher, in her efforts to settle in the newcomers in spite of empathising with the Reverend Cole on his views of city ways, was making a fundamental error. Even the children not related to the Parkers were beginning to steam with indignation.

The crate of milk was lifted out from behind the large iron guard which kept the children distanced from the heat of the coke stove. Storing the milk there was a winter practice, particularly necessary when the contents of the bottles had taken on the qualities of ice-cream. The milk, warmed by such proximity since half past eight, increased in sourness. Hannah grimaced as she took a long sip through the straw. School milk never tasted right. Nevertheless she sucked it down to the last bubbling dregs. Miss Spencer looked over her glasses which rested halfway down her nose. At her glance, a ginger-haired boy abandoned his blowing down the straw, hastily cupping the bottle in his hands to hide the bubbling evidence.

'It would make a pleasant change not to hear you drinking your milk. I've been in quieter pigsties. If you haven't finished your work, you'll have to catch up later. Now, who's ready to go out?'

The question did not expect an answer. It was a signal to sit up so straight that backs arched in the endeavour, arms tightly folded across each chest and heads set back at an exaggerated angle. It was an attitude which could be maintained only for a short time with any comfort. The waiting was agony as one by one the children were released from the torture into the dark dank cloakroom.

The class monitors, chosen for their reliability as well as their seniority, were put in charge of the evacuees. Needless to say, neither Dorothy nor her brother came anywhere near this criteria. For the time being Hannah felt safe as she was escorted out into the cold morning air.

'You'll be all right with me, duckie,' her companion said, reminding Hannah of Mrs Porter. 'Come on. I'll show you the girl's bit before there's a queue. You're not allowed to go in lessons unless you're desperate or have a note from your mam.' They rounded the corner of a bricked enclosure. 'This is ours, look. That one's the teachers'. It's always locked but you can see through the keyhole.'

Hannah followed her into a now familiar setting; the wooden box, the dangling string of newspaper squares and the unmistakable odour of an earth closet. This one was a little more complex in that the box was on two levels; one high for the seniors and the other at a lower level for half-grown children. The holes had also been cut with bodily size in mind. Beryl Morrison settled on the high one.

'Come on, duck,' she advised. 'Hurry up! They'll be banging on the door in a minute.'

Hannah gave a nervous giggle as she joined her companion, her face on a level with fat grufted[2] knees and concertinaed navy blue knickers.

Beryl's forecast of impatience was not long in materialising. Thumping on the door, accompanied by cries of 'Hurry up. I'm

---

2 ingrained with dirt

dying. Come on, it'll soon be bell time,' hastened their exit. There was a queue of jostling girls, and the sounds of boys shouting and laughing began to drift over the brick partition drowning out the impatient cries.

'Don't take any notice of them boys, 'annah. They always talk mucky. They'll cop it if Miss hears them.'

Hannah flinched away from the vulgarity of her words. Words which sullied their purpose. Beryl pulled a face in their direction and grabbed Hannah's hand, dragging her into the yard. The wind was beginning to blow bitingly cold. Hannah stood shivering and treading her feet on the rough concrete, watching the resumed game of tag and longing to join in. Tagged children stood with arms outstretched until released by those still free to run from the chasers.

'Quick, quick;' 'Me, me;' 'Over here,' came the yells of excitement.

Miss Spencer came out balancing a cup and saucer in one hand and clutching her coat collar over her throat with the other. She was accompanied by the infant teacher. Playtimes were cold comfort on days like this. The chasing became wilder. Miss Spencer grimaced at the sight and sound of their exuberance.

'The wind's got into them today,' she said grimly. 'Like wild animals the lot of them.'

Her young companion gave a wan smile. She had the beginning of another cold, an occupational hazard particularly linked with the reception group, who seemed to fall prey to every flourishing germ and had little regard for hygiene. It was her day for yard duty. Mondays, Wednesdays and Fridays were long days with no break and Monday always seemed to be the most trying.

'I'll leave you to it now, Miss Jenkins. Keep an eye on the new children and give them all an extra five minutes. It could be a wet dinner hour. Terrible weather for September!'

Miss Jenkins sighed and looked at her watch. It was always on one of her days. When it was Miss Spencer's duty on a cold day, the bell was rung on the dot or sometimes earlier than that if some miscreant upset her. At those times, apparently she didn't believe in children being too long parted from their books. The injustice of it all began to churn around in the young teacher's head, and she regarded the boy, who approached her holding his hand to his nose, with little sympathy at first.

Jack had been ambushed in the far corner of the playground as soon as the head teacher was out of sight. The game of tag was abandoned, and the only sound was the rattling of some corrugated sheeting in the paddock on the other side of the school fence. Was he going to tell? He'd better not or he'd be for it. The children watched as he reached the teacher who, alerted by the silence, was now aware of the blood oozing through the boy's fingers and running down the back of his hand.

'Goodness me! Whatever happened to you?' She recognised him as one of the evacuees. Miss Spencer would not be pleased.

'I fell over, Miss,' came Jack's muffled voice from behind the cupped hand. ''S'all right. My nose is always bleeding. Can I go in and get a wet cloth?'

The teacher nodded and playtime continued. The Parkers were satisfied that justice had been seen to be done. Jack had obeyed the rules, and provided that he did not step out of turn again, he would be tolerated. Not so, Hannah Flynn. She was already labelled 'teacher's pet'.

The assistant teacher checked the time again, torn between bringing the children to heel or following orders. She was not fooled by Jack's version of the truth. Six months' experience of this village life made her very familiar with the nods and winks and the closing of ranks against a newcomer. It was said that even twenty years was not long enough for an outsider to be accepted. She turned her face into the cold air that blew from across the flat field to the north. The children resumed their play but not with the same wildness of spirit. Some now stood pressed against the school wall, tensed with cold. Enough was enough, Miss Jenkins decided. She signalled for the bell to be fetched from the cloakroom and cleared her throat in readiness. The children were experts at recognising reticence, waiting for any weakness that would give them a loophole for defiance. On this day she had no need to set her face into stern-ness. The damp air had already done that, tightening the muscles around her mouth giving a mask-like expression.

Resentment hardened her resolution and was souring her good nature.

The children watched her as they stood in line. She had it in her power to bring the wrath of Miss Spencer down upon their heads. Young and pretty she might be but she was still a teacher. They stood like soldiers awaiting the command. Miss Jenkins was enjoying this unexpected feeling of power. Her back like a ramrod and her face grim, she remained stationary except for her eyes which glared up and down the four rows. One false move would have pleased her. A dog barked along the street. No one reacted.

'Come along, children. It's far too cold to stand out here.' Miss Spencer's voice rang out from the porch, a mixture of sympathy and condemnation. She sniffed loudly and went back into the classroom. The team leader in the first line looked across at the young teacher, a little smile playing at the corners of his mouth. Without waiting for her order, he set off for the door with the others following behind. Miss Jenkins fumed at this undermining of her authority. The game began again; the insolent looks, the hands in pockets, the scuffling feet. She wasn't a match for them. She was only the infant teacher after all.

She found her little ones, as she called them, sitting quietly in charge of the monitor. Her anger began to subside as she stood against the guard, her muscles relaxing in the warmth. The children chanted the two-times table in their sing-song voices. some only knowing the tune and not the lyrics.

Miss Spencer sniffed impatiently again as the sound drifted through the partition. She knew that she had acted out of turn but she resented the youthful figure, the unblemished skin, the dark curly hair; daily reminders of her own decline. 'She won't last long,' was her pronouncement when Miss Jenkins was appointed. How the governors were fooled by a pretty face and impressed by new ideas. 'The pendulum will swing back, you mark my words,' she'd said to old Miss Harvey, a retired teacher who lived in Stanley Cottage on the edge of the village. The seventy-year-old had nodded, and gave the fire a good poke.

Miss Spencer jabbed her finger in the air in memory, and raised her voice with a 'Right!' Some of the younger ones who were mouthing in time with the infants, pressed their lips together and sat up to attention with the rest. Jack rubbed his sleeve across his nose.

'Haven't you got a handkerchief, boy?'

'No, Miss, I forgot.'

The teacher went to the cupboard and pulled out the 'bit bag'. He was given a small square of flowered curtain material and she watched as he dragged it across his nose wincing at the hardness of the fabric. She made no further comment about his bad habits, and the Parker family relaxed.

'We are all going to describe our homes today. Let's think about the words we shall need.' The teacher stood near the big blackboard, a stick of chalk at the ready.

'Miss! Miss!'

'I shall only ask the quiet ones.'

Hands waved and bodies stretched up in the desks, legs trapped behind the hinged benches.

As she wrote her essay, Hannah's thoughts were back in Tennyson Street dwelling on its superior qualities. She had the urge to lift it on to an even higher status, borrowing features and details from Betty Turpin's detached house, where she had been once for a birthday party, and including Auntie Vera's new carpet, which her grandmother had described in great detail. The two fluted cups and saucers became a complete tea service, and a silver teapot, a legendary but misplaced family heirloom, was a thing of splendour on the sideboard.

The exercise books were collected, and the 'sandwich children' filed into the infant room. They were a small group coming from outlying farms. The majority of the village children went home to a hot meal. Hannah was the only evacuee to have a packed lunch and she sat on her own, picking at the fatty bacon sandwich. She looked around the classroom wishing that she could stay in this cosy atmosphere with its bright friezes and fairy-tale posters. Tears gathered, spilling over her lids. She rubbed them away and bit into the hard crust of the jam tart.

'How are you getting on, dear? Settling in?' Miss Jenkins was watching the child and noticing her apparent lack of appetite and the tear-stained face. 'You haven't eaten much. It's a long time to teatime, you know.'

Hannah's expression brightened. 'I don't like fat but I'm not really hungry.'

'I don't blame you. It seems to be all fat in the country. Would you like a couple of my egg ones? I've done too many.'

Hannah accepted readily. She was feeling hungry. They both sensed their compatibility. Mutual misery of injustice, rejection and a longing for more familiar surroundings hung like a thread between them. During the next half an hour they chatted, soulmates in spite of the difference in their age and station.

Miss Spencer, who preferred to eat in the school-house, returned early and looked in on the comfortable scene. The older children, warm and relaxed, were enjoying the games; snakes and ladders, the dolls' house, the plasticine, the jigsaw puzzles, claiming to be entertaining the infants, but happily reverting to those days when weekly tests were in the future and anxieties were cuddled away. They jumped at the sound of her voice.

'Why aren't these children outside? It's turned out to be a perfectly good day for outside play, Miss Jenkins. We want alert brains. You all look half asleep.'

The young teacher's cheeks flushed. 'Sorry, Miss Spencer. They were all being so good. It did look like rain.' She could hear the wavering in her voice and cursed her cowardice.

Miss Spencer studied her watch. 'You've got ten minutes before the bell goes and do wash your face, Hannah Flynn. You look like a chimney sweep.'

No, she doesn't, Miss Jenkins thought. She looks like a child who needs help. She tried to catch Hannah's eye to reassure her but that little thread had snapped. She belonged in the other camp once more, although both were shamed by the same source.

'Plasticine at your age!' scoffed the older woman as two of her thirteen-year-old pupils shuffled past her into the porch. She went into her own room, putting the pile of marked exercise books on her desk and then returned to the cloakroom. Hannah was drying her face and turned hurriedly towards her coat peg.

'Leave that, Hannah. There are one or two parts of your writing which need attention.'

Hannah followed her into the classroom, remembering her written lies and wondering if the teacher, like God, knew everything. What Miss Spencer did know was that she had in her grasp a potential scholarship child. They were thin on the ground in this village at the best of times, but this year she would be lucky if even one aspired to grammar school status at the age of ten or eleven. Genetic inheritance and home influences provided farming skills, home-making prowess and the ability to procreate and squabble. Occasionally one would break the mould both happily and unhappily in the divergence. Hannah was a free agent, ripe for development.

She pointed out a few spelling and grammatical errors. 'I want you to read out your composition to the class, so do your corrections now. There's no need for you to go outside, my dear, and in future don't waste your time in the infant room.'

The first period of the afternoon was used to discuss the essays. Each of the evacuees was called out in turn. Apparently the two brothers lived in a corporation house on a new estate. Rosie Dent described a house not unlike those in Tennyson Street, whilst Gloria and Jack Clayton came from an area where the front doors opened directly onto the street and with no garden at the back, just a concreted area which was known as the back yard.

Now it was Hannah's turn. She described her friend's garden, which bordered the house on three sides, rejuvenated the fixtures and fittings of her parent's house, and exaggerated the merits of their possessions. The imagined bathroom was luxurious, the water closet and chain were emphasised, and the black clocks remained hidden under the stairs.

When she had finished reading her account, she looked up at the sea of faces registering varying expressions. Some obviously were impressed, others hostile.

'Doesn't she speak funny, Miss?' said Jimmy Parker. 'I couldn't understand half of it.'

71

'They all speak funny,' came another voice from the back of the classroom.

'And you will speak when you're spoken to. That was very good all of you,' the teacher said, directing her last comment towards Hannah.

It was a wet playtime, depriving Dorothy Parker of any of her pleasure of bullying until a later hour. At a quarter to four the class was dismissed, with the evening prayer thanking God for all His blessings. The sky was heavy with black clouds, and the north-easterly wind raced across the playground. Hannah was loath to leave the shelter of the porch. She dreaded the long walk and the loneliness of Eastfield Lane.

'Get along home, dear. It looks like rain again.' Miss Spencer's voice came from behind her.

It wasn't home but it was the only home she had. By the time she reached the black wood, she was out of breath and trembling with anxiety. The dark shapes of the trees and the matted briars, which trapped twigs and dead leaves into an indefinable mass, seemed to be full of horrors. She didn't want to look, but felt obliged to be on her guard. A sudden whoop like a Red Indian war cry sent the gathering adrenaline into full flight. Dark shadows moved away from their hiding places.

'We're coming to get you,' yelled a now all-too-familiar voice.

'What shall we do with her?'

'Shove 'er in the mud.'

'No. Fasten her up in the haunted house!'

'I ain't going in there!'

'Cowardy cowardy custard.'

Hannah heard the yells coming hard on her heels. She staggered as she twisted her ankle in a pothole and felt icy water splashing up under her clothes. The next moment she gasped as she was pushed from behind and she cried out with the pain of grit scoring her knees. She was rolled over onto her back and through screwed-up eyes she recognised the face of Dorothy Parker who now sat astride her, knees pinning down her arms.

'Well, Miss Clever Britches. Are you going to be teacher's pet tomorrow?' She worked the spit in her mouth and leant over Hannah's face.

'Let 'er 'ave it. I'll hold her 'ead,' screamed Katy Parker.

'Someone's coming!' called the look-out. 'Quick! Let's leg it.'

Hannah didn't wait to find out who was coming. She scrambled to her feet, put her head down and ran, seeing only the track beneath her feet. Elsie calling from the gate gave her an indication of her whereabouts, otherwise she would have gone on running up to the farm.

'There you are. I was getting worried. It's gone so dark. Oh! Here comes the rain. Quick, before we get soaked.' Elsie's hysterical shrieks, which filled the air, were good to hear. They scrambled in through the open door and home or not, Hannah was glad of the refuge. Now, in the last dim rays of daylight, Elsie viewed her small charge.

'Goodness me, child. Just look at the state of you! Whatever have you been doing?'

Hannah, fear subsiding, felt again the pain in her lacerated knees and the stinging in her hands. Her torn stockings were laced with blood and mud, and the tassels of her scarf were spiky with water. She couldn't cry. She stood fixed in misery.

Elsie tut-tutted as she got the flannel. 'Take your stockings off, duckie. You didn't come across the fields, did you? That track's shocking when there's been a lot of rain. I know it's a short cut but best to avoid it at the moment.'

Hannah bit at her lip and shuddered. 'I fell over,' she said. 'I turned my ankle in a hole. I didn't see it. It was so dark near the trees.' Telling tales was discouraged both at home and at school. 'Tell-tale tit. Your tongue will split,' threatened her inner voice. Anyway, she didn't want Mrs Porter complaining.

Elsie was still tutting as she dabbed Vaseline on the inflamed knees. 'There. That'll help work the grit out. I've got rabbit for dinner. Mr Porter brought one in this morning. That'll be good, won't it?'

The thought was cold comfort. Hannah had had a pet rabbit when she was little. She called it Snowy.

Tom couldn't have been more sympathetic when he came in early

73

from work. The heavy rain had ended any useful occupation on the farm. He was glad of it, and the smell of rabbit pie baking in the oven at the side of the range completed his feeling of well being. Neither he nor his wife noticed the way that Hannah picked at her food. A third party was still not part of their programme. Still, heartened by what she considered to be a very successful day as wife and mother, Elsie suggested that she should give them a tune on the piano.

'What and spoil a good meal with indigestion,' Tom scoffed. 'Anyway, there's a good show I want to listen to after the news.'

Elsie sighed as he belched loudly and pushed his chair away from the table.

'I should get the kid to bed early,' he said on his way into the living room. 'Sleep's the best cure.'

'That blessed wireless,' Elsie muttered. 'It's the be-all and end-all of his life.'

Hannah offered to help with the washing-up and racked her brain for any more bedtime delaying tactics. 'I don't usually go to bed until eight. I do jobs for my mam and she lets me read or do a jigsaw. I like playing patience. Do you?'

'We ain't got any jigsaws nor any books you can read, and if you think I'm looking for cards at this time of day, you've got another think coming. Mr Porter's right. Your legs need to be up and rested. Your nightie's all clean again.'

Hannah's face flushed. It seemed like last week. She'd forgotten all about the wet bed. 'I'm sorry,' she stammered.

Elsie put her fingers to her lips and nodded her head in the direction of the living room. She was in charge again and could afford to be generous. 'Don't worry, dear. I expect it was all a bit of an upheaval for you. Don't let him know, that's all, and just watch what you drink. No cocoa tonight.'

Hannah decided to co-operate and went meekly to bed. Her resentment instead was directed towards the Parker family. 'Just wait, Dorothy Parker. You'll be sorry soon,' she murmured as she drifted into sleep.

Elsie Porter, all chores completed, sank down into the armchair and closed her eyes. She was tired, but it was a pleasant kind of tiredness. The day had justified it rather than frustrated it. A dry washday morning always put her in a good mood. Of course, she was irritated when first discovering the wet bundle under Hannah's bed as she checked the chamber pot, but she pushed these feelings aside, replacing them with compassion. She could recall such episodes in her own childhood when her mother threatened her with mouse pie. The threat was never carried out, but the horror of such a meal still lingered in the shadows of her mind.

She'd chatted to the farmer's wife whilst filling the buckets at the pump, and described her little Hannah. Pretty and clever, she said. That set her to thinking of her own youthful prettiness and she'd quickened her pace, causing water to slop down her wellingtons, remembering that she hadn't returned the photograph to its hiding place in the piano. She didn't want Tom to get his hands on it. He could be so cruel and would think nothing of tearing it into shreds.

She hurried into the house and began to hunt for it, panicking at its apparent absence. Eventually, she found it lodged part way down the back of the chest of drawers. She sank down on to the kitchen chair and smoothed away the dust, regarding the image for the umpteenth time. What secrets lay behind the gathers of the skirt! She fancied that if she cut a flap into the sepia surface and lifted it up her baby would be there, like a minuscule doll perfectly formed. She was about two months' pregnant at the time and rousing the suspicions of her mother with her dreadful morning sickness. She was vaguely aware of the significance of her monthly cycle. Her sisters were given the task of explaining this to her. 'Every month,' they said, 'unless you are having a baby.' Questions on that score were avoided with giggles and rolling of eyes. 'You'll know soon enough,' was the reply. It was sooner than any one expected.

Alarm bells began to ring and countless questions were asked. She gave no satisfactory answers. Her father was most concerned but not for her. How his guilt must have coloured his life and continued to do so until his death. Her childlike love for him became contempt, yet she could not betray him. Such a betrayal would destroy the bond between her parents, and equally damage the rather tenuous relationship that she had with her mother. That only hung by the thread of their shared musical ability.

She was the third daughter. Her gender was of great disappointment. It seemed that she was rejected from birth by her mother, cuddled only by her sisters during the early months, but then pushed aside in favour of her brother who was born less than a year later. She was always 'piggy in the middle'. Comparisons were frequently made. Apparently she would never be a patch on her sisters and her little brother was far more intelligent. She wore her sisters' hand-me-downs, the only new dress she ever had being the one in the photograph and that was for public gaze. Only when she gave a recital at the church, taking her mother's place at the organ, did her mother lay any claim to her. 'My Elsie,' she called her then. 'My clever Elsie.' Music was the only solace, and made seasonal work on the land and her contribution to the daily chores (more and more necessary to ease the burdens of her hypochondriacal mother), almost bearable.

It was a week or two after that photograph was taken that she was lashed with every insulting word her mother could lay tongue to. She was undoubtedly pregnant. How willingly her father supplied the gin; how scalding hot were the baths, how far the jumps from table to floor. They succeeded in saving the family name. No matter that she cried with the agony of it. Death was very close but no doctor was summoned. It seemed that her shame would go to the grave if needs be, or an institution if all else failed. She was sworn to secrecy and forbidden to mix with the young people in the village. It was made known that a bad bout of fever had laid her low and from then on her mother treated her like a servant, although her skills in that department were as lacking as was her ability to grasp scholastic learning.

She welcomed Tom's attention four years later. Times were hard and with her two sisters married it was decided that their room should be given over to a lodger. Tom was a godsend. His rough ways and speech were frowned upon by her mother, but he provided a welcome escape route from the bitterness of home life.

Her father constantly tried to make amends, and she used his fear of her betrayal of him in a kind of unspoken blackmailing game that extended beyond the death of her mother. She laid claim to the piano, and he did not protest even though it would have fetched a good price in the sale room. He begged for her attendance during his final days, but she refused. She exaggerated the effects of a cold on the day of his funeral and took to her bed. She couldn't forgive him. He would have to take his chances with his maker.

All the possessive affection which she had kept bottled up over the years for her aborted child, sought release. Her little Hannah. Clever little Hannah!

Now she opened her eyes and looked at Tom. Her secret was safe in the piano. She smiled at the idea of teaching Hannah to play. Her little girl would be musical. The thread would not be broken.

7

Jack Clayton

Similar scenes of such domesticity were being enacted in other households in this rural landscape. Animals were settled in for the night, black-out blinds were secured, and protesting children were given a good scrub or a lick and a promise depending on the circumstances and standards. Generally, eight o'clock was the deadline or even earlier on dark winter nights when parents were in desperate need of a respite from family duties. After all, 'early to bed...' did promise an abundance of blessings.

Jack Clayton was not used to such measures. His mother had little time or energy to be concerned for his health, and wealth was something enjoyed by 'them lot out of town'. Wisdom was something he learnt in the street, but although he was now setting out on a much narrower and straighter path, in a strange way he had a greater sense of freedom. Today he was given permission to listen to the wireless, and have a late tea after helping to sweep out the storeroom and carry boxes of provisions up the stairs. His mother would have been greatly surprised at his willingness to co-operate. He was the youngest of seven children, well skilled in the art of ducking and diving, and readily picking up on the backchat and the rules for survival. He never volunteered, content to merge into the background of the chaos which constituted the norm in his family. Now, for the first time in his life he had no competition. There was no one threatening his slice of the cake, his share of the blankets, or his opinions.

Mr Turner, the shopkeeper, was a quiet little man with a high-pitched voice and an acquiescent nature. He reminded Jack of the goat in *Rupert* annuals. Jack had a droll sense of humour appreciated by his peers but frowned on by adults, hence his frequent presence in the punishment line at school.

The memory of the first meal he enjoyed with his foster parents would stay with him for the rest of his life. The snowy white tablecloth, the polished cutlery, the silver cruet, the glasses and water jug were all like parts of a scene on the cinema screen. However, he was not intimidated by such splendour. Like the chameleon, he could adapt to his surroundings. It was all part of the game of life— something which he had learnt from an early age. His mother once said in a rare philosophical moment that he would end up on the stage if he didn't go to prison first.

Now he saw himself as a young gentleman, and played the role to his own ideas of perfection. Admittedly, his first thoughts when he learnt that his new home was the village shop, were how easy it would be to steal. He wouldn't need to wait until the shopkeeper was distracted. He could creep down during the night. It was all there for the taking. Yet, with no hunger pains gnawing at his stomach, there was little imperative to take chances, and new tactics could be more fun.

On the first evening, he actually enjoyed going to bed. Being clean all over felt good, and he pulled the crisp white sheets up to his chin and turned his face into the freshly laundered pillowcase. His room was sparsely furnished, but the emptiness was a luxury. In the bedroom at home, which he shared with his three brothers, there was hardly breathing space. His place was on a mattress on the floor with brother Jim, next in order of age. They were covered over with a coarse fraying blanket that had never entered a wash tub for years, and old curtains were added in the winter when the cold, combined with rising damp in the walls, made for fitful sleeping.

There was a great sense of order in his new home. Opening hours dictated the timetable and quiet periods were given over to cashing up and organising stock. The added burden of ration coupons to be counted and recorded left little time for relaxation, but Mrs Turner was meticulous in all things, and no one was allowed to shirk their duties.

Now, the radio programme coming to an end was a signal for Jack to go to bed. He didn't argue. It was a pleasure to wash in the bathroom and dry himself on the big white towel. He'd slept in his shirt the night before, a normal practice for him, but his foster mother was appalled at his lack of decent clothes, and earlier in the day had sorted through the clothes in the tall linen cupboard on the landing. Nothing was ever thrown away even in pre-war days. Things were re-cycled or donated to jumble sales to raise funds for the community. She pounced in triumph on the two pairs of wincyette pyjamas. She could see that they would be a little on the large side. Still, she reasoned, it would give him space to grow. She considered herself to be an expert on growing children. She put the pyjamas to her face testing for dampness. It didn't seem long since she had washed and ironed them and tucked her small sons into bed. There they were now, grown up and fighting for their country. She was never one to show affection but she wanted to run her mouth over the smoothness of the fabric and recall the scent of their young bodies.

She clucked over the evacuee as his limbs sought out the sleeves and legs, her sharp eyes behind the formidable glasses making a mental note of necessary alterations which could be done on the sewing machine when she had a minute or two. He certainly could do with some meat on his bones, she thought.

Jack tried to make a grand entrance into the living room, clutching at the pyjama legs, and proudly sporting a checked dressing gown with a gold silk cord. Mrs Turner smiled at his jauntiness, but the note of command remained in her voice. 'Right, young man. Say goodnight. Have you remembered your teeth?'

Jack said, 'Good night, sir,' as though addressing the headmaster. He was thoroughly enjoying his new role, with none of his family there to witness his compliance.

The bed was warm to his back from a hot water bottle and, as on the previous night, he sighed with contentment. His thoughts turned briefly to his sister Gloria and he wondered if she had to go to bed early. She'd be all right. She had the ability to make the best of situations. She was the capable one in the family and would be missed. No one would miss him except as a scapegoat. This school wasn't bad. The teacher was a teacher. There was nothing new about that. He frowned at the thought of Hannah and experienced a twinge of guilt. She was one of them, after all, even though she was a girl. Still, he did have to consider himself. He'd overheard Dorothy Parker's plans when they left at hometime. 'Take the short cut,' she'd said. 'We'll jump her at the spinney.' Her brother was bigger than him. Besides, how many were there in the gang? He wouldn't have stood a chance, and his silence, after the skirmish in the playground, had won him some breathing space. In spite of everything, survival was still the name of his game.

8

A Strange Encounter

Hannah had not slept well. Elsie's idea to put an old, cracked, kitchen table oilcloth under the bottom sheet was not very acceptable. The mattress was now so hard that it was like sleeping on the floor and her back ached with the ordeal. She awoke so many times that the night was a muddle of dreams, but one stood out clearly in her waking memory. She could still see Dorothy Parker crying, her face reddened with rash.

'Do you dream, Mrs Porter?' she asked as she sat at the table struggling with very lumpy porridge.

'Sometimes. Usually I go out like a light and don't remember nothing until the morning. Especially on washdays. If I do dream, I seem to be in an old building all falling down, or else I'm lost and can't find my way home. It would be nice to dream about something nice. Get on, duck. You'll be late.'

Hannah put down her spoon after her usual trick of spreading the remains of her meal around the bottom of the dish. 'I dream a lot. I take after my Grandma Hannah in Ireland. Mostly I can't remember much unless I have a special dream. I dreamt last night that Dorothy Parker had got the measles. I wonder if she has.' She studied Elsie's face for a reaction, disappointed at the continued blankness of her expression.

'Best over and done with, my mother used to say. Have you had the measles?'

Hannah nodded and Elsie looked cheerful for a moment. 'That's good, duckie,' she said, taking the dish to the washing up bowl.

Hannah's legs were stiffened by the scabs which had formed in the night on both of her knees, and she walked slowly along the lane. In the daylight she could make out the rough track between the spinney and the old house, and decided to try it. She had assumed that it was merely a pathway to the house, but realised last night after the Parker gang had reached their hiding place ahead of her, that it must be an alternative route to the village.

She stumbled along, jumping puddles, and was breathing heavily when she reached the crest of the hill. The track turned at an old barn and now she recognised the shape of the schoolhouse and the roof of the school rising beyond it. She stood and looked around, getting her bearings. The village nestled in the valley of the beck, the houses following the line of the village street as it wound its way past the church and up the steep hill to the school. At the sound of the bell, she broke into a run. The track, now brick surfaced, gave firmer footing, and she arrived just in time to join the last line of children marching into the classroom.

It was noted by everyone that she didn't lose a team point. Jack ignored her as he pushed past to reach his peg.

'Our Dottie's got the measles,' Katy Parker announced in a triumphant voice. 'I bet I get them next.'

Miss Spencer nodded and smiled. One day without the Parker clan was a joy. A week or two would be a blessing indeed.

Hannah was glad that her dream had come true. It gave her a feeling of power and she enjoyed the feeling. That would show them. However, the Parkers without their big sister were less of a threat. Jimmy, in spite of his size, was nowhere near as aggressive. Rather, Dorothy intimidated him, goading him into situations that he would have preferred to avoid. A game of football was more to his liking, and he worked hard at his sums anticipating a good kick around at playtime. Katy also was very much under her sister's thumb. She glanced anxiously at Hannah from time to time. Hannah ignored her gaze. She spoke to no one other than the teacher. It was the regular Tuesday timetable. The 'three Rs' in the morning and writing practice and history in the afternoon.

At home time she left quickly, taking the path behind the school which led to the cross-country route back to Eastfield Lane. She preferred the solitude of it, losing herself in the misty landscape which merged into the autumn sky. The sounds of happy cries of freedom from school bondage drifted away along the village street and down into the valley of the beck.

She dawdled along, stopping to investigate stones drawn up by the plough in the field along side. Miss Spencer had a collection of fossils that were passed around the class during the history lesson. Hannah longed to own one. She pressed her nail into the limestone glistening with tiny fragments of shells and contemplated dinosaurs. It was almost impossible to imagine a time when this lane was under the sea. Of course, she thought, the school wouldn't have been there then.

She was the only brightness in this landscape of greys and blacks. Her red woollen pixie hood and matching mittens glowed in the failing light, and her cheeks were flushed with coldness and exertion. She was so preoccupied with thoughts of the distant past that she scarcely noticed the old barn ahead. Then her eye caught a moving shape, which separated itself from the background of the building and became silhouetted against the low sky.

At first, she couldn't decide what or who it was, but as it drew nearer she observed the slow gait of an elderly person, head bent low against the wind, and body heavily shrouded in black. She stood still, ready to run.

'Who are you?' came a strong voice muffled by a scarf that obscured the lower half of her face.

She's a witch! She's a witch! The words repeated themselves over and over in Hannah's mind. She was surprised to hear herself answering politely as though nothing untoward was happening. Adults always expected an answer. Nevertheless, her reply was scarcely audible.

'Speak up, child. Cat got your tongue?'

Hannah was silent for a moment, fascinated by the ginger curls that hung down each side of the wrinkled face.

'I haven't seen you around here before,' the old woman continued. 'You haven't seen a cat on your travels, have you? Are you a gypsy? Tell your mother I've got enough pegs and I don't want my fortune read. I can do it myself.' She stepped past the child but Hannah wanted to explain, especially about not being a gypsy.

'Actually, I'm Hannah Flynn. I'm Mrs Porter's evacuee.' She felt somewhat reassured by her claim to a local guardian even though she had little faith in her foster mother's ability to cope with witchcraft.

'Oh, you're with Elsie, are you? And what do you think of that man of hers? Is he watching his temper?' She didn't wait for an answer but repeated a previous question. 'You haven't seen a cat, have you? Ginger. Answers to Nickodemus. Tell him to come home if you see him.' She muttered something else which was lost in a sudden gust of wind.

Hannah waited for a moment, trying to catch the words as the old woman stepped past her, but apparently the conversation was at an end. She screwed up her eyes as she hurried along the walled boundary of the ruined house, half expecting Nickodemus to leap out of the trees or a witch to appear from the darkening sky on her broomstick.

Elsie was waiting at the gate. 'I was just going to come looking for you,' she chided, irritable now that her anxiety had no substance.

'I had to stay behind,' Hannah lied. 'I didn't get my writing done.'

Elsie tutted. 'That Miss Spencer's a hard one. Fancy keeping little kids in late in such bad weather and with a war on as well. I'll go and have words with her, the clever madam.'

'Oh no, Mrs Porter! I'll get into trouble. I'll do all my work tomorrow and run all the way home.'

'We'll see. Some folks don't know what it's like to have kids to worry about, her not even married.' Elsie pushed wearily at her frizzy hair and tightened the knot in her headscarf. 'I'm just finishing with the livestock. Go and get your things off. We might have time for a tune before Mr Porter comes in.'

Hannah did as she was told, glad to be in out of the cold. She stood with her back to the fireguard, soaking up the heat from the range. Elsie hadn't lit the lamp yet and the room flickered with shadows. The clanking of the bucket outside the back door startled her, even though she knew it was only Mrs Porter. A flurry of leaves followed Elsie as she came in from the windswept garden. She rubbed the back of her hand across her nose and sniffed loudly. 'Oh! It's like the middle of winter,' she moaned. 'It's cold enough to snow. By the way, duckie, I've just remembered. It's Tom's darts match tonight so we'd best get on and leave the piano for now. I'll put some dumplings in the broth. That should line his stomach.'

She hung her coat and headscarf on the door and rubbed her hands on the roller towel before dipping her fingers into a measure of flour, fat and water. 'One for me, one for her, and three for him. That should do,' she said to the pot and then turning to Hannah, she gave instructions to put on the tablecloth and set three places. The dregs of the potato boiled up for the pig were drying into a hard crust in the old saucepan in the hearth, and the smell combined with that of the rabbit and dumpling broth made Hannah feel unusually hungry.

Elsie pulled back a chair and sat down. She looked across at Hannah who was staring into the fire. 'So what have you got to tell me then? Did you eat all your sandwiches? You're looking peaky. Some nettle tea would do you good.'

Thoughts of the meeting in the lane had distracted Hannah from the present domestic activity, but now she looked around, her eyes meeting the small dark blackberry eyes of her foster mother. Nettle tea! That old woman knew Mrs Porter. Called her Elsie and she knew Mr Porter. She decided not to mention any of it. She didn't want any alarming answers. 'Dorothy Parker's got the measles,' she said instead.

'So you were right. You'll be reading the tea leaves next, like old Mrs Knight,' Elsie laughed. 'I'm surprised she hasn't been up here. That cat of hers has. Coming to see his girlfriend, I expect. She spends her life worrying about those cats. Still, it's all she's got, these days.'

Hannah couldn't keep her secret any longer. Witch or not, she had to know. 'Is the cat a ginger one? Nick something?'

'That's the one. We'll soon know when Sootie has her kittens. Ginger and black, I bet. Anyway, how do you know?'

Hannah told her of the conversation with the strange woman.

'Ah,' Elsie said, 'that's 'er, all right. I expect she's been back to her old house. She often goes in there. Some say she's talking to her husband's ghost, but I reckon she talks to herself or those cats of hers. Last time I saw her, a few months ago, she had a cup of tea with me and read my tea leaves. She told me that my life was going to change and that I would have some good luck. Well, she was right, wasn't she? My life has changed now I've got a little girl to look after and do you know, the next day as I was walking back from the village, there on the ground was a ten-shilling note. Can you imagine it? Just lying there, it was. She's the best one around here for readings.'

'Is she a witch then?' Hannah asked, watching for Elsie's reaction.

But Elsie just laughed. 'Whoever told you that? She's harmless enough. Eccentric, folks say. Just gets lonely. I know how she feels. I talk to myself sometimes when Tom's snoring his head off.' She stood up and walked over to check the dumplings, stabbing at them with a fork.

'Where does she live now?'

'Just behind the school. You walk past her gate if you take the short cut. You won't have been that way yet. In any case, it's hard to see her cottage with all the elder. Don't you remember? I told you about it and all the cats. Anyway, get this down you. It'll put some meat on your bones. You need fattening up.'

Hannah thought of the pig and shuddered, her appetite suddenly gone. She picked at the food, moving it around her plate and investigating the meat for gristle and fat, which was in the habit of disguising itself as potato.

'Come on! Get a move on! There's nothing wrong with it. There's a lot of starving people out there would be glad of it. He'll be home in a minute.' Elsie abandoned her fond mother role and was the wife once more, anxious to please and mollify.

The transition was well timed for the doorknob turned and then Tom's large figure filled the doorway.

'Something smells good,' he remarked jovially, his red face creasing in good humour.

Making his peace in advance, Elsie thought cynically. A darts match was a red-letter day on the calendar and an excuse for over-indulgence and a stomach like a swill tub by the end of the evening. Still, he was out from under her feet and breathing his beer fumes down somebody else's neck. Now that Hannah was here, he could absent himself as much as he liked. He can bugger off for good, she thought.

He kept up the effort, trying to have a meaningful conversation with Hannah through mouthfuls of dumpling and gravy, escaping morsels punctuating the flow of his words. Hannah watched his rapid progress through the meal in fascination, and could hardly concentrate on his questions. She nodded or shook her head with the occasional 'yes, thank you' thrown in out of politeness. Elsie had baked a sponge pudding which, according to Tom, appeared to have fallen flat on its face in the oven. Elsie was not famous for her cooking skills, but the added plum jam and coating of custard proved her to be somewhat of an expert in culinary deception.

It was seven o'clock when Tom Porter left the house, transformed by his one and only suit. The trousers had been altered to accommodate what was commonly known as a beer gut, and the top button of his rather greying white shirt was made redundant in favour of the freedom of his double chin and the need to breath. A fraying necktie attempted to bridge the gap. He had cursed and fumed as he removed several days' growth of beard, dabbing at the blood which trickled down his chin. Elsie and Hannah made their presence as scarce as possible in the close confines of the living space.

Their sighs were mutual at the sound of his heavy tread and the creak of the gate, and then only the moaning of the wind around the cottage roof.

'Thank God for that!' Elsie said. 'I thought he would never go. Come on, duckie. Let's have a tune.'

Hannah was quick to learn the notes and attempted the first exercises in the old primer that Elsie found in the bottom of the piano stool.

'You'll soon get it,' she encouraged. 'I used to think I would never play both hands together but you watch me now.'

Hannah couldn't help but notice the change in Elsie. She spoke carefully and quietly as though someone else was taking her part and as she began to play it was obvious that she was in her element, her face glowing with an inner joy. 'Home Sweet Home' was an unfortunate choice but she was intent only on impressing the child and she crossed her hands effortlessly, reaching for low and high chords in her favourite piece of music. Gone were the drooping shoulders and the sagging facial muscles. A power now surged through her slight form, activating her fingers, and the room was filled with her joy and achievement.

Later, Elsie alone in her bed, was still warmed by the great happiness of the evening and the glory of recognition. Life could be so good without Tom and she cursed her dependence on him.

Hannah, also happy for the first time since she left home, stared into the blackness of the night and wished that Mr Porter was just a bad dream and gone by morning.

So deep and relaxed was their sleep, that only the mouse on its nocturnal pilgrimage to the pantry shared the obscene utterances as Tom fell over the threshold.

9

Seed Cake and Dominoes

There it was again. Hannah recognised first the note of pain and then the cat-like quality. With little concern for her own welfare, she followed a tramped pathway into the dark spinney. A rook flew up with a warning cry and dead twigs snapped under her feet. The cry came again and her young ears had no difficulty in locating the direction.

In spite of the gloom, she saw a flash of ginger fur at the same time as the creature gave another cry of pain. It could only be Mrs Knight's cat. Hannah gasped at the sight of the cruel snare and the leg wet with blood and saliva. Who could do such a thing? She thought of Mr Porter and the rabbit stew and felt very sick.

She tugged at the stake that secured the tormenting wire. 'There, there,' she murmured as she struggled to free Nickodemus. His amber eyes glowed with pain, yet her gentle tones soothed him, and he began to purr. She could feel the rasping in his throat, and carefully lifted him together with the snare. In spite of her hands being occupied, the way out of the wood was easier to navigate than the way in. She could see the light through the trees and retraced her steps over the trodden vegetation.

She heard the school bell moments before reaching the elder bushes which flanked a narrow pathway up to the old woman's cottage. She didn't run. The cat was far more important than team points. The pathway was becoming so narrow that it was like entering a tunnel and a sudden feeling of claustrophobia weakened her brave resolutions. She could leave the cat on the path she reasoned, or perhaps she could bang on the door and run. The sight of a besom propped against the wall heightened her fear, but the cat began his loud purring again and she felt reassured by her own virtue.

Before she could knock, the door opened and Mrs Knight came out carrying a large cane basket. She looked quite ordinary in daylight except for the ginger curls hanging down from under her black hat. She dropped the basket and gave a shriek of surprise and joy.

'Oh Nickodemus! Oh my little darling! Wherever have you been? You naughty little boy! Fancy leaving your mammy all this time.'

Hannah supported the snare while the old woman tutted and raved. 'This is going to take some getting off. Oh my poor little cat! Never mind. I've got just the stuff to make it better. I'll do the sticking later.'

'I must go,' Hannah said, retreating backwards along the path. 'I'm late for school. I'll be in trouble.'

'Don't I know you? One of the gypsies, are you?'

'No. Mrs Porter's evacuee. You asked me to watch out for him.'

'Oh yes. I remember now. Well, you tell that teacher of yours what you've done. You deserve a medal, never mind getting into trouble. Where was he?'

'In the spinney on Eastfield Lane,' Hannah shouted back. Her voice echoed from the elder tunnel and she felt that she was in a strange dream where nothing seemed to make sense. Whatever was the old woman going to stick?

But minutes later the sight of the school gates and then Miss Spencer's disapproving sniff were real enough.

'A cat in that state could have torn your hand to shreds,' she said. 'You should just have reported it.'

Hannah's opinion that the cat knew she was trying to help, led to the story of Androcles and the lion, which inspired the subject of the English essay. An hour was spent with 'One good turn deserves another,' then 'volunteers' were called to fill the remainder of the time with recitation.

'We'll hear the evacuees first,' Miss Spencer ordered. 'Gloria. What poetry have you learnt at your old school?'

Apparently, Gloria Clayton could recall nothing other than the first two lines of 'Drake's Drum' which she said in a broad East Yorkshire accent with its flattened vowel sounds. She stood red-faced at the front of the class unable to continue, her misery increasing as the children sniggered. Her brother Jack bristled. How dare they laugh at his sister. He volunteered to take her place.

Miss Spencer, surprised by his enthusiasm and recognising his act of chivalry, indicated a change of roles with an imperious sweep of her hand.

Jack faced the class, took a deep breath and gabbled out his contribution, half singing, half saying the words.

> 'Chin chin China man bought a penny doll.
> Washed it, dressed it. Called it Pretty Poll.
> Sent for the doctor. The doctor couldn't come.
> Because he had a pimple on his…'

'That will do, young man!' screamed Miss Spencer. 'Go to your place.'

Jack mouthed the same three repeating words that ended his poem as he swaggered back to his place and the children rocked with laughter.

'Get in the cupboard and stay there until the end of play,' the teacher yelled, striding across the room and flinging open the door of the storeroom which housed games equipment, art and craft materials and a box of percussion instruments. The cupboard was the ultimate punishment, windowless and a favourite place for large spiders.

'I ain't going in there,' Jack declared. Such confinement brought back vivid memories of nights spent in the small cupboard under the stairs during air raids.

'You will do as you are told, you wicked child unless you want the slipper as well. I don't think Mrs Turner would be pleased to hear about your rudeness.'

The last pronouncement moved Jack to total submission. Physical punishment was of little consequence. As his mother said, 'He'd cut his teeth on that.' But his new-found status as local errand boy with the monetary rewards and extra goodies could not be put at risk. Teachers didn't tell tales at his other school, not to his parents at any rate. They daren't, he thought grimly, his eyes straining against the darkness, and his ears aware of the unnatural silence beyond the cupboard door. His dad would make mincemeat out of the likes of her. Mr Clayton now appeared briefly as a hero, a kind of dockland Sir Lancelot.

The other children gaped in silence and at the teacher's 'Right!' jerked into the sitting-up-straight position. They heard the infants running out to the playground and every tick of the clock, while the teacher began to mark the table tests. The strain was too much for some of them, particularly those who had outgrown their desks. They relaxed, eyes fixed on the bent head with its tight knot of hair. At its slightest movement, they returned to the rigid position necessary for release into the playground.

Without raising her head, she gave the order to stand. Not being watched was even more nerve-racking than when she stared over the top of her glasses.

'Sit down again and this time stand without making a sound,' came her voice from the bent head.

The children co-operated, slowly lifting the hinged seats in the double desks. It was an exercise in slow motion. Some even stopped breathing in the effort to be silent.

'Lead out and I still don't want to hear a sound.'

They tiptoed out of the classroom and were well clear of the outside door before they dared to speak.

The whole of the class memorised Jack's 'poem' prompted by Gloria during the next five minutes. Miss Jenkins, who had shared in the cufuffle through the partition, overheard the chanting as she wandered around and guessed that it would be remembered long after the eight times table.

Jack was released from the cupboard at the end of the break. From then on, he was regarded by the village children as a kind of Robin Hood, William Tell and Richard the Lionheart all rolled into one. Only Hannah and the other evacuees fully understood the dreadful punishment of confinement in the dark.

Slowly the disastrous day came to an end. Hannah heard voices as she went in through the back door of Eastfield Cottage. She took off her outdoor clothes, listening to the murmur of words and recognising Elsie's high-pitched tones. The second voice was lower, more like a man's. It certainly wasn't Mr Porter but it sounded familiar.

'Is that you, Hannah? You've got a visitor,' Elsie called.

For a second Hannah's spirits rose, but the excitement was momentary. She would know her father's voice anywhere. She peeped around the door. The visitor was sitting in Tom's chair, leaning forward to share in the heat of the fire. The dark grey hair was short cropped like a man's yet the clothes belonged to a woman. A dress of dark brown serge gathered from the waist was bunched around the knees, and a black shawl covered the shoulders.

'Come and get a warm, duckie. You look half-frozen to death,' Elsie said in her newly acquired maternal voice. 'Have you got something to put some colour into her cheeks, Mrs Knight? I can only think of nettle tea.'

The visitor turned to examine the child, and Hannah saw that she was indeed old Mrs Knight without a ginger curl in sight. Had she changed herself into a man? She shrank from the extended hand.

'Brimstone and treacle's best in the spring,' the old lady said. 'There's nothing beats it. Clears the winter out of the blood and puts spring in its place.'

'Of course,' Elsie agreed. 'Come March, it was always brimstone and treacle.' She shuddered at the thought of it, for a few seconds back on the receiving end of the sticky laden spoon.

'But then nettle tea's best for now. She won't come amiss on that. Mr Knight used to swear by it. Bless his soul. Always used to leave a patch of nettles in the garden.'

It was all nettles now, Hannah thought, visualising the rough area around the old house. She frowned at the idea of all those stabbing prickles going down her throat. They were not going to make her drink nettle tea!

'Don't look so worried, my dear. We're not trying to poison you and they don't sting any more. I've been telling Mrs Porter about your kind act today. Did it get you into trouble?'

'No,' croaked Hannah, trying to clear her throat.

'That's good. I would have had to sort out that teacher of yours if she'd punished you.'

The idea of Miss Spencer changed into a frog entered Hannah's mind and she gave a nervous giggle.

'Nickodemus sent me with a message for you. He would like you to come for tea tomorrow so that he can thank you. Is that all right with you, Elsie? I'll see her safely home.'

Before Hannah could think of an excuse Elsie agreed. 'That'll be nice, won't it, duckie? Say thank you to Mrs Knight.'

Fear reduced Hannah's voice to a whisper.

Elsie fetched the black coat and hat. Folded inside the coat were several newspapers and resting in the hat, two sets of ginger curls. She helped the old lady on with her coat and waited whilst the newspapers were held against her chest, before doing up the buttons.

'What a good idea for keeping out the cold,' she commented, giving a quick smile in Hannah's direction. 'Did you have a scarf?'

'Yes, it's in my pocket but I'll get my hair sorted first.' She pulled the black felt hat low down on her forehead and over the tops of her ears before putting the ginger curls in place.

Hannah was fascinated by the two little fringes of curls attached to wire prongs which pushed up under the sides of her hat just in front of each ear. She had become the Mrs Knight of earlier acquaintance without using a word of magic.

'Poor old soul,' said Elsie, as they waved goodbye to the retreating figure. 'She's had a hard life and no mistake. You remind her of her grand-daughter who will be grown up by now. It was sad the way that adopted son left his wife and child. The old girl doted on him and couldn't see what he was really like.'

'Why did she adopt him?'

'Well, her little girl died. Drowned she was in the wash tub. That was terrible. Some reckon as how she did it but I don't think so. She worshipped the child. Found her head first, legs sticking out. Her other child, a little boy, was born deaf and dumb and ended up in an institution. I don't think she could have any more, or perhaps she daren't. Anyway, she adopted this little boy and called him George after her husband. He was perfect and turned all the girl's heads with his black wavy hair and charms.'

'Where is he now then?' Hannah interrupted. 'Does he live round here or is he in the war?'

'Timbuktu for all we know,' Elsie said, closing the outside door and beginning to clear away the evidence of an afternoon tea break. 'He took some of his father's savings and cleared off. His wife, she was a nice little body, stayed for a while but then went back to her folks in London and took the child with her of course. And that was that.' She stared at the wall recalling those distant events, then gave a little shrug. 'This won't buy the baby a new dress!' she exclaimed as she began to peel the potatoes.

Hannah smiled. Her mother used to say that. While the preparations for the evening meal progressed, Hannah entertained Elsie with the drama of the day. Elsie, enlivened by so much company, tutted and laughed. 'No sense of humour that one,' she pronounced, scraping the peelings into the pig bucket.

On the following day, time seemed to be accelerated. Hannah was told to go straight to Mrs Knight's cottage once school was over. She experienced a strange mixture of excitement and trepidation as the last lesson drew to a close. It had been a quiet day. Only one incident threatened the procedure. Someone had spit in the register inkwell during the dinner hour, causing the first two attendance marks to be rather thin and streaky, before Miss Spencer, from past experience, realised why. No one admitted guilt of course, but the teacher and the class had no doubts as to the identity of the culprit. The girls pulled faces, registering female disgust at the baseness of the male sex, while the boys gave broad grins of delight.

By a quarter to four the weather had brightened, but Mrs Knight's overgrown garden absorbed the late afternoon light, and

Hannah shivered with cold and apprehension at the front door of the cottage.

'Come in, my dear. The door's on the sneck,' the old woman called.

Hannah thought of Little Red Riding Hood waiting at Grannie's cottage with the wolf lurking inside.

'Come in,' came the voice again. 'I won't eat you. I'm not the Big Bad Wolf you know.'

Hannah drew in her breath sharply and her eyes widened. She turned to make a dash for the gate as the latch clicked and the door creaked open.

'Have you forgotten something?' Mrs Knight's blackness filled the small doorway.

Hannah was speechless for a moment and could only stare. A long wig replaced the black hat and ginger curls. Black hair hung down on to the sequinned bodice of a black satin dress. The long skirt obscured her legs, the hem rustling against the doorstep.

'Oh yes,' she lied, clearing her throat. 'My scarf. I've left it on the peg.'

'Oh never mind. I've got plenty if you need one. Come on in. We're all waiting for you.' She stretched out her hand and a large glittering ring sparkled and flashed in the light.

Hannah gave one last desperate look towards the gate and then feeling like a true heroine she resigned herself to her fate.

She was astonished at the cosiness of the room. A bright fire burned in the black leaded grate. A white tablecloth covered a round table, which was set with a delicately patterned tea service, and the air was filled with the smell of baking.

'Here she is, my darlings. This is the little Florence Nightingale who rescued Nickodemus. Come and shake his paw, dear. He has been so looking forward to your coming.' Mrs Knight swept grandly towards the armchair which was pushed close to the fire. There Nickodemus reclined, resplendent on a big cushion, his leg bandaged and his ginger fur glowing in the firelight.

Hannah was now aware of the other occupants of the room. Eyes, some green and some yellow, stared from all sides, following her every movement. Nickodemus opened one eye, stretched and miaowed.

'Say hello to him.'

'Hello, I hope you are feeling better,' Hannah said politely.

'There now. We can all settle down,' Mrs Knight said, rustling past Hannah. 'Do you like my dress? I thought it was an occasion to dress up. They are few and far between these days.' She rubbed her hand down her sequinned bodice. 'It makes me look quite young, doesn't it? And the wig just sets it off, don't you think? It's my natural colour. When I was your age my hair was as black as the fire back and so long I could sit on it. You ought to let yours grow. You would look like Rapunzel. Do you know that story?'

Hannah nodded, back in the realms of witches again. Mrs Knight gave a throaty chuckle. 'The children round here think I'm a witch. None of them steal my apples.' She grinned, showing a set of white even teeth, not a bit witch-like. 'Sit down, dearie. I've made honey sandwiches and a big seed cake especially for you. You do have a sweet tooth, don't you?'

She poured out the tea carefully, her gnarled brown hands making a marked contrast with the delicate porcelain pot. 'Oh just a minute,' she muttered and drew a large handkerchief out of her skirt pocket. She appeared to be wiping her mouth vigorously, but as the handkerchief was returned to the pocket, her teeth went with it. Now, with her nose in close proximity to her chin, she looked the picture of a fairy-tale witch.

Hannah tried not to stare at her and concentrated on eating the honey sandwiches and drinking the strong, sweet tea. That was all commonplace, but she eyed the large seed cake with suspicion.

'I never got the hang of them for eating.' Mrs Knight was chewing with her front gums and reminding Hannah of a rabbit. 'The crusts are a bit hard. You don't mind if I leave them, do you? You must eat yours. They make your hair curl.'

Hannah nodded. 'That's what my mam says.'

'Poor child. Never mind. How's Elsie Porter treating you? She's never been used to having children around the place and that man of hers doesn't help.'

'She's all right, thank you.' Hannah didn't think it was right to discuss her foster mother with a stranger. Instead, she talked about her own family and the air raids.

'Well I suppose anywhere is better than being bombed,' Mrs Knight commented, washing down the last of her sandwich with a noisy gulp of tea. 'Now for the seed cake. It looks the best one I've ever made. I'm a big believer in caraway seeds.'

Hannah daren't ask why. As her companion cut two large slices, she could see them dotted in the cake.

'That'll make you grow big and strong. Here we are. Eat it all up. There's plenty more.'

Hannah pressed her teeth into the cake and allowed a small portion to enter her mouth. Would she grow like Alice, she wondered? Or would she shrink? The strong taste of the caraway made her screw up her lips. She looked down at her plate and tried to think of a way to avoid eating any more. She picked at the pointed seeds and had another drink of tea. She didn't want to upset the old lady. She took another small bite and shuddered as a seed embedded itself in one of her molars.

'It's good, isn't it?' Mrs Knight said, her thought-reading ability apparently failing. 'I've about run out of them. Things are hard to come by these days. Still, it will all come right in the end.' She stared up at the ceiling and muttered under her breath.

Hannah followed her glance, but could see only a spider scurrying between the beams. It was a good opportunity to drop the cake on the floor. She was becoming an expert at getting rid of unwanted food, and with 'Oh dear! I'm sorry,' she got down under the table, making sure that the cake was no longer in an edible state.

'You should have told me you didn't like it. Mustn't waste food, you know. Must she, Tabitha? Not with a war on. Still, I've done the same myself. You do remind me of myself. Do you dream?'

'Sometimes.' Hannah whispered. She was embarrassed. The old woman seemed to know everything.

'I mean special dreams, not just muddles. They're very important, you know.' She leant forward across the table. 'They told me you were coming.' Her voice had become hoarse and mysterious.

Hannah wanted to ask who 'they' were but her courage failed her.

There was a silence for a while. The room seemed charged with energy, and waiting for her to speak.

'You do, don't you?' Mrs Knight said at last.

She knows already, Hannah thought, but felt obliged to answer. 'Well I suppose I do, but then everybody does, don't they?'

'No, not everybody. Some people never see the stars. They're too busy looking at their feet. It has been said that we're dreaming all the time. The truth is yet to come. Good things, bad things. Still we must leave it to the Dream Maker. He knows best. Shall we have a game of dominoes?'

'If this is all a dream,' Hannah persisted, 'then what happens when we wake up and who is the Dream Maker?' She wanted to ask if he was the sandman who put sand in children's eyes at bedtime, but she knew that that was just a fairy story.

'He's the captain,' Mrs Knight replied, ignoring the first question. She picked up the tea tray and went into the kitchen.

'Do you mean God?' Hannah called.

'A rose by any other name would smell as sweet,' came the answer.

Hannah sighed. The old woman was talking in riddles. Why didn't grown-ups ever answer questions?

Dominoes took her mind off the problem. She liked the patterns of the white dots on the black oblong shapes. They were so familiar, tangible and tactile. Her favourite was the double six. It made such an impact and her face shone with triumph when it appeared in her chosen set. They had four games and won two each.

'Goodness me! Just look at the time,' Mrs Knight exclaimed, turning her head in the direction of the fire.

Hannah followed her gaze to the large old clock on the mantelpiece which declared that it was half past two. 'What time is it?' she asked, confused but not surprised by its apparent eccentricity.

'It's six o'clock. I add four on and take half an hour off.' Mrs Knight laughed showing the white even teeth now back in her mouth, and Hannah felt a surge of affection for her new-found friend. 'Now, how about some magic?'

Goose pimples jumped up on Hannah's arms. The domino game had lulled her into a feeling of security. It was all so cosy and normal and, if she was honest with herself, disappointing. But now the panic was back. The cats seemed to be watching her and the log on the fire began to burn fiercely, sending sparks up the chimney.

'It's about time you decided to burn,' Mrs Knight muttered on her way to the sideboard.

'Pardon. What did you say?'

'Oh just talking to the fire. It's been as daft as daft all day. Ah here it is.' She took out a pack of cards from the drawer and came back to the table. 'Now, my dear. I'll show you how I can see through the cards. Put the first one face down on the table.'

Hannah took the pack of cards and pushed her thumb against the first one. 'They're a bit old. All sticking together!' she exclaimed.

'Yes they certainly are. I got them with some Craven A coupons—that's why they all have a picture of a man smoking a cigarette on the backs. That one's the Five of Diamonds. Turn it over. See. I'm right.'

She was and Hannah placed the next card down carefully so that there was no chance of her seeing the other side. Mrs Knight stared hard at it and then declared it to be the King of Clubs.

'I didn't shuffle them,' Hannah said.

'Well, give them a good shuffle. It won't make any difference.' The old lady laughed and Hannah felt a zigzag of excitement and panic travelling up her spine.

She continued to turn the cards, and her companion unfailingly named each one until the pack of exposed ones was stacked complete on the table. She even knew the Joker which appeared about halfway through. Hannah was mystified. Her father had taught her a number of card tricks that were easy to learn, but this one seemed impossible for a mere mortal.

'Can anyone do this?' she asked.

'Why? Would you like to do it?'

'Do you think I could? I've never really done much magic. What would I have to do?' Hannah recalled a conversation about someone who was in league with the devil. Sold his soul or something like that. It had made her feel very uneasy at the time.

'Just use your eyes and your memory, that's all. Let's begin with this card. What do you notice about it?'

Hannah glanced at it, turning it over and exposing its value. 'Well, it's the ten of hearts.'

'Now look at the back of it. What do you see?'

'A man smoking a cigarette.'

'Is it the same as the next card?'

'Yes, isn't it?'

'Look very closely. There is something different.'

'Do you mean it is torn at the corner?'

'Good girl! Every card in the pack is different. Some have creases. Some have damaged edges, and some have little marks on them. See, an extra line near the man's nose or one eye darker than the other or something in the background. I have made them all different and learnt all the differences.'

'Isn't that cheating?'

'It would be if I used them in a card game with someone else, but I don't. There's no one to play with. I just do it to amuse myself and keep my brain sharp. Now, you know that this one is the Ten of Hearts. I'll mix it into the pack and then we'll see if you can spot it.'

During the next half an hour, Hannah studied the cards, her sharp eyes noticing how each card differed from the rest. One card appeared to be perfect. 'I can't see what's wrong with that one,' she commented at last.

The old woman laughed. 'Sometimes, nothing is as important as something. Anyway, that'll do for now. By the time we've walked back to Eastfield Cottage it will be getting on for your supper and bedtime. We don't want Mrs Porter worrying about you or she won't let you come again and learn the cards. Whisper in the Mooncat's ear for a special dream before you go.' She pointed to the windowsill where a white pot cat sat staring at the black-out curtain. 'He likes to look at the moon. I put the blind up before I go to bed.'

'But it's not real! It's only an ornament.'

'What do you mean it's not real? It's made of what we're made of. The dust from shooting stars, the bones of a dinosaur, the autumn leaves. Everything going round and round. It's real enough.'

'No, what I mean is it…' Hannah paused, trying to think what she did mean.

'Hasn't got a soul,' the old lady interjected. 'Well, everything is not as it seems.'

'No! What I mean is, it isn't alive.' Hannah was determined to make her point.

'Are statues of the saints alive? People pray to them. They are like stepping stones to our creator and He's not flesh and blood either if it comes to that. He's pure soul.'

'What is the soul? Nobody seems to know.'

'Well the soul is a different kettle of fish from stars and dinosaurs. There's no substance, you see. It's like a shadow except that our shadows do what we do. Our souls can go where they like.'

Nickodemus meowed and the other cats began to stretch and sit up.

'They know. Don't you, my darlings? Never mind what folks tell you. You'll hear all sorts. You follow your instincts. Come on. Where's your things?'

Hannah put on her outdoor clothes and waited while Mrs Knight wrapped newspaper across her chest, put on her coat and pulled her hat hard down on her head. The padded shoulders and the collar pushed her wig out away from her face and her appearance became even stranger.

'I won't be a minute, dear. I'll find you a scarf.'

She disappeared through a door. Hannah could hear her slow tread on the stairs and crossed quickly to the window, turning the pot cat to face her. He had large round yellow eyes and put Hannah in mind of the first cat in the tinderbox story who had eyes as big as saucers. 'Give me a special dream about my mam and dad,' she whispered. She jumped back as she heard the creak of the stairs door. Mrs Knight glanced towards the windowsill and smiled.

It was a clear night and the air had a frosty coldness. The moon shone down unhindered by cloud, illuminating the track to Eastfield Lane. Hannah slowed her pace to keep in step with her companion. She was in no hurry. In spite of her earlier fears, some of which still flitted across her mind, she was enjoying the adventure. The air was cold in her nose and lungs as she breathed in. That was exhilarating, not only the sensation, but combined with the stillness of the night there was a feeling of unreality, secrecy and a kind of taking of liberties. Her breath hung like smoke as she breathed out. It all seemed magical; the dark silhouettes of the trees and hedges, the hooting of an owl, the smell of the wet earth, and the crunching of the rough surface under foot, yet the silence of the sky, so black but so full of stars. She stared up into the vastness, screwing up her eyes to see the moon as a great white ball turning in space, and wondered who was looking at her.

The old house, cold and empty seemed to be anticipating their arrival. Hannah imagined it sighing and waiting for company.

' "Is there anybody there?" said the Traveller.' Mrs Knight's voice broke into her thoughts and her heart leapt with the joy of a shared pleasure.

'We read that poem at school,' she said. 'I'm learning it for recitation.' A scuffling noise made her jump.

'Just a rabbit or maybe a fox,' the old woman reassured. ' "The Listeners". It's one of my favourites. Can you remember who wrote it?'

'Walter de la Mare.' Hannah said the name carefully, enjoying the sounds and the airing of her knowledge. Her hand was now clinging to the adult's arm. 'The Listeners are ghosts, aren't they? Do you believe in ghosts? My mam says it's all rubbish. She gets mad with me when I want to keep the light on.'

'You don't want to get scared. Ghosts have been ordinary people. What's frightening about that? The demons are in our heads. Think about good things when it's dark. I do and I soon go to sleep.'

A bat swooped low over their heads.

'I wish I could fly, don't you?' Hannah said, then wished she hadn't.

However, Mrs Knight made no comment. The seed cake had settled in a hard lump in the pit of her stomach, and she was desperate to get home for a large glass of elderberry wine, which worked wonders for her digestive system. Hannah wanted to walk forever, but Eastfield Cottage was in sight and Elsie stood like a dark stick at the gate.

The sight of her brought the child back to depressing loneliness. The cold air no longer excited her. She had the same kind of feeling when she was dragged back into reality at the end of a reading session, or when the lights came on at the cinema. She didn't want to communicate. 'Mardy' her mother called her. No one understood that feeling of wretchedness. It was almost a physical pain.

Elsie, visualising Tom's reaction, was half-heartedly suggesting a hot drink, but Mrs Knight declined.

'I must get back and see to the cats,' she said. 'They get worried if I'm gone too long. Don't fret, my dear. I'll soon be safely home.'

Hannah had no doubts on that score. Neither man nor beast would bother such a strange person.

'Goodness me,' giggled Elsie, as they went in through the cottage door. 'Whatever does she look like in that wig? All she needs is a broomstick.'

She's already got one, Hannah thought, part of her brain wanting to collaborate with fantasy, and yet reason telling her that the besom was for sweeping the path. She was almost sure now that Mrs Knight was not a witch, but she certainly was something.

10

A Moustache and a Miracle

At last it was the weekend. A letter had arrived from her mother and Hannah read the brief note over and over again, folding and opening it, until the creases in the paper became soiled with the pressing of her fingers. Her second prayer was answered. After dreamless nights, she was doubting the power of the Mooncat.

The contents of the letter made little impact in their brevity and showed no sympathy. Mrs Flynn hoped that Hannah was all right, and assured her that they all were all right. Apparently, she'd got a job at the shop at the top of the street. She made no mention of the war, apart from saying that Hannah's father was now in the army, and she promised to pass on Sally's address in her next letter. She finished with instructions to be good and eat properly.

Hannah would not have cared if the letter were written in Chinese. All that mattered was that her mother had written it. The physicality of the ink on the page produced by her mother's pen embodied the bond between them. She ran her finger around the word 'Sally'. She loved the shape of it; the capital S, the tall looping Is. The name was the person, the shape imprinted on her brain. If only life could go back to normal.

Elsie, who already knew the contents of the letter, watched her re-reading it, piqued with jealousy. It was all right for 'her', she thought unreasonably. 'Her' with her posh bathroom and her electricity and no kids under her feet and no husband to plague her. Plenty of money too with a job.

'Do you want this porridge or don't you?' she asked tersely. 'If you don't, I'll have it. I scarcely get enough to keep body and soul together.'

'Oh you have it, Mrs Porter,' Hannah pushed the bowl towards Elsie.

'You can jolly well eat it. I'm not wasting my time. I bet your mam wouldn't be pleased. She's told you to eat properly.' She stopped in embarrassment and then gabbled, 'I bet she's always telling you to eat properly and no wonder.'

After her morning chores, Hannah stood by the gate, picking at the flaking paintwork. The jangling of a bicycle bell drew her eyes and concentration along the lane. It was Jack Clayton balancing on the pedals of a large errand bike. He wobbled to a halt, steadying the heavily loaded box in the metal-framed carrier over the front wheel.

'Hiya, Hannah,' he called jauntily.

'Are you coming here?' Hannah responded with the same jauntiness, her spirits raised by the sight of a face which belonged if only briefly in her past.

'No. I'm delivering to the farm. Should get sixpence for this. Threepence from the farmer's wife and threepence from Mrs Turner if I keep my nose clean and she's in a good mood. I'm trying not to fall over. It's one 'eck of a job steering this thing. What a bloody awful road.'

Hannah looked around to see if anyone was listening, ashamed of his rough speech, yet possessive and protective.

'Can I come with you? I'm fed up.'

She was running now to keep up with him as he wove around the potholes, grunting and cursing. She bore him no grudges. He was guarding his own well being in the playground and he had defended her in the sum queue.

Jack, safely away from village scrutiny, was glad of her company. They spoke the same language–Yorkshire.

'I had a letter from my mam yesterday. I think we'll be going home soon.'

Jack didn't comment. Her words did not comfort him.

'You'd better wait there,' he ordered, considering the possible sharing of the reward.

Hannah waited at the gate until he re-appeared tossing a threepenny bit in the air. 'See. Told you,' he said joyously. He let her have a ride on the bike until the front wheel caught in a pot hole and she lurched into the grass verge. He pulled her to her feet and looked with concern at the blood which trickled down her leg.

'It's all right,' Hannah said shakily, fighting back the tears. 'I keep knocking the scab off.'

'You tell me if them Parkers hit you again. I'll put my fist in their faces.' Jack felt secure in his promise with no one else to witness it but still cast an anxious glance down the lane. 'Anyway, I'd better get a move on. I've got to sweep the yard yet.' His tone was boastful rather than complaining.

'I'll show you a short cut. It's a bit muddy but the middle's not bad. I'd better not come. She'll be looking for me.' Hannah quickened her pace, the pain in her leg forgotten until they had passed the cottage gate.

'No, and I'll have to pedal like bloody 'ell.' He grinned, exposing his freshly scrubbed teeth, whiter than they had ever been since they arrived.

'That's in a right state,' he said as they reached the old house. 'Has it been bombed?'

'No, just old I think. It's supposed to be haunted. Do you know Mrs Knight? Well, she used to live there. Do you think she could be a kind of a witch?' Hannah lowered her voice to a whisper, waiting for his reaction.

'Don't be daft, girl. She's just an old woman. They look funny when they get old. There aren't any witches any more. They've all been burnt up. I took her an order this morning. She gave me threepence.'

Hannah felt the colour rising in her cheeks and wished that she had kept her secret. Boys didn't understand. 'Well, don't tell anybody else I said that, will you?'

He didn't reply but jumped onto the pedals, the saddle jerking from one side to the other behind the seat of his trousers.

She watched until he reached the crest of the hill and the old barn. Then alone once more with her thoughts, she walked slowly back to the cottage and the peeling gatepost.

Sunday promised a change.

'All the kids go to Sunday School,' Elsie announced at breakfast time. 'It starts at ten, so by the time you've washed your hands and face it'll be time to go. Just got to see to the hens.'

Hannah was waiting outside ready to go when her foster mother returned along the garden path. It was easy to distinguish her goal from the neighbouring buildings. The red brick of the little chapel contrasted sharply with the stone cottages and the gabled end stood at right angles to the road, breaking the line of pantiled roofs. It had none of the outward splendour of the parish church, but the atmosphere beyond the plain brown front door was warm and welcoming.

Hannah stood for a moment, unnoticed by the group of children gathered around a rather stout lady near the raised platform.

'In your places, children,' the lady said, clapping her hands. 'We'll sort it out later. What's your name, dear?'

Hannah saw Rosie Dent waiting at the side.

'One of the evacuees, are you? Are there any more new ones?'

'Me, Miss,' called Hannah, now having the courage to join in. 'Hannah Flynn, Miss.'

'Oh lovely! Two more girls. No new boys, are there? Good. Well then I hope you can both sing. I'm Mrs Morris and this is Mr Morris.' She waved her hand in the direction of the small thin man who crouched in the corner studying his bible. He reminded Hannah of Sam, the rag and bone man, in a Sunday suit.

'Who are you staying with, Hannah?' Mrs Morris asked.

'Mrs Porter up at Eastfield Cottage.'

Mrs Morris frowned.

'She's not my relation or anything,' Hannah said quickly, recognising the signs of disapproval.

'No, of course not, dear. Never mind.' She signalled the children to stand and she sat down at the harmonium, warming up her fingers with a few chords and runs along the keyboard. 'Now, what shall we sing?'

The children sang lustily, putting in actions and clapping their hands in time to the music.

'I'm H.A.P.P.Y,' Hannah yelled with the rest.

'Lovely!' exclaimed Mrs Morris breathlessly. 'Now for the bible story. Loaves and fishes, I think.' Rationing was a heavy burden for her digestive system to bear. 'Sheila, dear. You can read today.'

It was a favourite story and everyone listened for mistakes, ready to prompt her.

'Now that was a wonderful story, wasn't it, children? Let's see if the little ones can remember what we call happenings like that. It begins with an "M".' The teacher pressed her lips around the sound and looked about for signs of inspiration.

'I know, Miss,' shouted Billy Brooks. 'It's magic.'

'No it isn't! It's not magic. That's in fairy stories.' She glared at Billy who bared his teeth in a defiant grin of embarrassment.

Hannah knew all about miracles and magic. She liked 'M' words and said them both to herself to see which one sounded the best. 'Moustache'. That was another one she thought as the teacher extended the sound to 'Mi...' and the hairs on her top lip bristled. She had never seen a woman with whiskers before and she stared fixedly at the gingery fringe.

'Come on! "Mir, Mir..." Oh all right then. Tell them, one of the big ones.' Mrs Morris looked at Hannah who was still staring at the strange upper lip and taking the glazed look to be a sign of ignorance, she turned away impatiently. 'Come on! Surely somebody knows. I've told you often enough.'

'A miracle, Miss,' Pat Craig said.

'Yes! It's a miracle.' The words rocked off her tongue and Pat Craig, perhaps feeling that it was a miracle she got it right, smiled smugly and shuffled her bottom on the hard bench.

'God can do any miracles can't he, Miss?' a little girl claimed.

'Yes anything,' the teacher assured.

'Why doesn't he stop the war?' Hannah asked.

'Well, God moves in mysterious ways,' came the quick reply.

'Amen,' said Mr Morris, who was deliberating on his text for the evening service. Whatever the theme, he always reminded the congregation of the evils of drink and of hellfire and damnation, with the wailing and gnashing of teeth. The platform was his stage and his wife, his leading lady.

That good lady beamed at her little flock. 'Have you enjoyed it, Hannah and Rosie? You must tell the others to come next week.'

Hannah couldn't imagine Jack enjoying it. Five days of ordinary school was enough for him. In any case, he would mess about. Boys could be such a nuisance.

'Now for a quiet prayer before we go. Who's sick in the village? Anyone off sick from school?' the teacher asked.

'The Parkers, Miss,' Rosie said without a trace of sorrow in her voice.

The others grinned widely.

'Anyone else?'

The children shook their heads.

'All right then. I expect they'll have to do. A silent prayer for them to get better.'

The children dutifully put their hands together and squinted through their eyelashes at Mr Morris grunting in the corner. Hannah's prayer was so silent that it became non-existent beyond 'Dear God'. Compassionate thoughts were out of mind. Her only awareness was of her closed lids and the contact of her hands pressing together.

'That child needs watching over,' Mrs Morris commented as Hannah went through the door. She's in the jaws of Hell. We must pray for her.'

'Alleluia,' Mr Morris replied, somewhat vaguely.

11

The Doll's House Dream

The next three weeks continued in much the same way, a familiar pattern now, but Hannah's feelings of wretchedness remained in spite of it. She sniffed and rubbed her nose vigorously on the remnants of an old pillowcase. Elsie, who had developed a heavy cold in the previous week, had infected everyone around her, and had kept Hannah at home for the last two days as much for her own convenience as for Hannah's comfort.

Now, Hannah sat on the rug by the fire and wrote a long letter to her mother. She couldn't understand why her cries for help were ignored. There had been only the one letter although she herself had written three more times. She couldn't contain her misery. Surely her mother would come and rescue her. She wouldn't have to work on a Sunday and Grandma and Granddad could always go to Auntie Vera's for their dinner. 'Please come next Sunday,' she wrote.

Elsie displayed no curiosity and made no comments other than that it was a long one this time. It can go on the back of the fire she thought. She had no intention of re-writing this one.

However, there would be no need for deception. The situation was about to change and this change was heralded by a sharp knocking on the back door. Elsie jumped up and Hannah gulped down a mouthful of slops as she craned her neck to see out of the back window.

'Oh, it's only Mr Bentley with the paper,' Elsie said, going to open the door.

Hannah strained to hear their conversation hoping that he was bringing news from home, but his voice was muffled behind his scarf and turned-up collar. She stood and went into the kitchen. 'Is it a letter for me?' she called.

'No. It's from your teacher. She couldn't manage to get up here. She's sent you a book. Here. Go and read it while I see what this letter's all about.'

It didn't take long for Elsie to read the brief note and her spirits rose.

'Dear Mrs Porter,' it said, 'I have been notified that Hannah Flynn's mother and grandparents have died as a result of a bombing raid. Could you break the news to Hannah? I will understand if her absence continues but the sooner she is back into routine the better. Apparently her aunt agrees to her remaining with you until it will be safe for her to return. If this is a problem, let me know. Yours faithfully, Miss J Spencer, Billeting Officer.'

Elsie relaxed her shoulders and stared at the letter. She was shocked yet excited by it. Was there only one aunt? Vera, wasn't it? Then there was the father. Perhaps they'd all get killed. That's wicked of me, she thought but then continued to dwell on the thought. She sat for a few minutes planning her next move. She would have a good day or two with the child, playing games and teaching her new tunes on the piano. It would all be jolly. She dabbed at her nose and pushed the letter down into her apron pocket, hiding it with her 'handkerchief'. Perhaps after another night's sleep they would all feel better. Yes, she thought. I'll tell her tomorrow.

Hannah was waiting at the foot of the stairs.

'What did she say?'

'Don't worry, duckie. She only wanted to know if you are all right and hopes you'll like the book. Now, finish your bread and milk. Do you want any more sugar on it? You can have my share. I'll do without in my tea. Then we could have a game of cards or else play the piano. You choose.'

Hannah finished the bread and milk, savouring the new-found sweetness. It soothed her throat and she returned to the fireside with her book and a feeling of contentment.

'You look like the cat that got the cream,' Elsie laughed rather shrilly. 'Is it a good book?'

'It's all about the Knights of the Round Table and Merlin. He was a wizard. Do you believe in magic? I don't know whether it's true. Sometimes things seem to happen by magic and I can't believe it.'

'I know what you mean. I have wishes that come true.' Elsie smiled fondly at her little girl.

The minutes ticked by, both absorbed in mental imaging. Elsie felt her eyes closing and sat up, shrugging away the tiredness. She mustn't allow Tom to find her like that and spoil the atmosphere.

'I'd better see to the hens before dark. You stay here, duck, and keep warm. It's like an entry under that back door. The wind blows straight at it.'

Hannah was so absorbed in her reading that she didn't hear Tom coming in from work or the low whispering voices in the kitchen. By the time she left King Arthur's court, Tom was sitting in his chair enjoying his pipe of tobacco. He asked her if her cold was better and told her about his day on the farm.

He turned to his wife, his voice changing. 'Have you shut the hens in, Elsie? There's a fox about.'

'Of course I have,' she snapped and then quickly smiled, looking across at Hannah. 'Hannah's getting real good on the piano. Do you want to hear her? Go on, Hannah. Play "Sunshine Showers".'

Tom looked at the clock and Elsie sighed. Don't you dare spoil it, she thought.

'Just a few minutes then,' he said.

Hannah sat at the piano and stumbled her way nervously through the notes but their joint applause boosted her confidence. Tom looked at the clock and Elsie stood up.

'I think that'll do now. We'll leave Mr Porter in peace and have a game in the kitchen. Then you can have some cocoa and take your book up to bed. There's a new battery in the torch.'

Hannah was astonished at her kindness. Still people were kind when someone was poorly. Her mam was like that. She remembered how she had sat up all night with her when she had the measles. Had she got some disease now? Even Miss Spencer was being nice. Fancy writing a letter and sending a book. She continued to read in bed, sitting up and making a tent of the covers over her head. The knights and the maidens in distress together with the magic of Merlin and the wicked Morgan-le-Fay stirred her imagination. Before the story began, there was a poem called "The Lady of Shalott". Hannah read how the Lady could see life only through a mirror and how Sir Lancelot rode past her window down to

'many towered Camelot…

…The mirror cracked from side to side.
"The curse is come upon me," cried
The Lady of Shalott.'

Hannah imagined herself floating down the river, dying from some dreadful disease and everyone sorry for making her suffer. The fantasising continued in her dreams, and she awoke, glad to see the light coming in through the sash window. The room, normal in its shabbiness and mundanity still surrounded her and she hadn't died after all. In fact, she felt full of energy. Her throat wasn't sore and she could breath through her nose.

She got out of bed and crossed to the window. Elsie was walking down the path with the bucket and bowl. The poem came back into her mind and she giggled at the idea of being the Lady of Eastfield Cottage. No one could mistake Mrs Porter for a splendid knight or a maiden in distress with her wellingtons splashed in the melted flurry of snow and, as usual, her curlers in hard lumps under her headscarf. Hannah was about to pull up the window and shout but changed her mind. She didn't want to go back to school yet. She hadn't finished the book and she wanted to practise 'Sunshine Showers'.

Elsie made no mention of school as she ladled porridge into Hannah's bowl. 'How's your throat, duck? You still look a bit washed out.'

'It's a bit sore.' Hannah swallowed hard on her lie.

'Never mind. It'll be better soon. The birds are singing. That's a good sign. We might have a walk later on. Go and see Mrs Langham, ay?'

The walk brought some colour back to Hannah's cheeks, and she enjoyed wandering around the farmyard whilst Elsie talked to the farmer's wife. She caught them looking across at her, and saw Mrs Langham shaking her head. Half an hour later the two of them ran back down the lane, jumping the puddles, and arrived at the cottage breathless and laughing. Then it was back to the book and The Holy Grail. An illustration of a knight standing in the Chapel Perilous where strange faces were carved in the organ pipes sent shivers up Hannah's spine, and she drew closer to the fire.

Elsie stirred the broth and smiled to herself. She didn't think she had ever been so happy. The letter in her pocket, still folded under her handkerchief, pressed against her stomach as she wiped her hands down her apron. It was no good. She would have to tell her. She cleared her throat noisily causing Hannah to look up from her book. 'Hannah, duckie, I've got something to tell you,' she croaked. She fished in her pocket and drew out the letter. 'I didn't tell you yesterday because you were so poorly but you've got to know.'

'Know what?' I can't have a disease, Hannah thought. I feel better today.

'It's about your mam.' Elsie hesitated and struggled to find the right words. 'Well, there was an air raid.'

Hannah knew what she was going to say. 'Our house has been bombed, hasn't it? I told you, didn't I? You know, the doll's house dream. Is my mam coming here or has she gone to Auntie Vera's with Grandma and Granddad?'

'No. I'm sorry. duckie. What I mean is they've gone to Heaven. Your mam and your grandma and granddad.'

'What do you mean? Do you mean they're dead? They can't be. They go to the air raid shelter. Who told you?'

'Miss Spencer.'

'How does she know? She doesn't know my mam.'

'She was told by the evacuation people or perhaps it was your auntie.'

Hannah turned away and stared at the primer on the music rest. 'I don't believe it,' she said. She stood up and went into the kitchen.

'Do you want a drink or anything?' Elsie asked anxiously following behind.

'No, thank you. I want to go home.'

'But this is your home now, isn't it?'

Hannah didn't answer. Her face was white yet calm. Her expression irritated Elsie. She wanted the child to burst into tears and then she could cuddle her better. She took a step forward and held out her arms.

'Come on, duckie. I'll make it better.'

Hannah ignored her and ran through the kitchen door into the passage and up the stairs. She stood by the bedroom window and looked out at the greyness of the afternoon. She couldn't feel the loss. Her mother played no part in this landscape. She belonged in the past, frozen in time. She was a thought in Hannah's head and nothing could take that away.

From then on, that memory extended into her daydreams. Her mother chatted with her grandparents, drank tea with Mrs Blenkin, went to the shops and continued with her household chores. She was like part of a never-ending loop of film, never changing, never ageing...

12

A Rude Awakening

It was on the second Monday of November that Elsie announced her intention to go to the Women's Institute meeting. She hadn't been for some time, but now, with her newly acquired status, she felt on equal terms with the other mothers of the parish. 'I need a break,' she told Tom and he didn't argue with the idea. Unbeknown to her, he had a half bottle of brandy hidden away. He'd seen the farmer's wife through the kitchen window in the act of having a secret nip, and had witnessed her furtive glances and guilty expression as she hid the bottle behind the flour in the back of the cupboard. He cunningly reasoned that she would not raise a hue and cry over its disappearance, and he waited until she went to feed the hens, before creeping in and pocketing it. At first, he experienced a dashing down of excitement as he read the label 'Blackberry vinegar 1939', but his nose was so finely tuned to the smell of strong liquor that one sniff of the stopper restored his anticipation.

Now he sat listening to the radio, distracted by his wife's comings and goings, and thought of the bottle hidden in the leg of one of his wellingtons. Blackberry vinegar! His mouth twisted into a smile. Crafty old cow! He wondered if she had noticed its absence. Medicinal, that's what she would claim. 'Medicinal, my arse,' he muttered.

'What did you say?' Elsie asked, stepping in front of his chair and smoothing her hand down her coat.

'Nothing,' Tom snapped.

'Do I look all right?' Elsie patted a curl in place and looked at her reflection in the mirror on the chimney breast.

'You'll do,' Tom said without looking at her. 'For God's sake, woman! They'll be finished before you get there at this rate.'

'Mrs Langham's calling for me. Oh, that'll be her now. You're sure I look all right?'

'I said yes, didn't I? How many more times?'

'I won't be late, and keep an eye on the fire.'

Hannah listened to the sounds downstairs—Elsie's high-pitched voice reminding Tom to keep the fire in; Tom's muffled reply almost drowned by the signature tune of his favourite Monday programme; then the banging of the back door and the creaking of the garden gate. This was the first time that she had been alone in the house with Mr Porter. She was enjoying the warmth in the small of her back where the oven brick wrapped in an old towel had rested for about ten minutes, and she drew up her feet seeking to share them in the warmth. The rest of the mattress surrounded her, a cold border encroaching on and dissipating that small patch of comfort. She huddled into sleep.

The next thing she knew was a tugging of the covers. Elsie was back and going through the now nightly potty routine she supposed hazily, part of her awareness still clinging to her dreams. The creaking of the bed under a heavy weight, and the contact of a mass of warmth, brought her fully to her senses. It was Mr Porter! She could smell him. She could taste him. His arm came round her compressing her ribs. She felt her night-gown being pulled up and the roughness of his hands on her bare flesh. She froze like a wild animal feigning death in the grip of the predator.

'Come on, duck. You little sweetheart. Let's have a cuddle.'

The lust and frustration were in his fingers, the brandy addling his brain. He pulled her against him and she could feel the hard nakedness of him. She lay like a thin reed, stiff and straight and unprotesting. She instinctively knew that a word or movement could

119

exacerbate the situation. His heart pounded against her, the rhythm passing through into the mattress. His breath shuddered, but then exhaustion followed fast on the heels of passion and his arm relaxed into a dead weight.

She was afraid to disturb him, breathing into the back of her throat just sufficient air to sustain herself. She was knowing but not understanding. Knowing that it was rude. Those bits were rude. Boys pulled at girls' skirts in the playground and shouted ,'Saw your knickers.' Well, that was boys, that was. This was a grown-up. She didn't understand.

Suddenly he rolled over and was now occupying most of the width of the bed. She pressed against the wall, the icy coldness contrasting sharply with the heat from his body. The smell of his sweat made her feel sick. He began to snore. Sharp rasping sounds as he breathed in, and then explosive blowings-out. Now the smell of alcohol and tobacco mingled with body odour.

She didn't know what to do. She tried to twist sideways but he was lying on part of her night-gown. She pulled slowly, carefully easing it away, stopping at a change in his breathing and resuming as his deep snoring returned. Free at last, she wriggled up, supporting herself with an elbow and looked over the mound that was the intruder.

There was a frost that night. The moon shone down unhindered by cloud. She could see her clothes on the chair and the door partly open. She eased herself out of the narrow space, still monitoring his breathing. He was lying with his knees bent and the foot of the bed was flat and navigable.

Her skills in night-time wanderings now played their part. She daren't open the drawer to get the torch. She scooped up her clothes and with all her senses on the alert opened the door wide, allowing as much space as possible in the passing of him. Her bare feet were sensitive to the creaking boards. She pressed against the staircase wall where the wooden treads were firm.

Now, with the moonlight showing only dimly through the landing window, night-time fears returned to compete with the terror upstairs. She opened the kitchen door and hurried into the colours

120

glowing in the light of the oil lamp. The sound of his snores just above her head were reassuring, but their sudden cessation propelled her into action. She grabbed the candle and matches from the chest of drawers, pushed her feet into her wellingtons, and, clutching her bundle of clothes, opened the back door and went out into the night.

She had no idea where to go. At first, she thought of the lavatory, but changed her mind deciding that he might need the use of it. She daren't look back. In her mind, the picture of him watching from the bedroom window was too alarming. She began to run towards the gap, her night-gown white in the moonlight, her wellingtons pattering on the icy path.

She reached the barn and squeezed in through the triangular opening, but then stopped, catching her breath, aware of the heavy blackness. With trembling hands, she opened the box of matches, and attempted to strike first one and then another, becoming more and more frustrated and tense. She remembered Elsie's habit which so annoyed Tom. 'Why do you put the bloody dead ones back?' she imagined him shouting. She felt for an unused one, rubbing her finger and thumb along until she located a smooth head. At last she succeeded in getting a flame, and now in the flickering light of the candle she walked towards the tea chests stored at the far end of the barn, under the hay loft heavily laden with straw bedding for the livestock. The sound of her feet crunching dead leaves and a quantity of loose straw was amplified in the stillness of the night, but once behind the packing cases, which she had pulled into a small enclosure a couple of weeks ago in a vain attempt to hide the kittens from Tom, she began to relax. She dressed quickly, comforted in the warmth of her woollen stockings and thick winter jumper.

Sooty appeared around the corner of one of the boxes giving her usual greeting. Innocently, Hannah's dilemma was her pleasure, and she nestled down on the straw, pressing her thin body into that of the child. The contact was reassuring. The mice and rats would give them a wide berth.

The candle flame flickered sideways in the draughts, and shadows stretched out long and thin along the wall of the barn. Hannah listened for the creaking of the gate. Mrs Porter had promised to be back no later than half past nine, but winter darkness gave no indication of time. Her eyes were dry with tiredness, and she closed them, feeling rested by the blackness behind her eyelids and confident with the access of light beyond. Her breathing deepened as she left reality and slipped into fantasy. Suddenly she kicked out against the horrors of a dream. The cat ran in alarm, knocking against the candle. The flame fanned out along the cobbled floor, quickly consuming dead leaves and loose straw in its path.

Elsie hurried alone along the lane. The meeting had finished later than usual and the farmer's wife was delayed with committee business. It had been good to relax with neighbours, feeling confident in her appearance and having a change of surroundings, but now she was anxious to get home to Hannah.

As she approached the cottage, a gust of wind carried the smell of smoke. They'd had a bonfire up at the farm, she recalled. It must still be smouldering. She fumbled her way through the gate, her nose turning in the direction of the smell. In the bright moonlight she became aware of a haze of smoke which hung over the area beyond the gap, and she realised that the source of it was much closer to home.

'Whatever has he been doing burning rubbish after black-out?' she muttered crossly.

The back door was open and lamplight was escaping along the path. She tutted at his neglect, ready to harangue. The downstairs rooms were empty. She trod swiftly up the stairs, the muscles tightening across her chest. The bedroom doors were wide open and from the small room came the sound of his snores. She flashed the torch light on to the bed illuminating his ruddy features and open mouth, and saw in the same instance that he was alone.

'Tom!' she shrieked. 'You bloody fool! What the hell do you think you are doing in here? Where's Hannah? What have you done? Oh my God! What have you done?'

She pulled back the covers which were huddled around his neck, exposing his unbuttoned trousers and bare belly.

'You bastard!' Her voice was low and venomous. She grabbed his hair and shook him into consciousness. Then she ran to the window, ripping aside the net curtain and looking desperately down towards the earth closet, aware of smoke drifting above the pantiled roof of the barn.

'Tom!' she yelled. 'It's the barn! It's on fire! Get up!'

She ran down the stairs, almost falling in her panic. The candle in its holder was not in its usual place. She rushed out and grabbed hold of a bucket, plunging it into the rain barrel and gasping as the water spilled forward and on to her legs. Tom, now wide awake was hard on her heels, filling the second bucket breathless and unsteady in his stockinged feet.

Elsie reached the barn and pulled at the gable door, cursing at its stiffness. Tom pushed her away lifting it clear of the ground and ran towards the blazing straw.

'Hannah! Are you in here?' Elsie's voice was harsh with fear.

Hannah, aroused moments before by the sound of the door opening was already scrambling from behind the tea chests. She stopped as she saw Tom lunging towards her.

'Go away!' she cried. 'Don't let him touch me. Please, Mrs Porter...' She retreated back behind the boxes and the encircling flames, hysterical with fright.

Elsie stood, bucket in hand, as Tom threw water over the straw. His trousers, hastily fastened at the waist, gaped open beneath, and she was remembering her anguish, the anguish of a fifteen-year-old girl. Tom became the old enemy, the thief of her innocence. Her face twisted with recollected pain, and the sound which came out of her mouth was, as the farmer's wife later described it, like the sound of a stuck pig. She ran, head down, female frailty replaced with demonic strength, and hit him full square in the back with the swinging bucket. Caught totally off his guard, he fell almost twice his length before hitting his head on the cobbles where the loose straw burnt fiercely.

'Burn in Hell!' his wife screamed.

Hannah ran past towards the safety of the door before looking back. Elsie, white-faced and arms waving, seemed possessed, the yellow light of the flames reflected in the wildness of her eyes. Her lips mouthed her hatred but her voice became lost in the sudden constriction of the throat as the smoke entered her lungs. The paroxysms of her arms slowed like a clockwork motor jerking into stillness. For a few moments, there was nothing other than the crackles and surges of the flames. Then the woman turned her back on the man.

'That's that,' she gasped as she stumbled towards the door.

'Shouldn't we get help?' Hannah urged, pulling at Elsie's arm and looking back fearfully at the burning body.

Elsie didn't seem to hear and pushed the child through the doorway.

'I've told him so many times. You know what he was like. Never could control the boozing. Fancy going down there at this time of night.'

Hannah strained to hear the gabbled words not understanding the rehearsal.

'By the time we got the buckets of water, it was too late.' She turned, shaken out of her ramblings by the sound of falling timber and cracking glass. The smoke was black in the moonlight, and flames sprang through the tiles as the straw in the hayloft burnt fiercely. She shrugged her shoulders and turned back towards the house. 'Come on inside, duckie,' she said. 'I think we need a cup of tea.'

Hannah resisted the pressure on her arm. 'I'll go and get help. I can run fast. Shall I?'

'You'll do as you're told,' Elsie snapped. Her face was white and strange. Hannah had never seen such a look before and tried to pull away from the hand that now tightened its grip on hers. At the same moment, they heard footsteps and the voice of Mrs Langham. She appeared at the gate and stood for a few seconds hanging on to the gate post and catching her breath.

'It's not an incendiary, is it, Elsie?' she called, seeing the two figures coming along the garden path.

Elsie didn't answer her, but continued to pull Hannah towards the back door.

'Go inside,' she hissed, 'and don't speak to nobody.'

Hannah was relieved to get into the warmth. She was shaking with cold and fear and now that the farmer's wife was here, she no longer felt responsible for Mrs Porter. Mrs Langham's large bones and stout physique radiated strength in comparison to the frailty of her more slightly built neighbour.

The child huddled up close to the range. The fire, left unattended, was reduced to a few glowing embers, but the metal bars retained heat from its earlier burning. Her throat was dry and the smell of smoke rose up from her clothes, yet only her sense of hearing was on the alert.

The muffled sound of a man's voice was at first reassuring. She strained her ears to identify it. Was it Mr Porter? She hoped it was, but then hoped it wasn't. She couldn't face the questions, the repercussions of the evening's events. It was with a sense of relief that the voice became identifiable when Mrs Langham shouted across the garden, 'Fred. Elsie thinks Tom's in there. She couldn't see for the smoke. Can you get near enough? Be careful. No! Don't go any nearer. The roof's going.' Her voice distanced itself out of earshot and Hannah began to cry. It was worse than a nightmare. Was it a nightmare? Nothing seemed real.

Suddenly the door creaked open. Hannah didn't look up. She knew it was Elsie. She recognised her breathing. The heavier breath of Mrs Langham followed behind.

'Sit down, Elsie,' that lady said. 'I'll make some tea.'

Hannah could sense Elsie's gaze. She didn't move. She was afraid to leave the security of the huddled contours of her body, guarding her inner being from the outside world.

'Why aren't you in bed?' Her foster mother's voice threatened in its tone.

'It's dark. I'm scared.' Hannah didn't look up.

'Oh come on then,' Elsie's voice had a calmer note yet the child gained no comfort from it. 'I'll shine the torch up the stairs but we're having no candles up there. We don't want this place on fire as well.' With her back to the farmer's wife, she narrowed her eyes and Hannah didn't argue.

In her neighbour's brief absence, Mrs Langham studied the untidiness of the living room and gasped as her eyes rested on the empty bottle at the side of Tom's chair. She lunged forward in a panic and picked it up. Seconds later it was out of sight under the Minutes Book at the bottom of her shopping bag, thus completing the circle of guilt.

'Best place for her. Poor little kid. First her folks and now this,' Elsie said in a wavering voice of contrived sadness as she re-entered the room.

'Never mind her. What about you? Is there anything I can do? I feel so helpless.'

'I could do with that cup of tea.'

'Oh of course! I can't think what I'm doing. What about Hannah?'

'It'll keep her awake.'

Sleep was an impossibility, tea or no tea. The blazing barn competed with the moon, which still shone brightly through Hannah's bedroom window as though nothing had happened. She could hear the sound of adult voices in the garden. Men shouting. 'No point in black-out tonight.' 'Let's hope Jerry ain't on the prowl.' 'Can't get near it, that's the trouble.' She wanted to look through the bedroom window but denied her curiosity. She was safe under the covers. A car was coming along the lane. The sound of the engine stopped and she heard the gate scrape across the ground. The voices left the garden and were now in the kitchen below. Her curiosity got the better of her and she crawled under the bed and pressed her ear to the floorboards as she had done on that first day, but the sounds merged into a symphony of highs and lows.

She drifted into sleep, relaxing on the hard boards with the ease of a cat, no longer able to sustain the tension. The bang of the door closing downstairs and the sound of footsteps drawing closer brought her back into consciousness. She didn't move at first, expecting the bedroom door to open. She longed to be coaxed from her hiding place but feared the only person with whom she could make contact. She heard the other door close and then there was silence. Now, fully awake, she became aware of her cramped position. Her limbs were stiff and cold and her back ached. She crawled out, slithering on to the bed and pulling the covers over her in one continuous movement.

In spite of the darkness under the blankets, she could still visualise the window with its view of the back garden, and the smell of Tom's body lingered in the sheets.

13

Chinese Whispers

Elsie Porter was up and dressed the next morning when Hannah went downstairs. She commented that it was a cold morning and best to wrap up warm for school. Hannah watched and listened whilst Elsie ladled out the inevitable porridge, waiting for her to sit down. Usually, at this time of the day, her foster mother was half asleep, but today she couldn't seem to keep still. She went to the window and looked out for the third time since Hannah had sat down for breakfast and suddenly began to sing in her rather shrill way.

'Has Mr Porter gone to work?' Hannah wanted to believe that the events of the previous night were a nightmare, although she knew the reality of them.

Elsie stopped singing. 'Of course he hasn't. How could he?'

'I don't know. I thought I heard him talking last night.'

'No. Not him. It would be Mr Langham or one of the others from the village. You saw him, didn't you? There was nothing we could do. He shouldn't have gone down there in such a state. He nearly set the house on fire once, you know.'

Hannah stared in disbelief.

'People who set fire to places go to prison,' Elsie continued, crossing over to the window again.

Hannah spread the remainder of her porridge around the bottom of her dish.

'Has he gone to prison?' she asked.

'No! He's dead. Now are you satisfied? He's dead. Gone from my life. It's just me and you and we both want to stay here, don't we? Prisons are bad places.'

Suddenly Hannah understood the warnings and from that time on they were both safe in each other's silence. It was a double-edged blackmail, one guilt hinging on the other. Exposure would be unbearable, yet there was no comfort in the guarding of their secret.

That day, the villagers were agog with the news. Death visited this small community on average only once or twice a year. Usually it was someone elderly and occasionally a mother or a still-born child who increased the occupancy of the graveyard. These country folk were a hardy lot, grown tough with the bracing air and fat bacon. Death by fire was a rarity in these parts, even in wartime conditions. The German pilots rarely risked flying over heavily camouflaged and defended airfields and there was little heavy industry in this rural community.

Mrs Langham told Mrs Turner what she believed to be the truth of the matter, omitting of course the 'blackberry vinegar'. Obviously, Elsie couldn't be held responsible. Poor long-suffering Elsie! 'I wasn't far behind her, as you know. What a shock for her! No one knows why he went down to the barn. Only he knows that.'

'And dead men tell no tales,' Mrs Turner said, with a note of satisfaction and triumph in her voice. She enjoyed trotting out such platitudes and that one was very apt.

'No, indeed,' replied Mrs Langham, nodding her head gravely. 'That is very true.'

It was the only truth and Elsie's lies were passed by word of mouth, growing and changing like in a game of Chinese Whispers. Some said that Tom had gone down to his hidden supply of alcohol. Others believed that he was making his own and had blown the place up. While a third source of speculation decided that the pig thief was involved. Mr Blake's pig had been stolen about three weeks earlier. Tom's reputation moved from alcoholism to heroics. Still, it was now universally declared that dead men tell no tales.

'Poor old Tom. He was a good un with the arrers,' one of the darts' team commented.

'None better,' agreed another.

Hannah arrived at school to find that she was the most popular person in the class, but she was a reluctant heroine. The children's questions were direct and she barely satisfied them with the briefness of her answers.

'Did you see his dead body?'

'No.'

'Is it in the parlour?'

'I don't know. I stayed in the kitchen.'

'Was he all burnt up then?'

'I don't know.'

'Did you see the policeman?'

'No. I didn't know there was one.'

'You don't know nothing, do you, gel?'

They began to answer each other's questions, some having picked up lurid details from their parents' careless and speculative comments.

Hannah tried to forget the sequence of events from Mr Porter's arrival in her bed, to his body in flames on the barn floor. The other children couldn't possibly know where his guilt truly lay; where it ended and her own began.

Miss Spencer was determined to carry on as though nothing had happened. Hannah was relieved to put all of her energy into mathematics and English exercises. She didn't want the workday to end, and volunteered to collect up the books and tidy the classroom. She helped Miss Jenkins to wash out the art palettes, welcoming the quietness.

'Are you all right, dear?' the infant teacher asked.

Tears welled up in Hannah's eyes and she struggled to fight them back, afraid of her emotions. Her resolution stifled her response.

'Yes, thank you,' she managed to say, and walked towards the door to escape the close scrutiny.

Miss Jenkins sighed. She understood her reluctance and felt helpless knowing the gulf that lay between them. She remembered the comments of mothers at the gate that morning. 'It's a blessing Elsie's got that evacuee,' one of them said. 'Yes, it'll keep her mind off things,' said another. 'There's nothing like a child to keep you busy.'

Miss Jenkins had wanted to interrupt and admonish. They were talking about Hannah as though she was some kind of object; a mere distraction. The teacher still felt little more than a child herself, and cast her mind back to the time when her grandfather died. His body was laid out in the parlour and death became more than a word. It was now a loss, a fear of future loss, a sudden chasm in her life. Yet no one seemed to recognise her part in it. 'Go and play, there's a good girl,' her father had said. 'You can have an early night tonight,' her mother added. 'We've got a lot to do.' The making of sandwiches and dusting of the parlour seemed to take precedence over all else, and she remembered wondering how anyone could eat and chat as though nothing had happened.

Hannah had similar feelings when she pushed open the cottage gate and was greeted by Elsie in the act of taking some washing off the line.

'As wet as when they went out,' she tutted. 'I've been doing a bit of spring cleaning in advance,' she explained. 'I thought we would have a change.'

Hannah followed her into the house. The living room furniture was re-arranged. Elsie's chair now occupied the place near to the fire, within easy reach of the radio, and the piano took up a central position along the opposite wall. There was no sign of Tom's chair.

'That looks better, doesn't it? And the piano will sound good now.' Elsie gave a twisted grin.

Hannah couldn't share in her sense of humour, but the absence of Mr Porter and his possessions was comforting. The living room door was closed when she went to school. She had wondered about it all day.

Elsie chatted on and the atmosphere in the house reflected her contrived cheerfulness. Apparently, her gloomy memories were swept away with the cobwebs, but every now and again, as the old house gave its customary creaks, she glanced fearfully towards the ceiling.

'I want to go to the lav,' she said, after they had finished their tea. 'Come with me and wait outside.'

It was raining heavily again.

'Hurry up, Mrs Porter. It's freezing out here.' Hannah stamped her feet. She hated going to the outside closet but not because of its primitive structure. It always seemed to be raining.

'You'd better go,' Elsie said.

When Hannah came out there was no sign of her foster mother. Mean thing, she thought. Why couldn't she wait? She ran back to the house giving Tom's wellingtons a wide berth. They stood side by side, banished from the kitchen. The coating of mud, a testimony to his past energy, was slowly being washed away by the heavy rain and reunited with the earth.

Later, while the newscaster's voice droned on, they half listened to national news and half-contemplated home-grown drama. Suddenly, a knock at the door startled them.

'Who the hell can that be?' Elsie said nervously.

'Perhaps it's Mrs Langham.' Hannah prayed that it was nothing worse.

'Who is it?' Elsie called through the closed door.

'It's only me, Elsie.'

Hannah recognised Mrs Knight's deep voice and sank back into her chair.

'Oh come in, Mrs Knight. Gosh you're out late. Not fit for a dog, this weather. We wondered who it was, didn't we, duckie?'

'I thought I'd pop in and see if you were managing. What a dreadful time for you. I couldn't believe it when I heard Mrs Turner telling somebody in the shop.' The old woman took off her scarf and rubbed her hand down her coat. 'Is it ever going to stop raining? I thought we were in for a dry spell with all the frost. If it freezes again though the road will be like a skating rink.' She looked across at Hannah and lowered her voice. 'I hear there's going to be an inquest.'

'Goodness knows why,' Elsie muttered. 'It's obvious what happened. Surely they can see that.'

'Well. The law's the law. It could have been arson, you know.'

Hannah listened hard. Her sharp ears picked up the word inquest and what did Mrs Knight just say? She didn't catch the last word.

'Go and get ready for bed, Hannah. Take the torch and read for a bit. You can come down and have some supper later. Me and Mrs Knight want to talk.'

'Do I have to?' Hannah moaned. 'I'm not tired. It's cold up there.'

Elsie smiled sweetly, looking across at Mrs Knight. 'I know, duckie,' she said. 'Just for a little while, there's a good girl.'

Hannah heard her say, 'Poor little kid. It's a shame this has happened. She was settling down so well with only me to mother her.'

'Ah, bless her.' Mrs Knight sympathised. 'Never mind, Elsie. You'll both feel better once things get sorted. Time's a great healer.'

When Elsie called Hannah down for supper, there were just the two of them once more. Elsie got two plates out of the cupboard, explaining that Mrs Knight had brought them a cake. 'That was nice of her, wasn't it? Folks are so kind.' Her voice wavered with the rush of self pity.

The next day, Miss Spencer gave the order that no one was to discuss the fire or Mr Porter's death. She said it was idle speculation and best left to the authorities.

Most of the children had no idea what the words 'speculation' or 'authorities' meant, although they were very familiar with 'idle'. Hannah was relieved to escape from further interrogation. She was frightened that she would say something to arouse suspicion.

Over the next week, schooldays resumed their strict routine, and the children were not spared from the daily tasks of conquering literacy and numeracy. The fire at the Porters' was stale news and, in the main, the hostility against the evacuees was a thing of the past. In any case, no one dared to challenge Jack. He had blooded Jimmy Parker's nose and now championed the 'townies', particularly Hannah. Some of the older boys teased him from a distance about his relationship with Hannah, which pleased rather than offended.

'She's a damn sight bonnier than Lincolnshire lassies,' he declared.

'Bonnier!' they scoffed. 'She's not a bit bonny. She's as skinny as Hell.'

Dorothy Parker had not recovered from the after-effects of measles. She was the worst case in the village, and chest and ear problems prolonged her illness. It was rumoured that she had been cursed by that old Mrs Knight because she had kicked one of the cats. But Pauline Thompson, a twelve-year-old staunch chapelite, said that they had all prayed for her four times at Sunday School and she knew for a fact that it only took three prayers to get rid of a curse. Hannah felt guilty. I couldn't help the dream, she argued, but then she had vowed to make the girl suffer. Perhaps Mrs Knight would know what to do. Perhaps she would ask the Mooncat.

Away from school, the evenings were spent by the fire listening to the radio, and they became so enjoyable that it began to seem that Mr Porter had never existed. However, on Sunday evening, Elsie announced that the funeral was on Tuesday.

'Tell your teacher that you won't be at school,' she ordered.

At playtime, Miss Spencer called her over. 'Now my dear,' she began gently, 'you told me that you will not be at school tomorrow. Is it the funeral?'

Hannah reacted to the unusual kindness of her tone. She longed for physical contact and the strength of an adult's love and compassion. She wanted to be gathered up and held against the starched white blouse, but the teacher couldn't oblige. Knowing this, she stood staring at the blackboard, her eyelids fighting against the threatened tears and waited.

'I don't think it would be sensible for you to miss your lessons. It isn't as if you're related, is it?' She stopped at the sudden pained expression on Hannah's face, and cursed herself for her carelessness and lack of thought. She wanted to reach out and put her arm around the narrow shoulders, but the arrival of two boys sent in for bad behaviour in the playground froze that compassion. Instead, she turned away and reached for a pencil and paper.

Elsie was indignant when she read the note, her thin lips pressing together, spite and anger increasing the tautness of her pale cheeks.

She had washed her hair and it hung wet and lank around her face.

'She can mind her own business, that one. Who the hell does she think she is? If I say you're not going to school, then you're not. If she doesn't like it, she can lump it!' she yelled, pulling the comb through the knots in her hair.

'It's because I'll get left behind on revision but it doesn't matter. I know it all anyway.' Hannah watched nervously as the comb snagged in the hair.

'Course you do. Better than those village kids. Pass me my box of curlers. I'll show them. Do you want rags in yours? You'd look like Shirley Temple. That would make them talk.' Elsie was giggling like a schoolgirl. The smiles changed to frowns as she struggled with the curlers and thought of the inquest. 'Death by misadventure.' Well, that was right. What else could it be and he deserved to have a misadventure, didn't he?

All the curlers in place, she sat down and switched on the radio. 'I wonder what's on tonight, duckie,' she said.

Only a handful of villagers, curious about Tom's family, paid their last respects on the following day, but they were disappointed to find no strangers at the graveside. Elsie had made no effort to contact Tom's relations knowing that there was little love lost between them, and in any case not wanting to answer to them.

However, it was a relief that none of them did turn up and her communication with the 'world' was bright and chatty. 'Fancy, not one of them has bothered,' she commented to Mrs Langham 'If we'd got some money put away they'd have been here like a pack of jackals sniffing around and offering to help.'

Mrs Langham nodded. She was as relieved as Elsie. She had never met any of Tom's family but if he was anything to go by they wouldn't be up to much. 'A rum lot,' her hubby said. She'd lent Elsie a black hat as a funereal accessory to her tweed coat. It sank down low on her small head, the brim almost obscuring her vision, but giving her freedom to keep her lack of pain from public gaze.

The grave was close to the boundary of the churchyard, well away from the area bordering the church. There, the marble slabs and imposing gravestones marked the passing of important 'sons and daughters' of this parish. Tom's remains belonged with the paupers. Even in death, it seemed that he was not allowed to rub shoulders with respectability.

Hannah, numb with cold, stood beside Elsie at the graveside. The rain soaked into her woollen hat and ran down the back of her neck. She rubbed the drips from her face and looked around at the adults, wondering if it was rain or tears on their faces. Would anyone cry over Mr Porter? In a strange way, she was enjoying the drama of it all. She pressed her feet into the wet earth and watched the mud creeping up the sides of her shoes. The vicar's voice droned on, mechanically mouthing the ritual words. She sighed and turned to look behind her. Who was Lucy, beloved daughter of John and Elizabeth Walters? She strained to read the words blurred by the growth of lichen: 'The Lord giveth and the Lord taketh away.'

The Reverend Cole was reaching his conclusion. Elsie stepped forward and stooped to gather up a handful of soil. Hannah gasped as it rattled on the coffin lid. What if it woke him? She couldn't get the idea out of her head. All she could think of was Marley's ghost in *A Christmas Carol*.

'Come up for a bite to eat, the pair of you,' Mrs Langham offered when ten minutes later they rounded the bend in the lane, but Elsie shook her head.

'No, we'll get in,' she said. 'Hannah 'll catch her death.'

14

Country Remedies

Elsie was determined to be a good mother and became increasingly possessive. 'Honour thy mother. It says that in the Bible,' she pointed out to Hannah one day. 'I'm your mother now. You don't need to call me Mrs Porter no more.'

Hannah didn't answer, but from then on avoided calling her anything. It was three weeks since the funeral and to the outside world all seemed well. Tom's death was seldom mentioned, the work and worries of everyday life becoming paramount once more and Christmas was on the horizon. For Elsie, routine jobs were the hardest to face. She couldn't walk beyond the outside closet and at first gave Hannah the job of feeding the pig and the hens. She helped to carry the bucket up to the lavatory door and then pushed Hannah ahead. The barn now stood blackened and roofless, and the smell of the charred timbers still hung in the air. Hannah always averted her gaze from the scene of their crime. She had mixed emotions when one day Elsie announced that they would have no further bother over livestock. Mr Langham had taken Mollie and the hens up to the farm.

'Well it was time for her slaughter and the hens are getting past it. We won't go short on eggs, he said, and we'll get a good share of the pig. So it's you me and the cat from now on. What's the matter?

You've got a face like a wet week. I thought you would be pleased. You grumble enough about feeding them.' Elsie glared at her foster daughter.

'It doesn't matter,' Hannah muttered. 'Don't expect me to eat any, that's all. I just want potato and gravy.'

'Oh do you now? You might get nothing at all, ya cheeky little bugger, and then where would you be? There's nothing wrong with eating pig. I might be out when you get home tomorrow. The key'll be under the bucket.'

'Where are you going?'

'I'm working up at the farm and I don't want you trailing up there. You can make yourself useful. Wash up and rake the ashes. We need some more wood for the fire. Don't light it, mind you. I know what you're like with fires. You'll have to keep your coat on until I get home and stop dragging your feet, for goodness, sake girl!'

'I can't help it. I keep telling you these shoes hurt and they let in water. Miss Spencer says I need some new ones.'

'Well she'd better buy you some then. Does she think money grows on trees? Bloody teachers!'

It was obvious that Elsie was working herself up into a mood. She alternated between cherishing her 'child' or blaming her for her own state of widowhood when a memory of a rare moment of affection with Tom would come to mind. She began to emulate her mother's sadistic zeal and to enforce her strict ideas on discipline. Hannah dreaded the days that followed apparent good humour. One evening Elsie would be hysterical with laughter and playing the piano like someone possessed, her fingers leaping across the keyboard, her foot jerking on the pedal and her body swaying from side to side. The next morning her face would appear to have become thinner overnight, her mouth mean and tight. On such mornings, Hannah daren't leave any of her breakfast although she almost balked on the last spoonfuls of porridge. Elsie would be waiting for such an opportunity to shout and bring her fist down on the table. On several occasions she took a comb to Hannah's hair instead of using a brush, viciously digging the teeth into her scalp and down her neck.

The standard of her schoolwork reflected Elsie's changing moods, but one word spoken against her foster mother could bring everything to public notice. As it was, her head was almost bursting with words, each one pressing against her tongue in desperation to escape. As each school day came to a close, her misery intensified and she walked back to the empty cottage knowing that a burnt pan, dishes from breakfast and ashes in the grate would be the only welcome.

This was now an established routine. At first, Hannah did as she was told, but the cottage was so cold and depressing that she began to stay late at school again, or if the teachers left early as they had done on this particular afternoon, she dawdled back along the field track.

'You're late. Not been in trouble, have you?' a voice called from behind the elderberry.

'No. Mrs Porter's working late. She won't be back until about half past five,' Hannah shouted back at the hedge.

A few seconds later Mrs Knight appeared at the gate without her hat and the ginger curls. 'Oh dear!' she exclaimed. 'You look perished. I'll make you a hot drink. What would you like and how about a sandwich?'

Hannah hesitated. She looked so old with her grey, cropped hair. The last time she had seen her was at the funeral and that seemed a long time ago.

'It's ages since I saw you. How are the cats?' she asked politely, intimidated by the stern-ness of her features yet hungry for food and a change of company.

'Oh they're well enough. It's me that's in a bit of a state. I've been like a creaky old gate these last few weeks. You don't look very bright either. Anyway, come in and tell me what you've been up to.'

Hannah offered to feed the cats and tidy up while Mrs Knight prepared some cocoa and sandwiches.

'I'll come and help tomorrow if you like. I only have to sort out the fire and wash the pots when I get home. Sometimes Mrs Porter doesn't get home until gone half past six.'

'And you all on your own. That's not very good. She ought to have asked me. You can come every night, dear. It'll be no bother to me. If you want to, of course.' She saw sudden hesitation which registered as reluctance to her ageing self-esteem. 'Still, I don't suppose you want to spend time with a crabbit old woman like me.'

'Oh it would be nice.' Hannah's frown changed to a smile. 'But I'll have to ask first.'

She hurried back and completed her chores minutes before Elsie stumbled in, irritable and tired and in no mood for a chat.

After school the next day she called at the old woman's cottage with a bogus message from Mrs Porter. 'Five o'clock and no later and thank you very much.'

By the end of the school week, a pattern was established. Hannah fed the cats and did the tidying and Mrs Knight prepared the tea. Then for half an hour or whatever time was left, they played dominoes or did card tricks. Before she left each afternoon, Hannah stroked the Mooncat's white head and looked into its big yellow eyes, with silent requests for the safe return of her father. This contact restored her spirits and prepared her for more chores and Elsie's changeable moods.

'I'm not going to work today,' Elsie announced one Friday morning. 'I'm going to get some shopping and do a bit of cleaning up. But don't dawdle home. There's plenty needs doing.'

Hannah nodded, trying to hide her feeling of disappointment. Mrs Knight had promised to show her some real magic after school and was making a junket for tea. She wanted to tell her about the strange dream she'd had on the previous night, where a big black dog had walked along the path with her and the Mooncat had come alive.

It was pouring with rain again when she walked home that night. Her eye throbbed. It's funny having a stye on your eye, she said to herself. I wonder who decided to call it that. Then she thought of Molly and the side of bacon which hung in the pantry.

When she reached the cottage she found the door locked and no sign of a key under the pig bucket. She banged on the door and waited, rain dripping from her fringe and down her face.

She must have gone to the farm after all, she thought. She picked her way around the pile of junk that had accumulated over the years, and stretched up to look through the kitchen window. Elsie's coat was draped across the table and her wellingtons were on the floor.

'Mrs Porter,' she shouted, rapping on the window.

'She's not here,' came Elsie's voice. 'I'm not called Mrs Porter.'

Hannah couldn't think what she meant. 'Yes, you are. I can see you. Let me in. I'm soaking wet!'

'Ask me properly then.'

'Please, Mrs Porter.'

'You don't call me Mrs Porter.'

Hannah was becoming impatient and angry. 'Oh all right then,' she yelled, 'Auntie Elsie. Please let me in.'

'Not until you ask me properly. Say, "Please, Mother, let me in." '

Her face appeared at the window. She was laughing and Hannah thought that she was in one of her giggly moods. 'You're not my mam, silly! Come on! I'll be washed away in a minute.'

'Go and sit on the lavvy then,' came the reply. 'You're not coming in.' Elsie's voice had changed and Hannah licked the rain off her lips nervously.

'There's a big rat in there. I saw it this morning,' she protested but with less defiance in her voice. There was a silence. She knew now that it wasn't a game. She pressed her lips to the glass and mouthed the required words. She could see Elsie crossing the room and waited back at the door for the sound of the key in the lock.

'Oh! You're all wet,' Elsie lamented. 'Come on duckie. Get your coat off and sit by the fire. I'll get you a towel. Look what I've made for tea.' She pointed to a plate of scones. 'I thought my little Hannah would like them better than Mrs Knight's cake.' Her voice harshened. 'You've been telling tales, haven't you?'

'No I haven't.' Hannah paled and drew back from the aggression. 'She asked me in the other day. I only told her about school. I didn't say anything about you.'

'I wonder what tales I can tell about you. She wets the bed. She wets the bed.' Elsie was working herself up into a frenzy and wagged her finger at the sheet drying in front of the fire. 'Didn't think I'd notice, did you? You know what cures that, don't you?'

Hannah shook her head. She was aching with cold.

'Mouse pie. That's the cure for bedwetters. You ask your precious Mrs Knight if you don't believe me. Now get to bed. I don't want to see you until morning.'

Hannah didn't argue. She'd never seen Elsie in such a bad mood as this. She often ranted and raved but now it was something else. She couldn't rationalise it, only knowing that the hard lump of fear was back in her chest. She ran up the stairs away from Elsie's shrill laughter and flung open the bedroom door. The bedroom was in chaos. The covers and pillows were strewn across the floor and Hannah's few possessions were scattered on top. She sat on the edge of the mattress for a little while, listening for any further sounds from her foster mother but all she could hear was her own uneven breathing. Then she began to shiver and reached for a blanket, pulling it around her shoulders. A creak on the stairs put her on the alert again, but even so she jumped and clutched at the blanket as the door slowly opened.

'It's only me, duckie,' her tormentor said. 'You didn't have any scones.' She held one in her hand. 'I'll read you a story while you eat it.' She picked up Hannah's book and flicked through the stories. ' "The Little Brother and Sister". That looks like a good one.'

Hannah's teeth were chattering.

Elsie began to read. It was Hannah's favourite story. She had read it so many times that she almost knew it off by heart. Each time Elsie struggled with a word or in some cases put a wrong word in, she wanted to correct her, but tension and fear inhibited her. Elsie's voice droned on, flat and expressionless.

'Conse—conse—' she stammered.

'Consequently,' the child said, forgetting her caution.

'Oh Miss Clever Dick! Read it yourself!'

Elsie banged the book closed and threw it across the room before stamping out.

By this time Hannah was too exhausted to even tremble. She drew the blanket over her wet clothes, the pressures of the last few weeks and her failing state of health inducing a long period of sleep so deep that no thoughts pierced the blackness of her mind. She lay there for hour upon hour. Then as her body began to recover, she fought against the sensation of falling down a deep hole, and awoke crying out in panic, trying to remember what she wanted to forget.

As her mind began to clear, she strained to hear any signs of her foster mother. She replaced her clothes with a clean jumper and skirt. Her coat was still damp but it was the only one she had. Once dressed, she began to breath more easily. She pushed her little Russian doll into her pocket and looked around for her *Child's Treasury*, her two possessions from the time before she came here. She tucked the book under her arm and carefully opened the bedroom door, staring hard at the door opposite and listening, willing it not to open. Elsie was not an early riser at the weekends. She forgot the third creak on the stairs and hesitated, one foot poised over the next tread. Nearly there. Just the kitchen door and the back door and then she could run. She slowly pushed open the kitchen door and then froze in horror. Elsie was sitting at the kitchen table.

'You're up bright and early for a Saturday,' she said grinning. Her teeth looked yellow against the pallor of her face. 'Not as early as me though. I've been up for hours. I've been baking just for you. You've got a special breakfast this morning.'

'What is it?' Hannah whispered.

'It's a pie. What do you think it is? Come on. Sit down and eat it while it's still hot.'

Hannah sat down at the table and poked her knife under the edge of the pastry lid, revealing what appeared to be a black length of string. On further investigation she found that it was joined to the shrunken body of a baked mouse. She screamed, pushing the plate away from her across the table and jumped up from the chair.

Elsie laughed. 'Mouse pie. I told you, didn't I? Once more and it would be mouse pie. You'll be glad of it I can tell you. It's a special one as well. The one that's been at the bread for months. Caught it this morning, the little bugger. It's a shame to waste it.'

Hannah began to wretch violently, clutching her hands across her stomach.

Elsie laughed again. 'That'll learn you,' she yelled. 'Thought I didn't mean it, didn't you? It'll be here at dinner time. You'll get nothing else,' she called as Hannah grabbed her book and ran out of the cottage.

She didn't know where to go. She thought of Mrs Knight. No, she wouldn't want her there all the time. She was too old to want kids. What about Mrs Langham? No, Elsie would go up there. She clutched her book to her side as she ran away from Eastfield Cottage. Her wet coat chafed across her wrists.

'Hey! Where are you going? Slow down!'

It was Jack riding up behind her, returning from an early morning errand to the farm.

'I'm running away. She gave me–she's trying to poison me. Is she coming? Can you see her?'

'Who? No, I can't see nobody.'

'It's Mrs Porter. I think she's gone crackers... Come with me, Jack. Let's go to Grantham and catch a train home.'

'Don't be daft, gel. I like it here.' Jack wobbled along trying to keep pace with her legs.

'Have you got any money then? Just the bus fare will do. I could hide on the train.'

'But where would you go? You can't go on your own. You'll get lost. Come back with me. Mrs Turner'll know what to do.'

'No. I'm going home.' She stopped talking and began to run faster than ever. She knew that she didn't have a home except the one she was leaving behind. The awareness of the death of her mother became a gaping cavern now that she needed her so desperately. She'd denied it, thought of it as a nightmare which would go away as soon as the war ended, but now she knew the truth of it. She didn't have a mother.

'Come on, Hannah. You can come back with me. I won't let that cow hurt you.'

'No! I'm going to my Auntie Vera's. She'll have me. She's got a big house.'

Hannah's mind was racing, realising that she had no idea where the house was. She couldn't even remember the number of the bus route. And she didn't really like her aunt. She wouldn't have Grandma and Granddad there. If she had, then her mam could have been evacuated with her and none of this would have happened.

'Well, I've got the money from the farmer's wife,' Jack said, shocked by the awful whiteness of her face. He got off his bike and fished in his pocket. 'I've got a ten-shilling note and ninepence. Threepence of that is mine so you can have ten and six. Will that be enough? I'll tell Mrs Turner I've lost it.'

'Thanks, Jack. Don't split on me, will you?' Hannah called as she ran along Eastfield Lane towards the bus stop on the main road.

Jack turned back towards the old house and pushed his bike along the rutted puddled surface of the field track. She always counted the money as soon as he got back. Perhaps he could sneak in and say that he had put it in the till. No, that wouldn't work. It would probably be locked anyway. He decided to stick with his original plan. He'd tell her that he had hit a pothole and had ridden into a ditch, the money came out of his pocket and sank in the mud and all he could find was his threepenny bit. Yes, that was a good story. He got off his bike and stamped in a big puddle, then scooped up some mud from the edge of the ploughed field and pressed it into his trousers.

Mrs Turner was sympathetic at first, rubbing a cloth over his clothes and checking his hands for any cuts and bruises.

Jack pretended to look for the money, expressing surprise and anguish at its apparent loss.

'Here, let me have a look. Come on, turn your pockets out. Ah! Here's something.' Mrs Turner fished out the threepenny bit.

'That's mine,' Jack said. 'It was a ten-shilling note and sixpence. It must have come out and gone in the ditch.'

He recognised the look of disbelief. No one ever believes me, he thought.

'You're lying, Jack, aren't you? I didn't know you were a thief.'

He shuffled his feet, desperate to tell her the truth but remembering his promise to Hannah.

Mrs Turner wanted him to be innocent. 'Turn your pockets out again. It may have slipped into the lining.' She felt around the bottom and smiled for a moment until her fingers retrieved a piece of blotting paper and the stub of a pencil. Her voice took on a fiercer tone. 'Come on! I can't do with liars. You'll have to go back home if you are going to start these games. Come on, Jack, there's a good lad.' The tone was pleading once more and Jack couldn't keep up the deception any longer.

'I gave it to Hannah.'

'Gave it to Hannah! What, that evacuee at Elsie Porter's? What did you give it to her for?'

'She's run away. Mrs Porter's trying to poison her and she's going back home.'

'Oh my goodness!' Mrs Turner gasped. 'Which way did she go?'

'She's getting the bus to Grantham and then catching the train to her auntie's.'

Mrs Turner looked at the clock. 'She'll have got the half-past-eight. Look after the shop, Jack. We'll have to catch up with the bus.

"Don't tell her I told you, will you?' Jack shouted to her retreating back.

He stood in the doorway watching Mr Turner backing out the car. This was the first time that he had seen it in action. I'll have a car one day, he thought as he stepped back behind the counter.

Once more the Porters were the subject of gossip.

'Edna Barrett was on the bus when the Turners overtook it and flagged it down,' Mavis Pattinson told her neighbour Sheila Watkins. 'Poor Elsie. As if she hasn't got enough problems.'

'Is she back with her then?'

'I don't think so. I don't know what's going on, but still, that's the teacher's problem, isn't it? She's supposed to be in charge of them. I'm glad we haven't got one.'

'Well, I don't suppose she'll stand any nonsense.'

'No. That's what they need. Ungrateful little buggers. That one could do with her backside tanning. That's what I'd do if she was mine. But then you know what they say. Too much kindness kills the cat.'

'Yes, that's true,' Sheila said vaguely, never sure of words of wisdom.

It was common gossip by the end of the day that the evacuee was with old Mrs Knight.

'She's taking on a lot.'

Mavis and Sheila were back at the garden gate.

'Yes, I was surprised when I heard. Surely somebody else could have her.'

'I don't think anyone else has got the space. Besides, I've heard that she's got dirty habits. You know, bedtime.' Mavis lowered her voice as she announced the crime.

'Oh how awful!' Sheila commented, painfully aware of a line of sheets and pyjamas which flapped on the clothes line in her own garden.

The villagers continued to speculate on the outcome of Hannah's ingratitude, until it was made known to the children that she would shortly be leaving the village.

15

Next Stop, Norbrooke

Once beyond Mrs Knight's tight embrace and the dark shadows of the elderberry, Hannah, with all her worldly goods packed into the small suitcase, walked towards the bus stop with no backward glances. Instead, she stared at the road which led out of the village and into the wide countryside. A cheery whistle nearly distracted her until she recognised it as belonging to Jack Clayton. He rode by on the shop bike, ringing his bell, but she refused to acknowledge him. She had vowed never to speak to him again after his betrayal. The approaching bus sounded its horn and he dodged out of the way, pedalling on to the junction. Miss Spencer took hold of the case and followed Hannah as she climbed the steps into the single-decker bus, and tutted once more at the state of the child's clothes. A proper little rag bag, she thought. Still, what could one do these days with all the shortages? It was the same at school. Why they had to eat their pencils, she couldn't imagine. Even an application of bitter aloes failed to deter the constant sucking and chewing.

The front seat was unoccupied and they sank down on to the grubby upholstery. Hannah sat by the window and stared out at the fields, ignoring Jack's frantic waving. It seemed a long time since the final nightmare had begun. Mrs Knight had done her best. She knew that. But the false teeth bothered her and the way she sometimes muttered to herself and the way the cats stared. There were no mice, not with all those cats, and no mouse pie. Would these new people believe in mouse pie? She continued to stare fixedly out of the window. Some gypsy children played on the rough grass verge near the group of caravans, and she envied them their freedom. 'I wish I lived in a caravan with a horse to drive like a pedlar man,' her brain chanted. She turned away and stared ahead at the partition that separated the driver from his passengers. His black jacketed shoulders and the back of the driving seat gave the glass a mirroring quality, and her reflection bounced up and down next to that of her teacher, distorting with each bump in the road. She turned her head from one side to the other and pursed her lips in silent communication with her mirror image.

There was a silence between them inducing an almost drug-like state, and although it was still early in the afternoon, the teacher nodded and dozed as the miles slipped by.

'We should be there soon,' she suddenly announced from her dozing. She looked at her watch for confirmation. She was not familiar with this area close to the city of Lincoln, and, with the directions removed from the signposts to confuse the enemy in the case of invasion, it was difficult to tell where one was these days. She sighed as the bus lurched around a sharp bend in the road. More houses came into view. 'Is this Norbrooke?' she asked the conductor. He shook his head.

'No, duckie. Quite a few more miles yet.'

The teacher's expression returned to its business of being long-suffering and the child sank back into her thoughts.

Kate Churchill pushed open the casement window, allowing the cat and the tobacco fumes from Harry's after-lunch cigarette to escape. She coughed in irritation. He'd promised to be here when the child arrived but, as always seemed to happen on a Saturday, his services were in demand. 'All grist to the mill,' he'd commented. Of course, he was right. It didn't do to turn work away. What was it this time? Oh yes. Jackson's barn roof leaking.

Harry Churchill was a kind of freelance artisan. 'A Jack of all Trades' was how he described himself, and in these days with the shortage of masculine strength and traditional male skills, he was kept busy enough. It was a pity he didn't lend his hand to home maintenance Kate thought, aware of the shabbiness of the kitchen decor. 'A sweep has his own chimney on fire,' he always joked as though that gave him absolution. The twenty years' gap in their ages was beginning to gnaw away at their relationship. People had warned her, but he was such an active man in his early forties and she had paid no heed to the warnings. It was the war, she decided, her irritation being replaced with self-reproach. He was a good man in spite of it all. Someone ten years his younger would balk at the effort of maintaining a large vegetable garden, greenhouse, a pig to fatten and another for breeding, bee hives, chickens and an overflowing workshop where he could turn his hand to an assortment of repair jobs. It was all a far cry from his days in the building trade but then beggars can't be choosers, as he would say.

There was still a quarter of an hour before the bus arrived. Perhaps there was time to reduce the marking. It would take her mind off worrying. She looked across to the pile of exercise books, which lurched untidily on the kitchen shelf. No, she couldn't face it. It would be Ella's weekend off! 'The best laid plans,' Harry said. He trotted out his clichés with unfailing regularity. She was back with her irritability again, her brows knitting into a frown. So what was so daunting about having a child in the house? She was supposed to be an expert with children, wasn't she? But it was different having the responsibility full-time. At four o'clock they were all back with their families, and their coughs and colds, mumps and measles were no concern of hers. What if this Hannah didn't like them? Apparently, she hadn't settled in her first billeting. Harry was all for having an evacuee. Poor Harry! How he'd longed for a family. If only Nigel had lived. He wanted a boy evacuee. But she couldn't bear the idea. No one could replace Nigel. She wiped away the tear that was creeping slowly down her cheek Why couldn't Harry be here?

'Passengers for Norbrooke,' shouted the conductor, nodding his head in the direction of Hannah and Miss Spencer. 'Can you manage, duck?'

Miss Spencer nodded curtly. She detested such familiarity and ignored the outstretched hand, tightening her grip on the suitcase handle. Hannah, sensitive to the rebuff, smiled her thank-you for the rough hand which guided her down the steep steps. The jolly little man, unaffected by the frostiness of her escort, gave an exaggerated wink, and she hid her giggle behind her hand.

'Thank goodness for a fine day after all,' the teacher said. 'Now, past the post office, turn left at the public house and we should see a white-washed cottage.' She walked at a rapid pace with the child struggling to keep up. They rounded the corner at The Marquis of Granby and searched for whiteness amongst a scattering of houses. 'That must be it at the end. Willow Cottage it's called.' Miss Spencer cleared her throat and strode along towards the gateway.

The five-barred gate was open and leant at a strange angle. It appeared to have become part of the hedge and obviously was seldom if ever used. There were other signs of neglect. The front windows and door were sadly in need of paint, and clumps of grass grew through the gravelled driveway. The teacher lifted the tarnished brass doorknocker and gave two raps on the door.

Hannah stared at the brass head with its deepset eyes and long nose, and remembered Jacob Marley's face which appeared in Scrooge's door knocker. She was feeling decidedly nervous now, but the house reassured her. It could have been in a fairy story for it had a kind of gingerbread feel about it, yet it seemed to have a comfortable aura, happy in its shabbiness.

There was a sound behind the door which was repeated several times and then a voice: 'Could you go round to the back, please? The door's stuck.'

Miss Spencer sighed and impatiently pushed her charge in front of her along the path. Hannah gasped with surprise. What a big house it was. The path zigzagged around parts of the building which jutted out, and numerous small squared windows suggested more than the normal living space. The back garden came into view stretching away, its complete length hidden by a large greenhouse. The glass glinted in a sudden burst of afternoon sunshine, inviting exploration.

The back door opened and a lady appeared. She was small and plump, and her shape put Hannah at her ease. There was something reassuring in her ample weight.

'Come in, Miss Spencer,' she said. 'I'm sorry about the door. It's rarely used. And this must be Hannah.' Her voice matched her contours, warm and flowing with no marked accent. She sounded pleased to see them. In fact, everything seemed pleased to see them, even though none of the furnishings or the decor had yet made any impact on Hannah's senses. She looked at the floor in that first shyness, remembering that it was rude to stare.

'We must do something about that door,' the lady was saying. 'It all gets so neglected at the front of the house as I expect you noticed. Still, one of these days. There are always a hundred and one other jobs to do but I don't have to tell you that, Miss Spencer. I expect you keep pretty busy.' Kate Churchill waited for a response, chiding herself for the dreadful feeling of inadequacy which was invoked by this lady's presence. Stop gabbling, she told herself.

'Yes, indeed,' Miss Spencer replied, giving a loud sniff. 'I've still got a lot of marking to do because of all this.' She nodded in the direction of the child.

'Me likewise.' Kate pointed to the pile of exercise books sprawling on the kitchen shelf.

Hannah gasped and looked up squinting under her eyebrows. She was a teacher! No one told her she was a teacher!

The two adults did not appear to notice the small sound and continued to converse.

'I expect you would welcome a hot drink before you go and how about a bite to eat? You've got half an hour before the bus comes back and there isn't another one until gone five. You're welcome to stay of course. It's dreadful, isn't it? We've got a car of course but that's not much good if there's no petrol in the tank. Still mustn't grumble. Do you want to take your coat off? You won't feel the benefit of it.' Kate stopped for another breath.

Miss Spencer declined, clutching her hands tightly across her coat as though the removal of it was a threat to her well-being. She half turned to look around the kitchen.

'Oh do forgive my manners. Sorry it's kitchen company. I've only just lit the fire in the sitting room. Do sit down. Oh you're back again. Off you go, Tiger,' Kate gabbled, pushing the sleeping cat towards the edge of the old armchair. 'Cats always choose the most comfy place, don't they?'

'It's all right. I'll sit here.' Miss Spencer stared pointedly at the cat hairs which were part of the upholstery and sank down on a wooden kitchen chair before reaching into her handbag and taking out a large envelope. 'These are her personal documents, identity card, ration book, et cetera. You will have to arrange a change of address but I've made it all quite clear. Oh one thing which I didn't mention in my letter. Actually, it's only just come to my notice. No late drinks if you know what I mean.'

The teacher didn't notice the child's quick jerk of the head, but Hannah saw the frown on the lady's face and felt her colour rising. How did she know? What else had Mrs Porter told her?

A man came into the kitchen and caught the tail end of the conversation. He stretched out his hand. 'Come on, poppet,' he said. 'Let's have a walk around the garden. Do you know anything about ducks? I need a bit of advice.'

Hannah nodded, wondering which kind of ducks he was talking about or whether he was joking. She wasn't too sure about this man. He was wearing dark-rimmed glasses which made his eyes look very wrinkly, and the same kind of wellingtons that Tom Porter used to wear. He was shaking hands with Miss Spencer, then he took hold of her hand and a warm feeling began to replace the tension in her stomach. She looked up into his twinkling brown eyes and somehow his glasses didn't seem to matter.

Kate Churchill stood by the gateway watching her fellow teacher as she walked along in the direction of the bus stop. What an unfeeling woman, she thought. She seemed to be more concerned with her own problems rather than those of the child. 'I hope I don't get like that,' she whispered, suddenly remembering her earlier thoughts. Miss Spencer rounded the bend and disappeared from sight. Kate turned and walked slowly back to the house, seeing the shabbiness and weeds as if through the eyes of a stranger. That could be a job for tomorrow if it was a nice day. There wouldn't be much more chance before the winter really set in, although it seemed to have been cold and wet all of that term She brightened at the thought of Sunday.

Poor little waif! Harry seemed to have taken to her. She'd better come in. The sun had disappeared behind a dark cloud and there was a late afternoon chill in the air. No doubt, he wouldn't have noticed. He never felt the cold. She went in to get her coat and was surprised to find them both sitting near the range. She couldn't hear what he was saying but, whatever it was, he was holding her attention. For a moment she felt excluded from the relationship, but then they became aware of her as the door latch clicked into place.

'Your teacher's gone and she told me to say goodbye and hoped that you would be happy,' Kate lied. 'Winston! Hannah does not want washing, thank you very much.'

The black Labrador rested his head on Hannah's knee and looked up into her face.

'You've got a friend for life here,' Harry laughed.

'I know. I've seen him before. I didn't know he was called Winston though. They didn't tell me that. Is that a dog's name?'

'Well I don't think you know Winston, dear. It's because our name is Churchill. Winston Churchill! It's a joke really.'

'Goodness me, Harry!' exclaimed Kate. 'How rude of us. The poor child hasn't been introduced. We're Mr and Mrs Churchill, but you can't call us that. No one around here calls Harry Mr Churchill unless they are pulling his leg. You must call him Uncle Harry and I'll be Aunt Kate except at school, of course.'

Hannah smiled, swallowing back a giggle. Her mum was always saying, 'You're like my Aunt Kate,' if she was muddled up between her left and her right. Aunt Kate never seemed to materialise and one day she asked where this relation lived. 'It's just a saying,' her mother laughed. Now there really was an Aunt Kate. Hannah found the coincidence intriguing.

'Don't you like that?' Kate asked, her confidence wavering.

'Oh yes,' Hannah hastily reassured. 'It just reminded me of my mam.'

Kate busied herself with preparing the tea and wished again that Ella was here. 'You'll have another auntie tomorrow,' she called across the kitchen.

'Of course,' Harry said. 'I'd forgotten all about Ella. She'll soon put some colour back in your cheeks. She makes wonderful Yorkshire puddings for a Lincolnshire lass.'

The reference to her poor state of health made Hannah feel tired and she searched her mind for something to say. 'Is she your daughter?' she asked, directing her question to Harry. She felt at ease with him but found it difficult to warm to Mrs Churchill, now that she knew of her profession. It was strange to see a teacher in a house. She looked on teachers as a race apart, never visualising them in any other role. They were at school when one arrived and usually there at home time. If they left school at the same time as the children, as Miss Jenkins sometimes did, the bags of books indicated a continuation of their way of life. Even the thought of them going to the lavatory was incredible.

'That would make her laugh, wouldn't it, Harry?' Kate was saying. 'No. She keeps house for us. She looked after her invalid mother for many years and when she died poor Ella was left on her own and in need of a job. She was too old to join up so she came to live with us and it leaves me free to teach. You'll like her. Everybody likes Ella.'

The two adults conversed far more than usual during the meal. Hannah contributed little to the conversation, giving brief answers to their questions. They found themselves wildly exaggerating the village amenities, addressing each other in an attempt to impress her. Kate watched her toying with the boiled ham, an indulgence at teatime, but intended to make this an occasion. Perhaps she doesn't like me, she thought. She seemed to get on with Harry earlier. She looked at the clock and wondered what time the child went to bed.

155

At last an uncomfortable silence settled on the little gathering except for the rattling and scraping of cutlery as Kate gathered up the plates, and Harry stirred his second cup of tea.

'Come on,' Kate said, her voice rising in an attempt to sound cheerful. 'Let's go on a grand tour of the house.' She led the way up two steep steps from the kitchen. 'It's all ups and downs,' she explained. 'It used to be three buildings and then somebody a very long time ago decided to join them all together.'

They were standing in a narrow passageway lit by a small window beyond the staircase. It reminded Hannah of Eastfield Cottage but the air was sweet, a mixture of floor polish and cooking.

'This is the dining room,' Kate announced, opening a door on the opposite side. 'I'm afraid it only gets used on high days and holidays.'

'She means Christmas Day,' Harry interrupted, grinning broadly.

'Well it takes a lot of coal to heat all the rooms, and anyway we like kitchen company. It would be a shame to cover up the table.'

Hannah ran her fingers over the polished surface of the oval table tracing the patterns of the grain. She had never seen such a wonderful piece of furniture before.

'It must be very old,' she said.

Kate was encouraged by her interest. Normally, children seemed bored by anything which came from the 'olden days' as they called the times of her youth.

'It was my mother's. I used to sit on that side with my back to the window when I was a little girl.'

What a stickler for etiquette her mother had been, Kate thought. She felt her presence in this room. She must be turning in her grave at such slipshod ways.

Hannah now turned her attention to the rows of delicate porcelain figurines that stood along the shelves of a Welsh dresser, and Kate, anticipating the clumsy investigation of small hands, stepped forward to intercept. But the child was keeping a safe distance, content to study the details. In that moment a bond began to form between them, a mutual respect for things of beauty.

'Come on!' Harry called from the passage. 'It'll be bedtime before we're done.'

'There are three bedrooms up there.' Kate pointed up the stairs. 'You can see those when you go to bed. Yours is the middle one opposite to the bathroom.'

'Is it a proper bathroom?' Hannah asked. 'Has it got taps and a chain to pull?'

'Of course and this is one for downstairs...' Kate opened another door on the left revealing the cloakroom as it was known.

'Two lavs!' Hannah exclaimed. 'Gosh, that's good.' She looked in awe at the toilet and washbasin in the corner and the assortment of coats that hung on a row of pegs on the opposite wall. The signs of neglect, the peeling paper under the window, the yellowing whitewash on the ceiling, were not important.

'It saves mud on the stairs,' Harry was saying. 'I have to use the tradesman's entrance. Round here, look. This is where I leave the garden behind.'

They turned sharp right at the end of the passage and stepped down into a large room.

'The old back kitchen,' Kate explained.

Hannah looked around, seeing the trappings of washday; a copper in the corner, a dolly tub, an old well worn mangle, and two clothes lines which spanned the beamed ceiling. A large scrubbed top table and a number of bentwood chairs occupied the centre of the room. There was a musty smell of age mixed with soap and Hannah stored the scent of it with her other favourites. A door on the opposite wall was open and beyond it was a gravelled back way.

'This is a pantry,' Kate said, opening a door in the end wall. 'It's where we store the jam and bottled fruit.'

Hannah had mixed feelings at the sight of the rows of neatly labelled jars and the side of bacon that hung amidst them.

Yet another little room was opened up to reveal shelves piled high with a miscellany of objects.

'The "Glory Hole",' Kate said apologetically. 'That's a job for a rainy day.'

In that brief glimpse before Kate hastily closed the door, Hannah spotted a box overflowing with remnants of material and a watercolour palette next to a jar containing a variety of paint brushes. She began to anticipate the pleasures of a rainy day until Harry commented that it had better be sooner than later before the mice ate the lot. They retraced their steps and were back in the narrow passageway. 'This is grandly called the music room,' Harry said, throwing open the next door on the left. 'Well, it's got a piano,' he continued, 'but it's really more of a reading room.'

The shelves on either side of the chimney-breast were crammed with books.

Kate noticed how the child's eyes scanned the rows of books and remembered Miss Spencer's comments about Hannah being scholarship material and a great loss to her examination group. 'Well that's about it,' she said, hearing Harry's sigh. 'Oh, except for Ella's room. She sleeps near the kitchen. Did you notice the door when we were having our tea? I expect you thought it was a cupboard. There's a little winding staircase up to it and a cellar underneath. That's a handy place for keeping the milk. I'll leave her to show you it tomorrow.'

Secret stairs and a cellar! Hannah could anticipate the mustiness. This was the next best thing to a castle.

'Go and sit with Uncle Harry now and I'll get the dishes washed.' Kate pointed along the passageway to a square entrance hall. 'Oh, silly me. You haven't seen that room, have you? We're leaving the best bit out, Harry. Follow me.' She walked ahead and threw open the door with a theatrical gesture. 'Voila!' she said.

Hannah stared in amazement at the large room dominated by an inglenook fireplace at one end and a gallery at the other.

'This used to be a barn,' Kate explained. 'And that was the hayloft. It's the warmest place in the house up there. Go and have a look. There's an assortment of books on the shelf, but be careful. The steps are steep and don't fall over the cat. I expect he's having a nap. It's his usual retreat after tea, away from Winston's teasing.'

Hannah looked and looked. It was a barn but not 'the barn'; a warm cheery refuge with no cobwebs, no rats and no Tom and Elsie Porter.

She climbed up the steep stairs into the gallery and looked down on the old chintz-covered chairs and the stone slabbed floor with the assortment of clip rugs. And it seemed that she had been waiting all her life for this moment.

16

Old Ways and New Ways

Ella Makepiece lived up to her reputation. She returned the next day, earlier than expected, in her eagerness to meet the new arrival, and at once put the child at her ease. Hannah likened her to a bright little bird. She was slightly built like Elsie Porter but there the resemblance ended. Her rosy complexion and sparkling brown eyes indicated a warmth and good humour.

A walk around the village in the sharp wintry air, leaving Harry to his radio and dozing by the fire, gave the three of them a companionable feeling and an appetite for Sunday tea, as well as providing Winston with a scent-filled ramble into realms outside of his everyday territory.

By the time Monday morning came, Hannah was part of the household. She regarded Kate as a friend rather than a teacher and walked along at her side with a feeling of excitement and possessive superiority. No one could hurt her now.

The months and years that followed merged into a period of bliss. At first there were the nightmares, but the doctor reassured Kate when she confided in him after church one Sunday. 'Shock takes a long time to get out of the system,' he said. 'The subconscious takes over at night and the demons escape. I'm sure they'll be gone soon now that she is in your capable hands.' He gave her arm a little squeeze and Kate felt the excitement of youth in that physical contact and a lifting of her spirits.

Hannah developed a great affection for all of them. Aunt Kate was her mentor both in school and out of it, Ella saw to her physical needs with a great deal of laughter thrown in, and Uncle Harry was a good friend, a champion of all country ways. He was a great storyteller and filled her head with adventure and fantasy in the spaces not taken over by her own wildness of imagination.

Village life was punctuated by a set pattern of red-letter days. For Hannah it began with that first Christmas. With little time to spare, her foster parents sought out second-hand games and a variety of books, and Hannah drew pictures, made things out of cardboard and scraps of material, and lavished much attention on a special calendar for the kitchen wall.

The winter gave way to spring and Easter celebrations. She learnt how to decorate eggs with onion-skins and leaves, all wrapped up in a cloth and immersed in water to be hard boiled. She polished the resulting orange marbled eggs, and they glowed like wondrous jewels in a cane breadbasket in the centre of the table on Easter Sunday. Then it was May Day when the chosen queen was pushed through the village in a decorated bath chair, and the children danced around the maypole, weaving intricate patterns as they skipped and turned. 'Come lassies and lads, get leave of your dads and away to the Maypole hi,' the children sang to an audience of proud mothers and tiny siblings.

'Will I have a turn when I'm one of the big ones?' Hannah asked as Kate wrote down the nominations for the May Queen.

Kate explained that it was tradition. 'You know, passed on from mother to daughter. You have to be a villager,' she added hastily, noticing the changed expression.

'But I am a villager,' Hannah protested.

'I mean born here. It would put the cat among the pigeons if I suggested you.'

There were no such reservations at the annual church garden fete in June. Then it was 'all hands to the deck' foreign or otherwise. Hannah helped Kate at the Lucky Dip stand and shared the excitement of the small children whose fingers searched in the sawdust for the largest or lumpiest parcels. The highlight of the day for the adults was the announcement of the winner for 'the bowling for the pig' event. This was a skittle game where scores were recorded until the fete officially came to an end. A young pig to fatten up was highly prized in the austerity of wartime. Every year Hannah thought of Tom Porter and shuddered. A fancy dress parade was always well supported. On the first occasion of Hannah's involvement, the theme was 'Characters of the war'. Fat people favoured Mr Churchill or Mussolini, and there were a number of thin Hitlers which posed quite a challenge to the judges. It was acceptable to cheer or boo but a 'Squander Bug', a fearsome lady with swaying antennae and a devil-like tail in the style of a familiar cartoon encouraging thrift, and a 'Dig for Victory' gardener with a placard covered with colourful representations of carrots, cabbages and beetroot, were given spirited applause. A small boy, who represented salvage collection, proudly pushed a wheel cart piled high with newspapers, and skipped triumphantly up to the announcer for his first prize of sixpence. Kate and Ella had dressed Hannah up in a home-made nurse's outfit, and she won a threepenny bit along with the other children in their assortment of costumes.

The Harvest Festival was celebrated with more enthusiasm and prayer than in pre-war years. Everyone obeyed the government directive to dig for victory. Not that food was in such short supply in the country. Most people had a back garden where rows of vegetables were grown and some kept hens and a pig if they had space. Uncle Harry taught Hannah a little rhyme about 'waste not want not' and she recited it at the chapel anniversary celebration.

'Dearly beloved brethren, isn't it a sin
That when you peel potatoes you throw away the skin?
For the skin feeds the pigs and the pigs feed you,
Dearly beloved brethren, isn't that true?'

Rabbits, rooks, pigeons and the occasional pheasant caught with some stealth and secrecy eked out the meat ration. Harry Churchill bred rabbits, both for the meat supply and for the pelts, which he cured and sold to the local cobbler for the making of gloves or as a warm lining for boots. Some people kept bees, both for the honey and for the extra sugar ration. Nothing was wasted, and milk which didn't survive in the summer heat was converted into cream cheese in little muslin bags left to drain outside.

Country people showed a great deal of gratitude when they thanked God for a good harvest.

And then it was Christmas again, the last big festival of the year, a mixture of religious worship and eating, with the added excitement of gifts. The majority of toys were second-hand, collected at jumble sales or passed from one family to another. Some enterprising people spent their evenings knitting dolls' clothes or sawing, hammering and gluing when the children were in bed. Few had the time to be miserable in houses where Santa was expected.

In between, there were the unexpected special days. The arrival of Red Cross parcels from America for the evacuees in the village caused a mixture of emotions. There were three other evacuees in the village and they and Hannah were greatly envied by the village children for their good fortune. 'It's not fair' was the common cry as the evacuees showed off their bags of shiny glass marbles, crayons, magic painting books where plain water changed the page into colourful pictures, and packets of bright clean plasticine. The evacuees wisely left the packets of sweets at home. Hannah hid hers in the newspaper rack, where they remained to be drooled over for several weeks until finally she gave way to temptation.

Wrapped oblong sugar lumps thrown by American troops passing the schoolyard in convoy did give the village children a share in the booty, and they scrabbled and screamed like a pack of jackals. Sweet rationing was the war as far as they were concerned. There had been few privileges and treats in their lives in peace-time, and games with marbles, old clothes lines for skipping, balls, hoops, old tyres and conkers still followed each other through the seasons. Bows and arrows were replaced with mock guns, and the whoops of Indians were a thing of the past. The Germans were the enemy now, and the boldest children longed to capture a spy and be honoured by the real Mr Churchill. Any stranger in the village was regarded as suspect and watched and followed.

Occasionally, documentary films were shown at the Land Army hostel. Uncle Harry employed a land girl on one day a week to help with the weeding and watering, and Hannah accompanied her to the film shows, almost beside herself with excitement. The clicking projector was indeed a magic lantern to the many children who had never been to the cinema, and the beam of light carrying all those pictures through the air was a source of wonderment.

But for most of the year, life followed a pattern comforting in its strict routine. In most households, Monday was a day of mourning for the passing of the weekend with the added torture of the weekly wash. A wet wash day depressed everyone, particularly during the winter. No one could see the fire for the festoons of wet sheets, pillow cases, towels and umpteen garments of varying size and colour, and the damp air seemed to cling to everything.

The clothes lines fastened across between the beams in the old back kitchen spared the occupants of Willow Cottage from such misery, but, nevertheless, there was much airing to be done, and Hannah's favourite place on such occasions was on the rug between the clothes horse and the kitchen range where the air smelt deliciously soapy.

A woman from the village was employed once a fortnight to help on big washdays when the bedding was changed. Hannah thought of her as 'the old washerwoman' and one day gave voice to her thoughts. Kate was not pleased. Not only did it show lack of respect, but it could also threaten the happy arrangement. Gertie Garton had been the mainstay of washday ever since Kate decided to return to teaching, and when Ella arrived on the scene a few months later, she was loath to lose the extra help. As she pointed out to Harry, who was quibbling over the expense, Ella would need a holiday or she might be ill or even decide to find other employment.

Probably Gertie Garton with her droll sense of humour would have found Hannah's description of her amusing. After having six babies under her apron in rapid succession and a husband whose chief asset seemed to be in fathering them, her face and figure were strangers to youth. Still, the stresses of life had strengthened rather than weakened her resolve, and she turned the mangle handle and ponshed the clothes in the dolly tub with a greater vigour than many of those half her age.

Now, with only vague memories of city life, Hannah had a sense of belonging. She was a country girl, and although the nightmares occasionally returned, poor health, fears of mouse pie and witches were mostly things of the past. The spaces in her imagination were now filled with glorious war-time adventures, when, single-handedly, she captured Hitler, and was recognised by the cheering crowds as the saviour of the world.

17

A Serpent in Eden

The events of one Saturday during the first summer holiday at Willow Cottage impressed themselves permanently in Hannah's memory. The day couldn't be described as a red letter day. Black would be more appropriate as later years would reveal. She was in her favourite place for being alone. The old willow tree at the front boundary was partly hollow and it was her den.

On this particular day, she had considered pretending to be Rapunzel, although she had never been allowed to grow her hair long, but memories of Mrs Knight led to thoughts of Elsie Porter and even worse Tom Porter. Fearing that such thoughts could somehow become reality, she abandoned the idea. Instead, she set about tidying the nooks and crannies which served as cupboards and shelves.

She became so engrossed in this pastime that she wasn't aware of someone approaching, until she heard the sharp sound of gravel underfoot. She ducked her head down below the rim of the trunk and waited for whoever it was to pass by, but the sound stopped. She peeped through the branches at a tall angular woman, who was looking down the drive towards the house. The woman turned her head, and Hannah ducked down back into the hollow.

She was a stranger! The children were warned not to speak to strangers. They could be German spies. It was forbidden to furnish them with information about the locality. 'Careless talk costs lives,' said the posters, together with 'Walls have ears'. This woman certainly looked very sinister. Hannah gasped as she heard the feet crunching in the gravelled driveway. Should she raise the alarm? She peeped over the edge of the trunk again. The stranger wasn't going to the front door. She was creeping around to the back.

Hannah decided that the best course of action was to approach from another direction. After almost falling from the tree in her haste, she ran across to the far side path, past the pear tree and her dangling swing. This path was seldom used by anyone other than herself, and followed the line of the old back kitchen which projected beyond the rest of the house. It ended near the greenhouse. Brambles grew unchecked from the boundary hedge and grabbed and snagged at her socks. She ignored the sudden stabs of pain and crept almost on her haunches along the end of the greenhouse, stopping and resting back on her heels as she heard voices.

'Hello, Margot. What a surprise! You should have let us know.'

It seemed that Aunt Kate knew the stranger and Hannah felt cheated, her expectancy of a chance for heroism fading into everyday mundanity. In truth, she was relieved, yet she clung to the last remnants of her fantasy. She didn't like this visitor, and, spy or no spy, she heard the hostility in Aunt Kate's voice.

'Harry. It's your sister, Margot,' Kate called as her husband came into sight at the end of the cabbage patch. He rubbed his hands down his trousers before raising one in acknowledgement.

His sister! Hannah leant forward taking the weight on to her hands. She knew he had a sister and some brothers somewhere. He often spoke of his childhood but somehow he seemed too old to still have them and especially one as young as this.

He looked pleased to see her and stretched out his arms to embrace her. She drew back giving a high-pitched laugh.

'All right, Harry,' she said. 'Hello will do. I'm not dressed for country smells.'

'Is it that bad?' Harry shared her laughter. 'You'll soon get used to it. I expect it's the pigs. I'll show you them after we've had a cuppa.'

'Not with me in these you won't,' she replied, pointing down at her elegant court shoes. 'I see wellingtons are the fashion here.' She nodded her head in the direction of Kate, who was wearing her weekend gardening gear—shapeless dungarees and wellingtons.

Kate had her back to Hannah, but the child could tell by her nervous movement from one leg to another that she was embarrassed. Poor Aunt Kate!

Harry followed his wife in the removal of the offending footwear, an act made easier with the help of a home-made aid, a length of wood with a V-shape cut out at one end.

'Ingenious, isn't it?' he said proudly, balancing with one freed foot on the step while he struggled to extricate the other.

'Brilliant!' You ought to send it in to the war office'. Margot followed her sister-in-law into the kitchen and out of earshot.

Hannah didn't particularly want to meet her but was loath to miss out on adult conversation. She went back along the side of the old kitchen and eased up the bottom sash of a window, which served little purpose these days in its position so close to the hedge. None of the adults seemed to have noticed the broken latch, and only Winston shared her secret. He followed behind her now, finding the back door firmly closed against his muddy feet, and pushed his cold nose against the backs of her legs as she clambered through the gap.

'Bad boy!' she hissed. 'All right then but don't bark.'

He gave her face an affectionate lick, and watched her pulling her dress back down and brushing away the cobwebs. After listening for a while with her hand on Winston's collar, she trod silently up the dark passageway that led to the hall. She could hear voices coming from the sitting room and crouched near the door listening, ready to stand up at a moment's notice. Winston sat with her, his ears pricking each time the visitor spoke. But it was the noise from behind which startled them, as Ella rounded the corner carrying a tea-tray.

'What are you doing? Aunt Kate's been looking for you,' she

whispered. 'You'd better show your face before she sends out a search party. You know what she's like and what's that dog doing all muddy? Go to your bed.' Her voice was still low but Winston knew that tone, and, giving Hannah a wistful look, he slunk off back to his old blanket behind the mangle.

Ella opened the sitting room door, carefully balancing the tray and its contents in her free hand.

'Lovely, Ella. Just what we all need and look who's here. Come on, you little monkey. We've been calling you. We've got a visitor.' Kate pointed to her sister-in-law as though she was establishing a heading on the blackboard. She was glad of the diversion. Margot's bereavement was filling her mind with pessimistic thoughts. Harry had just invited her to stay, and the spare room was badly in need of decoration. It wasn't until the child came into the full light of the window that she saw the state of her. Hannah had lost a ribbon and her hair hung down wildly over one eye. Her dress was ripped in her hasty descent of the tree, her shoes were scuffed and muddy and her socks casualties of the thorny path.

'So this is the evacuee,' Margot said. She made 'evacuee' sound like something less than human.

'Hannah! Wherever have you been? You look as though you have crawled through a hedge backwards. Where's your hair ribbon?' Kate snapped. Normally she wouldn't have taken much notice. Clothes were not all that important to her, but sensitive to her own dishevelled appearance and Margot's critical stare, her voice became unusually harsh.

'Young ladies shouldn't climb trees,' Margot commented, her eyes glinting with malicious humour.

Hannah glared at her. The stranger had seen her in the tree. That quick turn of the head. She hated this woman for knowing about her tree.

'Shall I tidy her up?' Ella asked. 'I'll leave you to pour the tea, Kate. I won't have any at the moment.'

'Do you let her call you Kate?' they heard Margot say as they left the room.

Hannah felt Ella's hand tighten on hers and looked up. Ella's mouth was set in a straight line and her brown eyes, which normally twinkled so readily, looked stonily ahead. She muttered something which became lost in the shutting of the cloakroom door.

'What did you say?' Hannah asked.

'Nothing. Come on. Let's make you look more respectable and just remember, no tales out of school. A still tongue in a wise head.'

Hannah didn't question her words. Life was full of little sayings. Instead she asked why this woman had come.

Ella rubbed the flannel vigorously across the child's face. 'Her husband has just died. Hold out your hands. Have you been digging the garden with your nails? You could grow potatoes in them.' Her voice rose in her impatience.

Hannah suffered the scrubbing with the nail brush in silence, wincing as the bristles caught in a cut on the end of her little finger. Then, curiosity overcoming pain, she continued to pursue the subject of the Margot woman. 'Was he killed in the war?'

'Now for your hair. I'll have to pin it back. You go through hair ribbons like a knife through butter, young lady.'

'Well, was he?'

'Was he what?'

'Killed in the war. Ouch! You're pulling!' Hannah shrieked in frustration and pain.

'Keep still, child. No, he wasn't. He was too old to be called up. He was ill for quite a while and no wonder.' She looked darkly towards the door. 'Now listen. Speak when you're spoken to and remember your manners. You could do with some clean socks on. Oh, you'll do. She's not the Queen of Sheba even if she thinks she is. Right, off you go for inspection.'

Hannah wondered about the Queen of Sheba as she walked slowly back to the living room.

'That's better,' Kate said. 'Now let's have some proper introductions. Margot, this is Hannah Flynn. Hannah, say hello to Mrs Sergeant.'

Hannah dutifully obliged and then sat down on a stool near the fireplace. She fiddled with the tear in her dress, pressing the edges together so that her bare thigh didn't show through.

'I see you've got some mending to do, Ella.' Margot's high-pitched voice broke the silence. 'It's a good job you've got some help, Kate. I can't get a daily for love nor money. Everyone seems to be doing war work these days. Still, I expect there'll be plenty wanting a job when this wretched war ends. I suppose you hardly know there's a war on, buried away here in the country.' Kate was about to protest, but Margot was intent on making herself heard and she returned her attention back to Hannah. 'I expect you're looking forward to seeing the bright lights again and going back home to your family.'

Hannah didn't answer and still fiddled with her dress.

'Cat got your tongue?' Margot persisted.

Hannah looked up in time to see Kate shaking her head and mouthing something. 'My dad will come for me soon,' she whispered. Her bottom lip trembled and she fought back the tears. Thoughts of her parents had not clouded her happiness for some time. She kept her two worlds separated and life was a daily affair.

'Oh well. I expect he'll be glad to get you back.' Margot showed no concern, although the discomfiture of the child was obvious to everyone. She changed the subject, now addressing her conversation to her brother. 'How's business?'

'Mustn't grumble,' Harry replied. 'The pigs bring in a good income and it's not been a bad year for vegetables so far. We had a fine crop of early potatoes and it looks like a heavy yield of fruit providing we get a bit more sunshine than of late. The tomatoes will need plenty of that.'

Margot had stopped listening and turned to study her sister-in-law. 'You look worn out, Kate.' She emphasised 'worn' and Kate pushed back her hair feeling all of her forty-five years.

'Whatever made you go back to teaching?' Margot continued. 'I thought you were comfortable these days, although having a child must make a difference. There's no way you would get me back into harness.'

Ella smiled at the idea of her foaming at the bit.

'Well you've come at the right time for the soft fruit,' Harry said. 'Do you remember how you used to eat more raspberries than went in the basket when you were a kid?'

Margot smiled but the amusement didn't reach her eyes. 'I suppose some exercise would do me good, although I must have walked miles backwards and forwards to the hospital. Perhaps the fresh air will improve my complexion. That's what they say, don't they? Although I don't particularly want a weathered look.'

Kate feeling decidedly weathered, noticed the texture of Margot's unblemished skin and sighed.

Hannah was sent to bed early that night. She didn't mind. Reading in bed was infinitely better than holding her tongue, and she could have a conversation with herself whether she was holding it or not.

It seemed that Margot Sergeant was here to stay for a while. She made a perfunctory effort at blackcurrant-picking after breakfast in bed and a late start each morning, and then spent the rest of the day attending to her personal needs. Eventually, boredom encouraged her to move on. Apparently an old schoolfriend in Northampton had extended an invitation and, as Margot put it, it would be rude to decline. Kate agreed, a little too hastily and added that it was always nice to see old friends.

'I'll not leave it so long next time.' Margot's promise was more like a threat and Hannah experienced a sinking feeling in her stomach. She could hear the low growl deep in Winston's throat as he pressed his flank against her leg.

18

More Secrets

One morning, nearly three weeks after VJ Day, a letter arrived for the Churchills from Hannah's aunt, Vera Morgan. Kate recognised the handwriting and clumsily tore open the envelope. The page of neat close writing shook in her nervous grasp as she screwed up her eyes in an attempt to focus on the words.

> 'My brother-in-law Martin Flynn has asked me to contact you with regard to the future of his daughter. He is in hospital after his release from a POW camp and hopes to be repatriated soon. However, his situation is not an easy one, having lost a leg and consequently suffering from ill-health made worse by deprivation. Of course, we are prepared to help, but we feel that until there is a little more stability in his life, it would be inadvisable for him to have the extra burden of a child.

> I know from your earlier letters that you would be prepared to keep Hannah with you and that this unhappy news of her father's disability would only unsettle her. I suggest that for her own good, we keep the news from her until Martin feels strong enough to find employment

and can set up a home for them both, or make alternative plans. I await your reply.

Yours sincerely

Vera Morgan

She doesn't want the extra burden of a child, that's what she means, Kate thought as she re-read the letter. And what alternative plans did she have in mind? She'd never taken much interest in her niece and from what Hannah once said, she had little sense of duty towards her own parents.

She showed the letter to Harry and Ella.

'Of course she must stay here,' Harry said. 'Why, she's one of the family. It would be dreadful if she ended up in some little back street, having to leave school early and becoming a little skivvy or being shoved into a children's home.'

'But what would Hannah want?' Ella asked. 'Don't you think we should tell her that her father is all right? Blood's thicker than water, you know.'

Kate glared at her and Ella suddenly became the hired help. 'No,' she snapped. 'Harry's right. She's happy at the High School and her education is important. We'll leave things as they are and not a word from you, Ella Makepiece.'

Ella shrugged her shoulders and turned the tap releasing a sharp jet of water on to the breakfast dishes.

Blissfully unaware of the tensions in the kitchen, Hannah bounced her ball against the wall outside. They would have been surprised to know that she had settled the situation a long time ago. It had worried her that her father would have nowhere to go and no job. It would be ideal for him here. He could sleep in the spare bedroom and work in the garden. Uncle Harry was always saying that he could do with some help. Just lately, she visualised him married to Ella. Ella was like a mother to her and it would work out like the ending of a story, all living happily ever after.

The following Saturday was the anniversary of Kate's mother's death. Putting flowers on the grave was a regular duty, but the yearly paying of respect demanded a special display and a short time of contemplation and reflections. Hannah saw nothing unusual in the suggestion to accompany her 'aunt' to the church. She liked the graveyard. The gravestones and narrow mounds meant little to her, but she shared the pilgrimage, wanting to experience a sense of continuity even if only by proxy.

They filled the vase with water from the standpipe at the back of the church, and Hannah arranged the asters carefully, admiring the soft mauves and pinks of the autumn flowers. As usual, they walked around reading the names and epitaphs. Hannah stood and looked at the small grave in the corner. She accepted that the occupant of the next grave, a Clara Smallwood aged eighty-four was in her rightful place, but William Smallwood, aged three, buried alongside her, evoked questions and the stirrings of doubt in the wisdom and compassion of the creator.

'Sometimes people die before we think they should,' Kate said, guessing her thoughts. 'But Jesus did promise us eternal life and we must all have faith.' She hesitated and cleared her throat. 'Lots of people have lost relations during the war as you have, dear. I got a letter from your Aunt Vera. She thinks your father may not be coming back.'

Hannah stared down at the small grave, pushing her toe against the coarse leaves of a dandelion growing in the rough grass. 'I didn't know you knew Auntie Vera,' she said at last. 'Where is he going then?'

Kate struggled to find words that were neither the truth nor lies. 'I don't know where he is. We'll just have to be patient.'

'Oh well. He could be in hospital and nobody knows who he is. That happened to a man in a story I read at school. He lost his memory. But he did get it back.'

Kate didn't want Hannah to entertain any hopes just yet. She walked back to her mother's grave and Hannah sensed her disquiet.

They were sending her back to Auntie Vera's! That's what it was, she thought. Auntie Vera! She twisted her mouth and frowned. Her mother didn't like her even though she was her sister. Why couldn't she have been bombed instead? Her thoughts sounded so loud in her head that she wondered if she had spoken them, and looked around the churchyard to see if anyone had heard. Her companion was stooping down to re-arrange the flowers and didn't raise her head.

'Aunt Kate,' Hannah said, stepping around the grave. 'Aunt Kate, do you think God hears our thoughts? I mean if we think something bad does He know?'

The nature of the child's question made Kate catch her breath. She eased her aching back into an upright position and searched for an answer.

'I don't think anyone really knows. I suppose everybody has bad thoughts sometimes. We're only human, aren't we?' She could hear herself gabbling. Her own feelings of guilt were causing a denial of her faith, and such a denial in the shadow of the church seemed akin to open blasphemy. She looked at the child and saw the doubt on her face.

'Oh, I thought God knew everything,' Hannah murmured. She turned away and walked towards the path. The small cracks that had begun to appear in the shell of her belief, now opened wider.

They returned to the village street in silence, both wanting to discuss the future, yet loath to leave the safety of the present. At last, Hannah could contain her fears no longer.

'I don't want to live with Auntie Vera. Why can't I stay with you? Don't you want me any more?'

Kate gave a little sigh and then her voice regained its surety. 'Of course we do! We want you to stay with us but we didn't know what you wanted. Your auntie says it will be all right for you to stay if your daddy doesn't come back.'

Hannah wasn't worried now. There would always be a place for him here. She continued to keep her mother locked securely in pre-evacuation memories and looked forward to a happy reunion with her father, shaped in every conceivable way in her bed-time fantasies.

19

Growing Pains

Life followed on in the same daily routine but Hannah was changing. It was a foregone conclusion that eventually she would use her school qualifications to gain entrance to a teacher training college. Typical teenage tantrums erupted and Hannah slammed every door on her way to sulks in her bedroom. 'I'll leave school then,' she shouted on one occasion when Harry declared that he had to earn a living when he was thirteen. 'I'll get a job and then you won't have to pay for anything. I didn't ask to be evacuated!'

Ella lived up to her name and tried to act as a mediator, but Harry, now in his late sixties, had little patience with the growing pains of a teenager. The ageing process was squeezing out his joy of living, making large spaces for self pity.

The moods and friction continued, and one Friday, a few weeks after her fifteenth birthday, Hannah didn't go to school and cried with pain from cramps in her stomach.

'Come on. Cheer up. You'll feel better soon,' Ella said, wiping her flour covered hands down her apron.

Hannah scowled. 'How do you know?' she muttered.

'Well I know these things.' Ella spooned the powdered coffee into the cups. 'Do you know about the curse?'

'What curse?'

'You know.' The colour rose in Ella's face changing the pink to almost purple. 'You know…every month.'

'Oh that. Course I know.' Hannah turned away embarrassed in spite of her apparent nonchalance. It seemed that she was the last to know at school. 'My mam and dad didn't do that,' she had declared when more adult matters were discussed during the mid-day break.

'Of course they did,' Sandra Atkins had retorted. 'How do you think you got here?'

'I saw my mam and dad doing it,' her friend Jean boasted. 'I got into a row for not knocking.' They giggled, putting their hands over their mouths as the duty teacher walked by.

Hannah's thoughts had raced backwards in time to Eastfield Cottage, and now she knew the truth. For a moment, she wanted to boast of her superior knowledge about the sexual act, but it was a rapidly passing fancy, a brief desire to raise her standing amongst her peers. The demon was imprisoned in the back of her mind, and there it must stay. She must not feed it any crumbs of encouragement so that it could gather strength and escape beyond her lips. Yet the recognition of it made her feel dirty and she went into the cloakroom to swill water through her hands and on to her face.

Now she watched Ella busy with the cutting-out of her pastry cases with an upturned cup, in readiness for the jam and curd fillings. The same old thing week in and week out, she thought. She speculated on how much Ella knew about sex. She wasn't married and Aunt Kate had no children, so they wouldn't know anything. What about Mrs Porter? No she was another one with no children. Mrs Knight though, she'd had some. That thought tarnished the memory of her. Her mother? Well only once. But Sally's mother…four times! She hadn't thought of Sally for a long time. She'd always said that she wasn't going to have any children. And to think I wanted four, she thought. 'Well I know different now,' she muttered.

'What did you say, duck?'

'Don't call me duck!'

Roxbourne Teacher Training College, the notice declared at the large barred gates. She hadn't taken much notice of the entrance when she came for the interview. In spite of this being the real thing now, she still felt disorientated.

A young woman greeted them in the entrance hall, taking particulars and handing them the key to her room, and the three of them walked up the stairs with her luggage, a single entity surrounded by the closeness of their relationship. But now that two of that unit had gone, she felt naked, threatened by the unfamiliar environment. She gave one last wave to her uncle and aunt as the car rounded the corner at the end of the cul-de-sac and joined the main road, and then hurried back into the confinement of the building.

The unadorned little room suddenly seemed like a prison cell. The door slammed behind her, and she sank down on the hard bed breathing unsteadily. The smell of Kate's lavender toilet water lingered in the air, offering some comfort. But it was bittersweet. She'd been horrid that morning. Aunt Kate was only trying to boost up her confidence, telling her to hang up her clothes straightaway to let the creases drop out. 'I know! I'm not a child,' she remembered saying, longing to be allowed to think for herself and to take full credit for it. 'I can't wait to get away,' she had muttered under her breath. Now, she couldn't wait to go home.

A bell began to ring in the corridor and she opened the door to investigate.

'Tea and sandwiches,' called a girl waving a long cigarette holder and blowing smoke out as she spoke.

'Do we have to fetch it?' Hannah asked.

'Not unless you want Matron on your back. No food in the rooms. It encourages mice. Follow me.'

Hannah ran down the stairs behind her. Ugh, mice! She was well used to the little field mice which wandered in and out of Willow Cottage, sharing the warmth on cold winter nights, but the thoughts of a permanent colony of opportunists with beady eyes and long tails produced an image of mouse pie.

The dining hall was at the end of the corridor and through swing doors. She sat down at the first table beyond the doors feeling that all eyes were upon her.

'It isn't a waitress service,' someone called from a table near the window. A group of girls giggled and Hannah turned away and pretended to be looking for something in her handbag. After a few moments she stood up and tried to walk casually towards a gap in the wall where a queue was forming. She could see large hatches and beyond them the kitchen. Apparently, a cup of tea, a sandwich and a small cake was the allocation at this meal. She hurried back with her tray to the table near the door, her stomach churning with nervous tension.

The sandwich was curling at the corners. She gave a little shudder at the sight of the filling; meat paste spread thinly on to a margarine backing. Still, eating passed some time. She nibbled slowly at the cake and listened to the voices around her. They all seemed to know each other. Second years, no doubt.

'Can I join you?' A girl with frizzy blond hair stood balancing her tray and pointing to the chair opposite. Hannah nodded swallowing the last of the cake.

The girl pulled a face as she lifted the corner of the sandwich. 'The usual "chance sandwiches",' she moaned, but grinning at the same time.

'What's that?'

'You take a chance when you eat them. Just a joke really. We get a good meal at seven. This just stops the old stomach from rumbling. I don't usually bother much during term-time unless I'm desperate for a cup of tea. What room are you in?'

'On the first floor. Twenty-six.' Hannah gave silent thanks for the quick recall.

'Oh you're lucky! I'm on the top floor again. I'm not kidding you. Two flights of stairs are the last straw sometimes, but I suppose it keeps us fit. I'm sure Matron has done it on purpose. You'll be having her rules spelt out to you after dinner. Have you seen her yet?'

'I don't think so.'

'There's no mistaking Matron. She's a right bossy cow. We think she must have been in charge of a concentration camp during the war. I'm Shirley by the way.'

'Hannah. Hannah Flynn.'

'Drink up then, Hannah and I'll show you the common room. I bet our gang are gathering in there.'

'I thought I would find you skulking in here,' Shirley responded to the enthusiastic greetings beyond the common room door. 'No one's given up the idea of teaching, then? This is Hannah by the way. I'm just doing the decent thing. Not that you lot would know anything about decency!' She pushed Hannah forward and the four young women acknowledged her with a wave of the hand and a casual 'Hi, Hannah,' before turning their attention back to their friend.

Hannah stood listening for a few moments, feeling awkward and in their way. She waited for a gap in the conversation before excusing herself.

'I'll go and finish unpacking, Shirley.'

Back in the safety of her room, Hannah sat on the edge of the bed listening to the voices along the corridor and the clattering of feet on the bare polished floorboards in the room above. First-years, she thought, probably as nervous as she was. This thought comforted her and she became more resolute, putting her books on the shelf and her brush, comb and tin of talcum powder on the dressing table. The top drawer was stained inside with spilt nail varnish and a coating of various shades of makeup. The smell of a mixture of perfumes rose up from the crevices and she relaxed with a feeling of shared womanhood.

After what seemed like an eternity, the bell rang for the evening meal. She cast a final despairing glance in the mirror and dabbed some powder on her chin. 'Well that's the best I can do with you,' she said to the anxious face staring back at her.

She joined a group of first-years recognisable by their quietness, and concentrated on eating, giving as little space as possible for communication. Matron arrived at the end of the meal as predicted. She was a strong-looking big-boned woman, dressed in a tweed skirt and a woollen twin set.

'The second-years can go,' she said with flattened Northern vowels sounds. 'Although by the conduct of some of you last year, you could do with refreshing your memories on the rules.'

The second-years did not take up her 'invitation' and hurried out before she could focus her mind on any specific subordination. Shirley pulled a face as she passed the first-year table and Hannah began to giggle. She turned to find Matron glaring in her direction, and rubbed her nose vigorously with her handkerchief in an attempt to intercept the penetration of that stern look.

'Right!' the 'prison warder' said, giving a loud sniff and drawing her top lip down in a strange grimace. Hannah thought of Miss Spencer and for a moment was back in the past and waiting for words of retribution.

'You are still under age,' Matron was saying, 'and as such you are my responsibility. Your physical well-being, that is. I leave the mental bit to the lecturers.'

Someone smothered a laugh and everyone turned in the direction of the sound trying to keep the smiles from their faces.

'We'll begin with the question of consideration,' Matron continued, glaring across the room. 'We are all living under one roof and sharing facilities, which means we keep the noise down and leave communal areas tidy. No food is to be taken upstairs and no washing is to be dried on the radiators or in the bathrooms. The laundry and the kitchen are more than adequate. All the students must sign the book before going to bed and the outside door is locked at ten-fifteen except on Saturdays when there is a half-hour extension. No men are allowed upstairs.' She made that declaration loudly, deliberating on each word as though it was spelt in capitals, and then continued in her normal rasping tone. 'Guests can be entertained in the common room on Saturdays. Lights must be out by eleven. Rooms must be kept tidy and beds made before breakfast on all days except Wednesdays when the bedding is removed for laundering. There is no restriction on bathing but please consider other people and keep your ablutions brief. Breakfast is at seven-thirty and will not be served after eight o'clock. This building should be vacated by eight forty-five each morning on weekdays unless you are medically unfit. I will be the judge of that and take the necessary steps. Any questions?'

Hannah's mind was drifting again, concentrating on the woman's face and the way her mouth opened and closed like an automaton, scarcely taking a breath. She kept her silence with the others. No one wanted to prolong the agony of listening to her harsh voice, or learning of yet more regulations. They shuffled out, sober under her watchful eye, and experiencing the early disillusionment of life beyond school days.

Hannah joined a group who went into the common room. She couldn't face solitary confinement again so soon. Shirley and her friends, who were monopolising the two settees and a large armchair, grinned at their long faces.

'Don't worry,' Shirley called. 'Rules are made to be broken. She comes down on us like a ton of bricks once or twice a term, but she doesn't look for trouble. Just makes the sounds. It keeps us all on the alert. Mind you. Men upstairs is a hanging offence.'

'You can do what you like with them anywhere else,' laughed the girl in the armchair.

'Meet Stephanie, our resident nymphomaniac,' Shirley joked. 'If you need any advice, she's the expert. Oh and if you report sick, Matron will ask you if it's the curse and if you admit to it, she will remind you of the British Empire and the women who stood by their men through thick and thin.'

'It's true,' her neighbour on the settee piped up. 'Just try it if you can keep a straight face.'

'And,' continued Shirley, 'if you have a cold, she'll get you over a bowl of steaming Friar's Balsam, pinned down under a towel until you gasp for mercy, grateful to be allowed to breathe again even if it is only through your mouth. No one ever complains of a cold twice. Believe me, if you haven't a raging temperature or you're not foaming at the mouth then there is nothing wrong with you.'

All the second-years nodded in agreement but the revelations caused so much merriment that Hannah didn't feel threatened. In any case, she felt very fit and knew that the occasional sinking feeling in the pit of her stomach or the quickening of her heart beat were, as Matron put it, 'mental'. She eased her back against the hard chair and listened to the conversations that drifted across the room. For a moment or two, she was back in the past recalling her own schooldays when teachers were a race apart. Could they ever have been so frivolous?

A lull in the conversation brought her mind back to the present. Matron was standing in the doorway with a bundle of papers in her hand. 'Has a Miss Maddison arrived yet? Miss Christine Maddison. No? Oh well, there's always one.'

The name stuck in Hannah's mind. That was three names she knew now but as yet only two faces to go with them.

Matron hovered in the doorway, her mouth drawing in breath for her final directive. 'Don't forget to sign in and it's about time you were making a move. A good night's sleep. That's what you want. Lights out at eleven and breakfast at half past seven.' She disappeared beyond the swinging door and for a moment there was silence.

Then, 'Good grief,' said Shirley. 'It's started all ready. It's only just gone nine. Don't anyone move. Let's have a singsong.'

She leapt up and ran to the piano launching into 'Ilkley Moor'. The first-years, full of schoolgirl inhibitions, glanced nervously towards the door, but Shirley's gang sang with gusto through all the verses. As they breathlessly came to a halt, Hannah stood up.

'I must go,' she said apologetically. 'I'm dead beat.'

'Me as well,' agreed a small dark-haired girl, studious-looking in heavy framed glasses.

'Oh well. Let the brainy ones go,' came a voice from the 'choir'. 'But be warned. This is our last night of freedom.'

'I really am tired,' stammered Hannah, her cheeks flushing.

'Of course she is, Pauline,' Shirley said. 'I can remember feeling whacked on the first day here. There's milk in the kitchen if you want a cup of cocoa, Hannah.'

Hannah threw her a grateful look and walked out, again with the feeling that all eyes were upon her. She decided to make do with water and found that the quiet solitude of her room no longer seemed like a punishment.

20

Peer Pressure

The Pauline girl was right. The next week was hectic. It took at least two days to learn the layout of the college block with frequent references to the timetable. Hannah was studying History and Art and Crafts as her special subjects combined with the general teaching course, and her evenings were spent in grappling with the first history assignment and the introductory section on child development.

She knew everyone by sight if not by name in their students' hostel, and after three days felt that she had been there for ever. Yet, there was a strange sense of unreality, as though she would wake up one day and find that everything had disappeared. She was acting out a role, doing what was expected, but always with a lack of inner confidence. Self-sufficiency was an adult status, and although being addressed as Miss Flynn was part of that status, it was only a veneer. The little girl trembled within, afraid to answer questions in case she gave the wrong answer and cursing her cowardice when the answer would have been correct.

It was on the following Wednesday evening during dinner that the now famous Christine Maddison arrived. She made her entrance halfway through the first course. A sudden silence began at the door and spread like a wave through the room. Both new and old recognised her as a stranger, but it wasn't only curiosity that drew their attention. She would have stood out from any crowd. Her appearance was immaculate. Her dark hair was cut in a short bob and her grey suit fitted without a crease. Her black high-heeled shoes clicked on the tiled floor, and it seemed to Hannah that confidence oozed from every pore in her body.

Shirley stood up to greet her as she emerged from the kitchen hatch with her plate. 'Christine Maddison, I presume,' she said, grinning broadly.

'Chris if you don't mind. I abandoned Christine in childhood.'

Shirley was speechless for a moment, but it was a condition so alien to her that she quickly regained her voice. 'Sorry, Chris. Come and join us. We've got a space on our table.'

Everyone stared. It was an unwritten rule that no first-years sat at that table even if there were spaces. They all returned to their meat and two veg but their voices were subdued as they strained to glean more about the newcomer.

Hannah ate quickly. She'd promised to telephone Aunt Kate mid-week and then wanted to finish her history essay before looking at plans for her art thesis. She queued at the hatch for the pudding course, loath to miss out on her favourite dessert, banana custard, and, as she walked back along the line of students, she glanced curiously at the new girl. For a moment their eyes met, but Hannah looked quickly away, aware of her own comparatively unkempt appearance. Her feeling of inferiority was both frightening and infuriating, and she bolted her pudding, needing to escape the clamour of voices.

She decided to wait until eight o'clock before going to the phone. Aunt Kate should have finished her marking by then. She wrote another few paragraphs of her essay and was just putting on her coat when there was a knock at the door.

'Who is it?' she called.

'Chris. Chris Maddison. Can I come in?'

'Oh—just a moment.'

Hannah quickly pushed her books into a pile and brushed her hand down her hair, giving an anxious look in the dressing-table mirror at the hideous blotch on her chin which repelled all medication. What on earth did *she* want? She opened the door, apologising for the delay.

'Sorry if I've interrupted anything,' the young woman said. 'I heard you moving about. I only want to know where there's a phone. Mother will be having a fit if I don't ring. You know what they're like.'

'Oh yes. I'm just going myself. The nearest one is on the next road from here.'

'Do you mean there's no phone in the hostel? I've been wandering around looking everywhere. What if someone wants to get in touch?'

'Matron's got a phone and passes messages on. You can give your family her number but it's emergencies only. Anyway, I'll show you where the public phone is. It's not far.'

'Is this your second year?' Chris asked as they went downstairs.

'Gosh no! I only came on Sunday.'

'And what about the ones at dinner? Are they first-years?'

'You mean Shirley and Co. They would be put out at the idea.'

'Oh. I just thought that they seemed very young. A bit silly, you know.'

'Through this passage, look. It's the short cut. Watch where you're walking. The flags are very uneven.'

Chris grabbed her arm. 'It's a good job I'm with you. I've got no sense of direction.'

'Me neither.' Hannah laughed.

'Oh well, it's a case of the blind leading the blind. Trust me to pick on a casualty!'

The shared infirmity drew them closer and by the time they reached the end of the passage that opened up into Alexander Road, they were at ease in each other's company.

'You ring your mother first. I'll look in the shop windows,' Chris said.

'It's not my mother. It's my Aunt Kate. My mother's dead,' Hannah responded and then regretted confiding in a comparative stranger. It could lead to a lot of questions and she felt that her orphan status would be regarded as second-class.

'Oh, I'm sorry. Well you ring Aunt Kate. This ironmongers looks riveting.' Chris laughed at her play on words and Hannah relaxed, sensing no personal attack in her humour.

She spoke all the right words to Aunt Kate and gave all the right answers. Yes, she was enjoying life. Yes, she was making friends. No, she wasn't keeping late hours. Yes, she was looking forward to the ball. She said goodbye and congratulated herself on her convincing performance.

'It's my turn to tell a few white lies now,' Chris joked. 'I set off this morning and should have arrived hours ago. I got on the wrong train. I daren't tell her that. She'll have a duck fit.'

Hannah smiled. 'What are you going to tell her then?'

'Oh I don't know. I had to go straight to classes and then there was my room to sort out. I'll just ramble on. She'll be all right once she knows I'm here. She usually does all the talking anyway.'

Hannah waited outside, watching her companion's head nodding and shaking.

'Phew,' Chris said, as she emerged from the phone box. 'I only managed one complete sentence. Is that a little cafe over there? Do you fancy a cup of something or are you in a rush to get back?'

'Well just for a while. I've got a history essay to finish,' Hannah said, flattered by the offer of her company.

The cafe was far removed from cordon bleu. Cigarette smoke hung in the air and ashtrays overflowed their contents onto the bare tabletops.

'This is a bit of a dive,' Chris enthused.

Hannah gingerly pushed the ashtray across the table and sat down.

'Tea or coffee?' shouted the proprietor.

'Shall we have coffee?' Chris asked. Then, 'Two coffees, white please.'

Hannah had never heard of coffee described as white before. Coffee was coffee. The balding man gave them a leery grin as he walked over with the cups, spilling part of the contents into the saucers.

They waited until his back was turned before pulling faces and giggling.

'Why didn't you come on Sunday, Christine?'

'Please! Not Christine. I hate it. I got lumbered with it because my father wanted another boy to safeguard the family name. You know, belt and braces. He decided that the baby would be called Christian. Goodness knows why. Perhaps a gesture to placate his Maker. So, when I arrived instead, I ended up as Christine. It's so ordinary. They could have picked a glamorous name like Ingrid or something. What's your name by the way?'

'Oh nothing special. Hannah Flynn.'

'Do I detect an Irish influence there? It suits you.'

Homespun, Hannah thought. That's what she means. Peasant stock. 'Are there just the two of you then?' she asked.

'No, there's Piers. He was a mistake I think. Still only fifteen. I bet you would like him. He's the artistic type. Dreams around the place and writes poetry. Anthony keeps trying to make a man of him, but Piers hates riding and sides with the fox.'

'I think I would as well. You know, side with the fox. It always seems so cruel to me.'

'It's not cruel. It's exciting, dressing up and parading about. There's quite a following.'

Hannah was pursing her lips in disapproval.

'Lots of the foxes get away,' Chris assured her. 'The old ones get caught but it's a quick death. Better than being maimed by a badly aimed bullet or left to die in a trap. It's the country code, you know. Or perhaps you don't. Where are you from by the way?'

'Oh, the country. I know what you mean. People protest about things but think nothing of eating a pork chop.' Hannah paused, hating herself for her compromise and turned the subject back to humans. 'Anyway, you still haven't told me why you are three days late. We kept hearing your name. You were becoming a kind of mythical creature.'

'Who would that be? Helen of Troy? Or was she real? What about the Medusa with snakes growing out of her head?' Chris rolled her eyes and lost that look of sophistication, a mischievous childishness taking its place. 'There's nothing mysterious about it. I had a kind of migraine thing which went on and on. I still feel a bit fragile.'

She took a silver cigarette case out of her handbag. 'Let's just have a cig and then I suppose you'd better get on with your essay.' She held out the case.

'No thanks. I don't smoke,' Hannah said.

'You don't know what you're missing. Mother doesn't approve, of course. It's all right for Anthony but not the sort of thing a young lady should do.' She blew a puff of smoke across the room. 'She'd have a fit if she could see me in this place.'

Hannah let her chatter on about her family, happy to keep her own lifestyle in the background. Apparently she went to boarding school and then spent a year at a finishing school in Switzerland.

'You lucky thing!' Hannah exclaimed. Boarding schools sounded so exciting in schoolgirl stories—midnight feasts in the dorms, and high jinks.

'Lucky! We were being groomed to make good society wives. I think they despaired of me. I returned home just as rebellious as when I left and pestered my parents until they agreed to let me have a career.'

'So why did you choose teaching? It's not exactly exciting, is it?'

'Too true! My real ambition is to get into films but any mention of drama school brought my mother out in a rash, so I'm having to be devious. Did you know we can do a supplementary drama course after our teacher training? I know it will take a long while but by that time I shall be twenty-one with the key of the door and all that jazz.'

Hannah was fascinated. It was like reading a novel. 'You mean you want to be a film star?'

'Why not? I'm not going to live like my mother—dinner parties, bridge and small talk. Being expected to give birth for the family line.' She dotted out her second cigarette, pressing the end down hard as if to obliterate her parents' expectations, then stood up, leaving the chair sticking away from the table. Hannah dutifully put her chair neatly back in its place and followed her new-found friend out into the street.

The essay didn't seem to matter now. It was so good to be in the company of someone that Hannah would describe as a kindred spirit. But still she needed to impress as she had done in those first days of evacuation and they spent another hour back in the privacy of Hannah's room talking about life before college or BC as it was known. Hannah described her background to her friend, skipping over the past with a few embellishments. Her father had had an antique business, she explained, but it was all lost in the Blitz. Aunt Kate's profession was worth mentioning, and the garden and menagerie became a flourishing smallholding. Mrs Garton, the village helper on heavy washdays was transformed into an old retainer, and the lad, who occasionally helped out at the weekend, was Bill the head gardener. She didn't feel guilty about such fabrication. After all, they were half-truths and who would know? Mention of the Maddisons' nanny encouraged her to talk about old Mrs Knight. She would have made a good nanny, she thought, and removed her from the little village into the large town house of her imagined pre-war years.

On Saturday morning, everyone was intent on preparations for the ball designed to welcome the new students. The required male partners were invited from a neighbouring college and Hannah was dreading it.

'Do you like dancing?' she asked Chris on the way out from breakfast.

'Yes. Why not? It's fun to dress up and make eyes at the men. Do you fancy a face pack? And how about soaking in water laced with oils from the orient? Let's dash into town this morning and explore the shops. I could do with a new lipstick and some more stockings. We could have a meal out and spend a few hours dolling ourselves up.'

Hannah hesitated. Funds didn't run to meals out. 'I don't think I'm going to the ball, and in any case I was going to use some reference books in the library while it's not busy. Remember we've got to work out our plan for our art thesis. Things will soon start piling up.'

'Oh Hannah! Don't be so stuffy. You'll be the epitome of the old spinster school marm if you carry on like this.' Chris dragged at Hannah's arm and broke into a hop, skip and a jump.

Hannah found her exuberance catching, but at the same time she chided herself for being so easily distracted.

'I don't know which dress to wear. What about you?' Chris asked as one hour later the bus wound its way through the country roads to the town.

'I only brought one and I don't really like it. Aunt Kate made it especially for me and I didn't have the heart to object. It makes me feel like a pink Sugar Plum Fairy.'

'Pink should suit you. I would hate it.'

Back in the hostel she regarded the frilly prettiness of the dress, pursing her lips. 'I see what you mean. How about wearing one of mine? You're slightly shorter than me but we could always tack up the bottom hem. I think I'm wearing the black, so you've got a choice between the turquoise silk or the cream brocade.'

'They must have cost a fortune,' Hannah gasped, as her companion held up each dress.

'*Desfilles*,' Chris said in a casual way, yet wanting to impress.

'Oh yes,' Hannah nodded, none the wiser but feeling obliged to be impressed.

'I've worn both of them once but they've escaped the red wine. I'm always spilling it much to my mother's disgust.'

'Does she allow you to drink?'

'Of course. Wine with a meal, that is. She wouldn't be too happy about a large gin and tonic. Still, what the eye doesn't see, et cetera.'

'The turquoise I think,' Chris continued. 'It shows off your fairness and is delicious to wear. You hardly know you've got it on. So, where shall we start? Face packs I think.'

They smeared the white paste over their faces, trying not to laugh. Talking was not advisable but inevitable all the same, and soon cracks began to appear in the shrinking masks.

'We look like ghosts,' Hannah commented, her voice emerging thinly through the stiffness of her mouth.

'We've got a ghost,' Chris whispered back. 'A young woman who wanders around in the part of the house which is shut off.'

'Is that why it's shut off?'

'No. It was a wartime measure to conserve heat. It's such a big house and we prefer to live in the newer section with all the mods and cons. I can remember sleeping in that part when I was little. We had a nursery and a big playroom as well.'

Hannah's close attention to her words pleased Chris.

'Have you seen her then?'

'Who? Oh the ghost. No, but I thought I heard voices once.'

'I think we've got a ghost at Willow Cottage. Just sounds really. It's a child crying. Uncle Harry said it most likely was the cat. But there's a "mama" sound in the middle. I've heard it three times and it was exactly the same each time.'

Just then Matron's strong northern accent fractured the air. 'Someone's been using that dreadful hair-removing stuff. I can smell it all over the hostel. For goodness' sake open the bathroom windows if you must use it.'

'I wonder if she will haunt this place,' Hannah giggled. 'Can you imagine it? "Turn the lights out." "Who's got a man upstairs?" '

'Are you mennerstrating?' Chris added, with an exaggerated accent.

Hannah laughed at the mispronunciation of the word which she herself wouldn't have repeated. 'She never asked you that, did she?'

'No. It was that little Jenny what's-her-name. You know. The one who always looks white and peaky.'

'Like Tim the Ostler.'

'Who the hell is Tim the Ostler?'

'In the Highway Man. "Where Tim the Ostler listened. His face was white and peaked." '

'Oh poetry again! For God's sake, Hannah, get back down to earth. That's where my face pack is, look. All over the floor. It's like an early fall of snow.'

Matron walked past them as they hurried to the bathroom, and glared at their strange appearance, no doubt linking them to the offending smells. In the safety of the bathroom, they shook with laughter and put paid completely to the crumbling facemasks.

'Of course it looks all right,' Chris assured her half an hour later as Hannah peered into the mirror through eyes heavily coated in mascara. 'It's just that you're not used to it. Everyone will be made up.'

Hannah did feel good in the dress, and she avoided any further scrutiny in the mirror.

The ball officially began at seven o'clock, but most of the students, not wanting to appear too eager, waited until a quarter past the hour, before emerging like a bevy of butterflies from their respective cocoons. Hannah was relieved to be part of the crowd crossing the hostel grounds and into the college block. The hall was lined with chairs and there was a scramble for places. Some had an eye for positions of greatest public exposure, whilst others, like Hannah, favoured the shadier corners.

'Let's sit here,' Chris ordered and Hannah found herself a third of the way along the wall to the left of the stage. Immediately, she took an immense interest in the small orchestra, staring until her eyes began to glaze with the effort. The pianist turned his head first to the side and then back to facing the sheet music in what appeared to be a routine, with a smile fixed on his face. His companions, two violinists and a cellist, seemed well past their physical prime and a younger man on percussion stared absently into the hall, raising and lowering his arms like an automaton.

As yet, no one was on the dance floor. It took great courage for even the most extroverted to step into that emptiness, but feet were beginning to tap in anticipation. Bedecked and perfumed young ladies pretended to be in deep conversation with each other, whilst dropping surreptitious glances for any likely admirer.

The quickstep slowed to a premature halt. 'Take your partners for the Dashing White Sergeant please!' enthused the lead violinist, apparently the Master of Ceremonies. 'That's right. A gentleman in the middle and a lady on each side.'

It was an old favourite, successful in encouraging many people to brave the terrors of the dance floor, and appropriate on this occasion when the ladies outnumbered the men. Chris pulled Hannah across the floor seizing a presentable young man en route. After a trial run in slow motion counting the steps and turns, all became expert, and the liveliness of the music motivated limbs and loosened inhibitions.

Hannah sat down out of breath and sorry that it had ended. Her eyes sparkled and her cheeks were flushed beyond the application of rouge. The band struck up again with a slow dreamy waltz.

'Can I have this dance please?'

She looked up into the face of the same young man who had just partnered them. 'I can't do this one,' she said, shaking her head.

'Oh go on, Hannah! Of course you can,' Chris yelled above the wailing of the violins. 'You only have to shuffle about.'

A group of second-years turned around and she could see Pauline King laughing. Oh well, let them laugh, she thought. At least she wasn't a wallflower. She stepped out determinedly on to the floor, grabbing her partner and pushing him back into the first step.

'I think I'm supposed to lead,' he muttered, changing the position of her hands and moving in the opposite direction.

'Oh gosh, I'm sorry,' she stammered, feeling the colour rushing back into her cheeks. 'I always had to do the man's steps at school. It was all girls, you know. No boys,' she added, as though he was having difficulty in understanding.

'Don't worry,' he advised, grinning and raising his eyebrows at a colleague on his left. 'We'll just shuffle like your friend said.'

She must have apologised half a dozen times before the music came to an end, resisting the pressure of his arm to draw closer and looking down at his feet to avoid the smiling faces of the non-dancers. After the pianist's final flurry of chords, she hurried back to the security of her chair, only to find that Chris had vanished. She rubbed her hand over her forehead now greasy with perspiration. The mascara was prickling her eyes and a pain, which had started at the back of her head, was now pulsating in her temples.

'I think I'm going to call it a day. Can you tell Chris?' she said to the girl in the next chair. 'I've got a headache starting. I'd best get an aspirin down me before it takes hold.'

Solitude would be like an oasis, Hannah thought and she quickened her pace as she left the building, although each rapid step produced a sharp jagged pain in her head. Back in the sanctuary of her room, she took off the dress, carefully hanging it on the hook behind the door. She rubbed her face with the damp flannel and looked at her reflection in the dressing-table mirror. The harsh light from the overhead bulb emphasised the feeling of wretchedness. 'God, I look awful,' she wailed. She'd rubbed her itchy eyes and spread the black mascara into unsightly blurs. Aunt Kate was right and if Chris wanted to be a film star then she was welcome to all the paints and powders. It was so much easier to be as nature intended. She felt somewhat invigorated by her detachment from the dictates of her peers, and ran a deep hot bath to complete both physical and emotional ablutions. It seemed strange to be lying in the water, the silence heavy around her. She was acutely aware of self and rubbed the soap vigorously between her hands, washing away the stickiness of both her own and her dancing partner's perspiration. Her thoughts wandered into the recent past. 'Remember, it's your body,' Aunt Kate had said in an embarrassing woman-to-woman talk a few days before she had left. Ella had joined in. 'My mother used to say keep your legs crossed and if you can't do that then keep your fingers crossed.' She'd giggled in a silly way and jumped up hurriedly to do the washing up when Kate snapped, 'Really, Ella. We need none of that talk.' Suddenly they seemed different—part of the world which she didn't understand. Not that she didn't understand, she mused. What she couldn't accept was that Kate and Ella were part of it and somehow removed from her childhood concepts of them. She didn't want them to be part of the sniggerings and the innuendoes.

She could remember as if it was yesterday, the time on the school bus when a book with a page marked by a turned-down corner was passed from seat to seat. She'd shared in the giggles not wanting to be different from the others. She'd read how the man's breath was hot and searing on the woman's neck, and then how his lips pressed passionately on hers. The following asterisks implied nothing to the innocent amongst the readers, who linked the announcement of her pregnancy on the next page directly with the passionate kiss. Of course, she now knew the truth of the matter, but kissing still worried her. What was the difference between French and English?

She still had an awareness of the pressure of the man's hands on her spine urging closer contact, and she sank back into the water allowing the warmth to flow over her shoulders. It was so comforting and the silence was so overwhelming, that she began to drift into sleep, brought to an awakening seconds later by the water going into her ears. She pushed herself up with the heels of her hands and began to soap her arms and smoothed the lather down her breasts. She liked being a woman. She wanted to be regarded as desirable, but she didn't want to be desired. Is that the same thing she asked herself? She was flattered by men's glances, but frightened of the predator behind them. The mixed emotions of pleasure and fear and then the guilt of it all led back, as always, to that childhood traumatic encounter with Tom Porter, and she shivered in the now lukewarm water.

21

Bosom Friends

For the most part Hannah was happy in her own company in the evenings, often finding her friend's lazy disposition irritating. But during the hours when her brain refused to co-operate, Chris did enliven her with her wild talk. They lived on the opposite sides of fantasy, neither of them accepting the world as it really was. Hannah wanted success to reward her foster parents, whereas Chris, intent on proving her parents wrong, consoled herself with visions of the cinema screen and her name in lights while her grades struggled to rise above the mediocre.

For Hannah, the end-of-term breaks were a welcome contrast to the institutional way of college life, and she soaked up the adoration of the two aunts, no longer feeling threatened by their attention. Uncle Harry was becoming less approachable. In spite of her youthfulness, he mourned her departure from childhood when he was her favourite storyteller and champion. It seemed to him to have become a house for females. Nowadays, he spent most of his time indoors, shut away with his television and Winston; both of them sharing in afternoon naps, both with the declining vigour of the elderly. His favourite response to enquiries about his well-being was, 'Oh, one foot in the grave, you know.' Hannah didn't miss his company and didn't think to question her attitude. His selfishness was the result of old age, she reasoned, and she could not see that her own singularity was akin to his, at the opposite end of the years. She thoughtlessly monopolised the attention of the two aunts. Three women content in a woman's world, the older, Kate, trying to recapture her lost student days, the middle-aged Ella satisfying her maternal instincts and her joy of tempting the appetite of her child, and Hannah, moved out from the shadows of self-consciousness and sunning herself in the limelight.

On one Tuesday shortly before the end of the summer term, Chris was in bed with a migraine. Matron was loath to sanction leave from lectures, advising a couple of aspirins and some effort in positive thinking, until Chris was sick on her new office carpet. It became the joke of the day and everyone laughed except Hannah.

She went into the cloakroom during the morning break, and was about to pull the chain, when her attention was drawn to voices on the other side of the door.

'They're a strange pair,' a voice said. 'Have you noticed? They're like Siamese twins. It was funny Chris Maddison throwing up all over Matron's carpet. How will Hannah Flynn survive all day without her?'

'Do you think she's pregnant? I bet Matron is suspicious,' another voice remarked.

'No! They never bother with boys. I think they're a couple of lesbians.'

'Do you really? I'd never thought of that. Now you come to mention it, they do spend a lot of time together. Still, perhaps they've got boyfriends at home. Chris anyway. She's the type to have it all arranged by her parents. Hannah Flynn would run a mile if she saw a man in his underpants!'

They went into fits of laughter at the idea of it and Hannah strained to put faces to voices.

'Anyway I bet you anything they're lesbians,' the first voice concluded as the door slammed behind them.

Hannah waited for a few moments until she was sure that they had gone. She was fuming at the scorn in their voices. What did they say? A couple of lesbians? She'd never heard the word before.

She went into the library, avoiding eye contact with anybody, and thumbed through the dictionary on the reference shelf. Was it one 's' or two? Ah, here it was. 'Lesbian (-z-) adj. Of Lesbos; of homosexuality in women (from the association of the island with Sappho, who was accused of this vice) Lesbian n. Homosexual woman.'

Homosexual. What did that mean? She turned to the 'h' section scanning down the hom's. 'homosexual adj. of, characterised by, sexual propensity for one's own sex. n. homosexual person.'

She was still confused, but the word 'sexual' and the memory of the laughter of the anonymous duo made her feel very uneasy. It was the same kind of feeling as when she knew that a joke came into the dirty category, but she wasn't sure what it was all about. She always laughed with the rest, despising herself for her cowardly complicity. Now, in the privacy of her own thoughts, this was no time for pretence.

Chris was still sleeping off the painkillers at half past four, but managed a cup of tea at eight o'clock that evening.

'I've been worrying about you all day. Has your headache gone?' Hannah reached forward to pat her friend on the shoulder, but then drew back.

'What's the matter? I haven't got some dreadful disease, have I?' Chris joked. 'Poor Matron. Still perhaps she'll believe me next time.' She pulled herself up from the pillow, her hair ragged about her face, the shadows under her eyes dark against the paleness of her cheeks.

For a moment Hannah wanted to comfort her physically. She looked so childlike devoid of make-up, but again she restrained herself.

'What is the matter, Hannah? You look like a frightened little rabbit. Migraines aren't catching, you know.'

Hannah stood up and went to look out of the window. 'Have you heard of the word lesbian?' she asked without turning around.

'Of course I have. Why?'

'Well I haven't. That is not until this morning. What does it mean?'

'Really, Hannah! Where have you been all your life? You know. You get these women who live together and don't like men.'

'Do you think we're lesbians?'

'What! Has someone said that? Who said it?'

'I don't know. I was in the lav at the time. I daredn't come out until they'd gone.' Hannah repeated the conversation

'They can't understand friendship. They have to make something of it. We don't have sex, do we?'

Hannah couldn't understand how that was possible, yet still felt guilty. 'But I am very fond of you, Chris and I don't really like boys. I always feel uncomfortable with them.'

'That's because you are shy. I'm fond of you but I don't want to go to bed with you.'

Hannah winced at the idea, then flushed at a sudden memory. 'But we did, didn't we?'

'What?'

'Slept together. You know. When I had that mouse running under my bed and I spent the night with you.'

Chris laughed. 'Oh that was an emergency, not some dark passion.'

'Yes, but I talked about it,' Hannah stammered, close to tears. 'No wonder everybody thought it was funny.'

'I'm sure they saw it in the same light as we did. It'll just be those two, whoever they are.'

'Still, perhaps we shouldn't go around together all the time.'

'Rubbish! Let them tittle-tattle all they like. We'll dance together at the ball. That'll give them something to talk about.'

'No, Chris. I don't want to go.'

'Rubbish!' Chris said again. 'All right then, suffer a few wandering hands if you want to restore your reputation. They'll be totally confused. They'll think you're bisexual.' She laughed, her cheeks flushing with the effort. 'This tea tastes foul. Go and make some cocoa. I've got a pint of milk in my wardrobe. It shouldn't have gone off yet and when you come back I've got something to tell you.'

Hannah went down to the kitchen finding to her relief that no one else was around, and when she returned, Chris was sitting in front of the dressing table pulling a comb through her tangled hair. 'Ready for the surprise?' she asked. 'How would you like to spend the first week of the summer vac at our house? I'm dying to show you where I live, and it's not much fun having two brothers and no sisters. Mother has already agreed. I've been waiting for a letter and it arrived this morning. Would Aunt Kate mind?'

Hannah's face was blank, her mind having difficulty in travelling from the traumas of the day to future plans.

'Oh well,' Chris snapped. 'It was just an idea. If you don't want to, it doesn't matter. We're not going to live in sin, you know.'

The sharp tone of her voice brought Hannah back into the present. 'Sorry, Chris. Of course I would like to come. I didn't expect it. What about your father? Won't he mind?'

'He doesn't know what's happening half the time. It would only be for a week. We're going to the States to see my aunt for the rest of the holiday. That is Mother, Piers and me. It won't interfere with your holiday plans, will it? Are you going anywhere exciting?'

'Not abroad. We may be going to Scotland,' Hannah lied, thinking of the vague plans of a camping trip in the Cotswolds. Aunt Kate would prefer a little luxury but Uncle Harry objected to paying for bed and breakfast when they had a perfectly good tent, and as to evening meals, well something could soon be rustled up over the primus.

Aunt Kate said that she was delighted when Hannah telephoned with the news, but Hannah could hear the doubt in her voice and was irritated by her questions concerning her clothes and luggage, and how she was going to manage. She doesn't think I'm capable of surviving without her rules and regulations, she thought angrily.

'You could ask her over here later on, dear,' Kate suggested.

'No,' came the hasty reply. 'She's going to America for the rest of the holiday.'

'Perhaps next half-term then.'

'I don't think she'll have time but I'll ask her.'

'Perhaps we're not posh enough. Never mind. Have a good week and let us know what train you're catching.' Aunt Kate put the phone down and Hannah stood for a moment caught offguard by her foster mother's perception, and feeling guilty at the truth of it.

'Just round the next bend. Here we are. Home, sweet home.'

The chauffeur-driven car swung in between two decorative wrought-iron gates, and continued along a winding drive flanked by trees and shrubs. Hannah gasped as the house came into view. 'Gosh! It's huge, Chris. You didn't tell me it was so big.'

'I suppose it is. I'm used to it. Like I told you, we only use one end unless we have a big do. I suppose it will be Anthony's wedding next and loads of relatives and notables will be milling about.'

They came to a halt on the gravelled area in front of a marble portico. Hannah got out and straightened her back, before going to the rear of the car for her luggage.

'Come on. George will see to all that. That's what he's paid for.' Chris waved impatiently.

Hannah looked at George, a man no longer in his prime she thought, wanting to acknowledge his service, but he stared impassively at the steering wheel, rubbing his hands with his handkerchief.

The entrance hall seemed nearly as large as half of Willow Cottage, and the staircase, which swept grandly up on the right-hand side, was like the setting for a period drama. There was no time to gain further first impressions as she was propelled by her friend towards a door at the end of the hall. 'Let's find Mother if she's up yet,' she said. 'I expect she's in the morning room.'

Mrs Maddison, who was sitting reading a magazine in the bright sunlight that flooded in through large french windows, jumped and put her hand to her head as her daughter bounded in.

'Freedom!' Chris shrieked. 'We're free for seven weeks.'

'Well you would go. And this is Hannah, I suppose.'

Hannah said the customary, 'Pleased to meet you,' her hand just managing to brush against the manicured fingers before they were drawn away.

'I've put her in the Pink Room—the small back room, Christine,' Mrs Maddison continued, speaking as though Hannah was no longer in the room. 'Francis may be here on Wednesday and she'll need the Blue Room with all her paraphernalia. May has aired the bed, and the window has been open since yesterday. You need to freshen up by the look of you.' Her eyes cast a critical look over them both, lingering on Hannah who felt decidedly sticky with nervous tension as well as travel. 'There's a cold buffet set in the dining room and dinner will be at the usual time.' She dismissed them with a wave of her hand and turned her attention back to her magazine.

It was a relief to escape her scrutiny, and Chris, who had become unusually subdued over the last few minutes, regained her exuberance and raced up the wide staircase. 'Come on, slow coach,' she yelled. 'I'll show you your room.'

'You'll have this bathroom all to yourself until Tony's fiancée arrives, so make the most of it,' she continued, flinging open a doorway along the landing. 'And this, as Mother insists on calling it, is the Pink Room. Pretty obvious, isn't it? Sorry, not your favourite colour but the best we can do.'

The small back room as it was described, must have been three times as big as Hannah's bedroom at Willow Cottage and she was glad that the Francis woman preferred the Blue Room.

'Right. I'll leave you to have a quick wash and brush up. We dress for dinner, so stay as you are for the time being. I'll be back in about ten minutes.'

After the door had closed behind her friend, Hannah felt free to stare around, allowing her mouth to round into incredulity and her breath to draw in sharply. She had never seen such luxury. The pink bedroom carpet sank and rose with each footstep, silencing even the heaviest step. The double bed was covered in a pink satin spread with matching lace-edged sham pillows. Lace-edged tablemats protected the mahogany dressing table from the cut-glass trinkets. Fresh air came in through the open window, wafting the snowy white voile nets against the heavy wine brocade draw-curtains. A long mahogany-framed cheval-glass stood in one corner of the room, and she caught a reflection of herself mirrored against the background of all this opulence. She turned away, depressed by the contrast, her cotton dress cheap and market-day looking. Suddenly, her friend's last instructions came to mind. 'We dress for dinner…' What on earth was she going to wear? There was a sharp knock on the door. Chris would tell her. In any case, whatever she wore she would need to press it back into shape. The art of packing was not one of her accomplishments.

'I've brought your luggage up, Miss. Shall I bring it in?'

She recognised the gruff voice of George and ran to the door. He seemed like an old friend and she thanked him profusely. He grunted, giving a quick jerk of his hand to his forehead and limped along the galleried landing, picking up Chris's expensive suitcases at the top of the stairs and making his way to her room. 'Oh, there you are, George. I thought you'd got lost somewhere. Just leave them there and ask May to come up and unpack. I'll need some pressing doing.' Her friend's high-pitched voice echoed up to the high ceiling.

Hannah was about to call along the landing when she heard another male voice. 'Oh you're back to plague us and with an orphan in the storm, I hear.'

'Don't be horrid, Tony,' Hannah heard Chris reply, her voice subdued but still audible. 'Keep your voice down! She's in the back room.'

'She's not another of your lame dogs, is she? The last one was a pain in the backside.'

'No she's not. I just thought it would make a change for her. It can't be much fun being an orphan and living with old people, especially a village schoolteacher.'

'Oh well. Have fun. You do know Francis is coming on Wednesday, don't you?'

'Don't worry. We'll remember our airs and graces!'

Hannah carefully closed the door as far as possible before the final click and waited, listening for further conversation. After a few agonising moments, she crept out on to the landing, and hurriedly opened the bathroom door feeling like a fugitive. The white tiles and fixtures, which had seemed so opulent, now represented coldness and she shivered with misery, longing for the shabbiness of the cottage bathroom with its assortment of meandering exposed pipes and the smell of fresh laundry in the airing cupboard. She couldn't escape her reflection in the large mirrors on three of the four walls, and she hastily splashed water on her face feeling that no amount of attention could lighten her spirits.

The atmosphere was a little strained, as half an hour later she shared the midday lunch in the dining room, both of them sitting at one end of a huge table and Chris chattering on nervously. She's wondering if I heard, Hannah thought, her irritability turning to sympathy.

They escaped from the oppression of the wood-panelled room to have a walk around the grounds and settled down for a while on a bench in what was known as the sunken garden, while Chris talked of possible activities during the following days. 'We could play tennis,' she suggested. 'That is if Anthony doesn't grab the court. Or perhaps George will be free to drive us into town. There's loads of things I shall need for next week.'

Hannah agreed to whatever she suggested, and they wandered back, shivering in a sudden drop in the temperature.

'It feels like rain. Let's go and explore the old part of the house,' Chris said, pushing Hannah to the right and along an overgrown path. 'This takes us round to the back and through a graveyard. The chapel is in ruins now, but there are some impressive gravestones.'

The sun had disappeared completely behind the heavy rain clouds. Trees stood tall and thick, crowding the back entrance. The door seemed unwilling to open. Chris kicked hard at the bottom, at the same time pushing against it with her shoulder.

'Is it left unlocked?' Hannah asked. 'Aren't your parents afraid of burglars?'

'Not really. You can see how hard it is to get in. This was the service area. It's bricked across inside now to conserve heat so if burglars did get in they wouldn't get far. I think Father has plans for it eventually. I'll show you the used area later on, but this is where the ghost is supposed to walk. We think she was a servant and something dreadful happened to her. Perhaps she was raped by the squire's son.' Chris dropped her voice to a hoarse whisper.

Hannah could feel the skin tightening on her arms as they walked slowly along the passageway lit by a small mullioned window. She should have enjoyed the musty smells and recaptured her childhood fantasies of secret tunnels in old castles, but there was something about this place which gave her a sense of dread. The old kitchen, festooned with cobwebs and with a thick coating of dust, did not invite curiosity and she remained standing in the doorway, whilst Chris brandished a large iron poker, shouting, 'Come out, wherever you are!'

Suddenly Hannah recognised the fear, her brain identifying the stored memory of that day when she had shivered in the cobwebbed shadows of the barn at Eastfield Cottage. She turned and ran as though the devil was at her heels, with Chris not far behind her. They gasped in the coldness of the heavy rain, which nevertheless reassured them with its normality.

It was the cue for a hot bath and a time for unwinding before dinner.

'I'll send May up if you want anything ironing although I expect she will be organising you already,' Chris said.

She was right. May had unpacked her clothes and hung her skirts and dresses in the wardrobe. Her best linen dress was creaseless now, and the rest of her clothes were folded neatly and put away in the chest of drawers. Hannah felt embarrassed and a little annoyed. She could have secrets packed away. Even Auntie Ella wouldn't intrude on her privacy these days.

She stretched out in the hot bath water, relaxed for the first time since she arrived and wished that she had never come. Perhaps she could pretend to be ill and Uncle Harry could fetch her. He wouldn't be too pleased about that. Chris would be upset as well. It wasn't her fault that she lived here. The soothing heat restored her spirits a little, and she dressed carefully, brushing her hair into its neat bob and pressing the damp ends into waves with her fingers.

Dinner was a challenge. She was introduced to Mr Maddison who she noticed was an older version of Anthony; dark good looks aged by jowled cheeks and a double chin, hair greying and receding, and eyebrows beginning to bristle, giving aggression to his stare. Anthony nodded and said, 'Good evening.' Hannah's mouth tightened around the smile which she had put on her face rather than letting it find its own way there. She turned to acknowledge the young person on her right, but he was left anonymous as the conversation moved on.

'You're from Lincolnshire, Christine tells me. Do you know the Crawford-Paintons?' Mrs Maddison asked, dabbing her napkin across her mouth and leaving a line of lipstick on the white starched surface.

'No. I'm Yorkshire really,' Hannah responded, as if that would excuse her from any such acquaintanceship.

'What do your people do? Farming, is it?' Mrs Maddison continued the inquisition.

'No not really. My uncle is a retired builder and does odd jobs and has quite a large garden but no livestock these days except for a few chickens.'

'Sounds a bit like old Mr Jessop, doesn't he, Henry? He was a Jack of all trades.'

Henry Maddison nodded and gulped down a lump of roast potato before answering, 'Salt of the earth. Couldn't do without them.'

Hannah didn't like the patronising tone in his voice. She wanted to say yes, as common as muck, just to shock them but it wasn't true. Uncle Harry was a gentleman by comparison. Instead, she concentrated on pushing the Yorkshire pudding away from the undercooked beef in the hopes of saving it from contamination.

'Of course, they're just your foster parents, aren't they? I remember Christine saying that you are an orphan.' Mrs Maddison was intent on probing into Hannah's line of descent, but before she could begin on the Flynn lineage Chris changed the subject.

'Art is Hannah's scene. She ought to be an artist, I think.'

'And starve in a garret,' Anthony commented, his face twisting into a sneer.

'She does lovely water colours; much better than I can do,' Chris continued, turning to her mother.

'Oh nothing too ambitious then,' Mrs Maddison said. 'You'll have to show her our collection of oils in the library.'

'I would like to do water colours.' Piers joined the conversation, his quiet voice contrasting with the strident tones of his brother and sister. 'Our paintings are hideous daubs.'

'Daubs or not, they would be snapped up at a London auction. The trouble with you, boy, is that you have no eye for value.' Mr Maddison stabbed irritably at another roast potato. 'You've got your head in the clouds. The only rich artist is a dead one. Dreamy! That description seems to crop up over and over again in your school report.'

Piers sighed and continued to eat his dinner, retiring from any further communication.

Again Chris moved the conversation on. 'I showed Hannah the haunted passage. It gave us both goose pimples. We didn't see anything though.'

'You're not likely to either. I should think Hannah is the nearest we've got to a ghost,' Anthony said, nodding at Hannah. 'Too much studying and not enough exercise. By the way, do you ride?'

'Don't be personal, Tony!' Chris scolded. 'Hannah likes the natural look. Besides she's fair-skinned.'

'But then nature does need a helping hand from time to time,' Mrs Maddison declared, and Hannah studied her heavily rouged cheeks and painted lips and thought of Ella's apple-pink cheeks and bird-bright eyes.

Talk of riding brought the conversation to fox hunting and then to shooting, and Hannah shuddered at the watery blood which still oozed from her slice of roast beef.

'What time are we going next Saturday? Is the flight booked?' Chris asked, attempting to break away from the male pattern of conversation and get her mother's attention.

'Everything's organised.' Her mother gave a small shake of her head and her mouth formed in a silent shush. The whole family seemed to be at war with each other, Hannah thought. Surely Mr Maddison knew about the trip.

Apparently what he didn't know was that they were going on Thursday instead of Saturday. 'There's no point in upsetting his apple cart,' she explained after they had finished their meal and retired to the drawing room. 'He hates me to be out of sight. God knows what he thinks I'll get up to!' She giggled. For a moment Hannah saw the young woman in her, and was reminded of Aunt Kate when she was intent on deceiving Uncle Harry. However, there the resemblance ended as Mrs Maddison's expression hardened, her high pencilled arched brows almost joined by the deep frown lines over her nose. 'There's been a change of plan,' she continued. 'Sarah rang and wants us there for Friday. She has some important guests for dinner. Connected with films, she said. So I'm afraid your friend will have to leave on Tuesday. There'll be too much to do.'

From then on Chris could talk about nothing else but the American trip. 'It's a must now to go shopping on Monday. Mother will be going. Do you fancy a day clothes hunting? You could get yourself all togged up for your holiday. I'll lend you some money until you see your folks.'

'You'll be better just with your mam. Aunt Kate likes to share in the shopping and to be quite honest it's not my idea of a good day out.'

'No, of course it isn't. I was forgetting your minimal tastes. Still, Piers will be here. Poor kid's got to get his holiday work done before we go. He's in Father's bad books. You could practise your teaching skills on him. Anyway, we've got tomorrow. We could do with an early night. Tony was right. You do look a bit peaky.'

'It's the atmosphere,' Hannah protested. 'There's going to be a storm. It always has a bad effect on me.'

They parted at the top of the stairs, and she breathed more easily in the privacy of the back room. The air was cooler on this side of the house, and she leant out of the open window and absorbed the stillness of the elm trees. She could see the small area of gravestones further along to the left and shivered as she recalled that dark passageway into the old kitchen.

The storm broke in the early hours of the morning, streaks of lightning forking down behind the trees, illuminating the bedroom with jagged flashes of light. Hannah woke from a strange dream, sitting up suddenly to witness areas of the room appearing in brilliant light and then disappearing back into darkness. The dream was overlapping into reality, and for a few moments she thought she was in the old passage. She tried to grasp the dream, knowing the truth of it, yet feeling it slipping away. It was a familiar feeling of sudden comprehension of the essence, so fleeting that it escaped before it could become consolidated.

She lay awake staring into the darkness and counting the spaces between the flashes of lightning and the thunder, which began to lose its threatening bangs and crashes, retreating into growling rumbles. She had retained her childlike conception of nature. The wind blew from the rounded mouths of the four winds, their cheeks puffed out with the effort, while Jack Frost painted the windows with his hoary breath and fingers and the demons of the storm appeared in the contrasting light and shade.

The early night had done nothing to restore her feeling of well-being and all she could think about was the cosiness of the rooms at Willow Cottage as she shared the breakfast table with her friend.

'Do you fancy going to church this morning? Mother goes and she expects me to make the effort,' Chris was saying. 'Piers is usually dragged along but I think he has too much homework left to do. No rest for the wicked and it's all a bit of a lark.'

In spite of her recent reservations about church dogma, Hannah was shocked by her blasphemous attitude, and her condemnation increased when Mrs Maddison surveyed Hannah's cotton dress and jacket with a disapproving eye. 'No hat?' she accused.

'No I don't wear them. Does it matter?' Hannah's voice wavered nervously in spite of her rebellious feelings.

'Of course it matters! People expect us to set a good example. Christine, sort her out a hat and hurry up. We don't want to gallop down the aisle.'

Hannah watched them kneeling dutifully, heads bowed in prayer, and wondered what part it played in their lives. Did it make them feel virtuous, free for self-indulgence? But then was she herself feeling virtuous in her condemnation of them? The self-analysis led to criticism of her own arrogance, but the disparaging thoughts were back as they drove away from the church. Chris and her mother were discussing their fellow worshippers. 'Did you see that Featherstone woman's awful hat?' Mrs Maddison's face twisted into a sneer. 'I think it must be the fourth topping it's had this year. Everything bar cherries!'

Chris laughed loudly. 'What about Mavis Humberstone then?' she giggled. 'You could climb the ladders in her stockings.'

Lunch was roast lamb followed by summer pudding, a favourite of Hannah's, although in her opinion it wasn't a patch on Auntie Ella's. Nothing was going to satisfy her now, not even Chris, who seemed to have changed from a Jekyll to a mild version of a Miss Hyde. Now they all occupied the enemy camp, even Piers and May, by reason of their association. She wanted an excuse to escape and she interpreted each glance in her direction as a criticism, making no effort now to converse, and answering any queries as briefly as possible.

'Do you feel like a walk?' she asked Chris, knowing that she would decline.

'Not really. You go if you like. It's quite a way round the grounds.'

Hannah had no intention of walking in the grounds. She had noticed a phone box at the crossroads and the plan to alert Aunt Kate to her state of misery would require the privacy of an outside line. She was out of breath with her determined striding along the country road and must have alarmed her aunt with her gasping explanation for telephoning. 'Ring me this evening and say that I'm wanted urgently and must get the first train possible tomorrow,' she gabbled. 'No! I can't explain. No, I'm fine. I just want to come home, that's all. I must go. That's the pips and I haven't any more change.' She replaced the receiver without a thought for the bewildered Kate, and walked back at a more leisurely pace, noticing the wild roses in the hedgerow and enjoying the freshness of the summer air like a prisoner released from jail

22

Paradise Regained

'Can you eat another egg?' Ella asked.

'Fresh from the nest,' encouraged Kate, as though new-laid eggs were a novelty in this house.

'I'd rather fill up on your scones Auntie Ella. You've no idea how I miss them,' Hannah said, leaning forward towards the familiar floral-edged cake plate and sniffing appreciably.

Ella beamed. 'Go on with you,' she said. 'You're only after my recipe and it's a closely guarded secret.' She'd said this many times over the years but that was Ella, her predictability, which had irritated Hannah in pre-college days, now feeling like a virtue; dependable and uncomplicated like life at Willow Cottage. There were just the three of them sitting down for tea in the kitchen. Uncle Harry had taken to his bed with a heavy summer cold and the meal became a casual affair, comfortable in its kitchen company.

'I can just imagine you sitting there with all those toffs. I bet your nose was wrinkling with that undercooked beef,' Ella giggled.

'Oh, it was awful, and all the questions as well. What do your people do?' Hannah mimicked Mrs Maddison's voice and the two women laughed hysterically at her accent.

'What did you say?' Kate asked, rubbing the tears from her eyes.

'Oh just the truth. What else could I say? Did you have a storm that night?' Hannah wasn't proud of her half-truths. 'It woke me out of a nightmare. I dreamt I was walking along the haunted passage and suddenly I was the ghost, trapped forever with the Maddisons. I feel sorry for the poor thing really, although she'll be in her own time, won't she? Still, from the story Chris told me, if it was true, she had a bad time of it. What a strange dream!'

'We know all about your strange dreams, don't we, Ella? Do you remember how she used to talk at top speed in her sleep and sit up with her eyes wide open?'

Ella smiled at the memory. 'And sleep walk,' she added. 'Perhaps you were walking in your sleep down the haunted passage. Was it near your room?'

'Oh don't, Auntie Ella. You're giving me goose pimples! No, you can only get to it from the outside, but I suppose some part of me must have been there else how could I dream about it with such clarity? Anyway, I told Chris about our ghost because she was bragging so much. Have you heard it or is it just me? I thought I did last time I was home.'

'You were dreaming,' Ella said sharply, giving a quick look at Kate who suddenly began to stack the plates together. 'What sort of work does he do?'

'Who?' Hannah couldn't fathom the change of atmosphere.

'Mr Whatsisname. Leave those, Kate. Come on. Sit down. You look tired out.'

'You mean Mr Maddison. Gosh! He would be upset to be called that. I'm not sure. I remember Chris saying that her grandfather was a Yorkshire mill owner and Piers said that he would have to work in the family business but nobody seemed to be doing much.'

'Oh, *nouveau riche*,' Kate said, sinking back into the old fireside chair.

'Noov what?' Ella asked, the anxiety leaving her face as her employer relaxed.

'Newly rich. The people who prospered during the Industrial Revolution. They had money but no class. Not like the landed gentry who were used to having money.'

'Piers isn't like that,' Hannah remarked thoughtfully. 'He's a real lamb to the slaughter. I wonder why he was born into that family.'

'Givers and takers,' her aunt replied. 'That's the way of the world. Perhaps he's there to soften their attitude.'

They cleared the table and washed up. Work didn't seem like a chore. They were so content in each other's company. Ella began to talk about her annual holiday. She always went to Skegness, feeling safe in the familiar surroundings, yet greeting it all each year like a new-found friend.

'Are we still going camping?' Hannah asked.

Kate sighed, blowing the air slowly through her lips. 'I very much doubt it. Harry is not really up to it. He's not a holiday person as you know, and these days it's a job to get him out of the house.'

'Couldn't we go somewhere then? Just me and you?' Hannah's voice rose with excitement at the idea. She didn't want to go camping anyway and now the world opened up in her imagination: Europe, America, Scotland. 'I wouldn't mind a week in Skeggy like Auntie Ella,' she heard herself saying.

Ella became caught up in her enthusiasm. 'Yes, why don't you, Kate? I'll look after Harry. It'll do you good to have a break.'

'Have you two been plotting behind my back?' Kate said in mock accusation. 'I'll have to see what Harry says.'

Ella tutted impatiently and pushed her chair noisily into place. 'Well don't blame me if you get yourself all keyed up again, that's all.'

Later, when Ella decided to have an early night, Kate and Hannah sat by the kitchen fire, more companionable than they had ever been before. They were content to have periods of silence, relaxing in the shabby comfort of the armchairs, which Hannah, less than a week earlier, would have condemned outright.

Kate broke a lengthy silence. 'I've decided. We will have a holiday. After all, I am the major breadwinner, and this is my property.'

Hannah stared. She'd assumed it was Uncle Harry's house. It was always the man who owned things like that.

'It was my parents' home,' Kate continued. 'They came here when I was about ten. Admittedly, Harry's done a lot to the place since we took it over, and bought extra land, but the house was left to me and it will be yours one day. If I want to spend some of my money on a holiday then I will. We'll see if Ella's guest house has any vacancies.'

Harry seemed indifferent to their plans, and the week spent at Skegness was wonderful, not only for the salt sea air, but for the indulgence in woman-to-woman talk. They walked along the sea front every day, wrapped up in warm clothes and enjoying the relaxing atmosphere with their fellow guests, who were also intent on putting aside everyday cares. By the end of the week they were all like old friends, promising to keep in touch, exchanging addresses and calling, 'See you next year,' as they went their separate ways. No wonder Ella enjoyed it, Hannah thought, suddenly aware of her auntie's and her own singularity.

Kate was a little piqued that Harry didn't appear to have missed her, but soon fell into the old ways of marital tolerance, happy in the company of her foster daughter and her paid companion. A week after they returned it was Ella's turn to taste the salt air. Hannah shared household chores with college work. There was the last section of her Child Development Study to finish. 'Adolescence – Emotional turbulence', headed the next chapter in the hefty book on psychology. She read it slowly. 'Often, seemingly as a preparation for deep emotional attachments leading to marriage, girls experience what is known as a crush on an older female, for example a teacher. This is not a sexual relationship neither should it be regarded as a lesbian relationship. It is obsessional and often painfully misunderstood, but it is a part of normal development in some young people.'

That didn't happen to me, she mused. Most of her teachers were old-fashioned and certainly did not inspire adoration. She continued to read. 'In late developers, the same admiration can be felt for a girl friend. A so called undying friendship, which often cools down when other interests such as a career or friendship with the opposite sex becomes paramount.'

She read the last few sentences again. Now she could relate to it. That was right. An obsessive friendship. She could see now how it had manipulated her opinions of Chris, and no doubt it was mutual, both wanting acceptance and reassurance. For Chris, it was a need for admiration. And how I admired her, Hannah thought. In turn, Chris gave her confidence and reassurance, but also distracted her from her work. This study should have been finished weeks ago.

She reproached herself for her weakness, letting people influence her as though she was on strings. Like Pinocchio, she thought, led astray by the cat and the fox, and feeling ashamed of his background. All those half-truths just to impress! It was a wonder her nose wasn't a foot long.

She began to work hard, resisting all the distractions which led to that old enemy, procrastination. The weeks hurried by until only days remained of the summer vacation. Then the anxieties returned. Could she cope with the final examinations and a month's teaching practice? And the thought of seeing Chris again was worrying her. Could their relationship ever be the same again?

She needn't have worried on that score. The matter was resolved soon after when a letter arrived. 'From America by the look of it. I expect it's that friend of yours,' Ella said as she brought it up to Hannah's bedside with a morning cup of tea.

In spite of her earlier reservations Hannah tore open the envelope and first gasped and then laughed at its contents. 'What do you think?' she yelled down the stairs. 'Chris has fallen in love with the son of a film producer!'

Later, Kate sat at the kitchen table trying to decipher the hurried scribble and smiled at the last words written in capital letters: 'HOLLYWOOD HERE I COME'.

'Well who knows?' she commented. 'You might see her name in lights one day, and then you can tell everyone that you shared part of her life, ghosts and all.'

'Yes, but I bet she won't be Christine Maddison. She hates her name, even when it's shortened. Perhaps she'll be Ingrid or Gloria.' Gloria Clayton. The name popped into her head followed by Jack Clayton. She hadn't thought of them for years. She'd hated Jack for his betrayal of her, but as things turned out he had done her a good turn, and now she could let her mind dwell on the way he had been her knight in shining armour once he had established himself in the pecking order. She tried to visualise his face, seeing his cheeky grin and wild head of hair. Her thoughts travelled further back to Sally. She was another one with her sights set on better things, Hannah thought—although she couldn't imagine her with her name in lights. She was probably married by now. That is, if she survived the war. A lot of evacuees didn't settle and went home. Perhaps she was part of the 'dolls house dream'. That seemed like a hundred years ago. She shrugged and returned her thoughts to the present, filing the letter under 'remedial reading aids' in her general folder.

The next bombshell arrived not long before Christmas. Again, it came in the form of a letter, this time from Aunt Kate. Apparently, unbeknown to the rest of the family, Ella had met a gentleman during her holiday. 'We were introduced to him last weekend,' Kate wrote. 'He's been on his own since he and his wife were divorced, and was having a long holiday with his daughter in Skegness. Ella says it was love at first sight! In our opinion, a bit late in the day for such romantic notions. He seems nice enough, although one can't help wondering why his wife left him. He's quite a lot older than Ella. I do hope she is doing the right thing. It all seems so rushed and I am sure it would be wiser to wait until the spring at least, but they are planning to marry by special licence as soon as possible. Then they'll be heading to his home in Hexam. I really don't see why she should uproot herself. She'd be much happier living locally, but that's what he wants. It's always the woman who has to be in tow. I'll give you some more details when you ring midweek...'

Hannah didn't need to read between the lines to know that Aunt Kate was thoroughly upset. Ella was like a younger sister to her, and since Harry now spent most of his evenings either watching the television or dozing by the fire, she was Kate's regular evening companion. Apart from that, there was the running of the house to consider. Kate was determined to continue with her job and Hannah knew that it wasn't solely to earn a living. She had once confessed that she dreaded retirement when she would become a housewife and Ella would no longer be required. 'Why can't you keep Ella with you?' Hannah had asked, and her aunt shook her head, exclaiming that Harry would have a fit at the idea of two women doing the work of one.

During her midweek telephone call, Hannah noticed the slightly hysterical rise and fall in Kate's voice, and the hint of bitterness when she said that she would pass the phone over to the blushing bride. The sarcasm was lost on Ella. Her voice projected pure joy in her good fortune. Hannah enthused with her, but as she walked back along the passage, she had the same misgivings as Kate for future life at Willow Cottage without her.

Three weeks later, she was back at Willow Cottage sharing the last teatime with Ella before that lady gained marital status.

'This time tomorrow we'll be on our way to York,' Ella enthused. 'I've never been that far north before.'

'If that seems a long way what about when you reach Northumberland? That's nearly into Scotland,' Kate said. 'You'll need plenty of warm clothes. There's a biting cold wind off the North Sea.'

'How long are you staying in York?' Hannah asked, embarrassed by the atmosphere.

'Just overnight to break the journey. Jim doesn't like to drive too far in one go and it will be nice to have a walk round the different streets although everything will be shut I expect. We can always go to the Minister.'

'She means Minster,' was Kate's acid response.

It was fine the next day and unusually mild for the time of the year. The ceremony at the registry office seemed very impersonal, the registrar reading the lines in a flat expressionless voice. Kate and Harry witnessed the marriage, and several of Ella's friends from the village sat a few rows behind in the drab cream-painted room. In spite of Ella's and Jim's fond smiles and glances, Hannah thought there was a funereal feeling, a sense of loss, almost of bereavement.

The friends were invited back to Willow Cottage for a ham tea and a glass of wine. Harry proposed a toast and Jim replied in his strong Newcastle accent which everyone found hard to understand except Ella, who hung on every word, her eyes sparkling and her mouth turned up in a smile which seemed to be painted on her face. The cake, which she had baked and iced, was very plain, her decorating skills never having progressed beyond silver balls and cherries on the yearly Christmas cake. She'd used the pink trim which had embellished the last birthday cake she had made for Hannah, and spelt out Ella and Jim with silver balls pressed into the white icing.

About half a dozen photographs were taken, and the conversation waxed and waned with a number of comments on how lucky they'd been with the weather and 'what a good job it didn't rain'. Soon, it was time for the departure of the 'happy couple' and for everyone to wish them well on their brief honeymoon and in their future together.

'Well, that's that,' Kate said, as they gave their last wave and turned back into the house. The guests offered to help with the washing up, but Kate was not in the mood for any re-digesting of the day and declined their offer. 'We'll manage, thanks. Hannah's a big help and I'd better get used to it, hadn't I?' She laughed and they laughed, but Hannah knew how her aunt was feeling. The conversation became so strained that after a few more 'Are you sure you can manage?', Ella's friends made their excuses and hurried away.

It was hard to leave Aunt Kate on the following Monday. Hannah became aware of the signs of age in her foster parents, a condition echoed in the increasing shabbiness of the decor. It was as though everything was in decline and there was little energy to put it right. Ella was the energy. Hannah realised that now. She was the catalyst and without her the household lost its sparkle.

'It'll soon be Christmas,' she enthused as they stood on the platform waiting for the train. Kate nodded, her mouth set in a tight line and that anxious frown deepening between her eyes.

As the weeks of the autumn term passed, a picture of that anxious expression stayed in Hannah's mind and haunted her in quiet moments before sleep. She telephoned several times a week now, trying to assess her aunt's condition, worried by the flat tones in her voice and willing the time to hurry to the day of their reunion. The roles seemed to have reversed. She was the protector now, murmuring reassurances.

During the Christmas break she became as selfless as her youth would permit, taking over many of the household chores and developing culinary skills.

'We'll make a housewife out of you yet,' Harry joked. 'I didn't know you had it in you.'

'Housework's not the be all and end all.' Kate snapped. 'Anybody can do that. Women need a worthwhile career.'

'Don't let it worry you,' Hannah said, as the two of them sat on either side of the range in the kitchen, enjoying each other's company away from the incessant noise of the television. 'You could like being retired. You never know. Why don't you go out at the weekends? Have a meal or go to the pictures or something. Life goes in chapters. You know, different ages like Jaques says in *As You Like It*. "One man in his time plays many parts." I always think of myself as "she" when I look back. One inside another inside another, like a Russian doll. I can't believe that that little girl was me. I wonder what the next "she" will be like.'

'I know what mine will be. To quote your Shakespeare bit, it'll be "sans teeth, sans eyes, sans taste, sans everything".' Kate sighed and struggled to her feet. 'I suppose we'd better make a move. It's nearly teatime.'

'Oh cheer up, Aunt Kate,' Hannah said, a note of exasperation in her voice. 'You're going to live until you're a hundred.'

23

Return of the Serpent

Hannah recalled that conversation as she travelled back from the hospital. Why didn't she realise how sick her aunt was? Kate knew of course. 'Sans everything.' That was in the material sense, but what about life ever after? Where was Kate now? This was the first time that death had caused such devastation. She was so young when her parents died and somehow so removed that it didn't seem real. Now her grief encompassed every loss in her life.

It seemed like another lifetime since eight o'clock when Matron came to her room with the message from Uncle Harry. 'Your aunt has had a heart attack and is in hospital,' she'd said. 'You're to telephone tonight.' She didn't think it was necessary to rush off. 'It's not close family, is it? Not like your mother.'

'She's like a mother to me,' Hannah remembered shouting at the red-faced woman with her expressionless face.

The train journey had seemed interminably slow, for no apparent reason coming to a complete halt between stations. It was as if something was holding her back, depriving her of that last contact with Kate. Finally, when she arrived at the hospital, there was only Harry looking old and bent, sitting in the ward outside the drawn curtains. She'd tried to comfort him and to take comfort from his physical presence, but there was no bond between them. She felt like an impostor. 'Are you related?' the nurse had asked her as she went into the ward. She had assured her that she was. Now she felt that she belonged nowhere.

They'd walked slowly to the parked car and as she sank down into the front seat—Aunt Kate's seat—she'd begun to tremble. Her teeth chattered now and she bit into her bottom lip, unaware of the pain or of the blood which trickled down her chin.

She dreaded arriving at the house without the welcoming warmth of Aunt Kate. There would be no Ella to greet them either. Kate had never been reconciled to her marriage. Harry had called Ella selfish, after all they had done for her. Not to her face, thought Hannah. What about all the things she had done for them?

His voice suddenly broke into her reflections and, as often seemed to happen with her companions, he was in tune with her thoughts, blaming Ella for the whole tragic set of events. 'She insisted on working, you know. I wanted to get someone in place of Ella but she would have none of it. Ella had no business to rush off like that. If she'd waited until the end of the school year, then Kate could have retired with a clear conscience. You know what she was like. A stickler for duty. Wouldn't have any help. Staying up until all hours marking books.'

Hannah wasn't listening. Instead, she was reproaching herself for all those arguments. Admittedly, they were the best of friends just lately, she tried to tell herself, but then memories of those traumatic times when she hated the sight of her aunt and longed to escape, leapt into her mind and the tears dripped down on to her clenched hands…

The cremation was like a nightmare. It was such a finality. The coffin disappeared behind slowly closing curtains and she wanted to jump up and run after it. The soft haunting notes of music were like a physical pain and the trembling was back, sobs choking in the back of her throat.

She could remember little of the journey back. There was no communication between her and her uncle but as the familiar landmarks at the edge of the village came into sight, they shared an increasing tension. Harry steered the car in through the gates of Willow Cottage with a 'Who the Hell's this?' at the sight of a red car parked at the end of the driveway blocking his route to the garage. Then, 'It's Margot,' he muttered.

Hannah recognised her immediately. Margot Sergeant had visited her brother the previous summer. Aunt Kate made no bones about the fact that she detested her, but Harry praised her virtues almost as though he gained pleasure from his wife's discomfiture. Hannah put it all down to ill-health, not recognising his 'feet of clay', but she couldn't extend such tolerance to his sister, and seeing her on this day aroused frightening emotions.

'Sorry, Harry,' she heard her call as she got out of the car. 'The traffic was sheer hell. Did it go all right?'

Insensitive cow, Hannah thought. Bloody bitch! Bloody insensitive bitch! Her thoughts tore across her mind, but she ignored the jags of pain, and ran up the path in front of the first greenhouse and alongside the old back kitchen to the sash window. She'd forgotten how much she'd grown, and cried out as she scraped her spine on the window bar in her struggle to get into the room beyond. Winston stood up to meet her. He became the embodiment of all the love she had known in this house, and she cried into his black fur as she sat with him on his blanket in the corner. He whimpered his sympathy, licking her hair and ear.

'Oh Winston! What are we going to do? How can we live here with no Aunt Kate?'

'We could all do that,' came a voice from the doorway. 'It's a blessing we're not all like you. Harry needs a hot drink and something to sustain him. It's a good job I'm here. I knew you would never cope.'

Hannah looked at the spindly figure silhouetted against the shadows of the narrow passage way, squinting through swollen eye lids. 'You didn't have to come,' she yelled, anguish replaced with anger. 'Aunt Kate was like a mother to me.'

'I'm glad you say like a mother. No relation of course. I was her sister-in-law.' Margot emphasised 'sister'.

'She hated you.' Hannah's voice was low now. She was shocked by the heartlessness of this woman. 'I'd stopped believing in witches.'

Margot stepped forward and raised her hand but then dropped it back to her side, and Hannah became aware of Uncle Harry standing behind her. He stepped forward pushing past his sister and rubbing his hand nervously across his head. 'I think you had better apologise to Margot. It's good of her to come,' he said.

'Apologise!' Hannah was shouting again. 'Apologise to her! What about me?'

'Kate wouldn't have liked you to make such a scene.'

'She wouldn't have spoken to me like this if Aunt Kate was here.'

'Well she isn't, is she?' Margot muttered under her breath.

'What did you say? Why don't you fly away on your broomstick, you evil bitch?' Hannah screamed, outraged by Margot's last words, and then appalled by her own.

'Oh dear. You are showing your roots, aren't you? It's easy to tell where you come from.' Margot turned around, pushing Harry in front of her. 'Poor you,' she said to the back of his head. 'As if you haven't had enough upsets for one day.'

Harry turned to look beyond her to his shaking foster daughter. He looked wretched, helplessly caught up in this jealous tangle. 'Come on, poppet,' he pleaded. 'We're all upset. Come and have something to eat.'

Hannah faltered, feeling a wave of compassion creeping in and cooling her anger, but Margot's next words rekindled the flames.

'Oh, leave her, Harry. She's got a lot of growing up to do. You're my chief concern.' Margot's voice was almost motherly, and Harry sank back into self-pity. He needed his sister's strength, and had very little energy or inclination to console.

Hannah listened to the retreating footsteps and the murmuring of voices. It all seemed so unreal. How had it all come to this? The security of the last eleven years negated in the space of a few days. The old back kitchen was cheerless, naked in its shabbiness. She used to feel safe in here, but now she felt lost like a little girl again in the poverty of Eastfield Cottage. Even Winston had abandoned her, anticipating his bowl of food.

She sat down at the old table and ran her fingers along the grooves in the wood. The light was failing fast and coldness began to stiffen her arms and legs. Her mouth was dry from stress and thirst and she looked around the door into the dark passageway. The grandfather clock ticked loudly in the hallway and she strained to hear any sounds beyond it. Reassured for a moment, and then unnerved by the silence, she tiptoed along to the foot of the stairs and into the wideness of the hall. She could hear voices now coming from the living room, and recalled her first encounter with Margot Sergeant. As she drew close to the partly opened door, she could hear those same brittle tones.

'You'll have to tell her, won't you? Surely she won't leave you on your own now.'

'I can't expect her to give up her career for me. She's got her finals next term.'

'Her duties are to you, aren't they? After all, where would she be if you hadn't taken her in?'

'Kate would never forgive me if she didn't qualify. You know how set she was on it.'

'Yes and more's the pity. She looked absolutely worn out the last time I saw her. It all shortened her life, no doubt. You were both too old to take on the responsibility of a child and all that expense.'

'She never got over losing Nigel. Having Hannah was the next best thing.'

'How old would he have been now?' Margot paused, apparently counting back over the years. 'Let's see. It must be over twenty.'

'Yes,' Harry replied. 'About the same age as Hannah. Perhaps nearer to twenty-one.'

Who was Nigel? Hannah strained to hear and gasped at Margot's next words.

'It's a pity you didn't take a boy. At least it would have been a help with all the heavy work. Kate should have retired years ago and as for that Ella leaving you in the lurch—another one who didn't know which side her bread was buttered.'

'Well we weren't to know. Goodness knows how Hannah'll

manage this place without some help when I'm gone, unless she marries a country lad who knows a bit about managing the land.'

'You're not leaving it all to her, are you? She's not even family.'

'Well, she's the nearest we've got to a daughter.'

'I'll make some more tea. I don't suppose she will think, daughter or no daughter. Oh, don't upset yourself again. I'll bring you a couple of aspirin.'

Hannah leapt back as the door was fully opened.

Margot looked slightly disconcerted but then regained her composure. She closed the door and faced her adversary in the half-light. 'You know what they say about listeners, don't you?' she said, her mouth pressing into a tight smug smile.

Hannah pushed past her and went into the living room. Harry jumped nervously. 'Ah there you are,' he said. 'Just in time for a sandwich. We've left you a round and Margot is making some fresh tea.' His voice wavered and he sank back into the chair.

Hannah shook her head. Anything that woman prepared would be like poison. She held her hands out in front of the fire, and the sudden sensation of heat made a shiver snake up her spine. She stared into the flames and the silence hung heavily in the room.

It was one of those times when someone must break the silence, yet words seemed inadequate. Harry was the first to speak.

'You look frozen. Try to keep the peace. I can't stand all this. She's only thinking of me, you know.'

'And blood's thicker than water,' said Margot, appearing through the door with the tea-tray, her eyes glinting with spite. Hannah stared at her, recalling how she'd once described those dark brown eyes as stony pebbles.

'Don't go on, Margot,' Harry pleaded. 'Things are said in haste and we're all upset.' He'd removed his spectacles and was wiping them with his handkerchief. Now, without the projection of the shiny lenses, his eyes appeared in reality sunken and shaded with tiredness. Again a wave of compassion swept over Hannah, and she wanted to sit on his knee as she had done as a child, cuddling into the roughness of his jacket.

'Your tea's here, dear. I didn't bring a cup for you,' Margot said, turning from her brother and glaring at Hannah.

Hannah ignored her. 'I'll keep out of the way if you don't mind, Uncle,' she said quietly. 'I think I'll write to Auntie Ella. It seems strange her not being here. She must be feeling really ill not to come.'

Thoughts of Ella were consoling, but, even so, it was difficult to write. She gave a brief account of the funeral and made no mention of Margot Sergeant. There was little point in worrying Ella. She must be feeling guilty at not coming. She promised to write more next time and hoped to visit in the summer holidays. Her mouth was dry and her tongue stuck to the gum on the envelope flap. She really needed that drink but having closed her bedroom door and distanced herself from the pain and injustices of the last hour, she couldn't bring herself to open it again.

The bedroom was cold. Aunt Kate would have liked central heating but such expense appalled Harry. 'You know what my father would say.' They all knew his father's answer to the problem. 'Put more clothes on.'

Hannah huddled under the counterpane. Her limbs ached and she felt very tired. She'd lain awake for hours on the previous night but yet her brain refused to relax. She looked around at the familiar possessions and reached down to her bedside cabinet for something to read. Her hands rested on her old favourite: *A Child's Treasury*. 'To dear Hannah on her fifth birthday' it said on the fly leaf, and underneath, 'With love from Grandma.' It had arrived in the post from Ireland and was a great surprise.

She loved the colour plates in this book and turned to her favourite, 'The Light of the World', tracing her fingers as always along the ivy growing up the wall, and noticing how the glow from the lantern lit up the face of Christ. The door was waiting to be opened into a secret paradise yet there was no handle. She drifted into sleep with her fingers resting on the page.

It was dark when she awoke. For a few moments, there was a feeling of normality. She had dreamt, that after hours of searching, she'd found Aunt Kate in a secret garden. Why hadn't they told her that she had been moved? She wasn't dead after all. She'd talked to her and begged her forgiveness. But as she became aware of the physicality of the dark surroundings, she knew the reality. She could hardly swallow for the dryness of her mouth. It must be early morning, she guessed. It had that feel about it. That intense stillness.

She got out of bed, and walked unsteadily towards the bedroom door. The knob was closer than she anticipated, and she realised without seeing it that the door was partly open. She imagined Margot's dark eyes looking at her as she lay vulnerable in sleep, and listened for sounds from the guest room, wondering whether *she* was listening too. Her memory became her eyes as she navigated the stairs and it wasn't until she was safely beyond the kitchen door that she switched on the light.

Drink was a priority and she filled the kettle with water, aware of every sound she made. The milk was in the cellar. Normally, she liked the musty atmosphere of this little subterranean room, but now she couldn't get up and down the stairs quickly enough, expecting spiders on every step. Her hand shook as she filled the jug. After the hot sweet tea and a bowl of cornflakes the shivering stopped. However, she daren't risk meeting Margot at what seemed like an unearthly hour, and instead of returning to her room, she went up the twisty stairs to Ella's old room at the side of the kitchen. The room was bare now, apart from basic bedroom furniture, but she felt close to Ella.

I seem to spend half of my time creeping around in the dark, she thought. Why does everything have to go wrong? She lay awake for hours, wishing for the night to end, with no joy in the anticipation of a new day. Sleep finally became the master of the situation, and when she awoke, sunlight was streaming in through the window.

She jumped out of bed and surveyed her crumpled appearance in the long wardrobe mirror, wishing that she hadn't marooned herself in this room away from her clean clothes and toiletries. She opened the door cautiously, and was relieved to find the kitchen deserted. Through the open curtains, she could see that Margot's car was no longer parked outside. A sound from the living room drew her attention; low muffled sobs, punctuated with moans. The door was open and Harry was sitting on his chair with his hands over his face. He looked up, sensitive to her gaze. He'd taken off his spectacles and again she became aware of the sunken eyes.

'Don't cry, Uncle,' she said. 'You've still got me.'

'You know,' he moaned, rubbing his eyes, 'we were just like Darby and Joan.' He began to sob again.

Hannah thought of Kate's dread of being like Darby and Joan. 'Jack Sprat could eat no fat. His wife could eat no lean.' The nursery rhyme popped into her head. Did opposites really attract and make good marriages, or was it divergence of interests which gave room for tolerance and later indifference? It was something that they had debated at college. Somehow her aunt and uncle did not fit into the Derby and Joan concept.

Harry moved his hands from his eyes and gained back her attention. 'Don't leave me, will you?' he pleaded, reaching out to her.

'No, of course I won't,' Hannah found herself saying. 'I'll look after you. Has she gone?'

'Yes. She's got visitors coming. She's not bad really, you know. I always think she's like the curate's egg.'

'The curate's egg! What's that?' Hannah drew back, put off by his regard for his sister.

'Don't you know that expression? The curate's egg. Good in parts.'

'No,' Hannah said coldly, shaking her head. 'No, I don't. Have you had something to eat?'

'Yes thanks but I could do with a cup of coffee, poppet.'

That was the beginning of her servitude. He expected her to continue the role of housekeeper, hen feeder and companion. His complaints varied, depending on the pain in his leg or the anguish and guilt of bereavement, and Hannah now saw the extent of his frugality. He never spent a shilling when sixpence would do and seemed to have lost touch with modern-day prices. She began to understand why her aunt was so unhappy. 'He's not the man I married,' she'd once said.

Hannah wished that she hadn't made that rash promise. She intended it to be a temporary solution, thinking that by the beginning of the next term he would have regained his strength and could face life without her.

The house oppressed her now with its dark corners. Its quaintness of different levels became wearisome inconvenience. She was sleeping badly, and on one particular night, when the sound of the wisteria tapping against the window and the scratching of birds under the eaves were setting her nerves on edge, she got up and went into the old back kitchen to do some ironing. He'd had his life, she thought, as she banged the iron down on the shirt collar. He's done what he wanted to do. Why shouldn't I? She found herself speculating on how long he would live and then hated herself.

'I'll have it out with him tomorrow.' She spoke out loud and Winston stared at her and twitched his tail. 'What else can I do, Winston?'

He raised his head and sniffed the air before relaxing his head back on his paws with a deep sigh.

She broached the subject on the next day during breakfast.

'I've only one term to go,' she said. 'Do you think you could manage if I get someone in to do the housework? I've an interview at that school in Lincoln and if I get the job I could do what Aunt Kate did and be with you every evening and at weekends of course.'

'I thought you had given up the idea.' Harry's voice was sulky and accusing. 'What do you need a job for?'

'Well you...well perhaps I won't have you to support me. You did rely on Aunt Kate's money, didn't you?'

'Of course we didn't. My business was the bread and butter and the luxuries. Kate's money wouldn't have gone far. Luckily I made some good investments and providing we are careful, there's no need for you to go out to work. A woman's place is in the home. That's what my father always said.'

How could he deny Aunt Kate's large contribution, Hannah thought, hating the arrogance of his father?

'Is there any more tea in that pot?' He picked up the newspaper and turned the pages slowly.

Hannah gripped the teapot handle and pressed on the lid, willing the tea to fill the cup. She had no intention of making another brew.

'I'm going down to the shop. Do you want anything?'

'No thank you. Whatever would I need?'

When she came back she could hear his voice in the hall.

'You know what it's like,' he was saying. 'These young ones don't know they're born. Still, I'm managing best I can.'

Hannah stood still in the kitchen doorway and listened. He was on the phone to someone.

'How are you then?' she heard him say. 'Got rid of your visitors yet?'

She picked up the clothes basket and went out into the garden. What did *she* want? Or had he rung her? Well that was the last straw. She would get in touch with that woman recommended by Mrs Travers at the shop. She'd been very helpful when Hannah asked if she knew anyone who did domestic work. 'Old Mrs Johnson's granddaughter,' she suggested. 'You know, the one with the illegitimate son. She's desperate for money I do know. She still owes me for last month. She was telling me that now she's got the kid to school, she's looking for work. Oh she's a good girl,' she continued, noticing the look of doubt on Hannah's face. 'Foolish she was, getting herself into trouble like that, but she's very particular. Her house is as clean as a new pin. You know where she lives, don't you? The second council house. Why don't you pop round or do you want me to ask her?'

Hannah had said that she would think about it and walked back feeling guilty again, but after hearing his remark about young people, she pushed all emotions except anger into the background.

She worked each night into the early hours and in the privacy of her room, catching up on her latest thesis, and feverishly reading through copious history notes ready for the final examination. Uncle Harry didn't appear to miss her after tea as he dozed by the fire, the television blaring out.

Alice Johnson was only too pleased to fill in the gap when the new term began. 'He'll be all right with me, miss. I'm used to their funny ways and hard work. I've been working hard for years.'

Hannah, sensitive to her 'student' label wanted to say that she was not the only one, but held her tongue. It wouldn't do to alienate an ally.

Her clothes were clean and pressed, packed ready in her suitcase.

She had a few precious possessions; some books, her diaries, her old doll, a necklace and an autograph book. She decided to take them all with her. They were not for outside appraisal.

As the day approached for her return to college, she became increasingly nervous, and it wasn't until the day before that she plucked up the courage to tell Harry.

He appeared shocked at the news, yet she sensed his indifference. He looked coldly at her, only saying, 'Oh, are you?' and turning back to his newspaper.

'Miss Johnson's coming in to clean up and do your dinner and tea. You'll manage the rest, won't you? It's only for just over two months,' Hannah gabbled.

He didn't look up. 'Don't worry about me,' he muttered. 'You do as you please. You always have.'

He avoided her for the remainder of the day and made no offer the next morning to take her to the railway station.

The morning bus came at half past nine. She could see him along the garden path and shouted, 'I'm going now. I'll ring tonight.'

She saw him step aside into the shade of the greenhouse. 'Oh tittle,' she mouthed, using one of her mother's expressions. She felt better for that and the mood carried her on the short bus ride to the station, but it was replaced with sadness of her loss long before she struggled in through the college gates, her suitcase heavy with additional luggage.

Part of her wanted to turn her back on the past, but her future was so uncertain that at the first opportunity she walked along the dark passageway to the phone box. Perhaps, after experiencing the efficiency and homely company of Alice, he would accept her plans for his welfare. She would be loving and full of reassurances. Surely he couldn't stay cross with her.

Her memory failed in recalling the phone number and she tutted as she apologised to the operator. 'Sorry, I've got that wrong,' she stammered.

'Take your time, sweetheart. You must be in love or something,' he joked.

'No nothing like that.' The man's humour grated, but had the effect of clearing her mind, and her memory didn't fail her at the second attempt.

'Trying to connect you.' He spoke now in the normal impersonal tone. She slotted in the required money, and waited for the familiar voice of Uncle Harry.

'Hello. Who's calling?' came the unexpected clipped voice.

Hannah couldn't answer for a moment.

'Hello,' came the voice again.

'Can I speak to Uncle Harry?' Hannah said, trying to steady the panic which lurched in her stomach.

'Oh it's you. Got a guilty conscience, have you? Mr Churchill is asleep and in any case he's got nothing to say to you.'

The phone clicked and Hannah slowly returned the receiver to its rest. She heard Margot's words over and over in her head as she walked back. Dismay, fear, anger, anguish, all merged into a jangle of emotions. For the rest of the evening she could think of nothing else. How dare she speak like that? How could Uncle Harry be taken in by her? Her own possessive feelings for Willow Cottage fuelled her hatred. That woman was in her house. Aunt Kate had promised that she herself should have it. She could go back and throw her out, but that would be giving in to Harry's unreasonable demands. It was Aunt Kate's house anyway.

She tried to relax in a hot bath and stayed in it until someone knocked on the door demanding to know if she was making her will in there. Again, she tried to suppress speculations on how long her foster father would live. They were ugly thoughts and she began to question her motives. Of course she wanted to own Willow Cottage. Who wouldn't want to own a house? When she was doing the various chores during the last few weeks, she'd day-dreamed about colour schemes and furnishings and visualised flowers growing round the house. Harry didn't like flowers. 'Only grow what you can eat', was his philosophy.

She emptied her case and prepared for the morning, but Margot had re-established the seeds of guilt, and by the time she got into bed, she had decided to relinquish all claims to Willow Cottage. In a way, it was like taking a great weight from her shoulders, but then again she questioned her motives. If she did try to contact her uncle, then why was she doing it? What did she feel about him? What did he feel about her? He'd used her and wanted to go on using her. He would rather have had a boy. Did Ella know about Nigel? Oh well. She didn't ask to be evacuated. None of it was of her choice, so she owed them nothing and would expect nothing in return.

That night she dreamt of Aunt Kate and woke up over an hour before the alarm call. He would be up and dressed by now, and no doubt Margot would still be in bed. Her eyes were sticky with tiredness as she took the familiar route to the phone box.

'Harry Churchill speaking.'

She pressed the coins into the slot. 'Hello, Uncle,' she yelled. 'Just to let you know I'm here safe and sound. How are you? Did Alice Johnson come?' Her voice trailed away. He'd rung off.

'Go to hell!' she shouted into the receiver. 'All of you. Go to hell!'

She banged the phone in place, and turned her eyes away from the curious stare of an old woman who was waiting her turn. 'These young uns,' she heard her mutter as she shuffled past her into the phone box.

24

The Past in Pieces

Hannah clapped her hands like a little child at the sight of the celebration cake. Ella surveyed her cake with its marzipan teacher and five jellybaby pupils. 'I ran out of marzipan,' she said, 'but you always were one for the jelly babies. You used to bite their heads off. Not a good sign for a budding school teacher.'

They both laughed at a shared memory as they sat down for afternoon tea.

'Fancy! You a school teacher. It doesn't seem long since you were sitting at the kitchen table doing your homework,' Ella commented. 'I wish you'd apply for that vacancy here. You'd get it, you know. Mrs Rollinson told me they're desperate. It was such a shock. Poor old girl! Fancy dropping dead in the lavvy. They had an awful job getting the door open. It would suit you down to the ground and you could live here instead of those gloomy lodgings.'

'It's a bed-sit, Auntie Ella and not a bit gloomy. I couldn't let the school down now. It would look bad, and anyway I prefer six to sevens. Reception doesn't appeal to me.'

'There's only about twenty in the class. They're nice little kids and only a handful of new ones. Five to sevens they are. Mrs Rollinson said it must be as easy as falling off a log.'

'Is she a teacher?'

'Good heavens no!' Ella laughed at the idea. 'She's the postmistress.'

Hannah felt a twinge of superiority. She liked her new status, even though she'd only practised at being a teacher. She noticed the way people hesitated when she announced her profession, like the woman on the train. She'd begun to speak carefully, dropping a few aitches in the effort and throwing a few more in at the wrong places. 'Come on. Let's tuck in. I'm starving,' she said, not wanting to extend the discussion about her future.

'That makes a change. Although it's for cake and scones, knowing you.' Ella poured the tea, and Jim joined them, leaving his hunched position close to the television.

'Don't you think she would be better up here with us, Jim? She won't know anybody stuck in the middle of a city.' Ella's voice increased in volume as though her husband was deaf.

Hannah saw the expression on his face. 'I'm better standing on my own feet aren't I, Jim? Anyway, it's where I was born. I spent the first nine years of my life there. It's like being in a foreign country up here. I could hardly understand a word the taxi driver said. You seemed to have settled, Auntie Ella. You're getting a bit of a singsong in your voice.'

'Call me Ella. Auntie makes me feel old. Forty-nine next month. Would you credit it?'

They chatted on and Jim aired his knowledge of the surrounding places of interest. He's relieved that I'm only here on holiday, Hannah thought. He needn't worry. No one need worry about her.

Later that evening, Jim went out to the working men's club down the road for a game of billiards. It seemed like old times sitting in the firelight talking, except that Kate was missing.

'I couldn't believe it when you wrote and told me about that Margot woman and what about Harry?' Ella grumbled. 'After all you did for him. I feel terrible you know. If I hadn't married, then none of this would have happened.'

'It wasn't your fault, Auntie, I mean Ella. Aunt Kate must have had a weak heart.'

'Yes I suppose she must, but then would it have happened so

soon? They should have had help. It was too much for her. Of course he wouldn't hear of it, and now Margot can't wait to get her hands on the money.'

'Do you think she will stay there? I can't imagine her mucking out the chicken huts or knee deep in mud.'

'Of course you don't know, do you? I've got a head like a sieve. Willow Cottage is up for sale.'

'It isn't!' Hannah gasped. 'Are you sure? I would have thought that's the last thing he would do.'

'Yes. Madge told me. Do you remember her? We used to go to chapel together. She's the only one I've kept in touch with. I've invited her to come and stay but her son's being a real worry at the moment. Got into bad company by all accounts and—'

'Where's he going?' Hannah interrupted impatiently.

'He's still at home. Oh. You mean Harry. He's already gone. The place is empty. Apparently, the removal van was a Nottingham firm, so it looks like he's gone to live with her.'

Hannah sighed. Well, that really was that.

Ella chatted on, unusually insensitive to her companion's signs of stress. 'Kate would have been turning in her grave if it had been a burial,' she said. 'All her hard-earned cash passing to the likes of that one. Still we'll have to wait and see. How are you off for money by the way?'

'I'll manage. Aunt Kate gave me two hundred and fifty pounds at Christmas. She was very secretive about it and told me not to broadcast it.'

'She did the same when I got married. Went on about keeping my independence and rainy days. She needn't have worried. Jim's very good. Of course Harry wouldn't have been pleased, and can you imagine what that one would say if she knew. You know, looking back, Harry was getting more and more like his father. I suppose old age doesn't do any favours.'

No, Hannah thought. Perhaps that was what it was. Neither of them spoke for a few moments, staring into the fire with their own recollections. Then Hannah asked, 'Who was Nigel?'

Ella looked up startled by the question. 'Who told you about him?'

238

'I overheard that woman talking to Uncle Harry.'

'Oh trust her! In a loud voice, no doubt. He was their son. He died when he was a toddler. It was some kind of stomach infection.'

'Infantile enteritis?'

Ella nodded. 'Yes something like that. I think Kate always blamed herself. Do you remember how upset she was when you said you heard a baby crying.'

Hannah didn't but remembered how Harry had insisted it was a cat. 'Oh dear,' she said. 'And then I talked about it again, didn't I, after I'd been staying with Chris? It wasn't a baby though. Older than that. Still it must have upset Aunt Kate.' She could visualise Kate jumping up to start the washing up. Now it all made sense. She was a replacement, like Margot said, but the wrong sex.

'Anyway, that's all water under the bridge. You've got black rings under your eyes. You are staying here for the whole of the summer holidays. We'll have no argument about that. I'll get some colour into your cheeks and fatten you up before you rush off into the wide, wide world, if it's the last thing I do.'

'You make me sound like a prize pig!'

'No. Just my dear little Hannah. We'll leave the pig category for a certain woman whose name will never be mentioned in this house again.'

'I like pigs,' Hannah protested. 'How about "serpent"?'

Ella was as good as her word, and by the end of the summer vacation Hannah felt both physically and mentally restored. The two of them walked for miles, breathing in the clean air which smelt of heather and pine needles, as the light breezes moved from heath to woodland and creased the marginal pools of the burn into curving patterns. It was a magical place, where, in the company of the familiar habits and chatter of her friend, Hannah could readily return to the fantasies of childhood.

In such happy circumstances time raced by, galloping into the future, and dragging thoughts away from those unhappy months when she felt that nothing would ever take away her sadness. It was now possible to allow her thoughts to wander back into the past, to think of that Hannah of Willow Cottage days as "she"; a layer of memories on which to continue building her life.

Ella's good food and company had filled out both flesh and spirit. Now she was full of anticipation, eager to prove her independence and worth to society. She leant out of the carriage window and continued to wave to the familiar figure on the platform until the curve in the tracks carried the train beyond the view of the station. Dear Ella. She was going to miss her. They'd got to know each other so well over the last six weeks. It was a new relationship with the generation gap narrowing, although both still held fast to their ideals born of different times and circumstances. Ella was her only close friend. She had consigned all other relationships into her own history, to be recalled if she chose to do so, or forgotten if she could.

Now, as she settled back in the seat, her thoughts turned to her one true relation. She opened her handbag and took out a folded piece of paper. She'd found it amongst a wad of old school paperwork in Aunt Kate's desk. At first, she'd read the address with a feeling of guilt at prying into her aunt's possessions, and noticed the date, May 3rd 1943, but her own name leapt out from the written words and she realised that it was from her mother's sister, Vera Morgan. She'd forgotten her married name. In fact, she couldn't remember ever having known it. She had a hazy memory of visiting her, recalling a bus ride out to the other side of the city. She tried to visualise her–smartly dressed and full of airs and graces—or were those her mother's opinions? They didn't see eye to eye, she could remember that. It was obvious now as she re-read the letter, a formal note enquiring as to the health of her niece, that Vera didn't want the responsibility of a child. She'd had a vague notion to make contact, but somehow the face of the forgotten Vera merged with that of the too well remembered Margot. She could manage perfectly well without her, she thought, and put the paper back into her bag, turning her attention to the flat coastal landscape which slipped monotonously by the carriage window.

After a few hours of reading, listening to conversations, looking out of the window and a welcome break at Doncaster to change trains, the journey came to an end. She indulged in a taxi ride to her new home, feeling rather unnerved by the seeming complexity of the bus station.

The bed-sit was gloomy. Ella would be pleased to know that she was right about that. It was passable for overnight accommodation when she came for her late interview and she was impressed by its closeness to the school. Mornings were not her favourite times of the day. An extra half an hour in bed was a serious priority, outweighing the disadvantages of a view of a bombsite and a shared bathroom on the landing.

She went over to the window and tried to focus on the patches of green and pink willow herb dotted here and there amongst the war-torn landscape. Obviously, it was a convenient place for dumping unwanted articles. Thistles grew through rusty bedsprings and a roll of cracked linoleum offered refuge to wild life, as well as providing something for children to jump over. A group of small boys chased and shouted in a game of cops and robbers. Two women walked along the well-trodden pathway, which had become established as a short cut to school and to the shops.

The building, which was now her home, cast a dark shadow over the neglected garden at the rear of the premises, where even the weeds struggled for lack of sunlight. Hannah suddenly shivered in the chilly surroundings.

A map of the city of Hull, on display at the railway bookstall, had seemed like a good investment. She opened it up on the bed, and located first Walpole Street and then her old address, Tennyson Street. After tracing her finger several times along the major routes, she folded up the map and pushed it into a carrier bag, still with little faith in her sense of direction.

She didn't know what to expect as some time later she walked along that road from the past. The open space in the terraced row appeared as a great gash, a wound healed into a pot-holed thoroughfare. The passageway of her childhood home which she shared with Sally was now part of a much wider convenience. A gang of young footballers played on the waste ground, and Hannah pressed her lips together and frowned at their unknowing act of sacrilege. She shivered. 'Someone's just walked over your grave.'

Her mother used to say that. She shivered again and could feel the hair standing up on her arms.

There was no need to search in her memory for details of the structure of her old home. The houses left standing gave immediate recall and prompted a speedy recollection of the back way and of her father's bike in the passage. She wanted to grieve for her mother, and arrange flowers on her grave, as she did when she'd accompanied Aunt Kate to her parents' graves. She felt cheated. There was nothing here, not even a brick as a memorial to past lives or to mark the site of her own birthplace.

The shivering was replaced with an ache of loneliness as she watched life going on in this street without her. Why didn't she write? Did she really care? The dregs of bitterness began to stir up again. Auntie Ella had tried to settle them one day when they were talking about mothers. 'Things are not always easy to understand,' she'd said. 'Perhaps your mam was poorly, or perhaps she had to look after your grandma. Days can slip by you know. It couldn't have been easy with bombs dropping, and she did try to make sure you were safe.'

It wouldn't have taken long to write, Hannah thought. She never did get Sally's address. Were the Blenkins killed, she wondered? It was a big gap. Fat, jolly Mrs Blenkin. She could visualise her large shape. They might have survived. It would be lovely to see Sally again. She thought of the fur coat and no washing up. 'Like her mother,' her father had jeered. 'Fur coat and no knickers.' She understood the sarcasm now. The brain seemed to have a special place for storing mysteries until the time of comprehension.

She could visualise Sally's face—her laughter really. The features were blurred. Personalities, that's what were remembered. Sally was like the popping of a champagne cork, released from the pressures of family squabbles as they ran to the park or giggled and jostled on the way to school.

A curiosity for the circumstances which led to this great change in her life, rose up inside her. She'd never thought about it before. Somehow it was as though none of it had happened, or it had happened to someone else. Did her mother and grandparents have proper graves? Were the bodies ever found? They must have been for them to be declared dead, she supposed. Or was it assumed? Did it really matter? Her mother was where she had left her in that back room. Did she really want to put her in some strange place removed from the realms of her imagination. But then the damage was already done. She couldn't see the back room now. The imagery was replaced with the reality of the bombsite. Sally would know. She had a great awareness of Sally still in the flesh. On a sudden impulse, she went up to the front door of the house at the end of the row and rattled the letterbox. The downstairs window was flung open, and a young woman put her head through the gap.

'What do you want?' she asked, her voice hostile with suspicion.

'I'm looking for the Blenkins. Do you know if they still live around here?'

Hannah flinched as the woman yelled at the top of her voice, 'Leave 'im alone, yer little bugger. I'll swing for you one of these days. Blenkin? Never 'eard of them.' The window banged shut and Hannah could hear screams as the unseen troublemaker made his escape out of the back of the house and down the ten-foot.

Oh well, she thought. Her father could have been right. Perhaps Sally was knee-deep in nappies, and hurling her resentment at her children like her mother used to do in those distant days now seeming to be tarnished by reflection. 'You can't turn the clock back.' That was what Ella said. Good old Ella. She was usually right with her homespun philosophy. The look of curiosity on the face of a little girl who was pushing her doll's pram towards her, made Hannah realise that she was talking to herself, and she put her head down and retraced her steps to the bus stop.

25

Picking up the Chalk

Walpole Street School was as old as the street itself. A late Victorian structure, which had survived the blitz, in spite of the prayers of local children. They had left this school now to try their hand at secondary education, but post-war babies, the so called bulge, were swelling the numbers of children in the infant schools and a mobile classroom covered a corner of the playground.

Hannah found that the headmaster had modern ideas, not popular with some of the old-timers on the staff. The reception class teacher, Mrs Gilbert, maintained that the old ways were best. Her colleague Miss Perry had similar views and Hannah sensed their disapproval of her youthful status. The children were all from working-class homes, but there was a great divergence in their needs. Some struggled with literacy, others with numeracy, many with both, but Hannah also recognised those certain little lost looks and a need for affection.

Sarah Pykett, the teacher in the top stream infants, was full of confidence. Her appearance was immaculate. She would have suited a model agency rather than a back-street primary school. It was obvious from her conversation that she came from a privileged background, although she emphasised that Daddy was a self-made man. Reflected glory, Hannah thought, forgetting past romantic versions of the truth of her own family. Or was it all a big pretence? Surely she would have preferred to teach in a private school. Another Chris Maddison? No, that wasn't fair. Chris had a sense of humour and a great deal of compassion. Jumping to conclusions again, she chided. Sarah was probably very nice underneath her airs and graces.

They stood together in the schoolyard watching the children. It was Hannah's first playground duty and Sarah was instructing her on the rules.

'Where do you think you're going to?' she shouted. 'Just watch them. They'll sneak into the cloakroom given half a chance and nothing's safe with some of them. No. Once out, they don't go back in unless it's a dire emergency like a broken leg or a split head. Why shouldn't they suffer the cold? We have to and we can't run around and keep warm.'

A little girl came up and stared at Hannah with frank curiosity.

'What do you want?' Sarah snapped. 'No! Miss Flynn does not want to hold your grubby little hand.'

The child turned and walked away.

'The latest of the Newtons,' Sarah said. 'I know the smell.' She put her finger and thumb to her nose. 'Phew! Wet beds!'

Hannah saw the child falter and half turn her head and knew the feeling. 'Poor little soul,' she said. 'How many are there in the family?'

'Oh who knows? There's a tribe of them. We've all lost count. It's a wonder you haven't got one. Right. I'm going in now. Blow the whistle at a quarter to. Haven't you got a watch?'

'No. They seem to go wrong on me.'

'I shouldn't rely on the school clocks. The caretaker sets them all at the same time from the other end of Juniors down to reception. 'Tortoise' is his middle name, so it's anybody's guess by the time he reaches reception. Mark Clayton!' she yelled and waved her arm. 'You've got a watch. Come here. A birthday present,' she said to Hannah. 'And his backside's hanging out of his trousers!' Hannah wasn't listening. Did she say Jack Clayton? The boy raced over and stood panting and displaying his wristwatch. 'Keep an eye on the time, Mark, and tell Miss Flynn when it's the end of playtime.'

The boy shouted, 'Yes, Miss,' to Sarah's back. 'I'll see to it, Miss,' he said to Hannah, giving a big grin. He reminded her of Jack. Could he be related? He was too old to be a son.

'Have you got a relation called Jack? You know. An uncle or somebody,' she asked.

'Naw. I did have, but I don't remember 'im. He got bombed.'

Hannah's heart lurched. No it wouldn't be him, would it? Surely he wouldn't have gone back home before the war ended. But what if she had caused trouble between him and Mrs Turner? She looked across at the present young Clayton who was scrutinising his watch, and stretching his arm out so that everyone could see it. He didn't bear any resemblance to Jack really. Most small boys had that 'Just William' look. Clayton was a common enough name, and what could be more common than Jack?

Hannah decided not to make Sarah her role model. How could anyone teach and have such an obvious dislike of children, she wondered.

Sarah didn't teach for much longer. She married the son of one of her father's business associates, and the following term it was Hannah's turn to show the new teacher the playground duties.

'I usually try to give some of them a little extra attention at playtime,' she told Brenda Curtis. 'Betty Newton for instance. Haven't you got a coat, my darling? You'll freeze out here.'

'I forgot it, Miss,' Betty said, cuddling up against the teacher's coat and holding her hand.

'I think she shares one with her younger brother although he seems to have it more than she does. I feel like buying her a coat from a jumble sale or something,' Hannah commented as the child ran off to chase with the others. 'But then the parents could get nasty about it. They don't like charity.'

'You'll soon get hardened to it,' Mrs Gilbert said one day when Hannah showed concern for a child with a black eye. 'We're here to teach them. Other people are paid to deal with home problems. Get them reading and writing. That's all we can do. At least it gives them a good start and we can only hope for the best.'

Hannah threw herself into her job, working up to the early hours after she returned to her bed-sit, making individual work cards and reading aids as well as checking her pupils daily work. Coping with a class of forty-five lively six-year-olds allowed little time for preparation and marking. Very often, she stayed in the classroom until gone five o'clock pinning treasured works of art on the walls or renewing history or Scripture friezes. Art was her favourite lesson. The children splashed the paint on to paper, and did paste and candle patterns with little or no regard for cleanliness. Most of the teachers avoided painting sessions, preferring more ordered periods with wax crayons or pencils, but when obliged to give paint a turn, they finished early to organise the cleaning up. Hannah became so engrossed in the activity that she lost all sense of time, and often helped the cleaner to mop up spilt paint and indulge her in light-hearted gossip.

'I don't know where she gets her energy from,' Miss Perry said to Mrs Gilbert on one such occasion, as they walked past Hannah's room on their way out. 'Hasn't she got a home to go to?'

'Just a bed-sit I gather. She's a bit of a loner, I think. She never talks about her family.'

'No men in her life either, it seems. I wonder why. She's pretty enough. The sort that settles down and has a family, I would say. Not the usual modern career girl. Mind you, I'm not saying she's not a hard worker, but she's always mothering the kids. I'd have to de-louse some of them first. That reminds me. The school nurse will be in tomorrow.'

Every major holiday was spent with Ella, who concentrated most of her time in the usual quest of restoring Hannah's complexion and appetite. 'You'll work yourself to death,' she said during the second summer break. 'Where have all the roses gone? I wish you would come up here. You've done two years at that place. They can't grumble.'

'I'm not a little girl, Ella. I like where I am. You get really fond of the kids, you know. I would miss them and it's a real change to come up here. I wouldn't have anywhere to go on holiday, would I?'

'Perhaps you're right. Kate would be proud of you. I curse that other one every time I think about her.'

'Well don't think about her then. I don't,' Hannah said, knowing that it wasn't true. Sometimes the injustice of it all occupied her mind so much that she couldn't sleep.

In truth, she loved the Northumbrian countryside and was loath to return to her newly acquired flat. Admittedly, it was a great improvement on the bed-sit, and the view from the fifth floor over the smoking chimneys took away the feeling of claustrophobia, but she missed the link with her past and the sweetly scented hillsides.

She thought of that gentle landscape on the first day of the new term, as she watched the assorted collection of children marching in. They were a mixture of old and new, some spending one more term with her before moving up into the juniors and others, whose brains were an unknown quantity, although she was familiar with their faces. Some were already making their presence felt, like wild things setting the pecking order. She felt sad at the loss of the older children, who would now transfer their loyalty to the junior teachers, and politely call her Miss Flynn instead of 'Miss'.

'They've appointed a man in Miss Hugh's place,' Miss Perry informed everyone in the staff room at the mid-day break. 'I saw him hovering outside "Sir's" room when I went up to the office.'

'That'll do some of those big lads good. They need a man to square them up. What is he? Young or decrepit like us?' Mrs Gilbert looked across at the clock. 'Only two more minutes of sanity. I've got some little monkeys this time. They get worse.'

'Is it that time already?' Miss Perry pushed the knitting needles into the ball of wool. 'He looks about fortyish. It's difficult to tell. He's started to get that distinguished look.'

'Oh! You had a good look then. It's the change, dear. She's getting restless.' Mrs Gilbert had turned and was unusually baring her teeth in a grin.

'I didn't know,' Hannah commented vaguely, not really following the conversation.

The two older women laughed. 'You'll know soon enough,' Miss Perry said. 'It only seems like last year when I was your age. Well I suppose we had better look willing. Another little Newton's arrived. He looks the image of Spencer.'

'He's not called Isaac, is he?' Mrs Gilbert joked, as she prised herself up from her seat. 'I could do with some advice on the laws of gravity.'

A couple of weeks into the term, Hannah was surprised to see the new junior teacher looking around her classroom door.

'Miss Flynn,' he said, 'I'm David Saxton. Class 10. You've been recommended.'

'Have I? What for?' Hannah asked rather sharply, agreeing with Miss Perry about the distinguished look, and liking the warmth of his smile.

He looked somewhat taken aback and she apologised, pushing her hair back away from her face. 'Sorry. I didn't mean to yell. You made me jump. I was miles away.' She waited for his explanation, noticing the smartness of his appearance and the way he raised one eyebrow.

'It's the pantomime. Back cloths, scenery, you know. Apparently you are nominated as the one most likely to volunteer. Handy with the paintbrush by all accounts.' He leant against the doorframe and grinned.

'Well as long as you don't expect too much.' Hannah gathered up her homework and pushed it into her bag.

'Can I give you a lift?' David asked, not too sure of the expression on her face. 'Where do you live?'

'Along Merton Road. It's not far. About a mile, that's all.'

'A mile! That sounds quite a way to me. I go that way. It'll make up for me taking up your time and for imposing my panto on you.'

Hannah accepted the offer. After all, he wasn't a stranger and that mile did often feel like two.

He enthused about the pantomime as they drove along the busy street. 'We decided on *Peter Pan* because there's an abundance of pirates and lost boys, especially in my class,' he explained.

'Not much for the girls though. Won't they feel left out?'

'Not with a pantomime. You know. It never strictly follows the story. I'm writing in a Santa's grotto scene where all the toys come to life. There should be plenty of scope.'

'It's the next turning. Just drop me off at the end of the street.

It's only a few yards down there.' She waved as she watched him head towards the traffic lights before she turned down Albert Street.

The next day, she was enthusing about art and drama in the staff room. ' I wonder if any of these kids have a potential that will never see the light of day? Did Constable know his tables?'

'If they've got any talent it will come out somewhere,' Miss Perry remarked.

Hannah wasn't in the mood to be convinced. 'Yes,' she argued, 'but once they get stuck in a humdrum life with a family to look after, will they have the time or money for personal development? Look what could be achieved if they concentrated on what they were really good at. Take Michael Higgs, for example. He's a brilliant artist already but he hardly knows one word from another in his reading book.'

'Well reading is a priority, isn't it?' Mrs Gilbert said firmly.

26

Old Scars, New Wounds

'Nothing too ambitious,' David said at the first meeting of the pantomime group. 'We're not competing with the West End. A lot of pleasure can come from innocent faux-pas.'

'I wouldn't have used the word innocent,' came a cynical comment.

David frowned. 'Let's start off by giving them ten out of ten. For God's sake, these kids need a chance to shine. There's more to life, you know.'

Hannah nodded. They were her sentiments exactly. She noticed how the others listened to him, yet he didn't try to dominate the conversation. His voice was quiet and controlled and he was sure of his facts; a natural born leader.

She listened to his directions as she sketched the shapes of the mountains and trees for the Never-Never Land backcloth, and looked forward to having him all to herself during the promised lift home at the end of the evening. She loved the way he spoke to the children, and it was obvious that they would do anything for him. Such popularity raised a stirring of resentment in some of the staff, particularly the other two men, but Mrs Timmins and Miss Wightman were willing slaves, answering his every beck and call. It's only me he's on Christian name terms with, though, Hannah thought, as

Miss Wightman reminded him for the third time that her name was Glenda.

'That's looking great, Hannah,' he said. 'Don't get too tired. There's plenty of time. I'll see you in about half an hour.'

She did begin to feel quite tired as the weeks progressed. Her six-year-olds were becoming wilder by the day, and there were the infant school's nativity play rehearsals too, times of great stress for the infant teachers, with declining feelings of goodwill to all mankind. The junior school highlight of the term finally arrived with only a few last-minute hiccoughs to contend with, and everyone on the staff sighed with relief.

'How about a celebratory drink?' David suggested after the last sounds of applause for the successful *Peter Pan* production had faded away.

Hannah agreed. Going straight home would be such an anticlimax.

An hour later at the Rose and Crown, they were on their third drink, the conversation moving away at last from the events of the evening.

'I'm feeling a bit drunk,' Hannah giggled. 'I'm not used to this. I really ought to be getting back.'

'Yes, I suppose I'd better call it a day. I'll end up in a ditch if I have any more. I think I need a strong coffee to sober me up. All the excitement and then that last gin has gone to my head.'

'I'll make you one. That is, if you're not in a hurry to get home.' Hannah could hear herself stammering again.

As usual, the lift was out of action and Hannah apologised as he panted his way up. 'Nearly there,' she said. 'I'm used to it. It exhausted me the first time.'

She apologised again, this time for the state of her flat. A tray with the remnants of the previous night's supper congealed on the plate, and a cup with dregs of tea in the bottom, were by the side of the chair. She picked up the tray and hurried into the kitchen. 'Find a seat,' she called. 'I won't be a minute.'

He pushed aside a pile of papers and books on the settee and perched on the edge. It certainly was untidy, yet interesting, not like the sterile neatness of his living room. She hurried in and thrust a cup and saucer into his hands, putting her cup and saucer on the floor, and resting her back into the chair with an air of fatigue.

They concentrated on drinking the hot coffee, both becoming embarrassed by the sounds of their gulps and swallows. 'I'd better be going,' David suddenly said. 'I'll be in trouble.'

Hannah said, 'Oh,' and he explained, rather hastily, she thought, that Penny his cat would be waiting in the porch. 'She gives me a hard time when I'm late with her evening meal. Doesn't speak to me for days.'

Hannah smiled. 'Cats are like that. I would like one but the rules forbid it.'

After the door closed behind him, she looked around at her untidy room, not really seeing anything. The last half an hour was on replay in her mind. She didn't know anything about him. They'd spent most of the time discussing the pantomime. She didn't even know where he lived. That bit about the cat didn't ring true. Well, why shouldn't he be married? He must be middle-aged. Or perhaps he lived with his parents. Couldn't he have said that then? Anyway, he was only doing her a favour giving her lifts home and she did invite him in for coffee. But then he'd asked her out for a drink. Just his way of showing his gratitude for all her hard work. Probably he wouldn't have much to do with her now the pantomime was over. Her head was beginning to ache and she felt guilty. It was like being back at college. 'No men in the rooms'. The memory of Matron's rule chafed at her guilt. Why did he have to lie about the cat?

She didn't see him to talk to during the remaining days of the term. There was always so much clearing up to do before Christmas. It was all such an anticlimax and the journey up to Hexham was tiresome. Ella's constant reminders of her tiredness and good intentions of 'feeding her up' were so irritating that she looked forward to a new term. And David, her thoughts reminded her. She wrestled with these thoughts, denying any interest in him. When Ella said for the umpteenth time that she needed a good man, she snapped, 'For goodness sake Ella! You think men are the be all and end all of life. I can manage perfectly well without a man.'

The spring term began as it meant to go on. A plague of ill-health hit children and teachers alike. Classes were doubled up as first one teacher and then another went down with either 'flu' or a stomach bug. The weather added to the gloom and the damp air drifted into the classrooms and fogged the senses.

The weeks dragged on, and by the half-term break Hannah had only caught fleeting glimpses of David over the fence which separated the two schools. Oh well, she thought. He just used her for his pantomime. He was like all males. She was just a convenience. However, his arrival at her classroom door one afternoon as she was packing up, threw her whole system into a complete panic.

'Do you want a lift?' he asked.

Thinks he can just pick up where he left off, she inwardly fumed.

'No thanks.' She smiled sweetly. 'I'm not going yet. I've got some cards to sort out. Some of the little ones seem to chew everything.'

'What a pain! I can't hang around tonight. Any time though. Don't do too much. You look done in.'

Hannah's tiredness was now a physical pain but she would have to give him time to leave. She went into the staff room and huddled in her coat, watching the minute hand move around the clock face.

She slept badly that night, waking several times shivering with cold. By the morning the dreaded infection had taken hold and it took a great deal of willpower to walk to the phone box and relay her symptoms to the school secretary. For the next few days she struggled with hot drinks and aspirin. The curtains remained undrawn, and sounds of life going on outside the flat seemed strangely distant.

A door slamming in the flat below roused her from a rambling dream. For a few minutes, she waited for Ella's voice at the door, and then as her eyes focused on the beige curtains, she returned to the present and the hunger pains in her stomach.

Her hair was lank with grease and she made a great effort, bending over the sink and scooping water over her head. She stood in front of the mirror combing the wet hair flat to her head. The mirror exaggerated the dark circles under her eyes.

A knock on the door startled her. 'Who on earth can that be?' she muttered, as though she was the last person on it.

'Anyone at home?'

She gasped. It was David! 'Just a minute,' she called, her voice harsh with the sudden dryness in her throat. She dragged back the curtains and scooped up her night-clothes and the wet towel from the settee. She struggled with the key in the lock and her stomach lurched with hunger and panic.

'You're not going to keep me out here, are you?' David protested, as she peered through a small gap. He thrust a bunch of flowers ahead of him and she opened the door wider, her eyes straining beyond him.

'You look terrible.'

'The dreaded bug. It caught up with me at last.'

'Have you had anything to eat?'

'No. I'm out of bread. I was just going to go to the shop.'

'You're cutting it fine. How about some fish and chips? I noticed that one on the corner is open. It'll save me the bother of getting a meal ready as well.'

His words encouraged Hannah to take pleasure in his company, and half an hour later they sat with trays on their knees enjoying haddock and chips, all washed down with tea which he insisted on making.

'I'd better go,' he said after a second brew of tea.

'You'll have the cat not speaking to you again,' Hannah joked, thinking how well he dressed and wanting to stroke the creases from his jacket.

'What? Oh yes the cat. He's probably given up waiting for me and has gone next door. Don't come in tomorrow. Get yourself fit.'

How could Penny be a 'he' she thought as she closed the door?

He came after school the next night with savoury pie and salad.

'Protein and Vitamin C. Just what the doctor ordered.' He didn't wait to be invited in and went straight into the kitchen to organise her meal. 'Can't stay long,' he shouted. 'Been invited to a meal out. It's a bit of an effort after a day with Class Ten. I hate small talk. How about you having dinner with me one night?'

"Oh I...I don't know,' Hannah stammered.

'I know a nice little restaurant on the York road. Do you know that side of town?'

Not on their own, Hannah thought with relief. 'No I don't. That would be nice.'

A message arrived with a junior, halfway through the following Monday morning. The children watched as she opened the envelope. She felt her colour rising and turned away to face the blackboard. 'How about tonight?' he'd scribbled. 'I'll pick you up at seven. Just write "Yes" and send this back.'

She turned back to her table, and, child-like, cupped her hand around the note while she wrote, 'Yes thanks.' The junior grinned smugly at the infants. They all watched intently as she stuck down the flap of the envelope with sticky tape.

It was difficult to concentrate after that and the future became the present in her thoughts.

Later that evening she was content to listen to his war-time adventures, and leave the ordering of the food to him. He was a great storyteller, reminding her in some ways of Uncle Harry. But there the resemblance ended. Uncle Harry would have been appalled at the cost of the meal. David indulged her sweet tooth, ordering a mouth-watering dessert. The drive home was a dreamy end to a perfect evening.

'It's been lovely,' he said as he stopped the car at the entrance to the flats. 'We must do it again sometime.'

She felt a pang of disappointment. The excitement was snatched away, and she likened herself to Cinderella as she hung her best dress in the wardrobe.

She went out of her way to avoid him during the next week and not really understanding why, hurrying home at night before he could come up to her room. But then on Friday the same junior arrived with an invitation to dinner that evening, and she didn't say no. She'd had a strange dream about him on the previous night. Now she could hardly contain her excitement.

They went to the same little restaurant. She wore the same dress, feeling that she was in some kind of time warp. Only this time there were longer gaps in the conversation, and she found him staring at her in a way which embarrassed her.

'You look tired. I don't think we'll hang about tonight,' he was saying, wiping traces of ice-cream from his lips. 'It's quite a drive home from here and I could do with an early night.'

'Don't worry about me. I'm fine but you ought to have said. We could have come another night.' Hannah had the distressing feeling that somehow she had burdened him with her company, bored him with her conversation. Perhaps the dream was an omen. She should have taken notice of it.

'Oh no! Sorry I shouldn't have said that. I've enjoyed every minute of it. No. Blow it! Why rush about?'

However, his impatience seemed to return on the way back. They encountered a long stretch of roadworks and he sat tapping his fingers on the steering wheel, waiting for the traffic lights to change colour.

' It won't be long.' Hannah stared at him anxiously. All of a sudden they couldn't seem to communicate in the same easy way.

He pushed the lever into second gear and accelerated away as soon as the lights changed. Hannah noticed that he was driving much faster than usual, and when he suggested a cup of coffee at her place, she jumped at the chance to get him away from the wheel and to calm him down before he set off again on his apparently long drive home. There were so many things she didn't know about him. When she asked, he evaded questions: 'You wouldn't know it' or 'There isn't time to go into that and you wouldn't be interested,' et cetera. Then he would change the subject back to incidents in her life and she found herself once more talking about college or school.

The lift wasn't working, and their footsteps echoed on the stairs. The stress of the drive had made Hannah feel extraordinarily tired. She had her usual struggle with the key and then sank into the armchair.

'You're a sleepy head tonight,' David said, back with apparent good humour and a teasing familiar note in his voice.

'Sorry, it was so stuffy last night. I don't think I'm really over that cold. They seem to hang on forever. I didn't sleep properly. Dreams kept waking me up. Do you think dreams come true?' She'd kept thinking about that dream all night and wanted to talk about it but didn't want him to think she was prying.

'No, not really. You get something on your mind and then it may seem like it. No, it's just a coincidence.'

'I knew an old woman when I was a kid. She could see into the future. She had a white cat.'

'Shouldn't it have been a black one, or was she a white witch?'

The sarcasm was wasted on Hannah. Her thoughts were too deeply in the past. 'It wasn't a real one. It was pottery with eyes as big as saucers.'

'It must have been a hellish big one!' David laughed.

'No! I'm just remembering how I used to think. You know the story. 'The Soldier, the Witch and the Tinder Box.'

'You've lost me. We're more into Biggles at our end.'

If Hannah was honest with herself, she had long since given up any belief in the powers of the Mooncat, shutting it away amongst childhood fantasies. But now his trivialising of it angered her. 'Well, I do think dreams come true,' she declared. ' It's happened to me quite a few times. No. Don't laugh. I'm being serious. It's important to me.'

'Sorry. I didn't mean to laugh. It's just that you wrinkle your nose when you are getting all serious. Go on then. You are determined to tell me, aren't you?'

She hesitated for a moment and then told him about her dreams, beginning with the 'dolls' house' one and then about Dorothy Parker's measles and about the night she dreamed that she came face to face with one of her teachers who had her arm in a sling and the next day there she was with a broken arm. 'I couldn't believe it,' she said. 'There have been so many times when I know what's going to happen next.'

'Dêja vue. That's common,' David said dismissively, waving the idea away with one hand. 'The experts think it is caused by a kind of mental gap in seeing and comprehending. Something like that anyway.'

'Well that doesn't explain my dreams, does it?' Hannah insisted, becoming more and more irritated by his attempt to rationalise the mystery. 'I knew a black dog was going to come into my life when I was a kid. Things seem to happen early in dreams.'

'Like I said. It's something on your mind when you go to sleep. It must have been a constant fear that your house would be bombed. I expect everyone was having nightmares like that, and was there a measles epidemic?'

'A few children I think.'

'Well there you are. It was on your mind.'

'I thought I made it happen because she was bullying me the day before.'

'The day before! Germs have to incubate. You know that. She must have filled your head with nonsense.'

'Who?'

'That old woman with her familiar.'

'Mrs Knight. She was called Mrs Knight and she didn't talk nonsense.'

'Mrs Knight! Oh that's the limit! Black as night. You'll be telling me next that she had a broomstick and flew over the chimney pots.'

'Don't be mean, David. She wasn't a witch although I did meet one later but there was nothing supernatural about her.' Hannah frowned at the memory of Uncle Harry's sister. 'Anyway, sometimes I have wide awake dreams. Not just fantasising. I've never told anyone this before but a few months ago I suddenly saw a man's face in the darkness. It was like a television screen.'

David grinned. 'Sounds like a ghost channel to me. Sorry. No, obviously it was an hallucination.'

'And what is that?'

'You know. It's a kind of mental aberration. Drugs can cause it. Alcoholics seeing pink elephants and that kind of thing. Probably you were over tired, or even asleep.'

'Yes but who really knows? People seem to think that if you give something a fancy name then it's no longer a mystery. Oh, just an hallucination. Who first said that word and who knows whether there's a difference between a vision and an hallucination?'

David sighed and looked at his watch. 'This is all getting a bit deep for me. How on earth did we get on to this subject?'

'Because I dreamt about you last night but I'm not going to tell you now. You'd only laugh.'

David's expression changed; the sardonic humour in his eyes replaced now with a look of curiosity as she tantalised his ego. 'Go on then, tell me,' he said. 'I promise I won't laugh.'

'It wasn't much really. I just thought you might be able to explain it. I was in a room and it was all dark, but I could see into another room which wasn't dark. There was a woman in the other room. She seemed to be very angry. I could see a grandfather clock, even though it was dark. You know how you do in dreams—see in the dark. Anyway, I knew the time was twenty past seven because I could see the hands of the clock. Then you came in and tripped over something. I wanted to help you but I couldn't move. I was in the doorway and you were shouting at the woman but I couldn't make it out. Then she went out and you went into the room with the light on. I called your name but you didn't seem to hear me. That's right, I remember now. It was a kitchen. You put the kettle on. That was about it really. It stuck in my mind. Not like an ordinary dream. They seem to fade quickly. What do you think?'

David was looking puzzled. 'Just got me on your mind, I suppose. It's a wonder I don't dream about you every night.'

Hannah jumped up. 'Was it tea or coffee?' she asked.

'Better make it coffee. Otherwise you'll be reading my tea leaves. Only joking!'

He followed her into the kitchen and as she reached for the cups, he put his arms around her pulling her towards him. 'Leave that,' he said. 'We'll have a drink later.'

She tried to move away from him but he grasped her wrist turning her around, and began to stroke her hair, his hand following down the curve of her shoulder. In that moment he became the predator. He became Tom Porter. His charm and attentions were weapons and the sparkle in his eyes mirrored the lust. 'Don't touch me!' she screamed, kicking at his shins and writhing her body to one side.

He dropped his hands, his mouth twisting with pain and anger. 'Come on, Hannah,' he shouted. 'For God's sake! I only want to kiss you. You must know how I feel.'

Hannah moved away from him, rubbing the reddened skin on her wrist. 'I like you, David,' she said in a low voice, feeling obliged to give him an answer yet frightened of his reactions. 'I really do like you. I like talking to you. Can't we leave it like that?'

'Oh come off it! What do you think I am? Don't give me all that Platonic claptrap. You've been flirting with me from that first day in the classroom. Christ! I've spent a fortune on you. I'm not some kind of charity!'

Hannah was shaken by his anger, and disappointed. 'And I thought you were a gentleman,' she said nervously pulling at her hair.

'Oh yes. A knight in shining armour I suppose, rescuing the fair damsel and riding off in search of the Holy Grail. You'd like that, wouldn't you?'

Hannah put her finger to her mouth. 'Someone will hear you,' she whispered. 'I'm sorry. I thought it was different with you. Not like the young ones just thinking about...' She hesitated, suddenly appalled at the expression on his face.

'Sex! That's what you mean, isn't it? You can't even say it, can you? And I thought your innocence was part of your charm but you want to keep it and still have fun at my expense. Well go and find yourself another meal ticket, if you can!'

'Don't drive fast,' Hannah murmured, frightened by his anger. He turned, hesitating for a moment and muttering something under his breath before walking out. The door slammed behind him.

Hannah was shaking. How could she tell him that she was afraid? He wouldn't understand. Had she flirted with him? She knew that she valued his friendship, was flattered by his attention and fearful of his disapproval. Was that flirting? She was still trembling as she poured the water on the coffee granules. It was like one of her bad dreams. What did he say? He wasn't a charity. She wished she hadn't told him about the dreams. She felt rather foolish and that increased her guilt.

She got ready for bed, unusually folding each article of clothing and placing it neatly on the chair. A bitterness crept into her reasoning as she lay unable to close her eyes. He was just having an affair. Punishing his wife. That was his wife in the kitchen. Was her name Penny or did they really have a cat? She could see now that it was all furtive; the glances around the restaurant, remote out in the country. She cursed herself for her feelings of guilt. It didn't matter what she did, she thought. She always ended up feeling guilty. Do you find the prisoner guilty or not guilty? Guilty, my lord. 'Oh for goodness sake!' she exclaimed. How dare he imply that she was some kind of prude destined to stay single. Why, he was old enough to be her father!

She flung herself over on to her side and drew up her knees, making herself into a tight ball against the mattress.

David had accelerated away from the flat along Albert Street and on to the main road. His heart, which had pounded first with passion and then with anger, began to steady its pace, and he lit a cigarette as he waited for the gates to open at the level crossing.

'Women!' he muttered. He thought of the row that morning with Julia. Well, she was extravagant. How could they have an electricity bill that size now that the kids had left home? She must have had the immersion heater on day and night. 'Oh Christ!' He braked hard as the car in front slowed down to turn to the left. 'Can't you indicate?' he yelled in the direction of the disappearing car. 'I might have known. Woman driver! Should be banned!'

As he left the city lights for the narrower roads of the countryside, he began to relax, lighting up another cigarette and reducing his speed. Would she be in bed? He was later than usual tonight, but not as late as he intended. She didn't question his after-school activities. Friday was his billiards night, not that she was interested. Middle-aged indifference he thought as he wound the window down and tossed the cigarette stub on to the road.

Hannah was different. A little strange tonight though. In spite of his attempts to rationalise her experiences, he still felt the hairs rising on his arms. It was funny about that dream. The grandfather clock was a family joke. It hadn't gone for years. 'Right twice a day at twenty past seven,' his daughter would say. How did Hannah know that? Had he talked about it? No. He'd avoided any mention of home. Just a coincidence. 'Come on, David,' he muttered. 'You'll be believing the tea leaves next.'

He swung the car around a sharp bend in the road. Normally he could see his house by this time, lit up like an ocean liner, but tonight there wasn't even a glimmer. She must have gone to bed. He sighed with relief. He couldn't take another scene today.

He opened the front door and clicked down the switch in the entrance hall. Nothing happened. He clicked the switch up and down again, still with no results. The door into the lounge was open. He could see by the light from the street lamp which shone through the glass panelled door. He tried the next switch at the far end of the hall. Surely both bulbs couldn't have blown. The kitchen light was on at the back of the house so it couldn't be a power failure. This was the last straw! Actually, the loose edge of the carpet in the lounge was his final undoing, and he lurched forward on his knees.

Julia came out of the kitchen as he struggled to his feet.

'What the hell's going on?' he yelled.

'Just economising. I've taken some bulbs out. I'm going to bed now. I'll manage with a torch.' Julia walked around him showing no concern for his knee.

'You stupid bat! It's that bloody heater, not the bulbs. I could have broken my leg!'

'Now perhaps you'll tack the carpet down. It's been like that for months. I could always go to the public baths and send your clothes to the laundry'

David staggered into the kitchen. 'God, I need that coffee,' he gasped. He knew that his life wouldn't be worth living unless he apologised. What a day, he thought bitterly. As he sat in the half-light, his thoughts returned to Hannah and he suddenly realised that her dream had materialised. What did she say? She sees things early—the dark room, his fall, the clock at twenty past seven. He looked across at the old clock, dark faced in the corner shadows. How could anyone see anything before it happened? Was she here now like a ghost standing near the door? He gave a violent shiver and felt the hair rising at the back of his neck. She was certainly weird. It was like being spied on. At least Julia had both feet firmly on the ground. Perhaps it was not too late for a good ending. Julia always seemed to be stimulated by a row and an abundance of apologies. He would try a bit of humble pie and if Hannah was watching, then perhaps she would learn what life was all about. He cast a defiant glance towards the open door and made a dash for the stairs.

27

'The Confessional Box'

'You're not looking very well, dear,' Mrs Gilbert commented, giving Hannah a searching look. 'You've not got your cold back, have you? These kids are lethal.'

'No, just a bad night.' Hannah stood up and went to the window. How would they react if she told them about David? She was dreading seeing him. She felt so guilty. Should she offer to pay for her share of the meals? Had she been very mean to him? These thoughts had tormented her all the weekend.

As though she was thought reading Miss Perry burst in excitedly. 'You know we were wondering about Mr Saxton the other day. Well I saw him on Saturday. I bumped into him in town. He is married. She was with him. He introduced me. Now, what was her name? Honestly, I've got a head like a sieve these days. Began with a 'J'. Janet? Jean? It'll come to me. She seemed very nice. Smart. The elegant sort.' She patted her shiny navy blue skirt as if apologising for its comparison with the kind of elegance she only dreamed of.

'About his age, was she?' Mrs Gilbert seized on a change of subject away from the confines of education.

'Excuse me,' Hannah said as she walked past them to the door. 'I'm on playground this morning.'

The anger stood on its own now, no longer diluted with guilt and regret. She blew the whistle long and hard, and the children, sensing her mood, stood silently awaiting her command to go in. The mood continued all day, robbing her of any feeling of well being.

She made up her mind on the way home from school. It was time for a change. Ella would welcome her with open arms. If there were no vacancies now, she could go on the supply teachers' list, or do something entirely different. She had never wanted to teach in the first place.

She would have to work out her notice and finish at the end of the term, but it was only a couple of weeks after half-term so there was still time. She would invite herself to Ella's for the weekend and spy out the lay of the land. On a sudden impulse, she ran for the bus as it pulled up at the stop a few yards ahead. She got off at the library and wandered aimlessly around inside, not seeing the rows of books, her vision still focused inwards on her plans. A special display had been set up at the end of the aisle, and she tried to focus her eyes on the large lettered heading. As she approached it, the name 'Hannah' leapt out at her, and captured her full attention. A poster was in the centre of the display announcing the library launch of a novel entitled *Hannah Childs, a Victorian Chamber Maid*. After the first impact made by her own Christian name, Hannah's eyes were drawn to another name and she gasped: 'Sally Blenkin.' She read on: 'Author returns to her home town and will be in this library to promote her highly successful novel. Leaflets available at the desk.'

Hannah ran across to the desk and joined the queue, her mind racing with excitement. There couldn't be another Sally Blenkin, surely.

'That's been and gone,' the librarian said. 'Sorry. We're a bit disorganised at the moment. I think we've got some leaflets left if you're interested in the book.' She sifted through some papers. 'Here we are. Looks like the last one.'

Hannah almost snatched it from her hand and stared at the rather grainy photograph. It was Sally! Her face smiled out from the leaflet, older of course but there was no mistaking that mischievous look in her eyes. She looked up to find the librarian still waiting for her reaction. 'You don't know her address, do you? We used to be really close friends but we've lost touch.'

'I'm sorry. We don't get private details. Actually, we didn't organise it. It was a writers' group. They'll know. Can you hang on while I see to these people?'

Hannah read and re-read the leaflet while she waited. She couldn't believe that her Sally had written a book, and was the name in the title in remembrance of those shared days or had Hannah Childs really existed?

The librarian opened a drawer and brought out a notepad. 'Here it is,' she said, after thumbing through a number of pages. 'Yes. This is the man who organised it—Mr Cummins. Give me that back. I'll write down his number for you.'

Mr Cummins was very helpful when she explained about the long-lost friendship, observing that it must have happened dozens of times during the war years. 'She moved away a while ago,' he explained. 'I can give you her phone number but I don't know her address. It's somewhere in London. That's all I can tell you.'

London! The name made the same impact on Hannah as if he had said New York, China or the moon. She wrote down the number carefully next to his on the back of the leaflet. 'Thanks very much, Mr Cummins,' she gabbled. 'I can't wait to speak to her.'

But she did wait. After all, it was such a long time ago and London seemed so alien and vast. Would Sally be interested? She would be mixing with important people, going to posh functions and wearing stylish clothes.

After two cups of tea back in the safety of her flat, she chided herself for her cowardice and returned to the phone box.

She heard a voice saying, 'Hello. Who is it? Hello.'

'Hello. Is that Sally? It's me. Hannah Flynn.'

'Hannah! Hannah Flynn? Where the hell have you been? I've been looking for you for a hundred years!'

Hannah giggled at her extravagant speech, already with added feelings of inferiority. She couldn't compete with such exuberance and explained quietly that she had seen the promotional poster in the library.

'Why weren't you there then? Didn't you hear about me? I'm famous. It was in the paper as well.'

Hannah began to explain, with Sally interrupting and sending one volley after another of questions, each one following the other with such speed that there was no space in between for more than a yes or a no. The pips began to indicate the end of the money. Hannah scrabbled in her bag.

'I've run out of change, Sally. I'll ring you again later.'

'Don't ring. Jump on the next train,' Sally shouted over the pips before the continuous buzz terminated the conversation.

For all her excited anticipation, she was feeling very nervous. It seemed so easy over the telephone. 'I'll meet you,' Sally promised. 'Go to the refreshment room if I'm late.' Hannah took the leaflet out of her bag and looked at the rather grainy photograph. It occurred to her that Sally would have problems in recognising her in the crowd, but later, when an oblong of cardboard waved above the heads of the people gathered at the barrier at King's Cross, her worries were replaced with a great burst of excitement. In big letters across the board was written 'Hiya Hannah'. That was typical of Sally. She giggled and waved her hand as high as she could. She couldn't see her friend but the disappearance of the board indicated that her friend had located her.

Sally's face appeared as the crowd began to disperse. 'You haven't changed a bit,' she shrieked above the station noises, seizing Hannah's hold-all and walking along with all the urgency of a city dweller. 'You don't mind the bus route, do you? It's only about an hour's run. My money doesn't stretch to taxis and anyway I can show you some of the sights from the top deck.'

Hannah was fascinated with the commentary from their seat at the front of the London bus. Here she was, miles from home and seeing landmarks that were only familiar on the cinema screen or in the pages of a book. She was beginning to feel rather travel worn, but the anticipation of seeing her friend's flat and sharing their memories gave her feet the same urgency of movement that this new world seemed to epitomise. She clattered down the steep stairs and jumped off the platform, feeling like a ten-year-old on a special outing.

It was quite a walk from the bus stop to the flat, zigzagging along streets which seemed part of a never-ending maze. 'Last one,' Sally gasped. Hannah viewed the long street with a critical eye. Her friend was successful, wasn't she? Surely she didn't belong in back-street mundanity.

'Sorry it's a bit of a dive,' Sally said, as if sensing her friend's disappointment. 'It costs a fortune living in London. I know Lambeth doesn't have streets paved with gold, but it suits me at the moment, and it's not a bad flat as flats go.'

The flat was surprisingly spacious; the first floor of a Victorian terraced house, with a large lounge, compact kitchen, a square bedroom and a diminutive bathroom.

'This is where I wash the London dust from my weary body,' Sally laughed, throwing open the bathroom door and revealing a half-sized bath.

Hannah laughed, comparing the room unfavourably with her own modern conveniences. Somehow, such a comparison restored her confidence, but Sally's next words began to undermine it again.

She spoke at top speed as if she didn't have a moment to spare and she seemed to have the energy of a spinning top as she suggested a quick freshening up, a cup of tea and a slice of toast and then a more substantial meal at a restaurant down the road.

Hannah, cramped into the small space beyond the bathroom door, washed her hands at the same time studying her face in the mirror. Country come to town, she thought. In spite of the recent years of city life, she still felt like a country bumpkin. Sally had all the sophistication and surety of someone worldly wise with her long bleached hair and stylish clothes. Her actions were direct and full of purpose.

Her voice came through the bathroom door. 'Come on! I'm dying for some reminiscing.'

'You start,' Hannah mumbled between two mouthfuls of toast some ten minutes later. She hadn't realised how hungry she was, and in any case she wanted to hear Sally's story. No doubt it was sensational compared to her own life. 'Where did you end up when we parted company?'

'You won't believe it.' Sally rolled her eyes in the same way as she had done as a child. 'Do you remember how I told everyone that we were going to live in a castle? I made that up of course. You know what we were like. Well, strangely enough, we did end up in a kind of stately home. We thought it was wonderful at first, a bit like being at boarding school, but the reality was three in a bed, and cold gloomy rooms. We became a cheap labour force and spent the weekends weeding the gardens, scrubbing floors and washing up.'

'What? Just the three of you?'

'No. It wasn't just us. There were about ten kids billeted with this posh couple. They must have thought that we older ones were a godsend. There was an elderly housekeeper with a biting tongue and a hard hand, and a charwoman who came twice a week. But the village girls, who would have provided a labour pool, were doing war work. So they used us instead.'

'Still, I suppose you did cause a lot of extra work.'

'Not really. We looked after each other, and our meals were very sparse even by wartime standards. I can still remember how my stomach rumbled. I'm sure they must have profited from the government funding and extra rations, clothing coupons as well.'

Hannah nodded. She didn't have any clothing coupons when she was re-billeted. Elsie must have seen to that. Sold them no doubt. 'Did you stay until the war ended?' she asked.

'Most of the kids went home when things calmed down a bit. I suppose, in spite of the benefits, her ladyship must have sighed with relief. Some of those kids were right little sods with no respect for history.'

Hannah smiled at her friend's easy use of a swear word, enjoying a feeling of liberation in her company, but seconds later experiencing the guilt of easy seduction.

'We were bombed as you know, of course...sorry, Hannah. I keep forgetting about your folks.' Sally reached forward and squeezed

Hannah's hand. 'Well, my mam escaped the full impact. The house was damaged beyond repair and she lost the baby. I learnt about that years later. Do you remember how ignorant we were? We thought you just had to order them from the Co-op!'

'I didn't. I thought I was found in a boat in the middle of a storm.'

'Typical of you!' Sally grimaced. 'Anyway she was sent to a hospital in North Lincolnshire to recover, and then it was easy to track us down. Good old Mam. For all her faults she did her best. The posh couple found us a cottage on the estate, and Mam worked at the big house and did land work to keep us going. Then when my dad came back, they stayed on there. Happy as pigs in muck! You'd think they were born to it.'

'So what took you back to Hull then?'

'Job opportunities. There wasn't much going on where we were. I'd always fancied writing and got top grades in English, so I applied for a job with the *Mail* and worked my way up from reporting on little shindigs. You know—baby contests and wedding anniversaries and such like. Then I moved on to heavier stuff, a bit more stretching but very often deadly boring. I liked the human stuff, especially from a woman's angle, so I set my sights on magazine articles and headed for the great metropolis. I thought I could conquer the world, but it's certainly a tough one. I freelance now and it gives me time to concentrate on my next book I've had some heartache on the way, but that's about it, apart from a few commas and just lately a lot of question marks.' She took a deep breath and brought the flats of her hands down on the arms of the chair. 'Now I'll make us another drink. It's thirsty work, all this soul-searching. It's your turn next.'

She took the cups into the kitchen and Hannah stretched up in the chair. She wouldn't have called it soul-searching. Sally's thoughts and emotions remained under cover. She wondered what the heartache or the question marks were. The time seemed to have moved on rapidly. Still, it wouldn't take long to fill in her gaps. She certainly wasn't going to mention David.

Five minutes later, she began to unearth her past, beginning at the same place and describing her first encounter with the Porters.

'I was only there for three months,' she said, taking a sip of her tea.

'Well? Did you like the place? Did you make any friends?'

'Don't rush me.' Hannah looked down at her hands, which were beginning to redden as she clasped and unclasped them. 'I've never talked about it before. It's hard to put into words.'

Sally's success in writing lay in her understanding of human nature and an insatiable curiosity. 'Don't you think it's about time you did?' she said gently.

Her sympathetic tone drew emotions to the surface and Hannah fought to hold back the tears. She wanted to tell someone. It had been a secret for too long. Suddenly the words came. It was like a crack in a dam; a relief of all the pent-up emotion and guilt. She restrained herself when she came to Elsie's part in Tom's death. Somehow, she still felt the threat of exposure in their shared guilt.

'Is this Elsie still there?' Sally asked, reaching forward to hold Hannah's hand.

'I don't know. I expect so. She couldn't have been all that old. I suppose she'll be in her early fifties now.'

'Do you think she was glad he died in the fire? I think I would have been. Still, you never know. Battered wives seem to have a compulsive loyalty to their partners.'

'I think she was at first. I didn't understand it all at the time but she must have known what he had done.'

'And then she began to blame you. That's pretty typical.'

'Yes, she had terrible mood swings and then, as I told you, the mouse pie was the last straw.' Hannah shuddered at the memory of it and took a large gulp of her tea.

Sally shook her head in disbelief. 'I've never heard of that for a cure. That wasn't one of my problems, but some of the poor little devils had their noses rubbed in it. God! When I think about it I could go back and commit a few murders. Did he actually rape you?'

Hannah was startled by her question and winced at the word, giving a nervous cough. 'I can't remember,' she croaked.

'He couldn't have done then. You would have remembered. You

would have been damaged. I should think it was drunken groping and then giving up on the idea and falling asleep. You don't want to dwell on it, you know. Dirty old men! There's plenty of them around. You have to develop a sixth sense. Our Lord of the Manor was just such another. He'd have his hand up your skirt as soon as look at you.' Sally swallowed a mouthful of tea and pulled a face. 'Ugh! No sugar! Must spend a penny. Don't go away!'

Hannah was glad of the breathing space, but her brain continued to torment. Rape and pillage. Pillage and rape. Destructive words. She thought of a rapier; cold steel, wounding and maiming, cutting through her childhood innocence. Sally's flippancy disturbed her. Whatever the truth of it, he had violated her. She closed her eyes in an attempt to shut out the pictures of her memories.

' Are you tired?' Sally was back. 'We can leave it all in the past, you know.'

'No. I might as well get it all off my chest. The next bad bit is more recent but the years in between are easy to talk about.'

She described the happy years of growing up at Willow Cottage with Aunt Kate and Auntie Ella. Sally noticed that she referred to Kate's husband as Mr Churchill and wondered why, but waited for the story to unfold.

'It was like the Garden of Eden,' Hannah said, 'until the serpent arrived.'

'That sounds dramatic.' Sally's curiosity was growing by the second. 'Who on earth was the serpent? Not Elsie Porter!'

'No, worse than her. She goes under the name of Margot Sergeant, but I think of her as Miss Murdstone.'

'Why?'

'Don't you remember in David Copperfield. Mr Murdstone was David's stepfather and he had a vicious sister.'

'Ah yes. So this Margot woman was Mr Churchill's sister!' Sally rolled her eyes in mock relief at reaching the answer.

Hannah nodded, ignoring her friend's droll gestures. She explained how matters came to a head and how she tried to make contact. 'Anyway, he's dead now,' she concluded, 'and she has inherited everything. Aunt Kate must be turning in her grave. The house and land were hers and the money it raised ended up in the hands of a person she loathed.'

'Couldn't you have contested it?'

'I didn't know he'd died until Ella got news of it. I had no legal claims to it and anyway I didn't want it.' She knew that that was not true. She would love to own Willow Cottage.

Sally's next words eased her guilt. 'But Aunt Kate wanted you to live there, didn't she? It would have made her very happy to know that you had a comfortable house to live in. What about the old lady and her magic cat? I bet she could have helped you. Cast a spell on Miss Murdstone and changed her into a Natter Jack toad!' Sally couldn't be serious for long.

'It's not magic!' Hannah protested, a picture suddenly popping into her mind of the Sunday School teacher pursing her lips around the 'm' sound as she prompted the answer 'miracle' and was given 'magic' instead. 'Actually I dreamt about old Mrs Knight last week. I was walking towards her and I spoke to her, but she didn't seem to know me and turned away. I woke up really miserable. Isn't it strange when dreams seem so real and if they come true it's as though everything is planned?'

Sally stood up. 'You and your dreams!' she said. 'I'd forgotten how you were always dreaming. I rarely do and, in any case, I can't remember the next morning. I'm not what you would call religious either. A cowardly agnostic I suppose. I used to think that if there was a god he should have done something about all the beatings I had. Sent down a thunderbolt or something. I think we make our own heaven and hell. Anyway, if you think it is all mapped out for us, then you have to accept it, good or bad.'

'Well, don't you think it was strange that I jumped on the bus and went to the library?' Hannah was so caught up in her ideas that she refused to be put off by her friend's cynicism.

Sally shrugged. 'Not really. If you were being manipulated, then you would have come on the day I was there. That would have been more certain, wouldn't it?'

'Yes I suppose so. But I still think it wasn't a coincidence. I might never have seen you again.'

Sally reached for her bag. 'You know what they say. There are a lot of mites in a piece of cheese. Anyway, what are your plans now or are you going to leave it to some omnipotent? I think our immediate plan should be to go and have a good meal. My stomach's rumbling like Vesuvius. Eating is my greatest pleasure. It used to be sex but I've decided to become celibate.'

They walked down the road to the high street and in spite of her recent vows to leave the past alone, Sally went into details of her love life. 'From now on,' she concluded as they approached the restaurant, 'men are out of my life for good.'

Walking arm in arm with her friend gave Hannah a delicious feeling of belonging. 'I thought you were going to marry a rich man and have a fur coat. Do you remember?' she giggled.

'Oh, I was just a kid. I do remember that family life appalled me. It was so chaotic. I can see my mother now, up to her ears in washing and knee-deep in fag ash. Wow! Something smells good!'

'So what about the men in your life then?' Sally asked, in between two mouthfuls of Yorkshire pudding festooned with a liberal coating of onions. 'You're too good-looking to have escaped notice.'

'I've had my share,' Hannah said, trying to sound convincing and pressing more mashed potato on to her fork.

'But?' her friend prompted.

'Well, the ones at college were out for a quick thrill, and one or two I fancied at pottery night class were married.'

'Pottery classes! Not the ideal place for passion. All that clay. The wrong kind of heavy breathing I should think. So, there's been no great affairs of the heart?'

Hannah reacted in her usual way, her friend's comments provoking that feeling of inadequacy which seemed to blight her life. She talked about her relationship with David, exaggerating the emotional highs and lows, and borrowing details from recalled scenes in literature. 'And then he told me that he was married and couldn't leave his wife because she was an invalid,' she lied.

'A likely story! The invalid bit I mean. And you had no idea?'

'Well, to be honest, I did suspect it. One or two things he said.'

'I know how you felt. It's a kind of safety barrier. You know the truth and yet you deny it. It adds to the thrill but there's still a way out. Men are slaves to their hormones, you know. Their hormones say jump and they have to jump. Anyway, we don't have to be their slaves. Poor things. They deserve a toast. To men. Who needs them?' she said, raising her glass of water.

Hannah copied her gesture but the guilty feelings were back. She'd really enjoyed David's company.

Sally yawned and looked at her watch. 'We'd better get back otherwise we'll be like death in the morning. What time will you have to go?'

'There's no need to rush. I planned to get the midday train but a later one will do.'

'Good! We can have a lie-in. You don't mind the settee, do you? I'm a bit short on clean bedding and it'll have to last until I can get to the laundrette.' Sally suddenly straightened up, her eyes widening with excitement. 'Why don't you come and live in London? You don't really want to bury yourself in the wilds of Northumberland, do you? There's plenty of work here, and I could do with someone to share the expenses.'

Three-quarters of an hour later, Hannah pulled the travel rug over herself and stretched out her feet as far as they would go before pressing on the arm of the settee. She didn't feel tired, and tiredness is a vital ingredient in the process of settee sleeping. Her mind wouldn't leave go of the new thoughts in her head, and re-digested countless old ones as well. She couldn't get that awful word out of her head. Did he actually? Well, did he? She couldn't remember. She didn't want to remember. She could only remember what she understood at the time. Did it matter anyway? Wasn't the abuse enough? 'Sex! You can't even say the word, can you?' David's voice loomed up from under the settee. She put her head under the tartan rug. Sally was right. 'Who needs men?' But then did she need a woman? 'A pair of Lesbians,' she heard the college-cloakroom voice say from the direction of the coffee table.

Right! Think of something else, she told her brain in her schoolteacher voice. She imagined that she was pushing the Fears back into that dark little cupboard and blocking their escape path along the telegraph wires by uprooting the poles. But it didn't work. It was like counting sheep jumping over a fence. Her sheep always refused to jump, and the frustration of it made her more awake than ever. If only the Mooncat was here. The Magic Mooncat. She pictured it, shiny white with eyes as big as saucers, and was asleep minutes later, her head sinking into the hardness of the kapok-filled, citrus green, fur-fabric-covered scatter cushions.

28

'Ghosts' Dead and Alive

They had their 'lie-in' in the morning and were attacking a plate of toast when the phone rang. Sally jumped up and crossed over to the coffee table near the window.

'Hi there,' Hannah heard her say. 'Just having breakfast…I know. You've been to the pier and back by now. Well it is Sunday… . You'll never guess who's here…Hannah… Hannah Flynn. You know, the Flynns from Tennyson Street… . Yes… . She hasn't changed much. Grown a bit here and there as we girls do! Are you sure? Where was that then?… . Did you speak to him? She didn't say…okay. Give my love to Gavin. I'll see you soon then. Bye.'

Sally put down the receiver. She looked puzzled and glanced uneasily across at Hannah as she returned to the table. 'That was my brother Michael just checking up on me,' she explained. 'Last time he called I cried bucketfuls over Paul. Do you remember Michael? He's a bricklayer and Gavin's an electrician. They share a little business back in Hull.' She nibbled on a piece of toast and stared at Hannah, her eyebrows pinching a small frown between her eyes.

'Is anything the matter? You look bothered about something. He's not in trouble, is he?'

'No. Why should he be? It's just something he said.'

Hannah said, 'Oh,' feeling that Sally's tone implied that it was none of her business.

'Did they ever confirm the death of your father?'

'What!'

'You know, you said that he was missing, believed dead.'

'No. I was never told anything.'

'Well, Michael said that he saw him in town the other day.'

Hannah stared, unable at first to take in her friend's words. Sally continued, speaking rather quickly to help Hannah over her confusion. 'Michael recognised him but obviously he wouldn't recognise Michael. He was only a little kid when we were evacuated. Anyway, Michael said, "Hello, Mr Flynn," and he answered him. He had a little lad with him in a pushchair and he seemed a bit lame. Had a walking stick, Michael said.'

Hannah shook her head. 'He must have been mistaken. Why it's years since he saw my dad. Like you said, he was only a little kid.'

'No, he was adamant. The man acknowledged him. Answered to his name. You haven't got an uncle, have you? Could he be a brother with the same looks?'

Hannah shook her head again, her brain racing to keep up with the pounding of her heart. How could it be him? Why would he abandon her? Who else knew that he was alive? Did Aunt Kate know and what about Ella? Was that why there had never been a legal adoption? She felt swamped by deceit. But then, what if he had lost his memory? She'd always felt that he wasn't dead, but the rationality of adulthood had finally laid her hopes to rest.

Sally used a little more logic in analysing the situation, suggesting that he might have felt so disadvantaged on his own with no house and no job that he felt it was best to leave things as they were. 'And,' she continued, 'if he was wounded, well…'

'Yes, I could understand that,' Hannah interrupted, 'but I'm not a child now. You would think he would have tried to contact me. Aunt Vera knew where I was.'

'Does she know that you have gone back to Hull? Have you spoken to her lately?'

'No. I didn't think she was bothered about me.'

'You know where she lives though. Why don't you contact her?'

Hannah reached for her bag and took out the folded sheet of writing paper from an inside pocket.

'No telephone number? What's scribbled on the back? That looks like it. Ring her up.'

'What, now? I won't know what to say.'

'Oh here. I'll do it for you. Give me the number.'

'Mrs Vera Morgan?' Hannah heard Sally say, and then, 'Oh. I'm sorry to have bothered you. You don't have a forwarding address do you? Okay then.'

Sally waved her hands as she returned to her anxious friend. 'Two years too late I'm afraid. They've gone to Australia. That was the new owner.'

'Perhaps I'm not meant to see him again. Perhaps I'm not meant to have a family.'

'Oh Hannah! Don't talk so stupid. Don't worry. You'll find him. I bet he wishes he could contact you. You never know. Perhaps he is looking for you at this very moment. We could hire a private eye except that we can't afford it.'

Hannah smiled, relaxing in Sally's lightheartedness, and knowing that she was doing her best to help. 'Mrs Knight would know. She seemed to know everything. I dreamt about her. Somehow it seemed significant as though I should take notice of it.'

'Well take notice of it then! For goodness sake, Hannah, have the courage of your own convictions.' Sally brought her hand down on the table, vibrating the coffee in the cups. 'Why don't you go and see her? Go and confront your ghosts at the same time. You never know. You may be in control of your destiny after all.'

A few hours later, Hannah was on her way home after a frantic rush to the station. She didn't want to think about her father any more. He'd been on her mind for hours and she felt as though she was going crazy with happiness, disbelief, anger and recriminations. It was all such a tangle. Now she wanted to dismiss him. He was as bad as the rest of his sex. He didn't care about her. None of them did. Even Jack Clayton couldn't be trusted, she thought bitterly, forgetting that in recent years she had been shocked by his possible death. Like Sally said, they could do without men. Her thoughts wandered to Chris Maddison as she stared out of the window at the fields and clusters of houses along the route. Chris was a lot like Sally. She still had moments of disquiet about that college friendship in spite of dismissing fears about her own sexual preferences. Now, in the solitude of her thoughts, she had stirrings of doubt. Was it a good idea to move in with Sally? She liked her zany sense of humour but they were so different. She began to feel weighed down by a cloud of depression which was echoed in the dullness of the landscape under the overcast sky.

She closed her eyes and fell into a light sleep, her elbow pressing into the table and her hand supporting her head. 'This is Grantham. This is Grantham,' the harsh voice announced over the tannoy system. A garbled message followed, made unintelligible by the opening and closing of doors and the shuffling of feet. The lady and the small boy, her companions at the start of the journey, had gone, and Hannah stretched her legs into the vacated space and looked across to the opposite platform and the station exit. That's where 'she' stood, she thought, and the little girl within her trembled with recollected anxiety of an uncertain future with strange people. And here I am in that future, she said to herself. Layers of growing. An accumulation of knowledge. How strange life was. Something could seem so commonplace, and yet it could be so important in the future. She frowned, suddenly recalling how Tess (in Thomas Hardy's book which she had recently read) contemplated birthdays and death days, wondering how many times she would pass ordinarily through that fatal date without knowing that one day it would be her last. Such gloomy introspection mirrored the doubts that had begun to cloud the excitement of the reunion. The cleansing effect of the confessional box was only skin deep, and the old wounds again began to pain her.

During the next few days, the cold virus which once more had hung over her like the sword of Damocles, finally descended and she sniffed her way through the days seriously contemplating life in a nunnery away from both children and men.

By Sunday evening, she felt sufficiently recovered to trudge to the phone box to telephone Sally whose bright voice lifted her spirits.

'So you've had to put it off. And there's me imagining all sorts of things. Oh well. Don't give up on it. You should be feeling fit by next weekend. Are you wearing a disguise?'

'I'll be a clown I think, I've already got the red nose.'

'Oh you poor thing! What you need is nettle tea or seed cake. Go and get a magic brew from your old witch woman.'

She giggled and then Hannah heard a man's voice in the background. 'Have you got a visitor?' she asked.

'No It's only the tele. Some crummy play. You could write one better. I'll turn it off. Hang on a minute. How's that?' she yelled. 'Now where were we?'

They chatted on until the pips went, Sally enthusing about her latest assignment and Hannah punctuating it with sniffs. Somehow the magic had gone and it wasn't just the effects of the cold.

During the following week, Hannah tried to throw off the infection, becoming unusually cross at a lack of handkerchiefs and pushing children away from her in the playground. She spent hours tidying cupboards and getting records up to date. Now that she had given in her notice, she didn't want to leave room for any criticism.

Her intention was to spend no more than an hour or two at Cragthorpe. It depended on whether Mrs Knight was still there. She couldn't think of anyone else she would want to see. It was all very well Sally telling her to confront her ghosts. She hadn't been half scared to death by the demented Elsie Porter. However, she did decide to make a weekend of it. Going to London had given her the wanderlust. She would find somewhere to stay and go to the cinema. It would be good to have no one else intruding into her fantasies.

On Saturday morning she dressed carefully in her smartest outfit. The two-piece, which she had worn for her interview, still fitted. There had been few occasions to wear it since then. She fluffed up her hair around her face. Curly hair suited her. Aunt Kate had preferred a neat straight bob, but such a style needed constant trimming. It was so much easier to pull the brush through the curls.

I'm getting quite a gad about, she thought. She wasn't too sure about her reasons for going. She felt that she should be searching for her father, yet somehow dreaded meeting him. Perhaps he wouldn't be pleased to see her. Who was the child with him? It all seemed like a good idea when she was with Sally. She made everything seem like a good idea. Where's your sense of adventure? she asked herself as a couple of hours later the train headed towards Doncaster.

It didn't seem long after she'd boarded the next train before it was pulling to a stop. 'This is Grantham,' came the familiar voice. Now, she stood on the opposite platform and remembered her thoughts from the earlier weekend. Her feet, in their younger days, must have walked along this concreted area with many others in that ordered little crocodile. She tried to remember the road leading from the station into the town, looking for any landmarks, but it was as though she had never set foot in the place. All she could recall were the feelings of anticipation.

According to the timetable at the bus station, there was a bus that reached Cragthorpe at two-twenty, and one returning at four-thirty. That would suit her plans very well, and she would have time to book a bed for the night at the little guesthouse on the corner.

'Here's your stop, duck,' the conductor called an hour later. A cloud covered the sun but she kept her dark glasses on and looked around, suddenly feeling very conspicuous in her solitude. Nothing seemed to have changed on this stretch of the road except that the village hall looked a little less dilapidated, with a coat of cream paint and neatly cut surrounding grass. She set off in the direction of Mrs Knight's cottage, and as she approached the village shop a young man came out and began to pick up trays of vegetables from the front paving slabs.

Somebody new in the shop, she thought. It would be safe to go in to get some mints. Her throat resembled sandpaper.

'You're not closed, are you?' she called.

'Any minute now. You've just made it,' the man replied. He gave her a friendly grin and stepped aside as she went into the shop.

'Sorry, I only want some mints.' Hannah cursed herself. Here she was apologising again.

'Humbugs?' He stood balancing a jar of sweets in one hand waiting for an answer, and with a big grin on his face.

Hannah stared at him. 'Jack! Is it Jack Clayton?'

He nodded his head at the same time studying her face. 'At your service, ma'am. Have I had the pleasure of your acquaintance?'

'I thought you were dead!' Hannah took off her glasses. 'Hannah. Don't you remember me?'

'Dead! Who told you that? Hannah Flynn! How did you expect me to recognise you in those glasses? I thought you were a tourist or a film star at least.'

He was the same Jack, treating life as a joke and apparently bearing no grudges.

'How did you know I was here?' he asked.

'I didn't. Like I said I thought you were dead.'

'Oh! So the disguise wasn't for me then. Are you afraid someone will recognise you? Now, Elsie Porter is dead. Did you know? And you've just missed Mrs Knight's funeral.'

She experienced sadness and gladness in the same moment. She had desperately wanted to see Mrs Knight again, but it was a relief not to have to risk coming face to face with Elsie. He was answering all her questions before she could ask them. Her exercise in tying up loose ends was not going to take long at this rate.

'What did she die of?' she asked.

'Old age I suppose. Oh, do you mean Elsie?'

Hannah nodded.

'Died in hospital suddenly. It must have been, let me see.' He thought for a moment and she noticed that he still had that habit of staring up in the air for inspiration. 'You won't find it written up there, Jack Clayton!' Miss Spencer used to scold.

'About five years ago. Yes, that's right, because it wasn't long after Mr Turner died.'

'Oh dear. Is he dead as well and poor old Mrs Knight? It was her I came to see. I dreamt about her and it seemed like a good idea to come. I suppose I felt guilty at not keeping in touch. She didn't know me in the dream.'

'Still the same old Hannah, dreaming away. When did you have this dream?'

'About five weeks ago.'

'That follows. She had a stroke and didn't know who anybody was after that.'

Hannah sighed. 'She must have been very old. She looked pretty ancient when we were kids.' It was strange that she could visualise her clearly, yet other people's faces in her past had become a blur.

'Look. Just wait here,' Jack said in a gentle voice, bending his head and looking at her downcast face. 'I'll finish closing up. I do it early these days. Everybody knows they can come round to the back if they are desperate, and then we could have a walk round the village. The exercise will do me good and I am the village shopkeeper. I have a right to know all your business.'

'The village shopkeeper! Is this all yours, Jack? I think you have got a lot of explaining to do as well. Here, let me help you with the boxes.'

'You don't lift a finger not in that outfit. I thought you were a model when you walked up.'

'Oh don't be silly, Jack,' Hannah giggled.

She watched him packing up the boxes. It was such a relief to find him alive. Still, if she hadn't heard him speak, she wouldn't have recognised him. She could have passed him in the street. Obviously, it wasn't the sound of his voice. That was very deep now. It was the way he expressed himself. But then she could see the small boy in him. In his eyes, she decided. A greeny-grey, weren't they? Eyes which danced with devilment or could become dark with concern.

'I'll just lock up,' he called, disappearing into the shop. The lock clicked into place. She could see him bending down behind the closed sign and the advertising stickers on the glass door, and heard the bolt being drawn across. A few minutes later he appeared on the side path.

'Right,' he said. 'I'm all yours. Which way do you want to go?'

She pointed in the direction of the school hill and he set off with an enthusiastic surge of energy.

'Hey. Slow down! My legs aren't as long as yours,' Hannah gasped.

'Sorry,' he said, looking down at her. 'I'd forgotten how little you are.'

'I'm not that small. Average actually. You've grown like a beanpole.'

They were like a couple of kids again, and now that she had caught her breath she had the impulse to run up the path, dodging the cracks in the pavement.

'Do you remember when you got shut in the cupboard?' she asked.

'As if I could forget.'

'I bet it was dark in there.'

'You're not kidding. It was like the black hole of Calcutta. I felt as though I was locked away in a little corner of the universe. Everybody sounded miles away.'

Hannah laughed, but not at the humour of it. It was his fanciful way of talking. She could have said that. 'Is she still here?' she asked.

'Miss Spencer, you mean? No. She retired early and had to find somewhere else to live.'

'What about the infant teacher? She was nice.'

'Too nice really. The kids messed her about. She didn't stay long. Her replacement was more of the old school, like Miss Spencer. They were like chalk and chalk. Do you get it? School teachers. Chalk and chalk.'

'I'm a teacher,' Hannah said.

'Whoops! No offence intended.'

'None taken,' she replied primly.

'You don't look like a teacher.'

'I don't feel like one. What does a teacher look like anyway? You only have to say that you're a teacher and people look at you as though you have two heads.'

'Well two heads are better than one,' he joked, feeling that he had offended her.

'What about your family then? Did they get bombed?'

'No, they're still there in the same house. They weren't really bothered about me and I dreaded going back. I wanted the war to go on forever. So when Mr and Mrs Turner offered to adopt me, everyone was happy.'

'They didn't have any children, did they? I can't remember seeing any.'

'Oh, they did. Two sons. Both in the airforce. Didn't you see the photographs? Still, I don't suppose you ever went in the house, did you? They were both aircrew and killed within a few months of each other. It was a dreadful time. Mr Turner never got over it. Neither of them did, but he was not a strong man and died a few years later. So now it's just the two of us.'

They were back to their silent contemplations again, separated by individual thoughts yet still a single entity, keeping in step and detached from their surroundings.

Jack was the first to break the silence. 'Yes, the war certainly did me a good turn. I don't know how I would have ended up. There's the old water pump, look. Obsolete now, and here's the school. Expanded a bit since our day. All mod cons now.'

They followed the path that led to the back of the school, and Hannah gave a shriek of anguish at the sight of Mrs Knight's cottage, totally exposed to public view.

'It is a bit naked, isn't it?' Jack commented. 'Her son's put it on the market.'

'She must be turning in her grave. Did he have to chop everything down?'

'It was almost impossible to walk up the path. You know how elder grows and the birds planted new ones every year. She was a bit like the Sleeping Beauty except that she got the kiss of death, poor old thing.'

'Don't joke about it,' Hannah retorted, anger rising in her voice. 'That little house was the best part of my memories…'

'Sorry,' Jack interrupted, patting her on the shoulder. 'I didn't mean to be flippant. It upsets me as well. George suddenly arrived on the scene a few months before she died. Did you know about him?'

'Yes. Mrs Porter told me he was a bit of a bad lot. I didn't know it was her house.'

'She was a dark horse. I don't think anyone really knew her.'

'But very kind.' Hannah described how Mrs Knight had looked after her when she was ill. 'Goodness knows what was in those concoctions but they worked. I've never had another stye since.'

'Where did you go when you left here?' Jack asked. 'I've often wondered.'

Hannah went into brief details of her re-billeting but didn't mention Margot Sergeant. 'They're both dead now,' she concluded, 'and Ella lives in Northumberland, so I've had to make a new life for myself.'

They'd reached the shortcut to Eastfield Lane and Hannah stopped and turned around.

'Don't you want to go any further?' Jack asked. 'Don't worry about me. I'm not in a hurry.'

'I'm worrying about me. I don't think I can face walking up there.'

'It's all empty, you know. Just an old cottage. Nobody wants to live without mains services these days. It'll put different pictures in your mind. Houses are nothing without people.'

Hannah knew that he was talking sense. It was like seeing a room in daylight after being scared in the dark. This was one of those loose ends. The trouble was, did she have the courage to tie it up?

The ruined house near the little wood was now reduced to a few layers of stone.

'It's gradually disappearing,' Jack explained. 'The roof collapsed and I think people must sneak up and take the stone. It's expensive to buy. Probably it's part of some townie's rockery or garden wall now. I expect they congratulate themselves on tidying up the countryside.'

Hannah wasn't listening. She could see the hawthorn hedge and the sycamore tree further along the lane. They drew closer, and she half expected Sooty to come out calling for milk. The cottage gate, as if tired of hanging on to the post, was propping itself against the hedge. She slowed down, her eyes drawn towards the back door at the end of the path.

Jack went on ahead of her, stepping over thistles, which grew out from the overgrown garden, barring the way. Very tall nettles grew in a large patch near the door, and waved in the light breeze, reaching their stinging leaves towards his face. He picked up an old sweeping brush, which had become half buried in the soil, and beat them to one side. 'Here you are. It's quite safe,' he called back. 'Just a little house.' He knocked jauntily on the door, at the same time saying, ' "Is there anybody there?" said the traveller.'

Hannah had stopped several yards away from the door. 'Don't, Jack,' she said, this time with no anger, only fear showing in her voice.

'Sorry, I always say that when I come past here. I've never forgotten you standing up in front of the class reciting it. You gave me goose pimples.'

'Do you think my ghost is in there listening on the dark stair?'

'Not really, silly. You've got to die first.'

'Well I don't know. I often think we leave part of ourselves. You know, like a fossilised footprint, recording a piece of time.'

'But that's nothing to do with ghosts.' Jack had another go at the nettles, and Hannah wanted to tell him to stop in case he woke the dead.

'Listen, I'm trying to explain,' she said instead. 'Ghosts don't have new hauntings, do they? They don't necessarily haunt where they spend their last days. Perhaps I'm looking down on you from the leaf-fringed sill.' That poem seemed so relevant. She pointed up to the small back window, but daren't raise her eyes.

'The door's open,' Jack said. 'Come on. Stop being so gloomy. There's nothing in there but dust.'

'There was always plenty of that. Don't go in, Jack! Let's go.'

Jack took no notice, pushing the old door open as far as it would go and squeezing through the gap. 'I'm surprised this has been left,' Hannah heard him say. 'I could do with this in my office. A rub down and a lick of paint. Not bad at all.'

Hannah leant forward. 'What is it?' she asked.

'An old chest of drawers. Do you remember it?'

She remembered it well. She could see it clearly in her mind's eye; dark green paint, badly chipped, two small drawers across the top and two full drawers underneath. It seemed to have contained remnants of the whole of Elsie's life.

'No sign of woodworm. The drawer sticks a bit. Oh bugger! Sorry,' he laughed. 'That slipped out with the drawer.' He pulled at the door making the gap wider and pointed to his foot. 'Right on my big toe,' he complained.

'Serves you right,' Hannah whispered, looking fearfully beyond him.

Jack picked up the drawer and struggled to push it back into the space. 'What's stopping it?' he grunted, feeling into the back. 'Oh! No wonder! There's a wad of papers or something. They're letters. Miss Hannah Flynn, c/o Mrs Porter, Eastfield Cottage.'

'Letters for me? You're joking, aren't you?' Hannah gasped.

'Look for yourself.'

Hannah snatched them from his outstretched hand. Her mother's handwriting almost leapt from the first envelope. She stared at it, joy, confusion, disbelief all present at the same time.

'That must bring back some memories,' Jack said, anxious now at the effect such a find might have on her.

'I've never seen them before,' Hannah said in a hoarse little voice. There were two of them, each one addressed in her mother's hand.

'What? You mean you never got them? Do you think they were lost in the post? Or perhaps Elsie didn't want you to be upset after your mother died.' Jack was getting out of his depth.

'How could she, Jack? She's opened them and read them but then hid them away. She knew I was miserable and thinking bad things about my mam.'

One envelope seemed bulkier than the other. She lifted the creased flap and drew out the contents. A photograph of her mother and father appeared smiling at her from a time before war was declared. All those years they had been prisoners in the back of the drawer. Most of the time she had accepted their deaths, but sometimes, when her life lacked stability, it seemed that they had never existed except in her imagination. Now it was as though they had been resurrected, only to be taken away again in a realisation of the reality. But then not her father. It had worried her that she would not be able to identify him if she did catch up with him somewhere. She looked at the image of her mother and suddenly her bereavement was tangible. A dull ache began in the pit of her stomach, tensing into a sharp pain as a deep sob welled up in her throat. 'That woman robbed me,' she said, staring at the photograph. She thought that she had forgotten what they looked like. The memory of their faces had become so elusive, every now and again a fleeting glimpse snatched away in a fraction of a second. But now, as she recognised those familiar features, she knew that their images were locked away in her subconscious. They were part of her and she was part of them—Hannah Flynn, daughter of Martin and Sylvia Flynn. She unfolded the page of writing, seeing mere shapes of black on white through a blur of tears.

Jack put his arm around her to steady her as she swayed in the doorway. Her head began to clear, and she put the photograph and letter back in the envelope, pushing the little bundle into her handbag. She pulled away from Jack's grip and began to walk quickly to the gate. Jack followed her and called her name. She stopped at the gate and began to pick at the peeling paintwork, her fingers agitated and her breathing heavy. Jack was reminded of that day when he had seen that lonely little figure standing with the same posture, her nails chipping at the layer of paint. It was the first time that pity had moved away from himself to someone else and it had always stayed in his mind.

'I don't think she meant to hurt you,' he said gently. 'She desperately wanted a child.' He offered a reassuring hand on her shoulder again.

'Well she wasn't much of a mother, was she?' Hannah replied bitterly. 'What about what I wanted?'

'There are some things you don't know about Elsie. I didn't until a few years ago after she took her own life.'

Hannah drew in her breath sharply at his last words, but then shrugged and pulled away.

'I remember some time after you'd gone,' Jack continued. 'I dropped a few groceries off for her. She didn't usually have deliveries because she never spent much money, but she was ill and as I was going up to the farm anyway, Mrs Turner waived the rules. I was waiting for the money and wishing she would hurry up, when she came out of the living room with a photograph. "This is me and my baby," she said.'

'I remember a photograph she showed me,' Hannah said, her breathing returning to a normal pace. 'But there wasn't a baby on it. I didn't know she ever had a baby.'

'Well I'm coming to that. There wasn't a baby. Just a picture of her when she was a young woman. She was very good looking. I asked her where the baby was and she said that they got rid of it.'

'Who got rid of it?'

'Just listen. I was a bit embarrassed. I was just a kid and nobody talked about pregnancy and that sort of thing then. I didn't tell anybody. I suppose I thought that she was a bit funny in the head and I was scared. There was a lot of talk after you went. Then, what was it? Four, no five years ago, She was rushed to hospital. Mrs Langham found her collapsed with an empty bottle of sleeping tablets, and as I told you, she died there a few hours later. We were all shocked but not really surprised. She had become almost a recluse. Mrs Langham tried to help and sat with her sometimes. Apparently she used to ramble on about the past, and after she died Mrs Langham confided in Mother, Mrs Turner, and this is where the photograph comes in. It seems she was pregnant at the time it was taken, but her parents dosed her with gin and went through all the tried and tested methods to bring on a miscarriage. You know what I mean?'

Hannah nodded. She was shocked at the graphic details. It wasn't really the sort of thing for a man to talk about. What was he going to say next? What else had Mrs Porter told her friend?

Jack didn't seem to have noticed her embarrassment. 'The thing was, her father was responsible,' he continued. Her expression was blank and now he began to feel embarrassed. 'You know.' He waited for a reaction but she still stared with no apparent comprehension. 'He was the father. The father of her baby.' He talked quickly, feeling obliged to finish the story. 'Apparently she couldn't have any children after she married because of the miscarriage, and that's why she wanted to keep you.'

Hannah knew exactly what he was saying. Her blank looks were not from ignorance but from enlightenment, as she stared fixedly into the past. That night in the barn—Elsie crazed with hatred. She could understand now. It was an old hatred, simmering for years and emptying like molten lava through a fault. She knew my fear, she thought. What a torment! She finally had a child to care for but the accompanying guilt was too high a price to pay.

'Of course, Mr Porter setting himself on fire must have been a terrible shock,' Jack was saying.

'Nobody ever knew why, did they?'

'No, that will always be a mystery.'

Hannah turned and looked back at the cottage. Now it dreamed away in the sunshine. Just an old building, enhanced with the unchecked growth of ivy, the garden wild and beautiful with weeds. 'I've changed my mind,' she said. 'I'll just have a little look inside.'

She wandered through the kitchen, avoiding the imagined pig bucket and wellingtons. The living room seemed smaller than she remembered. She went over to the corner and recalled how she loved to watch Elsie crossing her hands as she played her favourite 'Home Sweet Home'. That was her claim to fame. Was it enough? 'I'll never tell about how Tom died,' she whispered. 'It's our secret, Elsie.'

Jack was waiting outside. He didn't speak, and she appreciated his sensitivity. They walked along, back the way they had come. At last, Hannah found her voice as they were nearing the 'Black Wood'. 'It looks so small. I used to run past it. Do you remember?'

'It's been cleared out just recently. It was a tangle of undergrowth in there. You can actually see daylight through it now. I expect that's why it seems smaller, although things do seem smaller years later, don't they?' Relief at a return to everyday topics relaxed his voice, but Hannah's thoughts remained in the past.

'It reminds me of a board game I once had. Do you remember the kind? Landing on square nine meant leaving the road and being side-tracked through the wild woods. There were strange little animals and goblins jumping out. I used to like being diverted, even if it meant losing the game. It was boring keeping to the straight path.'

'Mrs Morris would have tutted at your choice. "Keep to the straight and narrow, children." '

'This is where the Parkers jumped out at me. What are they up to these days?'

'Your guess is as good as mine. They went before the war ended. Their old man used to work for Callums over on the West Ings. Mr Parker was a bit of a rum 'un and got involved with sheep stealing. The police collared the gang and he got the sack, and lost his cottage. It went with the job and so off they all had to go, lock stock and barrel. Nobody missed them. They were at the root of most of the quarrels in the village. Are you intending to settle down or are you a dedicated teacher?'

' I'm moving down south and I don't know what the job prospects are at that end.'

'Down south? Whatever for? I can't imagine you down south. Do you mean London?'

Hannah told him about the reunion with Sally and of their decision to share the flat.

'How do you know you'll get on? Don't you think it ought to be on a trial basis? There's a lot of water gone under the bridge since you were kids.'

No more than you and me, she nearly said, and then thought that was foolish of her. She wasn't contemplating sharing a flat with him. 'She hasn't changed,' she said instead. 'She was always courageous and independent. Some people might take it as brashness, but she's the kind of person who grasps life by the horns.' She knew she was exaggerating Sally's attributes.

'But you've only spent one day with her. She can't always be like that. I've found that those kind of people can be very moody.'

'You don't know her. I've read her book. I can tell. Anyway the dominoes always fit together.'

He gave up trying to follow her reasoning. 'Oh well. It's your decision,' he muttered.

Yes, she thought. It was her decision. She was in charge of her life. She had made up her mind. She stepped a little to one side, a physical gesture distancing herself from outside interference, suddenly irritated by his familiarity.

'Sorry,' he apologised, sensing her change of mood. 'Now, there's a view for you. Does that bring back memories?'

'It would make a good jigsaw puzzle,' she said. 'Do you like doing jigsaws? I always think life's like a puzzle. Important bits and dull bits like people, and lost pieces making holes in the pattern.'

'That's a bit profound for me,' he said, laughing. 'What am I in your picture then? A bit of grey sky?'

'No. You would be more important. An edge perhaps or a corner.' Hannah felt sorry for sounding so irritable and suddenly wanted to please.

'What's all this about "would be"? I'm one of your oldest friends.'

'You know what I mean. Anyway, it's just one of my silly ideas.'

'What are you in my jigsaw then?'

She didn't answer, becoming aware that she must sound very egotistical.

'Well?' he persisted.

'Oh, it's a stupid idea. We are all part of one big picture.'

'Yes but how do you see yourself?'

'I don't know! A tree on the horizon.' She said the first thing that came into her head but her answer was very revealing.

Jack was determined to bring her closer. 'My scene isn't a landscape. I'm not one to wander. I think it'll have to be a garden full of beautiful flowers. What's your favourite flower?'

'That's easy. A corn poppy. I love the colour. One day I'm going to paint a poppy picture.'

They had reached the end of the shortcut now, and once more the sight of Mrs Knight's cottage encouraged conversation about the past.

'Did she give you seed cake?'

'No, but I remember the carrot cake. I ate a hell of a lot of it, but never did get the hang of seeing in the dark.' He looked at his watch.

'What time is it? I don't want to miss my bus.'

'Oh there's no panic. I can give you a lift back. I'll have to go in soon and get a meal sorted. You can stay and have some tea with us, can't you?'

They broke into a brisk walk down the steep hill, leaving Hannah with little breath for conversation, concentrating instead on Jack's spasmodic running commentary.

'Come and see the back way before we go in,' he said as they reached the shop. He pointed to the path that ran along the side of the building.

Hannah was curious. A high gate had always blocked the view of the back way. 'You didn't say it was a field,' she chided. 'Fancy having a big garden like this and not doing anything with it. I love gardening but all I've got these days is a window box.'

'You look the sort to have green fingers, when they're not covered in chalk Unfortunately it just can't be a priority with me. The shop and house take up most of my time. But one day I would like to spend a lot more time out in the fresh air.'

'I don't have much time either these days. I talk to my window-box flowers sometimes. It's supposed to make them grow.'

'I can just imagine you,' he laughed. 'They don't know their tables, do they?'

'Oh don't remind me of teaching,' Hannah said, thinking of David, whose image still hovered like a black cloud in the back of her mind. Her eyes focused on an old stone building that marked the right-hand boundary of the garden, and she asked if it belonged to the shop. Jack explained that it was once the bake house in the days when Mr Turner's father provided bread for the village. Now, it was used for general storage purposes. 'Come and have a look,' he said, pushing open the stout old door.

Hannah sniffed at the familiar smell of old mortar and dusty stones. 'What a wonderful building!' she exclaimed. 'It must be very old. Do you think it could have been stables once? You can almost smell the horses.'

'The floor in the next part is cobbled. It could well have been stabling.' Jack opened a door and led the way into the adjoining area. 'There's an old friend of yours in here,' he said.

'An old friend? Whatever do you mean?'

296

'Over there, look.' He pointed to a deep windowsill.

Hannah's eyes followed the direction of his finger and then she squealed with excitement. 'Oh! It isn't, is it? How long have you had it?' She ran over to the window and rubbed her hand down the back of the white pottery cat.

Jack shared her excitement, grinning with delight. 'I rescued it from the bottom of a box of jumble. When Mrs Knight's adopted son George came to claim the cottage, he brought a box of oddments in and asked me if I was interested. I suppose he thought I could sell them. He was happy with a quid. Most of it was of little value. You can bet your life anything valuable went in the back of his van. Most of the jumble will come in useful for the white elephant stall at the fete, but I decided that that was no place for a white cat. Not this white cat at any rate.'

'It's Mrs Knight's Mooncat, isn't it? Did you know it's a Mooncat?'

'Yes of course. I used to whisper in its ear like you did.'

'How did you know that?'

'The old lady told me. I think she talked about you every time I went.'

'Do you believe in predestination, Jack? Everything planned?' She didn't wait for an answer. 'I can't believe that all the things which have happened are by chance. If I hadn't seen Sally's photograph I wouldn't have come here today. She said that I ought to come back. And then I wouldn't have found the letters or the Mooncat. Don't you think it's strange?'

And you wouldn't have seen me again, Jack thought.

'Mrs Knight used to say that the Dream Maker knows best. Sally thinks we have freedom of choice. I'm not sure,' Hannah continued.

'I think I agree with Sally,' Jack said. 'Although I know what you mean. Perhaps it's like that board game of yours. The roll of the dice.'

'Do you think so?' Hannah considered that for a moment before saying, 'Yes, but then who's controlling the dice?' She turned her eyes away from the cat and looked at Jack. 'It's fascinating, isn't it? When we start looking back, the past seems to leap forward to meet us, almost as though lines are drawn from one thing to another.'

He was staring at her, his eyes dark in concentration, and she turned away, suddenly embarrassed. 'You must think I'm a bit crazy,' she said.

'I think you are—very interesting.'

They both turned towards the door at the same time, knocking into each other and apologising. 'Better get in,' he murmured. 'Mother gets miserable on her own.'

How easily he calls her mother, Hannah thought as she followed him into the house. Still, she almost made that claim when Matron told her about Aunt Kate. People who mothered were entitled to be mother figures. Poor Elsie! She had desperately craved that recognition.

Mrs Turner looked frail. The dark-rimmed glasses, which had appeared so intimidating in the past, were now replaced with steel-rimmed ones, matching her grey hair and taking away the fierceness of her expression. However, there was still vigour in her voice.

'You didn't tell me we had a visitor, Jack,' she said, waiting for an introduction.

'You'll never guess who it is.' Jack beckoned Hannah forwards towards the armchair.

'It's not your sister, is it?' Mrs Turner asked, peering short-sightedly at Hannah. Her tone implied little pleasure at the prospect of entertaining anyone from that family, perhaps fearing latent loyalty.

'No, but she is a ghost from the past. You remember Hannah Flynn, don't you? That little evacuee who got me into trouble.' He turned apologetically to Hannah and winked. 'Sorry,' he said. 'Just jogging her memory.'

'You don't have to jog anything, thank you,' Mrs Turner retorted. 'It's lovely to see you again, Hannah. I've often wondered what became of you.'

'She's a school teacher now, Mother, so we'll have to watch our Ps and Qs.'

'I'm not at all surprised. This one didn't do so bad, you know, once he stopped playing the fool. I'd be lost without him. Jack, go and open a tin of salmon. Do you like salmon, dear? You're not still living on bread and jam, are you?'

'How did you know that?' Hannah asked.

'Nothing ever escapes her,' Jack called from the kitchen.

Hannah fed Mrs Turner's curiosity with brief details of her life and then of the surprises of the day.

'Fancy that!' the elderly lady exclaimed as she looked at the photograph of Hannah's parents. 'I can see a family likeness. A bit of both I think. That was very wrong of Elsie Porter, but then she wasn't thinking straight, was she? Still, we can't turn the clock back.' She glanced across at the photographs of her two sons and her husband, and for a moment her face saddened. Hannah wanted to reach forward and hold her hand, but already Mrs Turner was back in the present.

'Come on, Jack,' she called. 'You're not having to catch that salmon, are you? He's a good boy, you know. A great blessing to me.' Her voice dropped to a whisper. She seemed to shrink with her voice as she leant forward and Hannah noticed the gauntness of her jaw and shoulders.

'Here you are,' Jack announced. 'Now just stop talking, Mother, and get one of these sandwiches down you. You know what the doctor said.'

Hannah, at least, pleased him with her appetite and she didn't spoil it by disclosing that it was the first substantial food of the day. Mrs Turner was amazed at her guest's request for three sugars in her tea. 'How do you manage to stay so slim?' she asked. 'It was always a losing battle with me, although I think at last I'm getting a decent figure.'

She laughed, but Jack did not share the joke, offering her another slice of cake. She shook her head. 'Well you will, won't you, Hannah? It'll only go stale.'

Cake was never a problem and Hannah helped herself to another large slice. 'Did you ever have seed cake, Mrs Turner?' she asked between mouthfuls of the thick sponge cake.

The conversation turned to the past again and the eccentricities of the late Mrs Knight.

'She was a kind old lady,' Mrs Turner said. 'And she thought the world of you two. "Two of a kind," she used to say. What do you think she meant? Perhaps that you were both evacuees.' Her eyes twinkled behind her spectacles.

'She could see a lot more than most, couldn't she, Hannah?' Jack commented, and Hannah felt the colour rising in her face and turned her eyes away from the dark look in his.

'Is that the time? I'll have to be going. Let me help to clear away,' she gabbled.

'Stay the night if you like. Unless you have plans for this evening. That would be all right, wouldn't it, Mother?'

Mrs Turner nodded, but Hannah could see the signs of fatigue in her face.

'No, Jack. Thanks all the same. I don't want to outstay my welcome. In any case, I've booked a room for the night. Just an elderly couple earning a few extra pounds I think. She'll have made the bed up now. I want to make an early start in the morning. There's a train at half past nine.' She could hear her words coming out in short bursts, and began to stack the plates to cover her embarrassment.

'You must come again,' Mrs Turner said, generous now in her relief. 'Give us some warning next time, and we can get the spare room aired.'

'And don't make it another fifteen years.' Jack's mouth lifted at the corners, but his eyes were unsmiling, an expression which made Hannah's stomach give a little jolt. She stood up, holding the plates, and turned to go into the kitchen. 'You don't have to do that, silly. Guests aren't expected to do the dishes.' His hand brushed against hers as he took the plates and put them down on the table. The pressure of his arm on her back when he led her to the settee near the window had a kind of paralysing effect on her leg muscles, and she sank down quickly into the soft cushions, straightening her skirt over her knees.

Mrs Turner drifted off into her after tea nap, and Hannah became aware of a change in the atmosphere. He had been the Jack of her childhood, an old friend remembering the past. Now, she felt that he was a stranger; someone new in her life, an unknown quantity. Their conversation became strained and polite, and she fidgeted uneasily, pulling at the sleeve of her blouse and pushing back her hair. She was fearful of letting her eyes meet his. The clock struck the half-hour.

'What's that? Half past six? I think I'll have to go soon, if you don't mind,' she said, getting to her feet.

Jack didn't argue. 'We'll leave her to finish her nap,' he said. 'I should be back by the time she wakes up.'

Hannah was disappointed at his compliance. He made no effort to help her on with her jacket, and stood waiting at the door, jangling his car keys in his fingers.

'Say goodbye to Mrs Turner for me.'

He put his fingers to his lips and closed the door quietly after her. They drove in silence for a while. Hannah was aware of his every movement. She studied his hands on the steering wheel, strong and sure of direction. Eventually, she chose a topic well removed from herself and her plans.

'Mrs Turner looks so tired, I didn't want to be a bother to her. You mentioned the doctor. What's the problem?'

Jack didn't answer for a moment and braked hard at the next bend in the road. 'That's a tight one,' he said. 'They are supposed to be straightening that bit soon. Mother has cancer.' His voice had become harsh with emotion and he cleared his throat.

'Oh. I'm sorry, Jack. I wish you had told me. She must have been very tired with my chatter.'

'Not at all. She needs all the pleasure she can get.'

'Does she know?'

'I think so. No one has said anything but you can see that she tries hard to put a brave face on things. Life would be hell for her without regular pain killers. I expected some opposition when I got Mrs Dexter to come in and do some cleaning but she never said a word. Oh yes. I'm sure she knows what it is.'

Jack lit up a cigarette and wound down the window. They had reached the edge of the town now and he concentrated on navigating the traffic lights and the narrow roads finally pulling up outside the guest house. 'I hope it's comfortable,' he said. 'It looks a bit of a dump.'

'It'll be okay. It's only for one night.'

They were talking like strangers again. Hannah didn't want to get out of the car. Loneliness was so threatening. He turned suddenly and grasped her hand. 'Give me a ring. Hang on a minute. Let me write down our phone number.' He fished in his pocket for a pen, and scribbled on the back of a card given to him at some time by a commercial traveller. 'There. Let me know you have got there safely.'

She meant to say that she would, but heard her voice resorting to flippancy. 'I am used to travelling on my own, you know. I'm not a little girl now.'

He got out of the car and went round to open the door. 'Here we are, madam. That will be three and six, please.' There was no humour in his voice.

'I will ring you,' she called as he accelerated away, but she wasn't sure if he'd heard her. She stood for a few moments caught up in a kind of limbo; his abrupt departure on one side and the brown closed door on the other.

'Come in, duck,' the landlady said. 'I'll be having a cuppa later on if you want to come down. I usually wait until gone eight after my other half nods off.'

The narrow old staircase was steep and Hannah sank down gasping on the edge of the bed and looked around her. She was used to austerity. Her flat was sparsely furnished, but there was a wholesomeness about it. This room was reminiscent of Eastfield Cottage, depressingly drab, the air stale with a mixture of tobacco smoke and body odour.

Such reflections reminded her of the letters. She'd forgotten about them. How could she? She read the first one, finding no response to her cries for help. 'I'm glad you like Mr and Mrs Porter,' she read. 'The house sounds posh.' She couldn't remember saying that! It continued with a brief description of her job and ended with Sally's address. The second letter, the one which included the photograph, chided her for her handwriting and spelling. 'I hope you are not falling behind with your work. Is it just a little village school?'

Suddenly it dawned on Hannah. Of course, Elsie had re-written the letters. She must have opened her letters, not liked the contents and substituted ones of her own. Now she came to think about it she had never actually seen the letters put into the hands of the postman. No wonder she had hidden the replies. What a tangled web of deceit!

She felt sick and sticky with the heat of the room and went over to open the window. The sash cord hung down at one side, frayed and defunct, and no amount of lifting would move the lower sash. The top sash was firmly embedded in a layer of old paint. Hannah sighed and looked through the dirty glass at the back ways of the terraced houses. A pot of daffodils crouching in a corner looked completely alien to its surroundings. Like a good deed in a wicked world, she thought, and wondered how people could live surrounded by so much decaying junk. Beyond the walled concrete enclosures was a car park and the bus station. She had a mental picture of red poppies and then grey eyes, flecked with green.

She sank back on to the bed and pulled her book out of her bag, turning the pages with little interest. Finally, after reading one sentence three times in an attempt to follow the plot, she gave up. A sound outside drew her back to the window. Mrs 'Duck' was pushing rubbish into the already overflowing dustbin. Hannah felt a desperate need for company and went slowly down the stairs, listening for sounds beyond the living room door. The 'other half' was snoring. It must be gone eight o'clock, she thought and wondered which was worse, misery or snoring. The matter was resolved by the old woman coming into the passage and looking up the stairs.

'I thought I heard you coming down. I'm just putting the kettle on. I expect you're ready for a cuppa. I know I am. Dry as the Sahara desert.' She laughed, her lips drawing back and displaying false teeth and a lot of gum. 'We'll be best in the kitchen with him snoring like a pig.'

The kitchen, which projected into the back yard, had a view of the boundary wall, old red brick, coated at the bottom with green mould.

'Are you on holiday, duck?' the woman asked, as she poured the dark brown liquid from the large aluminium teapot.

'No. Just the weekend,' Hannah replied, not wanting to go into details. 'I'm going to London soon,' she added, with a sudden desire to impress.

Her hostess obliged with interest. 'My word! That's a long way! I've never been myself, but I had a friend who went once. She didn't care much for it. Too many people, she said. No. I like it here. It's good enough for me.'

Her negativity prompted Hannah to enthuse, although she was having misgivings about it all. 'I'm going to stay with a friend,' she said. 'Well actually, she's a novelist. Quite famous in fact. I'm going to help her with her next book.'

'Well I never! Now that's something I couldn't do if you paid me an 'undred pounds.'

Hannah choked back a giggle and stored the words up to entertain Sally. 'I've got lots of things to do and places to see before I settle down,' she said, watching the landlady pouring herself another cup of tea.

'There's nothing like a cup of tea. You could travel round the world and not find nothing better than a cup of tea. Mind you, a glass of stout takes some beating, especially with a game of cards in the local. Why make life hard? That's what I say.'

Mrs 'Duck' rambled on about the strength and failings of her drinking companions, inducing in Hannah a need to detach herself from the human race. She yawned and got to her feet. 'If you don't mind I'll go up now, Mrs er…'

'Onyon dear. That's onion with a "y" .'

Hannah choked back another giggle. The word onion was closely followed by shallot in her train of thought. Suddenly a clear image of Elsie Porter in her tweed coat and curlers, and walking down the garden path like a bizarre Sir Lancelot, came into her mind. She was back at the little bedroom window at Eastfield Cottage. That was still a sobering thought in spite of recent revelations. Whatever had kept that picture so clearly in her head, she wondered, and the answer came back instantly. She had become familiar with the poem

'The Lady of Shalott', on the day before news of her mother's death. The poem was of death and tragedy. She pressed her fingers against the bulkiness of the envelopes in her handbag. Life, at the moment, was going round in circles it seemed. Or had she landed on square nine and was following the twisting path to where the strange goblins lived?

29

Alice and the White Rabbit

The night had become morning before her brain gave up contemplating the events of the day, and she awoke with the sound of a rapping on the bedroom door, accompanied by a voice announcing that breakfast was in a quarter of an hour. Her ears, which had been closed to all sounds, were suddenly aware of traffic and the twittering of sparrows under the eaves. After a cursory splash of water on her hands and face in the grubby little bathroom, she went downstairs. She could smell the frizzled bacon before she reached the ground floor.

'Just in time,' Mrs Onyon declared. 'Another five minutes and it would all have spoiled.'

The undercooked egg, swimming in grease and slithering on the plate next to two strips of hard bacon was enough to deter the strongest stomach. The sweet tea and toast were a help, but even so most of the egg had spread out into a congealed layer when she put her knife and fork down.

'Not much of an appetite,' Mrs Onyon said reproachfully. 'Here you are, you little tinker. You're in luck today.' She put the plate down on the floor, and Hannah watched as a small brown mongrel licked it clean. 'That won't take much washing up now,' Mrs Onyon cackled.

It wasn't long before Hannah paid her bill and was on the other side of the front door breathing in the comparatively sweet smell of exhaust fumes from a passing car. The summer Sunday morning had an air of pleasurable expectancy, and she relaxed as she walked slowly along the road. She stared at a display of ladies' fashions in an impressive double-fronted shop, and was reminded of the need to extend her 'wardrobe' for the move down south. The thought of it was worrying. She wasn't sure whether Sally really wanted her to move in. One or two little comments, the tone in her voice, seemed to imply some reluctance and regret. Perhaps she was just feeling sorry for her. Perhaps the lame-dog tag was showing. Probably she was laughing now about the Mooncat. Anyway, she didn't want to go. She didn't really know where she did want to go. A little voice in her head said, 'You want to go back to Cragthorpe.' She couldn't do that—not today at any rate. Besides, no doubt he had a girl friend, a good looking bloke like him. They hadn't discussed relationships. She moved away from the clothes shop and stared aimlessly into a shoe shop. The chimes of the town hall clock alerted her to the passing of time. 'Oh no,' she gasped when she reached it, 'twenty past nine!'

Many railway stations, by nature of their comparatively recent development, are a good walk from the town centre, and this one was no exception. By the time she reached the ticket office the train was steaming out.

'Eleven thirty-five duck,' the ticket man said in reply to her query. 'The buffet's open. You've got plenty of time for a four-course meal!'

Hannah didn't respond to his humour and, with the overdone bacon and the greasy egg still lying heavily on her stomach, she shunned the buffet and sat in the general waiting room. The station no longer fascinated her with its importance in her past. It was now very much in the present with its dreary green and cream paint and hard seats putting nothing good into new memory.

As the hands of the clock moved nearer to the scheduled time of the next train arrival on the north-bound line, people began to arrive, their chatter and movements energising the atmosphere and encouraging Hannah to stretch her legs and find a place on the platform. The 'voice' came over the tannoy system, and at first there was a general disregard for what seemed like a routine announcement, until the word 'cancelled' triggered a ripple of silence. The message was repeated. 'The eleven-thirty-five train calling at Doncaster and Newcastle has been cancelled owing to unforeseen problems on the line.'

There were a few moans and sarcastic comments about the service and one man, with a bristling moustache and an air of leadership, strode across to the ticket office 'to get an explanation' as he called back to his companions. Soon, 'the explanation' had passed from one to another and Hannah learnt that there had been a major accident and all trains on the main line going north were not continuing beyond Grantham. Apparently, there would be an announcement as soon as suitable arrangements could be made.

Half an hour later it transpired that the only solution, bearing in mind that it was Sunday, would be for passengers to take the local train to Lincoln at two ten, and travel from there to Doncaster on whatever trains were scheduled to run. 'It'll take hours,' the man with the moustache said. 'These little country trains meander all over the place.'

He was right, as it seemed he always was, and Hannah shouldn't have been surprised to see familiar landscape as the train rattled along the tracks. 'I was here yesterday,' she said to the woman sitting next to her. 'It's like *Alice Through the Looking Glass,* isn't it?' The woman paused halfway through knit two and looked up quizzically. 'You know,' Hannah said, 'Alice on the train never seeming to get anywhere.'

'I suppose so,' the woman replied with a kind of shrug in her voice returning to her knitting.

Hannah leant forward to look for familiar fields and buildings. She could see the top of the church spire and one or two outlying farms, but the rest of the village lay hidden in the fold of the land. She had a fleeting urge to jump off the train but common sense prevailed.

There was much starting and stopping, changing trains and waiting for connections before she sank wearily into a taxi on the last stage of her journey. The taxi ride was an indulgence she couldn't afford. She could have had ten bus rides for the amount she was charged.

The lift was working and that was a blessing. The flat had a deserted chill to it, and she turned the gas fire full on before making a strong pot of tea. In spite of her earlier protests, it was good to be back in her own domain. She took off her shoes and stretched back in the chair. Within minutes, she was asleep, the cup of tea untouched at her feet.

It was dark when she forced open her eyes, which felt heavy and sore in the overheated atmosphere. For a moment, she couldn't think where she was. The room was dark except for the glow from the fire. She stumbled across the floor, narrowly avoiding the cold cup of tea, and pressed down the light switch. Her weekend case and the carrier bag containing the parcelled-up pot cat were just inside the door.

'Jack!' she exclaimed. What time was it? The alarm clock had stopped in her absence and she opened the outside door and looked across the landing. Her neighbour's door was slightly ajar and then opened wide as a lady came out with her empty milk bottles.

'Time? It's just gone half past ten,' Mrs Humphreys replied in response to Hannah's query. 'You look terrible. You ought to get an early night.'

Gone half past ten! Mrs Turner would be in bed. Jack wouldn't thank her for ringing up at this time of night. It would take another ten minutes to get to the phone. If she'd not indulged in that taxi she could have got off the bus at the stop near the phone box. Now he would think that she didn't care.

In spite of her neighbour's comments, those three hours of sleep had taken the edge off her tiredness, and she did everything she could think of to pass the time until she felt sufficiently tired to sleep. Finally, at a little after one, she and the cat went into the bedroom. She put her old friend on the windowsill and whispered a request for a special dream. 'I'll leave it up to you,' she said, turning it around to face the black sky.

As dawn approached, she dreamt of Jack who seemed to be

somewhere in front, and she ran and ran, trying to catch up with his disappearing figure. Things kept happening to slow her up, and then she became Alice and Jack became the White Rabbit, running and running but always ending up in the same place.

She woke up in a panic, her eyes flying open. It was daylight. Now what time was it? 'The time is seven-thirty,' said the radio. She threw on her clothes and bolted a thick slice of bread and jam, chewing the last remnants of it as she ran to the phone box.

Jack answered the phone, and the sound of his voice made the adrenaline rush to join the bread and jam in her stomach.

'Hannah!' he yelled. 'I've been worried sick about you. Where are you? Were you injured in the crash?'

'No Jack. Listen! I wasn't on that train. I got the next one.'

'Oh thank God! I rang up but no one could tell me anything. Was it one of your premonitions?'

'No. I lost count of the time. You know what I'm like. The train was just leaving when I got to the station. We were re-routed all over the place. We actually came through Cragthorpe. I nearly got off. Anyway, by the time I got home it was gone seven and I collapsed for three hours and then I thought you would be in bed.'

'I think your guardian angel made you miss the train. I hardly slept a wink and when I did I was looking for you in my dream.'

'You were the White Rabbit in mine.' His concern for her was so uplifting that Hannah wanted to laugh and cry both at the same time.

'Can you come over again before you go to London?' he asked.

'I'm not going now. You were right. It's not the place for me.'

'No. You would be like a fish out of water. Come next weekend then and bring your paint box. I've asked some tulips if they will pose for you and they've promised to stand up straight.' His voice was full of laughter now.

'Yes but do they know their seven times table?' Hannah joked.

She almost skipped back to the flat, and ran up the stairs as lightly as a child. The postman had delivered a letter. She studied the postmark. It was from Sally, she guessed with a twinge of guilt. The brief note, obviously hurriedly written, explained that Paul had come back into her life and all was forgiven. His job was being re-located to Manchester, and she was going with him. 'I'm sorry our plans have been disrupted,' she wrote. 'We must meet up again as soon as I am organised.'

Hannah smiled and looked across at the Mooncat. 'I'd already made up my own mind, hadn't I? It was my decision, wasn't it?'

The Mooncat made no reply of course, but continued to stare with eyes as big as saucers, over the chimney pots and into the future.

30

The Magic Mooncat

It was Hannah Clayton's fiftieth birthday and, sharing the company of her daughter-in-law Sarah, she was suddenly feeling her age. Sarah was American, good-looking and with all the sureness of a modern-day young woman. Hannah knew, without any need for physical proof, that Sarah would look smart in an old sweater and shabby jeans. She was just that kind of a girl. They had it all made for them, Hannah thought. A relationship where marriage was optional even with a child, and then when they thought the time was right, a stylish wedding and a no-expenses-spared honeymoon.

Mark was with his father on a tour of the grounds, and young Leigh was having an afternoon nap upstairs in the family cot, which had been retrieved from the loft.

Sarah, armed with what Hannah had heard was a typical American preoccupation, was keen to explore Mark's roots as she put it. At her request, Hannah had unearthed the old family photograph album. They hadn't looked at it for years.

'Are they in chronological order?' Sarah asked.

Hannah nodded.

'Well then. Let's start at the beginning,' her daughter-in-law enthused, pressing the clip open on the small brass lock. 'Men are hopeless about such things, aren't they? All they seem to care about is today and tomorrow.'

'My father and mother. 1939 I think,' Hannah said. The faces of her parents looked out at her from the past, held now in the grip of the pages rather than in an envelope in the confines of Elsie's chest of drawers.

'Ah 1939. That's a date to remember. Mark told me about the bomb, but that was later, wasn't it. I'm a bit vague about the war. Sorry, I hope this isn't upsetting you.' She hesitated and Hannah was heartened by the show of sensitivity. However, Sarah didn't wait for any response. 'You must have been so sad. I can't imagine life without my mother. And then your father losing his memory for such a long time. Gosh! I can see Leigh in him. That's what I mean about investigating the past and tracing ancestors.'

The thought of her father as an ancestor made Hannah feel older than half a century. Now Sarah had turned the page to reveal the wedding photographs. Hannah pushed back her hair nervously in anticipation of probing questions. All the family, except for Jack of course who knew the truth, believed her story about her father losing his memory. It had always been her favourite solution to the mystery right from the end of the war, and the explanation fell readily from her lips. What was the point of telling them that their grandfather had been hell bent on destroying himself with alcohol? Jessie was a godsend, an angel or a good fairy whatever was one's belief, and by the time Jack found Martin's name on the City Hall registers, he was restored to rationality.

'Who are these people? Hannah! You're miles away.'

'Oh sorry. It's years since I had this out. Those were my evacuation parents, Kate and Harry Churchill and that's Ella. They were all so kind and loving.' Hannah smiled in memory of those happy days—memories no longer clouded by the intolerance of youth.

'So that's Ella. Mark wants to take me to see her. You're right. I mean Mark does look upon her as a grandma. North Country isn't she, wherever that is?'

'Very much so now, although she was Lincolnshire born and bred.'

'And this old lady. Is she on Jack's side of the family?' Sarah pointed to Mrs Turner.

'Yes, his mother.'

'He doesn't favour her, does he? Is he more like his father?'

'I don't really know,' Hannah said truthfully. Oh dear, she thought. This was weaving into quite a little web of deceit. It wasn't the right time to explain about Jack's natural family, especially as Jack's father died in prison.

'And the black woman. What did she have to do with the wedding party?'

Hannah's shoulders stiffened. 'That's my stepmother, Jessica. She's lovely. Only a few years older than me. More like a sister.'

'Really! Mark never told me.'

'That's Patrick,' Hannah continued quickly. 'The little boy on the front row. He's my half-brother. He was only three then so he's very close in age to Mark. Little monkey! He used to insist on being called uncle.'

'So that's Patrick Flynn. Mark has mentioned him. I somehow had the idea that he was Irish with a name like that but obviously not.'

'No. He's Yorkshire,' Hannah said sharply. 'Like me and proud of it. He's good to his mother and always keeps in touch. Jessica has gone back to full-time nursing since my father died last year and Patrick has become the man of the house.'

'Oh I see.' Sarah's gaze moved on to the honeymoon snaps and Hannah felt a growing sense of irritation. 'So this is the old family business.' Her daughter-in-law had turned the page and was now studying a photograph of Hannah and Jack standing in front of the shop. Hannah nearly pointed out that it was the day that the sign writer had replaced 'Turner's Village Stores' with 'J.& H. Clayton'. They'd left the name-changing for a long time. Jack said it would be like dancing on her grave. She'd best keep quiet about that. 'That was the year Mark was born,' she said instead. 'He was hiding at the time.'

'I can see that. He must have been a big baby. It looks like any minute now!'

They both giggled and Hannah relaxed.

'It didn't put you off then,' Sarah said. 'Did you want four children?'

'Oh yes. I always said I would have four. Two of each.'

'And you did. How clever of you. One's enough for me. Pregnancy takes over your life, doesn't it? All the check-ups and tests and those wretched antenatal classes.' She rolled her eyes in comic disapproval.

Hannah suddenly was reminded of Sally, and she couldn't resist poking fun at this brave new world. 'We didn't go in for all that puffing and panting. I had all my babies at home and we just let nature take its course. I didn't even know what to expect when I had Mark. It was all a bit of a taboo subject.'

'Really! Oh of course, I was forgetting. Things are a bit behind here.'

Hannah smiled. 'Well we are talking about the 'fifties. We hadn't reached the swinging 'sixties, and by the time we did, it passed me by unnoticed. I was knee-deep in children and teaching part-time. Life didn't really change much in the country.'

Sarah nodded in agreement, as though that was perfectly understandable in these back woods. 'I had everything I could at the birth. If it had been invented, I had it. But I still screamed my head off. Never again.'

'Oh, I quite enjoyed giving birth. It was so exciting seeing a new human being after all those months of waiting. Although I must admit the first time was a bit daunting. An old customer of ours told me it was like being constipated.'

Sarah screamed with laughter at the idea, and tears of hysteria ran down her cheeks. 'That must be the understatement of the century,' she gasped, carefully dabbing the tears away with her handkerchief.

'I'll tell you something else that'll make you laugh. She told me that my illness would soon be in my arms.'

Sarah looked baffled.

'She meant the baby,' Hannah explained. 'The baby was the illness.'

'Good God! What ignorance!'

'Not really. She'd had ten children. She knew what it was all about, I can tell you. It was the old strict code of decorum. A kind of indirectness and sensitivity. My own mother would have been a little shocked at my profile on this photo, and my grandmother would have been outraged.'

Sara didn't look convinced, and returned to her own suffering. 'It was the postnatal depression that floored me. That's the worst bit, isn't it?'

'I never had that. It hadn't been invented in my day.' Hannah's eyes twinkled at Sarah's sheepish look.

'You sound just like my mother,' the young woman protested with a wry twist of her mouth. 'Who is this then?' She had flipped over the page and Sally's face merging into the yellowing shabbiness of the leaflet, was given a rare public airing.

'An old friend.'

Sarah read the details of the book signing. 'Interesting,' she commented. 'Does she still write?'

Hannah shrugged. 'Probably. I've lost touch, but no doubt our paths will cross again one day.'

'Ah. I can recognise Mark in this one. He hasn't changed much, and you can see he and Simon are brothers. But the girls are different, aren't they?'

'Yes. Rachel favours my mother and Emma is more like I was at her age.'

'You must have been very pretty. You still look good. Nowhere near fifty. More like-well—forty-five at the most.'

And I hoped it was forty, Hannah thought ruefully. 'That one was taken just after we came here.'

'Oh yes. What made you sell the shop?'

Hannah explained how they were very cramped living over the top of the shop, and that Jack had always wanted to work in the fresh air. Shop hours were so long, and gardening, which was his favourite occupation, had to take a back seat. 'Then we went camping down south and had a walk around a garden centre. It was something new for us. Jack had a long chat with the owners and came back fired with enthusiasm, and a few months later we moved here.'

'I guess it was a miracle you found this place,' Sarah said. 'It's just perfect and what a success you've made of it. It would be worth a small fortune back home. It's so old and fascinating.'

Just then Mark rapped on the window. 'Dad wants you to see his prize chrysanths, Sarah,' he called, pressing his mouth on the kitchen window.

'Excuse me,' Sarah said. 'Don't put it away. Oh, and be a pal and listen out for Leigh. He usually only gives me an hour's peace.'

Leigh. That's a posh name, she thought. *'Did your mam get it out of a book?'* For a few seconds Hannah's thoughts were back in Eastfield Cottage hearing Tom Porter's words and seeing his red grinning face. She shuddered and flipped the pages of the album back to the wedding photograph. How young they looked and what a strange kind of family history the children had inherited. Somewhat twisted roots, she thought wryly. It was quite a hybrid family tree; a mother, three foster mothers and a stepmother, a father who came back from the dead, a foster father who died in apparently mysterious circumstances and another foster father who was bewitched. And the added bonus of a half-brother. Then on Jack's side, two lots of parents, two unknown foster brothers, and the siblings whom he had 'buried' in his past.

Clever to have had two of each, Sarah said. Did I know that I would have four children, she wondered, or was it a case of self-fulfilled prophecy? But two of each. She'd had no control over that.

And there was Sally again. She hadn't thought of her for a long time. Sarah reminded her so much of her old friend. She flashed across my life like a comet, she thought. Would she return or was she a catalyst pointing in the direction of Jack and then disappearing forever? The trouble was that neither of them knew where the other was. How long had the gap in their relationship been before? Between 1941 and 1955. That was fourteen years. Well one orbit had gone and the next one was due next year. She smiled at her fancifulness but nevertheless popped it into her 'memory cupboard'.

She was back to her thoughts of predestination. Nowadays her ideas were beset with conflicting philosophies. The concept of predestination worked wonderfully if it was based on one's own life, but became impossible when it involved the rest of humanity. Could she seriously believe that Tom and Elsie Porter were born merely to influence her life? If she hadn't lived with them for those few months they wouldn't have died so early, or would they? Surely not in the way that they did. If Hitler had never existed, then she wouldn't have known any of them and she wouldn't be here with Jack. Did her mother die in war-time so that all this could happen? No. She couldn't consider herself queen and everyone else pawns in her destiny. What about the chaos theory? A book she had read recently was totally unconvincing. Evolution was all right up to a point, but could all the millions of different forms of life evolve from a series of genetic accidents? Which came first, the chicken or the egg? Perhaps it was a bit of both; chaos interspersed with divine intervention.

She turned the pages of the album, smiling at a holiday snap of them all up at Ella's house. Mrs Knight said that life was all a dream and the reality was yet to come. Perhaps the reality would be the knowledge. She'd never forgotten the old lady's words—the Dream Maker, the captain. 'Do you mean God?' she remembered asking. The reply had puzzled her for quite a long time. 'A rose by any other name would smell as sweet.' Now, she always seemed to be saying it herself. 'What's in a name?' she mouthed silently.

She looked out of the window, noticing how the sun glinted across the panes of glass in the greenhouse. How beautiful the garden looked, and how lucky she was to be here. That was another clue. Was it a coincidence that Mr Gregory's car broke down outside the village shop and he came in to use the phone, chatting for a while as he waited for the breakdown van to arrive? If they hadn't met him, would they have known that he was the owner of Willow Cottage and had just put it on the market? Was it a coincidence that she and Jack had decided to retire from the retail business and sell the shop? No, she thought. It was all meant to happen. But why didn't she just inherit Willow Cottage as Aunt Kate had wished? Well, she would not have encountered Jack again would she, or would she?

That encounter was so black and white. Love at first sight. She knew now that it wasn't just a physical thing, although that side of their marriage was as vital and natural as breathing. No need to debate as to how and why on that score. Dear Jack. He was so down to earth, maintaining that life was for living, and everyone was responsible for their own way in life. But she knew that he stroked the Mooncat when he thought no one was looking. 'That reminds me,' she said out loud. 'I'd better put you in a safe place out of harm's way.' She picked up the white cat from the windowsill and sat it on the kitchen shelf. It was Sally who had labelled it 'The Magic Mooncat'. Perhaps it should be 'miracle' rather than 'magic'. As Sarah said, it was a miracle that they had moved here, and that wasn't the only miracle.

A sudden bang brought her back into the present. She jumped up, steadying herself for a moment, and went into the hallway. There was a rattling noise and then the wail of a child. 'Of course,' she said to the coat stand, 'I'd forgotten about Leigh.' She hurried to the foot of the stairs and listened. He gave another loud wail and then, 'Ma—ma.' Hannah immediately experienced that familiar strange prickling at the back of her neck. A crying child! The crying child! She knew it! That cry she'd heard all those years ago. It was the same. Without a shadow of a doubt it was the same cry. So it wasn't a ghost from Aunt Kate's past. After all, she'd never heard it, had she? A voice from the future? But so far into the future? Was it possible? Could time be shuffled out of sequence like a pack of cards?

At that moment, the grandfather clock in the hall sounded its prelude to the hour. Hannah's nerves had become so on edge that it startled her.

She was trembling as she climbed the stairs. Leigh was standing up, holding out his arms for a quick release from the confines of the cot. 'Ma—ma, ma—ma,' he moaned. Sarah was right. He was definitely a Flynn. The image of her father. He'd announced his coming all those years ago. But why then and why not since? Mrs Knight would have had an answer. She'd always said that time was a funny thing and no doubt Grandmother Flynn in Ireland would have had something to say about it.

Her legs felt wobbly, threatening to give way, and she sank into the kitchen armchair breathing heavily. A sudden thought startled her with its clarity. What if it was all about Leigh? His big picture? His jigsaw puzzle? And she was a pawn in his destiny? That was a chastening thought! God! She was getting all fanciful again. Jack was right. Now is what matters.

Leigh snuggled his face into her neck and she rejoiced in the tenderness of his skin, sharing the dampness of his recent tears. Suddenly, he jerked his head around and looked across to the kitchen shelf, pointing and laughing.

Was it a trick of the light, or did the Mooncat wink an eye?

Oh well, she thought.

Miracle or Magic Mooncat—a rose by any other name—